"YOU'RE A REAL BASTARD, LUCAS McCAIN," MEGAN SPAT AT HER CAPTOR.

"It's about time you figured that out," he replied.

Megan launched into a string of curses, all of them cut short by Lucas's hand over her mouth. She bit down hard, making him yelp and release her.

"That ought to teach you not to touch me." She smiled, proud of her triumph.

But with lightning speed, Lucas grabbed her and backed her up against the wall.

He towered over her, his body pressing into hers, sending shivers down her spine. But suddenly she no longer wished to escape.

"I want you," Lucas growled. "Do you understand what I'm saying? I want to take you to bed."

Megan hid her smile. This big, strong bounty hunter talked too much. Why didn't he just shut up and kiss her?

Other *Leisure* books by Heidi Betts:
CINNAMON AND ROSES

A Promise of Roses

Heidi Betts

LEISURE BOOKS NEW YORK CITY

A LEISURE BOOK®

July 2000

Published by

Dorchester Publishing Co., Inc.
276 Fifth Avenue
New York, NY 10001

ISBN 0-8439-4738-1

The name "Leisure Books" and the stylized "L" with design are trademarks of Dorchester Publishing Co., Inc.

Printed in the United States of America.

Prologue

Cubilo del Diablo
The Devil's Lair
Leavenworth, Kansas, 1885

Lucas McCain tossed back his sixth shot of whiskey, surely the cheapest rotgut on earth. But what more could he expect from this hole-in-the-wall that passed for a saloon in a town half the size of a deer tick? Especially one that catered to the dregs of society, men who were running from one thing or another and didn't want to be found.

Lucas raised his eyes to stare at the four men occupying a corner table. Shouts of laughter came from the group, and Lucas cursed his streak of bad luck.

If he had left this one-horse town a week ago as he'd planned, he wouldn't be facing this dilemma. If Brandt Donovan hadn't saved his miserable hide on more than one occasion, he might have been able to shrug off the man's request. But Brandt was his best friend—had been for more years than Lucas could count. That was the only reason Lucas hadn't torn Brandt's letter to shreds. The only reason he was even contemplating this asinine stunt.

Except that it wasn't asinine, and Lucas knew it. Brandt knew it, too, or he never would have asked the favor in the first place. So now Lucas had to face the cold fact that he couldn't go on as he had been. This last year of tracking Silas Scott had drained him of every penny he had to his name. He had hardly enough coin to pay for the drink in his hand.

Whether Lucas liked it or not, he would have to take Brandt up on his offer. But surely there was some way of making money better and quicker than taking a secret-investigation job for the Union Pacific Railroad. God knew they had employees of their own who could handle the assignment, Brandt being one of them.

But, damn it all, the fates were working against Lucas. He hadn't gotten out of town soon enough, and the gang of outlaws Brandt wanted him to track down had stumbled right into his path. It was too good an opportunity to pass up.

All the old instincts of his bounty-hunting days surfaced, priming his brain like a thousand tiny pinpricks. For the first time in a long time, Lucas felt his blood flow hot. The exhilaration of the chase, of infiltrating this band of robbers, burned beneath his skin.

Lucas blinked several times, clearing his eyes of an alcohol-induced haze. He still had it. He could still drink enough hard liquor to fill the Gulf of Mexico without dulling his senses. It amazed him how quickly he could once again become the predator, stalking its prey.

He ran a hand through his hair, surprised to find that it fell well past its usual length. As soon as he finished this assignment, he would have to get it cut. He stood and ambled toward the four men.

He would do as Brandt asked so he could collect his pay. And then he would get back to searching for Silas Scott. The bastard who had slaughtered his family.

Chapter One

"I ain't gonna do it, Miss Megan. I just ain't."

"Hector, for God's sake, the outlaws won't try to rob you today."

"You don't know that, ma'am, and I'd just as soon not find out."

Megan Adams gritted her teeth and tightened her hands into fists at her sides. Three of her five stagecoach drivers had already quit because of that blasted gang of outlaws. The Adams Express was at serious risk of going under, and if Hector didn't take this run, the customers were bound to bad-mouth her business right into the ground.

"I'll give you all of next week off."

"No, ma'am."

"I'll make sure both you and Zeke have weapons."

"No, ma'am."

"I'll double your pay."

"No, ma'am."

"Blast it, Hector, you know how bad things have gotten lately. I'm not asking you to walk through fire. I'm just asking you to drive the damn stagecoach."

"No, ma'am," he said with a shake of his dirty brown hair. "Nope. I ain't doin' it no matter what you say."

"If you don't take this run, you're fired."

"Aw, come on, Meg. You fired me twice last week, and I'm still here. That threat just don't wash no more."

Megan tapped her foot in agitation, wondering if an ass full of buckshot would change his tune. She doubted it.

"I'm asking one last time, Hector. Begging you. Please take this run."

Hector shuffled his feet uncomfortably, keeping his gaze on the floor. "I'm sorry, Miss Adams, but I can't. I'd be more than happy to keep an eye on the office for you, though."

"Fine." She plucked her Stetson off the desk behind her, slapping it against her thigh. "But don't expect your usual pay for sitting around selling tickets," she said as she stormed out the door.

She tugged her worn hat down over the pile of curls atop her head, pulled a pair of leather gloves from the waistband of her tan trousers, and went to the door of the Concord waiting just outside the depot. "Sorry for the delay, folks. You'll be on your way in a minute or two. If it gets too dusty for you, let the window covers fall shut." Giving the passengers a smile, she made her way around the team of horses at the front of the stage.

Megan climbed onto the tall vehicle and took hold of the reins. "Looks like I'll be keeping you company today, Zeke."

"That young upstart giving you trouble again, Miss Megan?"

She smiled at the graying, potbellied man for his intuitiveness. "Nothing I can't handle, Zeke," she said, patting the six-shooter strapped to her right thigh.

Megan motioned to the shotgun lying flat across

Zeke's lap. "You keep that thing cocked and loaded, just in case."

"Always do," Zeke said with a grin.

Megan took a deep breath to stiffen her resolve, slapped the reins, and set the stage in motion. She had lied to Hector when she assured him the outlaws wouldn't attack today. In truth, there was a good possibility that they would. She was carrying a strongbox full of railroad payroll, after all.

She cursed under her breath. But how the hell did they find out? It seemed that every time her stage was carrying one, they took great pleasure in relieving her of it. Worse, she was the only person who knew precisely when the payrolls were being transported. Her stage picked up the boxes at the Kansas City station, then delivered them to the Union Pacific offices in Atchison. She kept all the information confidential, the paperwork under lock and key. So how the hell did they find out?

The stage took a sharp turn around a high, smooth expanse of rock face. A perfect place for outlaws to lie in wait, unseen.

"We got trouble," Zeke said, lifting his shotgun.

Megan didn't have to turn her head. She could see riders approaching them from all directions, clearly aiming to surround the Concord. Slapping the reins, she drove the horses faster, hoping to outrun the men closing in on her.

"It's no use, Miss Megan," Zeke called over the noise of the rattling stage. "I've been through this before. They'll catch us no matter what you do." He got off a shot, but the riders were moving so fast, his bullet was bound to miss its mark.

Megan didn't say anything but urged the team to ever more dangerous speeds. The outlaws raced beside and behind the stage. One reached out and tried to halt the horses, to no avail. Then a shot rang out, and the lead mare dropped to the ground, pummeled and dragged by the other animals until they had no choice but to stop.

As she tugged on the reins to slow the heavy vehicle, Megan yelled for the passengers to stay inside the coach no matter what. She couldn't stop the bandits from halting her stage, she might not even be able to keep them from taking the railroad payroll, but for damn sure she wasn't going to let them hurt her customers.

"Nice to see you again, mister." The man who spoke to Zeke seemed to be the leader. His mount pranced nervously at the scent of blood from the lead mare. "Mind throwing down your weapon?"

Zeke did as he asked without argument.

"You killed my horse, you bastards!" Tired of letting the bandits have the upper hand, Megan reached for her gun. But before she could aim it at any particular target, the pistol flew from her grasp, and a sharp, stinging vibration ran through her fingers.

Damned if one of the bastards hadn't shot the gun right out of her hand! She raised her eyes and glared with icy disdain at the bandit guilty of disarming her. A thin trail of smoke floated up from the barrel of his Colt revolver.

"Must be a new driver," the leader called out. "He thought he could get the drop on us. Nice shot, Luke."

The man named Luke remained silent. Even with a brown bandanna hiding the lower part of his face, Megan could see cold disinterest in his blue eyes. He leaned forward in the saddle, an arm lazily draped across the pommel. It seemed to annoy him that he'd even had to remove the Peacemaker from its holster.

Megan stared at him long and hard, memorizing every detail from his pale eyebrows to his scuffed boots. She might not be able to identify all the members of the outlaw band, but she was going to make damn certain she could pick this particular man out of a crowd.

"Throw down the strongbox," the leader commanded.

"Over my dead body," Megan spat.

The leader shrugged. "Don't like to hurt anybody if I can help it, but since you seem so determined, I'd be happy to oblige." He raised his gun and aimed it at Megan's heart.

"Just throw down the damn box!" the man named Luke called out.

His voice sounded tense, and Megan wondered why he should care whether she was killed or not. She stood and pushed Zeke across the seat and out of harm's way. With a clearer view of the leader, she put her hands on her hips and lifted her chin a notch. "Over my dead body," she said again.

"Christ, this one's a real pain in the ass." The leader cocked the hammer of his pistol and pulled the trigger.

Megan held her breath and waited for the searing pain to rip through her body. After a second, she realized the bullet hadn't hit her. He had only shot her hat off.

Lucas cursed under his breath when the shot rang out. He thought for sure Evan planned to kill the boy, or at least make him wish he were dead.

"Son of a bitch!" another member of the gang yelled. "He's a woman!"

When a veil of midnight-black hair fell around the driver's shoulders, Lucas lost his train of thought. The hot July sun brought out streaks of auburn in the waist-length mass, and its owner's brown eyes shone with angry defiance. Damn it, the chit had more brass than brains. Didn't she know better than to hassle a gang of gunmen?

Obviously not.

The woman grabbed her Stetson from the shotgun rider's lap and shoved it back on her head. She turned to Evan and straightened her spine, once again ready to do battle.

"Frank," Evan said, "take care of her, will you?"

"Right, Ev." Frank swung a lasso above his head and tossed it around the girl's slight frame, quickly tightening the rope so that her arms were pinned to her sides. Dismounting lazily, he climbed aboard the Concord and plucked her from the stage, dangling her in the crook of

15

his arm. With his free hand, he loosened her gun belt and let it fall to the ground.

"Let me down, you son of a bitch! I'll see you all hanged for this, I swear to God."

Frank simply got back on his horse, redistributing her weight on his arm.

Hanging upside down, she continued ranting. Lucas couldn't contain a chuckle at her colorful language.

"Okay, old man," Evan said. "We'll take that money off your hands, and you and the passengers can go about your business. Dougie, unhitch that dead horse so these people can be on their way."

Zeke didn't move as one of the bandits climbed up behind him and dragged the heavy black strongbox from the stage. When they all began moving away from the Concord, he cleared his throat and asked, "What about Miss Megan?"

"Well, seeing how Miss Megan here gave us so much trouble, I think we'll be taking her with us for now." Without giving the man time to argue, Evan raised his gun and fired several shots into the air, spurring the horses forward and causing Zeke to struggle with the reins to regain control of the team.

"Tommy, you take the money. Frank, keep a tight grip on that little gal. Everything taken care of?" he asked, looking around the area of their latest robbery. When no one said anything, he continued. "Good enough. Let's go."

They started out at a brisk pace but soon had to slow due to the weight of the strongbox and the struggles of one Miss Megan Adams.

Maybe his luck wasn't so bad after all, Lucas thought, allowing a smile to spread behind the cover of his bandanna. So this spitfire was Megan Adams. Imagine that.

In his letter, Brandt had been adamant that the Union Pacific Railroad suspected the Adams Express proprietress of being involved in the robberies. Not just involved, Lucas amended, but likely the ring leader. As the head of railroad security, Brandt was damn sure

Megan Adams was feeding information to the bandits, telling them when and where it would be easiest to rob the stages of the payrolls being transported to the railroad office in Atchison. The problem was, since she'd seen his face before, Brandt could hardly infiltrate the gang for proof of Adam's complicity.

Lucas had thought he would have to gain information from the outlaws first and then go after Megan Adams, but as fate would have it, she'd fallen right into his lap. Yes, this assignment was coming along better than he'd hoped.

Why, though, had Megan been driving the stage? It was odd enough for a female to be running her own business.

Lucas looked at the woman slung over the front of Frank's saddle. They were less than half a mile from the band's hideout, and it seemed that she'd quit fighting. So perhaps there had been a reason for her to drive the stage today.

He shook his head. Of course. That hellfire-and-damnation rant had all been an act, contrived to convince everyone that Megan was being taken against her will, when in reality she had planned to meet up with her cohorts.

Any other time, Lucas would have considered the idea far-fetched. But Brandt had sounded quite certain that Megan Adams was involved with the robberies. And why else would she have driven the stage? Why else would Evan decide to take Megan when he had, by his own admission, never before taken a hostage? Besides, if Brandt believed Miss Adams guilty, that was enough for Lucas. The sooner he wrapped this up, the better. He had more important things to do than save a few bucks for the bigwigs who owned the railroad.

It was bad enough that he'd been saddled with this pack of bandits. He'd never seen such empty-headed idiots before. They used their real names in front of their victims, only covered their faces when they remembered to, and had accepted him as a new member of their gang much too quickly for his peace of mind. The only one who had a lick of sense was Frank, and he was downright intimidating. Frank was mean enough and tough enough to get out of any situation—his many scars attested to that.

Single file, the horses threaded through a thick patch of trees and undergrowth until a small, slanted shanty came into view. The men dismounted, tethered their mounts, and went inside. Lantern light made the place seem livable, but it also illuminated the dirt and grime that covered the plank floor.

Megan walked into the shack on her own, guided only by Frank's hand pressing into her back. She looked around, wondering how six people—five rather large men and one fair-to-middling woman—were supposed to be comfortable in such a tiny space.

"This is nice," she said sarcastically.

"We like it," Evan replied.

The men still wore their bandannas over their noses and mouths. Megan noticed and commented, half hoping they would opt to keep them on so she wouldn't have to see their faces. She didn't have much hope that they would be easy to look at.

"Yeah, Ev. We don't gotta keep these dang things on, do we?"

Evan cocked an eyebrow, holding Megan's gaze. "Nope. Our little prisoner here won't be telling anybody who we are. Will you, Meggie?"

"Of course not," she answered. She had no intention of describing these men to anyone—except Marshal Thompson, the *Leavenworth Daily Times*, and the *Kansas Weekly Herald*.

But now that the outlaws were revealing themselves to her, she had to do some serious planning on how to get away. She wasn't naive enough to think they would let her live after she'd seen their faces.

Evan pulled his red handkerchief down around his neck and gave Megan an engaging smile. She had been fully prepared for the outlaw leader to resemble the back end of a bull moose. Instead she faced a handsome, dark-

18

haired man with sparkling brown eyes. Without a doubt, Dougie was Evan's younger brother. They had the same chestnut hair and high cheekbones.

Frank made Megan's skin crawl. His black hair fell far past his shoulders in matted tangles. She thought the ends might have dangled into his supper on more than one occasion. A scar circled his neck, but she wasn't close enough to determine if it had been caused by the blade of a knife or an uncomfortably tight rope. Either way, he had escaped from some sort of deadly trouble. Megan made a note to avoid Frank as much as possible.

Tommy seemed to be about Dougie's age—sixteen, if she didn't miss her guess. Hair the color of summer wheat tumbled into green eyes filled with adolescent excitement.

And then there was Luke, the one who had shot the pistol right out of her hand. He was a good shot, she'd give him that much. He hadn't so much as nicked her with that little trick. His bandanna remained over the bottom half of his face.

When he noticed her gaze upon him, he gave a wink and tugged the brown material down over the bridge of his nose, the pale pink of full lips, and the slope of a strong chin in need of a shave. Megan swallowed and lifted her eyes back up to his. They shimmered like chips of ice melting in the hot summer sun. Oh, yes, she would remember him.

"Have a seat, will you, Meggie?" Evan waved to the four chairs surrounding a lopsided table. "No sense acting like complete strangers, now is there?"

Megan arranged one of the chairs at an angle so she could keep the whole room in view. Frank leaned over, lifted the table, and pulled a deck of cards out from under a leg. The table thudded back to the floor, teetering precariously.

"Deal me in." Dougie straddled a chair and rested his elbows on the table, which then slanted to the other side.

"We need some grub," Frank said, but he made no move to do anything about it.

Evan nodded. "Tom, Luke, you go into town and see what you can find. Take money from the strongbox if you need it."

Tommy bent over and shook the padlock.

"Don't bother," Luke said in a low voice. "I've got some cash on me. No sense getting into that yet."

"I agree," Evan said. "After we get a bite to eat, we'll divvy it up."

"No hurry." Luke shrugged. "It's not like we're going anywhere for a while."

Evan chuckled. "Right. Luke's the sensible one," he pointed out for Megan's benefit. "Glad you came along, Luke. Mighty glad."

Megan watched the door close behind the two men, then turned her attention to the game of poker going on at the scarred, lopsided table. Frank raised a booted foot to rest on one corner, and the spur dug deeply into the wood. Well, now she knew how the surface had gotten so scratched, Megan thought a moment before asking to play.

"Think we got enough supplies here?" Tom asked, glancing down at the two sacks of fruit and meat and cheese in his arms.

Lucas didn't answer but kept his eyes on the scraggly black gelding standing in front of the makeshift saloon of Cubilo del Diablo. Why the town just outside Leavenworth carried that name, Lucas would never know. He hadn't seen that many Mexicans in residence. But then, the outlaw crowd of Diablo stuck around about as long as a long-tailed cat in a room full of rocking chairs.

Lucas stopped in the middle of the street and handed the overburdened Tom the sack of bread and eggs he'd been carrying. "Take this to the horses. I'll be right back."

"Where ya goin'?" the boy asked.

Lucas ignored him. When he reached the gelding, he

ran a hand over its rump, stroking the ridge of a long, straight scar. The hair hadn't grown back after the injury.

Lucas clamped his jaw shut. He adjusted his hat to conceal his face and took slow, sure steps as he made his way into the saloon, keeping his eyes down the entire time. The press of customers inside the small building made it easy for Lucas to sidle up to the bar and remain inconspicuous.

"What'll ya have?" The bartender yelled over the roar of voices.

"Five bottles of your strongest whiskey," he said over his shoulder, holding up his fingers for the man to count. He kept the brim of his hat low and scanned the room.

Disappointment rushed through his veins when he didn't find what he was looking for. And then he heard a bark of laughter. His eyes narrowed as he focused on a table near the stairs.

A group of scantily clad women clustered around the occupant of that table. A dusty black hat sat atop the customer's head. His black beard held a hint of white that hadn't been there when this all began.

Hatred, thick and vile, pooled in Lucas's gut. He hated this man with every fiber of his being. With every thought, with every motion, with every breath, he wanted this man dead. And Lucas intended to see it done.

But not here. Too many people. He wanted to kill Silas Scott out in the open, where the man would have nowhere to run, no one to interfere. He wanted to make the bastard beg for mercy.

Lucas turned around. "Who's in charge of the girls?" he asked the barkeep.

"Gracie." He arched a thumb in her direction. "End of the bar."

"Watch the whiskey for me, will you?" Lucas said.

Gracie turned out to be a large, flaxen-haired woman with exceptional hearing. "Lookin' for me, hon?" she asked, keeping her eyes on the group of girls surrounding Silas Scott.

"You Gracie?"

She nodded.

"Then, I'm lookin' for you. Do you usually let that many of your girls work on one customer?" Lucas asked, making sure he honored her position as the saloon's madam.

"One customer doesn't usually throw money around the way he's been doin'." Gracie stuck out her ample bosom, which looked ready to pop from the tight white satin camisole she wore. "What's it to you?"

"Well, I've got a proposition for you. If you're interested, that is." Lucas knew that if it involved money, she would be interested.

She slanted her eyes in his direction but didn't answer.

"I'd like you to keep that man entertained for a while."

"I have a feeling he's going to be plenty entertained."

Lucas chuckled. "Yes, I imagine so. But, you see, I'd like you to keep him entertained until I get back."

"What for?"

"That's personal."

"I take it you don't want him to know."

"No."

Gracie shrugged a plump shoulder.

"You get your girls—as many as it takes—to keep him liquored up, and I'll make it worth your while."

"How worth my while?"

"Very. I'll pay for the whiskey and the girls. Double."

"You mean you're willin' to pay me twice what it costs to get him drunk and happy?"

"That's right. All you have to do is make sure he stays here till I can get back."

"What're you gonna do then? I don't want you stainin' my sheets with blood or nothin'. That stuff's a real bitch to get out."

"No blood. As soon as I get back, you can go about your business and let him leave the saloon."

"That's it? I'm supposed to go to all the trouble of keepin' him here and then just let him leave?"

"Yep. I'll take care of the rest."

Lucas and Gracie both watched as Silas stood and started none too steadily up the stairs, flanked by a blonde and a redhead.

"Looks like he's about to be entertained," Gracie said.

"And you're about to make a great deal of money."

Chapter Two

Megan jumped when the cabin door flew open. Tommy came in and dropped his burdens onto the table, oblivious to the game of cards that promptly slid out of order. Frank let out a curse, then threw down his hand. He grabbed one of the burlap sacks, dumping its contents. Six apples rolled out, along with a hunk of cheese, a slab of salted bacon, and two unmarked tin cans.

Evan looked into the other bag and sighed. "Good thing you didn't turn this one over, Frank." He pulled out a loaf of bread and half a dozen brown eggs tucked in a bed of straw within a small wooden crate. "Where's Luke?"

Tom smiled. "He's a thinker, that's for sure. He done bought us all whiskey to celebrate."

The man under discussion chose that moment to step through the doorway. He held two bottles by the neck in each hand. He'd tucked the fifth into the waistband of his tan trousers. "Drink, anyone?" he asked with a wide grin and proceeded to gift each man in the group with his own bottle.

"None for me?" Megan asked, her mouth turning down in a pout.

Slowly, like butter melting over hot corn on the cob, Luke pulled the whiskey out of his waistband. He tilted it toward her and in a silky-smooth drawl said, "Be my guest."

Megan smiled, wondering if he expected her to refuse his offer. Maybe this was a test to see if she actually had the gumption to drink with them.

She reached out and, as leisurely as he'd removed it from his pants, took hold of the bottle. "Thank you."

She wiggled the cork loose and set it on the tabletop, then lifted the bottle in silent salute to the bandits before taking a long swallow. Her body seemed to go up in flames. The liquid burned down her throat, taking several layers of vital tissue with it. Her eyes began to water. She held her breath to keep from letting out a strangled scream.

Luke looked at her with twinkling blue eyes.

Megan would not let him see how much pain the alcohol caused. She blinked to clear her vision, then forced a smile. "That is the worst-tasting whiskey I've ever had." She heard the strain in her own voice, and, before she could change her mind, she took another swig of the nasty liquor.

"That it is," Evan agreed after drinking from his own bottle.

Frank grunted. "Tastes like horse piss," he said, lowering his bottle from his lips.

"Well, now, Miss Megan," Luke said, removing his hat and wiping an arm over his forehead, "nobody said you had to drink it."

Megan stared at the man. Half of her wanted to strangle him. The other half wanted to run her fingers through his sandy-blond hair. This was the first time he'd taken off his hat, and her heart did a little flip when she saw the whole of his attractive features.

From the start she'd thought his eyes surpassed the blue of a summer sky. But together with the dark gold of his hair, they formed a package that was almost too much to handle all at once.

The trail-worn condition of his clothes no longer hid the handsomeness of the man. Something happened when he took his hat off; it was like flinging back a curtain to fully reveal a work of art. Tan skin covered cheekbones that now seemed finely chiseled rather than menacing.

Luke reached for the bottle. Megan let him take it.

"Who's winning?" he asked. The question was directed at the men, but he kept his eyes on her.

"She is," Dougie said with a moan.

"Meggie here is quite good," Evan added.

"I'll bet."

There was a double meaning somewhere in the conversation, but Megan didn't have the energy to figure it out. Her body felt flushed, and she didn't think it was a result of only two sips of whiskey.

They dealt Luke in and continued to play poker, their hunger forgotten now that they had liquor to fill their empty stomachs. Megan maintained her winning streak—which she pretended was beginner's luck—for well over an hour. When her eyes grew tired of concentrating on the different suits, she folded her hand, settling back to watch the others.

Megan didn't even realize she'd fallen asleep until she felt herself being lifted carefully and just as gently laid down on a rough, threadbare blanket that separated her from the hard floor. She tried to open her eyes to see who was playing the part of a gentleman, but her lids felt like lead weights. With a long sigh, she rolled to her side and pillowed her head on her hands.

It seemed only a minute later that someone shook her awake. She mumbled an obscenity under her breath at being disturbed, snuggling away from the pest. But the slight pressure on her shoulder persisted, and a harsh whisper sounded in her ear. When she opened her mouth to tell her annoyer where to go, a strong hand clamped over her face.

"Shut up. I'm taking you out of here, but I don't want to hear a peep. Got it?"

Megan strained to make out the features of the man who knelt over her, but the room was darker than a tomb.

Before she could argue, her abductor stuck a strip of cloth into her mouth and tied it behind her head, then wrapped another over her eyes. He warned her again. "Not a sound."

He lifted her and tossed her over his shoulder. If his threat hadn't sounded so dire, she would have moaned in indignation. Only a minute later, she felt herself being transferred from his shoulder to the seat of a saddle. At least he allowed her the dignity of riding astride rather than slung over the horse like a felled piece of game. But he quickly grabbed her wrists and tied them together on either side of the pommel.

She listened closely as he went back into the cabin. He returned and lifted her arms at an awkward angle, shoving something heavy and hard beneath them to press against her upper thighs.

Megan was beyond trying to figure out what was going on. First, five outlaws kidnapped her from her own stagecoach, and now one of them was spiriting her away in the middle of the night. The only thing that kept her from struggling, despite her bonds, was the fact that she felt more capable of escaping from a single captor than from a group of them.

Megan only wished she knew which one she had to deal with. She couldn't identify his harsh whisper. Evan or Tommy wouldn't intimidate her too much, but the idea of being thrown over Frank's shoulder made her stomach churn. There was no telling what kind of critters crawled through his filthy hair. Or what he might do to her.

"Take it easy," she heard. He gave her knee a pat. "I have your horse in hand. You don't need to do anything but hold on and be quiet."

Leather squeaked as he climbed into his own saddle.

Megan lurched backward as they started away from the tiny shack at a slow pace. She listened carefully, and although the horses' hooves made little noise on the brush of the deep woods, she knew instinctively when they came to a clearing. With her horse urged into a lope, Megan tightened her grip on the saddle horn, feeling unbalanced by the blindfold and heavy box on her lap.

The first sign that they were nearing civilization came in the form of a tinny, off-key piano and high, feminine laughter. Megan tried to ask about their destination, but the question came out muffled. The man leading her horse brought himself up alongside, so close she felt his leg brush her own.

"Hush," he said. "I have some business to take care of, and I need you to be still until I come back."

But where are you going? she wanted to ask. From the sounds of it, they were nearing a saloon or bawdy house. Megan didn't know of any other establishment that stayed open so late at night or attracted such a rowdy crowd. How did he expect her to just sit here and wait? What if some drunk decided to make her his evening's companion? Megan generally considered herself well able to defend herself, but even she would have trouble with her eyes and mouth covered and her hands tied.

Lucas brought their mounts to a stop behind the Diablo saloon and swung his leg to dismount. His feet hit the ground with a soft thud. Tethering the horses, he raised his eyes to Megan Adams. She sat ramrod straight, her head held high. With any luck, he would be able to turn her in to the Leavenworth authorities by morning.

"I'll be right back," he said and turned for the back door of the saloon. He wasn't worried about leaving her alone. If there was any trouble, it would be in front of the saloon, not back here. And no one had seen them ride into town.

He saw Gracie as soon as he stepped inside. He sneaked up behind her and blew in her ear. She whirled around to face him. Red tinged her complexion, and she looked like she'd just swallowed a bug.

Lucas's stomach clenched. Something was wrong. "What is it?" he asked.

"Me an' the girls tried to keep him here. Poured whiskey down his gullet like water. But after he had his fill of Tilly and Priscilla, he done took off. We couldn't stop him for nothin'."

"Damn it," Lucas swore. He pounded a fist on the bar.

Gracie cleared her throat. "Like I said, we tried. And even though he ain't here, you still owe us our money 'cause we did what you asked."

"Did he say where he was going? Did you see which way he headed?" Lucas asked as he fished into his pocket.

Gracie flipped through the money and then tucked it between her breasts. "Pris watched him ride out. Said he was goin' west. Left about two hours ago."

"Son of a bitch. Thanks, Gracie," he said and walked out.

Damn. Now what was he going to do? If he took Megan to Leavenworth to hand her over to the marshal, he'd lose Scott's trail. Damn it, he couldn't let that happen. He'd been after this bastard for too long, lost him too many times.

"There's been a slight change in plans, sweetheart," he said to Megan as he mounted. "I hate to say it, but you're coming with me."

Until he'd called her *sweetheart,* Megan didn't know who her abductor was. But that slow, textured drawl could not be mistaken; it was definitely the one named Luke. And now that she knew, she wasn't sure how to feel. Should she be happy not to be in Frank's grimy hands? Or should she be furious that handsome Luke would take her hostage?

Before she could decide on a proper reaction, her body seemed to give out. All of a sudden her muscles ached, her hands tingled, her back threatened to snap at any moment, and she couldn't feel her legs because the weight of the box on them had long ago cut off her circulation. She let out a low moan as she swayed. With no strength left in her legs to hold on, she began to fall.

She felt an arm grab her waist and haul her from the horse. The strongbox clattered to the ground, causing the horse to whinny and pace about. The next she knew, she sat cradled in the V of Luke's lap, the saddle horn poking into her hip.

"Christ, why didn't you tell me you were falling asleep?" He ripped the blindfold from her eyes.

She blinked and tried to get her bearings. Then she proceeded to answer him. It came out as a strangled bleat of grunts and groans.

"Guess you don't need this anymore," he said, slipping the gag down to hang around her neck.

"—yellow-bellied son of a bitch!"

Luke's eyes widened a fraction of an inch, then he started to untie her wrists. "I should have left the gag on a while longer. Quite a mouth you've got there, sweetheart."

"Do not call me *sweetheart,* you maggot-infested, grub-eating, yellow-bellied—"

"Son of a bitch. I believe you said that already."

Megan clamped her teeth together. "Let go of me."

"Gladly," Luke said, and did just that.

Megan hit the ground like a hundred-pound bale of hay. She groaned and looked up to see Luke grinning at her. "I can't believe you did that," she said.

"You wanted me to let go."

"You didn't have to dump me on the ground."

"I didn't dump you. I simply let you go."

"And let me fall on my ass."

"A pretty little ass, too, I might add."

"No, you might not," Megan snapped. "Help me up."

"You wanted down," Luke said, his smile widening.

"I did not want down. I wanted you to let go of me."

"I did, and now you're down. Maybe next time you'll be more specific in your requests."

Megan grumbled under her breath, inventing a few new nasty names for the man sitting so high and mighty on his chestnut gelding. She moved to her side and tried to support herself on her hands and knees. Damned if they didn't feel as limp as wet noodles. Tingles stabbed through her limbs as they began to regain feeling. With a sigh of defeat, she rolled back on her hip.

Luke jumped down from his horse to crouch at her side. "Why didn't you tell me you were tired?"

"I am not tired," she said, knowing her supine position betrayed her.

"That must be why you can hardly move."

"I wouldn't be in this condition if you hadn't tied me up like a Christmas goose. I'm an excellent rider, for God's sake."

"I'm sure you are."

"I am."

"I don't doubt it," Luke said a bit more sternly. "But I don't have time to let you prove it." He lifted her to her feet and held her as she struggled for balance.

"They probably aren't even awake yet," Megan said, clutching Luke's shoulders for support.

"Who?" He looked thoroughly confused.

"Evan and the others," she answered. "They won't know you took off with their money for another two or three hours."

"That's the least of my problems right now."

"Then what's so all-fired important that you have to toss me over a horse and drag me half across the state?"

Luke chuckled. "We haven't even gone ten miles yet."

"Well, it feels like fifty," she said, rubbing her bottom.

"Can you stand?"

"Of course I can stand, you idiot."

"Good." He removed his hands from her waist.

Megan's legs wobbled, and she grabbed at his arms.

31

"Christ, you should have said something." Luke eased her back to the ground and went to pick up the strongbox.

"I'll remember that. The next time some cold-blooded outlaw kidnaps me, ties my wrists, gags and blindfolds me, I'll be sure to mention that my hands and feet are falling asleep. I'm sure he'll be terribly concerned."

"I don't know why anyone would be concerned about you with a smart mouth like that."

"You're one to talk, Saint Luke, Robber of Stages." Megan watched as he steadied the box on the saddle of her horse, securing it with a length of rope. "Where the hell am I supposed to sit? If you think I'll be walking behind you and your precious railroad payroll, you're out of your itty-bitty bandit mind."

Luke threw her a quelling look and checked the ropes again. "You can ride with me."

"You are an idiot," she said, forcing her stiff body to obey her commands. She got to her knees and struggled a long minute until she stood upright. "I am not riding with you."

"I don't think you have much choice in the matter," Luke said, patting his double six-shooters.

The guns on his hips didn't impress Megan. "You might as well shoot me and get it over with, Mr. Big Bad Bank Robber. Because if you make me go with you, I'll make your trip a living hell."

"You already have." He took a step toward her. "And I have never robbed a bank."

"Stage robber, bank robber—it's all the same. You're still going to hang." He moved forward. She took a step back.

"I won't hang," he said.

"You will if I have anything to say about it."

He laughed. Megan didn't know what could be so funny about a noose tightening around one's neck, but he obviously found the possibility amusing.

With little warning, Luke swooped Megan up over his shoulder and mounted his horse. She pounded his back for several minutes until she realized the uselessness of her efforts. When she stopped, he slid her down his body and helped her get comfortable in front of him.

"It's going to be a long ride," he said. "You might as well get some sleep."

Megan stiffened her spine, determined to remain awake. She didn't care if she stayed on this horse for a month straight; the last thing she would ever do was fall asleep in this man's arms.

Chapter Three

Megan awakened to the gurgle of swiftly running water. She opened her eyes and looked around only to find herself sitting with her back to the thick trunk of a cottonwood tree. Both horses stood ankle-deep in a crystal-clear stream, drinking their fill. She didn't see Luke anywhere.

She stretched, testing her muscles and joints. They seemed to be in better shape now than they had the night before. Megan frowned. How long had she slept that it would be light out already? It didn't really matter. She had to get away.

Jumping to her feet, she raced into the water and grabbed the mare's reins.

"Goin' somewhere?"

The deep male voice froze Megan in place, one foot in a stirrup. She lowered her leg and turned to face Luke.

"You weren't thinking of running off, now, were you?"

"Of course I was, you dolt. You didn't expect me to just sit here awaiting your return, did you?"

Luke laughed. "There's something to be said for honesty, anyway. Why don't you come on out of there before your toes turn to ice. You can help me with the money."

Megan sloshed out of the creek and crossed her arms over her chest. Luke dragged the strongbox from beside the tree where she had been resting, then drew his gun. He aimed it at the padlock and pulled the trigger. Megan whirled to see if the noise had spooked the horses, but they seemed undisturbed as they continued to drink.

"How about putting the money in these?"

She caught the fawn-colored saddlebags Luke tossed her.

"Count it, too. There should be close to three thousand dollars."

"Four thousand, six hundred," Megan said.

A golden eyebrow arched upward. "And just how do you know that?"

"I own the stagecoach company." Megan shot him a glance, curious to see his reaction to the news. Most people just about swallowed their tongues. He didn't so much as blink.

"So you would be privy to all kinds of information, huh?"

"Anything concerning the stage line or its passengers."

"Or its cargo."

"Yes."

"And I suppose you knew ahead of time how much money the railroad wanted transported."

"Of course. But what does that have to do with anything?"

"Nothing. I was just asking."

Megan watched him a moment longer before turning her attention to the cash. She counted the coins and bills before stuffing them inside the pockets of the saddlebags and handing them to Luke.

Luke kicked the strongbox into the thicket. Then he looked toward the stream, gave a long, sharp whistle, and called out, "Worthy!" The gelding came at the sound of his name and nudged Luke's shoulder. "Good boy," Luke said, patting his muzzle. The black mare followed, wanting the same attention.

"Is that his name? Worthy?"

"Yep," Luke said, arranging the bags on the back of his saddle.

"Why do you call him that?" She saw a muscle in Luke's jaw jump.

"My wife named him."

For some reason, that announcement stung more than Megan cared to admit, though she knew Luke's being married shouldn't affect her one way or the other. "You're married." It was more a statement than a question.

"Not anymore. She's dead."

"I'm sorry." Megan didn't know which hurt more, the fact that Luke had been married or the thought of him losing someone he loved. She knew from experience that the pain could be almost unbearable.

"Why—" Megan cleared her throat. "If you don't mind my asking, why did she name him Worthy?"

"She thought he looked like a trustworthy mount." A hint of a smile reached his lips. "I couldn't decide what to call him, and before I knew it, the name stuck."

"What was your wife's name?" Megan's throat felt scratchy, her palms damp.

"Annie." Luke's voice turned rough. "And don't even think about asking another damn question. Mount up. We've got plenty of ground to cover before dark."

Before dark, it dawned on Megan that, despite her claims to excellent horsemanship, she had never ridden a horse to the extent that Luke expected. He stopped only once to water the animals, and he made Megan keep up a conversation from the bushes so he could be sure she didn't use the call of nature as an excuse to escape. Then he pushed them another twenty miles if he pushed them an inch.

The sun had gone down an hour earlier, but not until

now did Luke decide to make camp for the night. He tethered the horses, then came back to help Megan down.

"You gather kindling for a fire. I'll see what I can do about finding us something to eat. Don't wander off. If you run, I won't think twice about putting a bullet in your back."

Megan waved a hand, clicking her tongue. "What a charmer you can be, Mr. Luke." She hoped to see a small smile, but his face remained impassive.

"My name is Lucas, not Luke."

"What's the difference?"

"I don't like being called Luke. I don't mind Lucas or McCain."

"I see. So why have I only heard you called Luke up till now?"

"I sometimes use Luke with . . . certain people. You can call me Lucas."

"Why just certain people?"

"It's a long story."

Megan cocked one hip. "I'm not going anywhere," she tossed out, reminding him of his earlier order.

"I am," he said. "I'm going to see what I can find for supper. Don't be scared if you hear a shot."

"I would not be even remotely frightened by a gunshot, Lucas McCain."

"Good. I'll be back."

Megan watched him walk out of sight before starting her own search for brush and twigs to build a fire. She cleared an area, made a ring of stones, and piled her kindling inside the circle. Then she went to her mare and dug around in the bags attached to the saddle. Since the other pouches contained the railroad payroll, she assumed Lucas's belongings were in these.

An extra shirt, a gold pocket watch on a worn leather fob, a packet of tobacco and papers. Megan rebuckled the flap. She went around to the other side of the horse to root in that bag. Her fingers bumped something solid, wrapped in a soft piece of wool. She knew she shouldn't pry, but even as that thought raced through her brain, Megan took the object out of the leather satchel. She let it rest in the palm of her hand for a moment before pulling back the folds of cloth.

She stared at the picture inside a beautiful silver frame etched with delicate vines and blossoms. A gentle-looking blonde sat in a medallion-backed armchair, a young child on her lap. The woman's smile lit every fine feature of her face, including her pale eyes.

Filled with curiosity, Megan turned the tintype over and slipped it out of the frame. Scrawled on the back in flowing letters were two names and a date: Annie and Chad, 1879.

Annie. Lucas's wife. Chad must be their son. But where was the little boy now?

Megan sensed Lucas's presence and turned to see him standing a scant yard away. His usually light eyes looked dark and stormy, more gray than blue. A muscle in his jaw twitched. He held a rabbit by its hind legs in his left hand. Funny, she didn't remember hearing a shot.

"What are you doing with that?"

His question came out in a low, calm tone, but Megan wasn't fooled. The words sounded raw, enraged. She quickly replaced the picture in the frame and rewrapped it in the blue cloth.

"I'm sorry," she said, returning it to the saddlebag. "I didn't mean to pry. I was looking for matches."

Lucas reached into his pocket and pulled out a small metal box. He tossed it to her.

Megan didn't move. The case landed in the dirt at her feet with a tiny clink. She held Lucas's cold gaze.

"There are your matches. Go start a fire."

She bent down and retrieved the box, then moved to the pile of kindling. Bits of reddish rust corroded the hinges of the metal case, and it took a minute to get the lid open. A leather pouch rested inside. Megan worked the tight drawstring loose and pulled out a match.

She lowered herself to the ground, crossed her legs,

and struck the sulfur tip on the sole of her boot, lighting the dry brush she'd collected. Smoke whirled up for a moment before the flame caught and spread.

By the time Lucas showed himself again, Megan had a good-size blaze going. He shoved two Y-shaped sticks into the earth and rested the long, straight one with the skinned rabbit skewered on it across the top.

Megan kept her eyes averted, still feeling guilty for nosing around in his belongings. Lucas's past was none of her business. She didn't even care. The fact that he'd been married and had a child didn't bother her in the least. Why should it?

"Is Chad your son?"

Lucas gritted his teeth so tightly, Megan imagined she could hear them grinding. Long seconds passed, and she decided he didn't intend to answer.

"He's a very cute little boy." *Shut up, Megan!* her mind screamed. *Why in God's name do you want to know so much? This man is a criminal. He robbed your stage, kidnapped you, dropped you on your bottom in the dirt, and you're asking about his family as if you're old friends.*

"I'm sorry. I don't mean to pry." Lord, she'd said that already. And here she was with chisel and hammer, pounding away at his tough outer shell, trying to peek inside.

He remained silent.

"I wasn't snooping. I really thought the matches would be in your saddlebags."

"I carry them with me," he said, keeping his eyes on the flames that licked at the meat.

"Here," Megan said, handing his match case back to him. "That's a very good idea. Keeping them in that oiled leather pouch and then putting them in the metal box."

"They stay dry that way."

Megan swallowed and rearranged her legs, searching for a comfortable position. "I really am sorry," she said again.

No answer.

"Damn it, I said I was sorry." Her last shred of patience snapped and sizzled like the rabbit's juices dripping into the fire. "I'm sorry I started digging in your saddlebags. I'm sorry I found the picture. I'm sorry I was curious enough to look at it. I'm sorry your wife died. I'm sorry you can't stay home and spend more time with your son. I'm sorry you can't find a decent job and have to rob stages for a living. I'm sorry, I'm sorry, I'm sorry. Now would you please say it's okay and accept my apology?"

A minute of tortured silence passed. Megan wanted to rip the hair right out of her head. Damn his stubborn hide, she wasn't going to apologize again. Eating too much crow gave her a rash. Megan scratched a spot on her elbow as if emphasizing the thought.

"My son is dead, too."

Her fingers stilled. "Oh, God. I'm sorry," she said, breaking her most recent vow. She buried her face in her hands. "I've made a terrible mess of things, haven't I?"

Lucas chuckled, and Megan lifted her head, sure she'd imagined the sound. But the smile on his lips was real. And devastatingly charming.

"Why do you say that?" he asked.

Megan struggled to remember what she had said. "I had no right to touch your things. Your past is your business. It's personal. I never should have asked about it."

"No, you shouldn't have. Have you ever lost anyone you loved, Miss Adams?"

"Don't call me that," she said, wrinkling her nose. "It makes me feel old. Call me Megan."

"All right. Have you ever lost anyone you loved, Megan?"

"Yes."

"Who?"

Now look who's prying, she thought. Well, she supposed it was only fair after the Gatling-gun questions she'd thrown at him. "My father," she answered.

"When did he die?"

"Two years ago."

"How?"

"The doctor said his heart gave out on him."

"And how did you feel when he died?"

She squirmed. "It was his time to go, I guess."

"That's not what I asked, Megan. How did you feel?"

"Sad."

"Do you miss him?"

"Of course I miss him," she said, tears clouding her eyes.

"It's lonely when someone leaves you, isn't it? It's not like when friends marry or move away, because you know they're still there, no matter how far they go. When someone you love dies, it's a hundred times worse, because they're never coming back."

Megan sniffed, holding back the tears that threatened to fall. She hadn't cried since the day of her father's funeral. It seemed pointless; tears never solved anything. Her father was gone, and nothing she did would ever bring him back.

"What about you?" she asked stiffly, a little embarrassed by her near bout of feminine waterworks. "How did you feel when your wife died?"

"I'm not done asking about your life yet," Lucas said, reaching out to turn the rabbit so it would cook evenly. "What did you do after your father died? Do you have any other family?"

"Of course. My mother lives in New York. She never liked living out here in Kansas—she says it's desolate and savage—so she stayed in the city."

"Anyone else?"

"My brother and his wife live just outside of Leavenworth. Caleb and Rebecca built up their own cattle ranch after their son, Zachary, was born. Now they have two children. Zach is four, and little Cinnamon Rose is less than a month old." Megan frowned. "I still don't know why they named her that; Caleb refuses to tell me. They call her Rose."

"It sounds like they're very happy."

She nodded. "They tried to get me to move in with

them after Papa died, but I didn't want to leave the house empty."

"You live all alone?"

"Yes. Sometimes it seems terribly quiet, but other times I like the privacy."

"And now you run your father's stagecoach company."

Megan shrugged. "It's not so hard. Over time Papa and Caleb taught me all about the business, and I gradually took over. It wasn't as if I was forced into it suddenly after Papa's death. I already ran the Express pretty much on my own."

"People don't shy away from a female stage driver?" Lucas asked, one side of his mouth lifting.

"I don't usually drive. I know how, and I could do it every day if I wished," she defended herself, "but I hire men. The passengers seem to like that better." She gave an unladylike snort. "They don't believe a woman driver could get them to their destination in one piece. I ought to tell them a few stories about Hector. Then they'd think twice about putting their lives in his hands."

"So why were you driving the day we stopped the stage?"

"Robbed it, you mean."

Lucas shrugged. "Robbed it."

"Hector wouldn't take the run with the railroad payload aboard. You and your outlaw friends have him afraid to do his job."

"So you decided to drive the stage yourself."

"What else could I do? The damn railroad is putting me out of business as it is, stretching their lines all across the country. A canceled run would only cause passengers to find an alternate mode of transportation. I can't afford that. The railroad wants to run tracks right through Leavenworth from Kansas City to Atchison, to Topeka—everywhere. If they do that, there won't be much use for little ol' me and my out-of-date stage line."

"You must hate that."

"I won't let it happen."

"And just how do you intend to stop it?"

Megan leaned forward to touch the crisping meat, then stuck her finger in her mouth as much to taste the rabbit as to cool her heated skin. "I'll do whatever it takes."

"Including stealing railroad payrolls?"

She frowned. "What?"

"You said you'd do whatever it takes to save your business, to keep the railroad from making the Adams Express obsolete. Does that include masterminding robberies to steal the railroad payrolls?"

"The smoke from this fire must be fogging your brain. That's the most outrageous thing I've ever heard."

"That's why you've been able to pull it off so flawlessly. Who would ever suspect you of sabotaging your own coaches?"

"Nobody. Because it's a stupid and ridiculous idea. How did you ever come up with it?"

"I didn't. The railroad figured it out. They sent me to stop you."

Chapter Four

Megan stared at Lucas, her mouth falling open. "Have you always been this creative? I'll bet as a boy you told your mother one tall tale after another."

"I'm not making this up."

"You're with the railroad? You? I'm sorry to be the one to tell you this, Lucas, but you can't work for the railroad and steal from them at the same time. It's just not done. Employers frown on that sort of behavior."

"I agree. Union Pacific has been frowning on your behavior for some time now."

"Why is that?"

"Because you're robbing them blind."

"Stop saying that!" Megan jumped to her feet. She crossed her arms in front of her, tapping a foot in agitation. "I don't know why you persist with this nonsense, but it's making me very uncomfortable."

"It should. When I get you back to Leavenworth, you'll be arrested. Your friends, too, as soon as they can be rounded up."

"What friends?"

"Evan, Frank, Dougie, and Tom."

"They're your friends, not mine."

"Drop the act, Megan. The railroad knows all about the information you've been feeding the gang. You tell them when and where, then they show up and take the strongbox. Pretty slick plan, but they figured it out."

"I'm telling you, I have no idea what the hell you're talking about. I admit I have a grudge against the railroad, but I'm not stealing the payrolls. That would be downright stupid of me. Union Pacific has already made it public that I can't protect their cargo; the number of passengers I transport has dwindled to half of what it used to be. Robbing my own stages is not exactly a brilliant plan to keep myself from going under."

Lucas levered himself up from the ground and stood face-to-face with Megan. "But then, why bother running a legitimate business when you've got thousands of dollars of railroad payroll hidden away? Minus the cut for your accomplices, of course."

"Hector and Zeke are hardly accomplices."

"I'm talking about Evan and the boys," Lucas said through clenched teeth. Damn, but she made his head spin. She was a good little actress. If he didn't know better, he'd almost believe she had no clue of what was going on.

"I don't know Evan and the boys. I never set eyes on them until they dragged me to that shack in the woods. Need I remind you, Mr. McCain, that you were with them, not I?"

"I was under orders by Union Pacific."

"You were under a mask," she snapped.

"I'm working for the railroad. Brandt Donovan had a pretty good idea who was robbing the stages. He was also fairly certain you were involved."

"Brandt Donovan? That first-class joker? He couldn't find his ass in an empty room!"

"Watch it, Megan. That's my friend you're talking about."

She threw up her hands. "Why does that not surprise me? You couldn't find your ass if it perked up and started singing 'Dixie.' "

"Brandt wrote and told me there was a good chance you were involved in the robberies. After all, you're the only one who knows when the payrolls are shipped, right?"

"Yes."

"Then you're the perfect candidate to be leader of the bandits."

"Leader? I told you, I've never seen those men before in my life. Did it look like I was in charge? Because if so, I'm afraid I missed it—hanging from Frank's arm and all."

"That was an act. They decide to take you hostage, you put up a fight, and the guy riding shotgun and all the passengers get to tell how the outlaws dragged you away kicking and screaming. It was a good plan, but I don't buy it."

"Do you actually believe that? I've never heard anything so ridiculous. If anyone should go to jail, it's you. You were riding with them when they robbed the stage. You have the payroll with you right now. If that's not guilt, I don't know what is."

"Shut up," he grated.

"I can't believe you actually intend to take me to jail for being kidnapped. Not only by that gang of thieves, but also by you. I've been abducted twice in the same day, and you have the gall to accuse me of being a criminal."

"Sit down and shut up."

Grudgingly, she clamped her mouth closed and dropped to a sitting position in the dirt.

He lifted the rabbit from the fire and pulled a long knife from inside his boot. He cut off a sizable piece and handed it to her, oblivious to singeing his fingertips. "Eat."

Megan took the meat and immediately dropped it on the ground. "It's hot," she said in an accusing tone.

"Of course it's hot. I just took it out of the fire."

Megan looked around and picked up a fairly flat rock, rubbing it on her pant leg in lieu of washing it. She balanced the stone on one knee. "Give me another piece," she said.

"I already gave you a piece. You dropped it in the dirt. Wipe it off and eat it."

She picked up the meat with two fingers and tossed it into his lap. "You eat it. I want a different piece."

Lucas grumbled under his breath about stubborn females and getting drunk, then cut her another hunk of rabbit. She used the rock as a plate and pulled the meat apart to eat in small strips.

"This is very good," she said with her mouth full.

He nodded.

"Are you really working for the railroad?"

Another short, dismissive nod.

"You don't look like you work for the railroad. I can't even picture you in a suit and tie."

Lucas shrugged. He shouldn't have assumed the simple act of eating would be enough to keep her quiet.

"Do you really know Mr. Donovan?"

He nodded again.

"You said he was your friend. Are you really friends or do you just work together?"

No nod or shrug would be enough to answer that. Lucas swallowed a bite of rabbit and took a moment to think of a short reply. "Brandt and I have been friends since before Annie and I married."

"Did he get you your job at the railroad?"

Didn't she ever shut up? "I don't work for the railroad."

"But you said—"

47

"I just took this one assignment for them. Brandt offered me the job as a favor."

"You really needed work, huh?" She tipped her head back and held a strip of rabbit above her mouth.

Lucas watched as she bit off the very tip of the meat, then slowly licked the grease off her lips. Her tongue darted to one corner, then traveled over her full bottom lip, returning across the top. Heat suffused his body and gathered between his legs, causing his manhood to strain against the confinement of his trousers.

Megan lowered her head and met his eyes, blissfully unaware of his response to her innocent actions.

"So you needed the work?" she asked again.

Lucas gave his mind a sharp order to get his body under control. "No."

Her brows puckered. "Then why did Mr. Donovan offer you the assignment?"

"He thought I might be short on cash."

"And were you?"

"Yes."

"Then you did need a job."

"Not the way you think." She didn't say anything, and Lucas decided to continue before she piped up again. "For the past year, I've been following someone. Every time I think I'm close enough to grab him, he disappears. I was using my life savings and the money I got from selling my house and cattle, but that ran out a while ago. Brandt knew and wanted to help me out."

"That's sweet of him," she said, licking her fingers.

It was the most sensual act Lucas had ever witnessed. He forced himself to concentrate on his own meal so he wouldn't be tempted to grab Megan Adams and kiss her senseless. He groaned at the picture that thought painted in his head.

"Are you all right?"

He straightened. "Fine."

"Did you burn yourself?" Megan asked, her eyes filled with concern.

"I must have," he said. She looked at him a minute longer. He blamed his raging pulse for making him give such an asinine answer.

"Who are you following?" she asked, drawing his attention back to the conversation.

A conversation Lucas would rather avoid.

"A man," he said.

Megan rolled her eyes and reached for the canteen Lucas had filled with fresh water and set between them. "I gathered that much. Who is he?"

"The man who murdered my wife and son."

Megan coughed and sputtered, choking on her mouthful of water. Lucas didn't move a muscle as she gasped for breath. Such a gentleman, she thought, racing to a lady's aid that way. After several seconds spent thinking she was going to suffocate, Megan got hold of herself. "Your family was murdered?"

Lucas inclined his head.

"When you said they were dead, I thought you meant they'd been the victims of some sort of epidemic. I never thought . . . Murdered? That's terrible. I'm so sorry."

"Would you do me a favor?" Lucas asked.

Megan studied him warily. "What?"

"Stop apologizing."

She didn't respond.

"Look," he said, "you don't have anything to be sorry for. You didn't cause their deaths. If you feel the need to say you're sorry, apologize for the fact that I have to drag you along and that you're slowing me down."

Megan bristled visibly. "If I'm slowing you down, why don't you let me go?"

"I can't do that."

"Why not?"

"Because Brandt would never forgive me."

"Then why don't you take me back to Leavenworth and let me deal with him?"

Lucas shook his head. "That would take too long. I can't risk losing Scott's trail."

"Who is Scott?"

"Silas Scott is the man who slaughtered my family," he said with a hard edge to his voice.

"I think I'm confused," Megan said.

Lucas gave a bark of laughter.

"It's not funny," she reproached. "If you're so hot on the heels of this Silas Scott person, why did you take the time to work for the railroad?"

"I lost Scott, so I figured I could make a little money before picking up his trail again."

"Then why are you in such a rush now?"

"I picked up his trail again."

"Here?"

"Not here, exactly. Back in Cubilo del Diablo."

"He was there? How did you know?"

"I saw him when I went for supplies with Tommy."

Understanding lit Megan's dark eyes. "That's why you came back with all the whiskey. You wanted to keep the bandits off their guard."

Lucas shrugged one shoulder. "They were pretty proud of themselves for pulling off the robbery, anyway. I just helped them relax with some liquor is all. They didn't suspect a thing when I offered to take the first watch. Once they were asleep, it was easy to sneak off with you and the loot."

"Well, I know you brought me along because you think I'm a criminal and need to be duly punished, but why bother lugging the money around?"

"A couple reasons," he answered. "First, so I can turn it in right along with you. Second, so I'd have money to travel on."

"Isn't that stealing?"

"Nope. The railroad's reimbursing me for any money I spend on the job."

"But technically, going after Scott isn't included in working for Union Pacific."

"Brandt will understand. He wants this guy caught as

much as I do. They can take it out of my pay if they want. I don't care."

"You don't care about much, do you?"

At Megan's low tone, he raised his head and met her eyes. "Catching Silas Scott is the only thing that matters."

"And what will you do once you catch him?"

"I'm going to kill him. Nice and slow, so I can watch him suffer."

Megan swallowed, her heart breaking for the man in front of her. It was none of her business, but she felt compelled to question him further. To find out just what made Lucas McCain, a man of so many contradictions, tick. He took a job to bring a gang of lawbreakers to justice, and yet he was stalking Silas Scott with the intention of committing murder.

"Did he make your wife suffer?" Anguish shone in his eyes, and Megan instantly regretted giving in to her penchant for being nosy.

"Yes."

"Will you tell me about it?" she asked in a soft, soothing voice. He looked at her a moment, as though deciding if she could be trusted with what was certainly the most painful memory of his lifetime.

"I used to be a bounty hunter," he started, his tone distant and devoid of any hint of emotion. "But Annie thought it was too dangerous, and with a new baby, she worried something would happen to me. Said she didn't want to raise Chad alone.

"We needed the money, though, until the cattle we were raising started to turn a profit. I worked another year, but to ease Annie's fears a bit, I only went after the least dangerous bounties.

"Finally we had a large enough herd to ship east. Got a good price per head, too. And since it looked like the ranch would make us a comfortable living, Annie begged me again to quit bounty hunting. One last trip, I said. I promised I would lay down my gun just as soon as I brought in Ted Mercury. I'd been after him a while, and it had become kind of personal. He wasn't dangerous, just hard to find.

"I kissed Annie and Chad good-bye one morning and promised to be back in less than a week. I kept my promise," he said, as though his honor were in question. "I was back in only five days. I had a bouquet of flowers in my hand for Annie, a hobbyhorse tied to the saddle for Chad. My rifle and pistols were all unloaded, and I'd taken off my gun belt—for good, I thought.

"I rode up to the porch and called out, but they didn't answer. So I went around back, hoping to surprise them. The kitchen was empty, which was odd, because it seemed Annie always had something in the oven—she loved to bake. I left the flowers and hobbyhorse there and started to search the rest of the house. I wasn't even worried—I just thought they were taking a nap or had gone for a walk or something.

"And then I opened the door to the dining room."

Megan saw him flinch, and she steeled herself for the rest of the story. Already she felt tears stinging the backs of her eyes.

"Annie was slumped over the table. She looked so beautiful, so peaceful. Even when she didn't move, I still thought everything was fine. But the closer I got, the more I realized something was definitely wrong. Her hands were behind her back, tied to the chair. I cut her loose and lifted her face in my hands. Her eyes were still open, just as soft and blue as ever. But the front of her dress was soaked in blood. There was so much, it had run down her body and pooled beneath the chair. There were so many knife wounds, I couldn't count them all.

"For a long time, I just stood there, staring at her. I don't think it had hit me yet that she was dead. And then I thought of Chad. I tore the house apart looking for him. He wasn't downstairs. He wasn't in our bedroom. I prayed so hard that he was in his room. That Annie had put him down for a nap and he'd slept through everything.

"He was in his room, all right. Wrapped in his favorite blue blanket. But the blanket and mattress were both covered in blood. His throat had been cut."

Megan bit down on her hand to keep from uttering a sound. She didn't want to distract Lucas, who seemed to be off in his own world, reliving the happenings of that day. Tears coursed down her face. Her sleeves were already drenched from wiping them across her face. A sob escaped her, and Lucas looked in her direction, as if only now remembering her presence.

"Why are you crying?" he asked. He sounded perplexed.

Megan shook her head. "How . . ." She sniffed. "How do you know who did it?"

Lucas's face turned to stone. "Scott wanted me to know. He left his wanted poster next to Chad's body. On the back, he wrote that he'd enjoyed spending the afternoon with my wife but that Annie hadn't cared for his choice of entertainment, so they'd put the baby to bed. I don't know if it was just a taunt or if he raped her."

The muscle in his jaw twitched, as Megan noticed it did whenever Lucas was angry. Right now he was furious, she could tell.

"I've often wondered if Scott made Annie watch when he killed Chad."

"Oh, God," Megan moaned, dropping her face to her knees. "What kind of animal would do something like that?"

"Silas Scott. He wanted revenge. He figured hurting my family was a good way to get it."

Megan raised her head and waited for him to continue.

"I'd put him in jail a few years before. For murder. He broke out of prison and came straight for me. But then I guess he decided it would be just as easy to kill my wife and son as to track me down. Since then he's been having a fine old time crisscrossing the state with me on his heels."

"You have to find him," Megan said, understanding now why tracking this man was so important to him.

Lucas nodded.

"And when you do . . ."

"I'm going to kill him."

Chapter Five

Megan dipped the bandanna into the stream and wrung it out, draping it over her eyes to relieve some of the pressure pounding there. She couldn't recall ever crying so much at one time. But then, she had never heard anything as heart-wrenching as the story Lucas had shared with her. And to think that it was true. He had seen it unfold firsthand, had loved the victims.

His own son. Oh, God, how horrible.

A lump formed in her throat as she fought to keep from sobbing again.

"You all right?"

She heard Lucas come up behind her but couldn't bear to face him. He had looked dumbfounded when she broke into tears. And after finishing his story, he'd handed her his brown kerchief with a brusque order to go to the stream and wet her face before her eyes swelled. Megan imagined it was already too late to stop that from happening.

He moved to her side, crouched beside her, and lifted

the bandanna. A small smile touched his lips. "You look like a raccoon."

She sniffed. "Thank you."

Lucas dabbed at two fresh tears that broke free. "I didn't mean to make you cry," he said.

"How can I not cry?" Megan asked. "That was the most tragic, horrid thing I've ever heard in my life."

"Yeah." He turned away, submerging the cloth in the racing water.

"I understand now why you have to follow this man. If you want to dump me at the next town and move on more quickly, that's okay. You can even just give me some food and water and point me in the right direction."

He grinned. "You're not getting off that easily. You're coming with me."

"But won't I slow you down?" Megan thought his dedication to the railroad noble, but if he was so close to catching Silas Scott, why did he want to encumber himself by dragging her along?

"Not too much, I hope. It may be rough riding at times, but I think you can handle it."

"So where are we headed? Or maybe I should ask where you think Silas Scott is headed."

"I'm not sure. He's traveling west, veering south a bit. If I'm lucky, he'll stop in Big Springs. There's a whore there he took a liking to when he was a kid. He goes to visit her every once in a while."

"How do you know so much about him?"

"I make it a point to find out as much as I can before I kill a man."

"You've killed that many?" Megan asked. Somehow she couldn't picture Lucas as a cold-blooded murderer. Sure, he wanted to kill Silas Scott, but that was out of righteous revenge. And while she didn't agree with his idea of vengeance wholeheartedly, she could certainly understand his reasoning.

One side of Lucas's mouth lifted in a semi-smile. "Only in self-defense, and I can count those cases on one hand."

"That's nice to know. So if I upset you along the way, you won't shoot me full of holes, right?"

"Wouldn't dream of it," Lucas said. His grin widened. "I would, however, consider staking you out for the buzzards and coyotes."

Megan licked her lips. "Oh, good. Then I'll have something to look forward to."

Lucas chuckled and rose to his feet, holding a hand out for her. "It's getting late. We'll be breaking camp early, so you'd better get some shut-eye."

Megan accepted his assistance. She brushed the dirt off the back of her pants and walked over to the fire. She watched as Lucas shook out his bedroll and spread it on the ground.

"There's only the one blanket," he said.

She noticed a devious twinkle in his blue eyes and knew he expected her to put up a fuss. Instead, she sauntered forward, swinging her hips in what she hoped was a seductive manner. She had seen other women use their feminine wiles, but she'd never actually tried it herself.

"It's so kind of you to sacrifice your own comfort for me," she said in her friendliest voice. "I really do appreciate it." Then, before he could so much as open his mouth to reply, she stretched out on the edge of the blanket and brought the other half over to cover her body, tucking the scratchy wool under her chin and snuggling in.

"I didn't mean for you to hog it. I thought we could share."

Lucas sounded like a little boy who'd just had his favorite toy taken away. Megan smiled, pulling the blanket higher to hide the response. She didn't answer.

"Fine," he said. She heard his footsteps as he stomped off to settle beneath a nearby tree. "But if it gets cold, I'm coming under there whether you like it or not."

The deep, resonant sound of snoring woke Megan. At first she thought she was responsible for the racket, and even half asleep, she blushed. But when she turned her head to brush long, tangled strands of hair back from her face and open her eyes, she realized the noise continued unabated. She was on her stomach, one arm bent awkwardly beneath her body, the other resting on something warm and . . . moving.

She jerked upright, her vision suddenly crystal clear. Her cheeks burned when she realized she'd been sleeping right beside Lucas McCain. Draped across him was more like it, she realized with chagrin. Thank God they'd both been fully dressed. She wiggled away from him, trying to pull the blanket from beneath his legs.

Lucas mumbled and rolled onto his stomach, pinning the blanket even more securely. His arm reached out, as if searching for something to hold. When he didn't find it, his brows came together in a frown. He turned onto his side and levered up on an elbow, looking at Megan through heavy-lidded eyes.

"It's not time to get up yet," he said. "Go back to sleep."

She gave the blanket another tug, hoping to free it and move to another spot.

"Come on," he said, grabbing her arm and dragging her down next to him.

Megan wiggled to get loose. Even though he really hadn't done anything untoward, she didn't think it was proper for them to sleep so close, even if she was his "prisoner."

"Settle down," Lucas said in a stern if sleep-laden voice. He wrapped an arm around her waist and rested his chin on the top of her head.

Megan remained rigid, trying to keep her body from touching his. She didn't care if he had already fallen back to sleep; she was not going to relax against his long, masculine form.

It was the last conscious thought she had before drowsily snuggling closer to his warmth.

They reached Topeka late the next afternoon. The hot sun beat down, drenching them in their own sweat. Megan had long ago begun bargaining with the Devil for a bath. She would give her firstborn child for a porcelain tub and a bar of rose-scented soap. By noon she'd agreed to give up the Adams Express, her home, and all her earthly belongings for a quick dip in a shallow creek. By four, she'd promised all that *Lucas* owned for just a splash from his canteen.

And as if the heat wasn't bad enough, Lucas seemed to be in the foulest of moods. He'd done nothing but curse since a rider heading in the opposite direction told him someone fitting Scott's description had passed him a while back. What if Silas wasn't going to stop off in Big Springs after all?

"What are you going to do now?" Megan had asked Lucas.

He swore and started mumbling under his breath. She never did get an answer.

Rather than ride straight through the middle of town, Lucas had them skirt the main thoroughfare and come around to the rear of the livery. He flipped a coin to a young boy for stabling their mounts and led Megan back outside into the bright, busy street.

His grip on her arm was strong but not painful, and she had to take two steps to equal one of his long, quick strides as he moved toward the Eat 'n' Sleep Hotel. The man behind the desk greeted them with a broad grin. His smile faltered, however, when Megan removed her hat and smacked it against her leg to dislodge several layers of dust. She looked up to see him staring at her now-scraggly, waist-length hair.

Lucas gave her an ominous glare before turning back to the clerk. "A room for me and my wife," he said.

The man quoted a price, and Lucas dug into his shirt pocket for the money. Megan peeked over his shoulder when he signed the register, curious when she saw him write *Mr. and Mrs. Luke Campbell* in tall, flowing letters.

"Send up a bath, will you?" Lucas said, then took her arm again, picked up the key the clerk slid across the counter, and started up the stairs to the third floor.

The room was larger than Megan had expected, most likely because Lucas had signed them in as man and wife. In the middle of the room stood a wide four-poster, on it a quilted bedspread covered in white eyelet lace, with several fluffy pillows stacked against the headboard. One window faced east, the other south, and in front of each sat a burgundy brocade armchair. Megan noticed that nothing in the room matched. White bedspread, burgundy chairs, sunflower-yellow curtains, blue-and-purple flowered wallpaper, and a worn, once mahogany-colored carpet. None of it went together well, but Megan liked the individual pieces.

Mainly, though, as she stood just inside the door, she wanted to fall facedown on the bed and sleep for a hundred years. Still, she was loathe to soil the immaculate white lace with her filthy, dust-covered clothes, and the same went for the brocade chairs. She was about to collapse on the faded carpet when a knock sounded on the other side of the door.

Lucas answered it, moving aside as several young men carried in a porcelain tub and buckets of steaming water.

Oh, she'd died and gone to heaven—she just knew it. She chewed on her bottom lip, wondering if the Devil would someday come to claim her firstborn. Certainly he realized she'd made the promise under duress; she couldn't be expected to comply. Besides, she would probably never have children of her own.

And then a mobcapped older woman came in with a pile of fluffy white towels, and Megan didn't even care anymore.

"Anything else, sir? Madam?" the woman asked.

"Nothing," Lucas said.

Megan grasped the plump woman's arm before she could leave and whispered in her ear, "I'd kill for a bit of rose soap."

The maid nodded and said, "I'll see what I can do."

Lucas's brows were drawn together, and he seemed less than happy. Megan didn't waste her time trying to figure out what was bothering him. He'd been grumpy all afternoon. She felt confident he'd get over it.

"Go ahead and get in the tub," he said. "I'll be back in a bit."

Megan had just tossed her hat onto the bureau and started yanking at her boots when he reappeared in the doorway. She lifted her head and waited.

"I'm locking the door behind me, Megan. Don't even try to run away."

"I assure you, I haven't the strength to run any farther than that bath. I intend to stay there until my skin is as wrinkled as raisins or I melt, whichever comes first."

"Good," was all he said before closing the door.

She heard the key turning in the lock and couldn't have cared less.

Lucas hadn't planned on leaving Megan alone so soon, but he suspected she was up to something, and he wanted to know what. He caught up to the maid as she reached the landing of the second floor.

"May I help you, sir?"

"Yes," Lucas said, wondering how to go about quizzing her without setting her curiosity on edge. "Back in the room, my wife said something to you."

"Yes, sir," she said, not elaborating.

Lucas shifted his weight. "What did she say, exactly?"

"She wanted a bit of rose soap is all, sir." Her mouth drifted down in a frown. "Is there something wrong?"

"No, not at all," he said, relief washing through his tense frame. "Is that all she asked for?"

"Yes, sir. I'm on my way to look for it now. Should I not give it to her?"

"No, that's fine. In fact, why don't I come with you? If you find any, I can take it back up to her."

The woman turned and made her way down the next flight of steps. Lucas followed, his mind racing as it cooked up what he hoped was a perfect story to explain the oddities of their stay that the hotel staff—and other

61

guests—might notice. If he started the rumor now, likely this maid would fill everyone else in.

"I don't mean to seem overprotective," he began. "It's just that my wife sometimes acts . . . rather strangely. It's to be expected, of course, after her terrible ordeal last year."

The woman cocked her head, and Lucas knew he'd drawn her in.

"She was kidnapped, you see. By a band of dangerous, murdering outlaws." A startled gasp reached his ears. He had to press his lips together to keep from laughing. "It . . . changed her. She gets confused now. Sometimes she even thinks I'm one of her abductors."

The maid stopped and turned to look at him with wide, astonished eyes.

Lucas shook his head sadly. "I'll warn you now not to go into the room if she's alone. It's best if I'm there . . . in case she gets out of control. You might want to tell the rest of the hotel staff, too. Better to be safe, you understand."

She nodded, her mouth falling open.

"About that rose soap?" he said, bringing her around.

"Oh, yes. Yes, sir. Your wife . . . she, uh, likes rose soap, does she?"

"Loves it. She says the scent reminds her of better times. I think she believes that if she uses enough of it, it will wash away the touch of the outlaws."

Another terrified gasp. Lucas winced, afraid he'd gone too far trying to convince the maid to keep her distance from Megan.

"They didn't . . . harm her, mind you. She wasn't violated. It's just that sometimes she can still feel their presence, their threat."

"Here, sir," she said, producing a much-used sliver of soap from a hallway closet. "Not much left of this bar, but I'd be happy to buy some more for your wife, if you'd like. I mean, if that's her one luxury after such suffering, I wouldn't mind spending a bit of my own pay."

"Thank you very much," Lucas said, touched by the woman's compassion—and her willingness to believe his trumped-up tale. "That won't be necessary. I'll go out and buy her some new things this very evening. Do you think you could have our clothes laundered, though?"

"Sure thing, Mr. Campbell."

Lucas smiled. Good. News did travel fast on the hotel grapevine. This maid already knew who he was—or, more precisely, who he'd said he was when he checked in mere minutes before.

"I can pick up the bundle a little later." Her eyes bugged out, and she stammered to correct herself. "After . . . after you get back, that is. I wouldn't dare bother your wife while you're gone."

"Yes, that's wise of you. I'll gather our things for you, and why don't I just set them outside the door? Would that make you feel more comfortable?"

"Yes, sir. Sad to say, it would."

"All right, then. And, miss?"

"Sir?"

"I probably also ought to warn you that, well, in her agitation my wife sometimes has to be restrained."

"Restrained?" the maid squeaked.

"She becomes delusional at times, and I have to tie her down. As barbaric as it sounds, it's the only thing that keeps her from hurting herself or others. Don't be worried if you see her like that. And don't pay any mind to her rantings. She sometimes says strange things."

"I understand, sir. I'll tell everyone the circumstances."

"Very good," Lucas said, turning to head back to the room. A smile tickled the sides of his mouth, begging to be let loose, but he wouldn't allow the grin until he was in the deserted privacy of the hallway outside the door.

He paused, listening for any sign of movement from within.

Nothing.

Lucas twisted the key in the lock and stepped into the room. The sight that greeted him froze him in his tracks.

He had never seen anything as sensual, erotic, and arousing as lithe Megan Adams drowsing in the yellow-trimmed porcelain tub. Her head rested against the back, her hair cascading over the rim in a fall of black and auburn, sparkling in the light that filtered through half-drawn draperies. In some dim recess of his mind he remembered that he hadn't closed the door, and he reached back to do so silently.

His breath caught as his eyes traveled lower, to Megan's bent knees. One leg was folded inside the tub, but the other was draped over the edge, tiny droplets of water sliding off her toes to form a wet circle on the rug. A twin spot grew beneath the slim, elegant fingers that brushed the soft carpeting.

Heat shot through Lucas's body, firing an almost painful hardness between his legs. And then his gaze caught on her breasts, bobbing just beneath the surface of the water, their pink tips appearing with each intake of breath that raised her perfectly formed chest.

Jesus, if you don't get out of here—and soon—you'll pull her out of that tub and have your way with her in a matter of seconds. Get out! his mind roared. Yes, he had to get out, get away from such a desirable display of womanly beauty, and clear his head.

Lucas swallowed and squeezed his eyes shut, trying to conjure an image that might erase Megan's from his mind. Nothing seemed to work.

Don't bother, man. Cuff her and get the hell out!

He searched the room for his saddlebags and rummaged around inside for the cold metal he knew had to be there. He went back to Megan, kneeling to fasten one end around the clubbed foot of the tub—she'd never manage to lift the full tub and slip it off—and the other iron ring around Megan's limp wrist.

There. Let's see her get out of this, he thought, rising to his feet to examine his handiwork. He took in Megan's elegant, milky-white skin, the clear water encasing her, caressing her, then fought the groan welling up from his gut. He looked at her dainty wrist and the heavy metal weighing it down.

With a rueful half smile, he set the sliver of rose soap on the pile of towels beside her and walked out. He was glad he would be gone when Megan awoke and found herself handcuffed to the tub. No doubt she'd bring the walls down around her, cursing him to eternal hell.

Chapter Six

Lucas plucked a plain white cotton shirt in his size off the pile and laid it on the counter with a polite nod to the pinched-faced proprietor's wife. Then he moved down the aisle to the stacks of trousers. He chose a pair in sturdy denim and slung them over his arm.

He wanted to get a change of clothes for Megan, too, but he had no idea what she would wear. She'd been dressed like a man for the past two days, so he didn't figure she could be too particular about her wardrobe. But somehow it didn't seem right to hide the gentle swells and curves that Lucas now knew lurked beneath her baggy shirt and pants. It wouldn't kill her to wear a dress, at least while they stayed in town. She could change back to her wayward-urchin look later.

With that determined thought, Lucas headed for the racks of ready-made feminine apparel. It was only as he flipped through the dresses that he realized he didn't know what size Megan wore.

He turned to the proprietress and cleared his throat, giving his most polite smile. "Do you think you could help me pick a dress for my wife, ma'am?"

She pursed her lips, and for a moment Lucas thought she might refuse to leave the relative safety of the counter. But then she crossed her arms over her chest and moved toward him.

"What size is she?" the woman asked.

"I'm not sure," Lucas said, frowning. "Her waist is about like this," he said, making a circle with his hands. "I'd say her hips are an inch or two wider. And her breasts would just about fill a man's hands." His mistake hit him like a brick to the stomach when the woman narrowed her eyes and gave him a freezing glare.

"It's odd that you don't know your wife's size," she said.

He shrugged, hoping to smooth over the blunder. "We haven't been married all that long. And we've been traveling, so I haven't learned all her little secrets yet. She would have come herself, but she's plumb tuckered out. I left her alone to bathe and rest before dinner."

The woman gave a disbelieving snort. "Maybe you would be better off getting her a skirt. The buttons can be adjusted if it doesn't fit just right."

Lucas nodded. "Sounds good."

"What color does she prefer?"

"I'm not sure." He had only seen her in a brown and red plaid shirt made for a man. "She's very soft and feminine," he said, wondering if God would strike him dead for such an outrageous lie.

The woman held up several choices. "This pale yellow is nice, but it gets dirty easily. The light blue is just as bad. Then there's this forest green, but it draws the heat like an iron skillet."

Lucas had half a notion to ask why the hell the store bothered to carry any of the garments if they were so troublesome. Then the flash of another color caught his eye. Tiny blue and yellow flowers danced around on the fabric of a red skirt, and Lucas knew the combination would suit Megan much better than any of the other, plainer prints.

"What about this one?" he asked.

The woman inhaled so deeply, her buttons threatened to pop. "Red is a shameful color, meant only for trollops and ladies of lesser morals."

"I like it," Lucas said. He could already picture the skirt on Megan. "Give me the yellow one, too," he said to appease the woman's sense of propriety.

"Will you be wanting unmentionables to wear with them?"

"Huh?" Lucas could have sworn the stodgy old lady blushed.

"Unmentionables, sir. Undergarments."

"Oh, you mean drawers and such." Yep, the old lady definitely blushed three shades of red.

"Does your wife need them or not?" she snapped.

"I suppose. A couple of blouses, too."

Lucas watched the woman fold the two skirts and add them to his pile on the counter. Then she picked two blouses, one plain with no frills, the other ruffled from neck to waist and around the wrists.

He smiled and dug into his pocket to pay for the purchases. But she wasn't done yet. She seemed to take great pride in building the stack of clothes until it wobbled precariously. Then she simply started another. He ended up buying drawers, chemises, camisoles, stockings, garters, and something that looked like a bear trap, which the woman insisted no decent female should be without.

Too stunned and out of his element to argue, Lucas simply handed over the money, asking to have everything wrapped and delivered to the hotel. At the last minute, he remembered that he'd wanted to get Megan some rose-scented soap or perfume or the like, and he started digging into his pocket again. Whatever she could find would be fine, he assured the woman. He scooped up his things—a mere pittance of the full order—and started down the street for the bathhouse.

Lucas let out a long sigh as he lowered himself into the steaming water. Nothing eased the aches and pains of the trail like a hot bath. It would have been nice to take advantage of the privacy of the hotel room, but he didn't think Megan would appreciate his presence.

Of course, he didn't much care what Megan thought. At least, he shouldn't. He was still fuming over the expense of kidnapping a woman. A man never would have cost him so dearly or given him so much trouble.

A man's leg never would have looked so damn good hanging over the side of a tub, either, he reminded himself.

And that had been one damn fine leg.

Lucas cursed and forced himself to relax, letting the heat seep through his stiff, tired muscles. He lathered his hands with a chunk of the brand-new soap he'd paid extra for and scrubbed every inch of his body. When he finished, the water was nearly as dark as his boots. He felt ten pounds lighter as he walked next door to the barber shop.

Half an hour later, Lucas had a hard time recognizing his reflection in the mirror. With a clean-shaven face and neatly trimmed hair that barely brushed the collar of his new shirt, he looked almost human again.

He paid the barber and started for the Eat 'n' Sleep, humming an old tune his mother used to sing. In the hotel lobby, a bloodcurdling scream stopped Lucas in mid-stride. The young man behind the desk blanched, and Lucas's stomach clenched. He cast an apologetic smile toward the hotel clerk and quickly made his way up the two flights of stairs.

People were gathered in a tight group outside his room. The mobcapped maid he'd spoken to earlier crouched in front of the door, talking through the keyhole in soothing tones. "Hush, now, Mrs. Campbell. All's well. Your husband will return directly, I'm sure."

A frightfully calm voice drifted out of the room. "You'd better hope to hell he doesn't come back, because when he does, I'm going to rip out his liver and feed it to him for supper." Less than a second passed before Megan started screaming again. "Lucas McCain, you bastard, let me loose!"

"I warned you that she gets confused," Lucas said, annoyed that she'd used his real name when he was trying to maintain a modicum of anonymity in this town.

The maid whirled around. "Oh, Mr. Campbell, your wife's been hysterical for nearly an hour now. We've tried to calm her down, sir—told her you'd be back in a wink—but nothing seems to work. She must be out of her mind again, Mr. Campbell, calling you horrible names."

He could imagine. A high-pitched screech sounded, followed by the most foul language Lucas had heard in a long time. Where had Megan learned to talk like that?

"Thank you for trying to help," he said, pulling the room key out of his pocket. "Some packages should be delivered soon from the mercantile. When they arrive, will you please bring them up? And I think it would be best if my wife and I remained in our room this evening. Could you please send two steak dinners up within the hour?"

The onlookers remained, wide-eyed, waiting to see what he would do. "If you don't mind. I'd rather not deal with this in front of an audience," he said.

"So sorry, sir," the maid said with an amateur curtsy, waving the others away. "I'll make sure you get your meals and parcels. Just leave your dirty laundry in the hall, and I'll take care of that, too."

Lucas turned the key in the lock, took a deep breath, and opened the door. He wasn't sure what he thought he'd see, but he sure as hell hadn't expected Megan to be standing in the middle of the room completely naked. Her position was awkward, hampered as she was by the handcuffs.

"You son of a bitch! How dare you lock me up like some rabid cur!"

He didn't respond. The carpet was soaked from the water that had sloshed over the sides when she'd tried to move the heavy tub. She had obviously jostled it considerably more than he'd expected. His gaze drifted from the wet rug to the handcuffs attached to Megan's arm. Her wrist was red from her struggle to get free.

He tried to keep from looking at the rest of her, but it was damn hard to avoid doing so. Her veil of hair didn't cover even a portion of what he shouldn't be seeing. Hills and valleys of creamy flesh. The slight scent of roses drifted in the air.

With a low oath, he crossed to the bed and ripped off the coverlet, throwing it at her. "Cover yourself."

She flung the quilt aside, standing as straight as possible. "Unlock these damn cuffs."

He turned to face her, his body buzzing with unleashed tension. "If you're smart, you'll wrap up in that bedspread before I forget I'm a gentleman."

She glared at him, her maple-syrup eyes shooting daggers. "Gentleman? Hah! You'd better sleep with one eye open, Lucas McCain, or you may wake up dead."

He cursed and stalked over to the discarded bedspread. He draped it around her, pulling it about her neck. "Hold this," he said, bringing her free hand up to the bunch of fabric. He kept her fingers in place and retrieved the key to the handcuffs, holding it up as a peace offering.

She set her jaw, and Lucas crouched to remove the cuff from the tub.

Megan straightened, and he released her wrist from the shackle. Rather than rubbing at the marred skin, she gathered the bedspread about her and regally stalked away.

Lucas watched as she climbed onto the bed and

71

propped herself with wounded dignity against the pile of pillows. "I'm sorry about the cuffs," he said. "I didn't want to give you a chance to escape."

"What makes you think I would run away?"

Lucas dropped into one of the armchairs. "It's been my experience that criminals will do almost anything to keep from going to prison."

"I'm not a criminal."

He chuckled. "Funny. Most of them say that, too."

"So what does that mean? You don't believe criminals when they say they're innocent, because they all claim to be. But you don't believe innocent people, either, when they say they've been wrongly accused."

"That's what judges are for."

"I'm guilty until proven innocent, huh?"

"Yep. Don't forget, I saw you with those outlaws."

"I saw *you* with them," Megan said.

"I told you, I was masquerading to capture the real culprits," he said.

Suddenly Megan became aware that they could go around in circles with this argument until Armageddon. Lucas believed she had been the mastermind behind the payroll robberies, and his opinion wasn't likely to change. She would have to try another tactic.

"All right," she said, shrugging. "You were masquerading, and you caught me red-handed."

Lucas met her gaze. At least she had his full attention.

"You've got me, Lucas McCain. I'm guilty."

Megan thought she saw a spark of surprise in the blue depths of his eyes, but his face remained impassive.

"I admit it," she said. "I planned the whole thing. And I would have gotten away with it if it hadn't been for you." Megan couldn't believe her own ears. But Lucas's cocky I'm-right-and-you're-a-criminal attitude had finally gotten the best of her. Maybe if she confessed, made up a story so ridiculous that *no one* could fall for it, he would finally come to his senses.

"Do you want to know *how* I did it? It was brilliant, if

I do say so myself." She didn't wait for a reply. "I met Evan one night on my way home from work. His horse had thrown a shoe. It was late, so I invited him to stay the night. We had a quiet dinner and made small talk until neither one of us could deny our urges any longer. We didn't even make it upstairs; we made love right there on the steps. Hot, sweaty, passionate love that left us both gasping for air."

Megan lifted her gaze and looked at Lucas. His eyes gave nothing away, but the muscle in his jaw jumped.

"I didn't go to the Express the next day, and Evan didn't take his horse to town. We stayed in bed for hours, pleasuring each other. A pounding at the door woke us late that afternoon; Dougie and Tom had spotted Evan's horse in the corral and wanted to know what was going on. That's when he told me they made a living by robbing stages.

"The timing couldn't have been better. I wanted to get back at the railroad for trying to put me out of business, and these boys could help me. It's just like you said—even if the Adams Express did go under, I'd have the payroll money to keep me comfortable for the rest of my days.

"I explained my plan to Evan, and he convinced the boys to make me a full partner. I wasn't going to split the booty with them evenly, of course; that would have been downright stupid on my part. After all, without me telling them when the payrolls would be on the stage, they wouldn't have been able to steal a dime. I convinced them to keep all the money stashed away until we could sit down and divvy it up. Then we would go our separate ways.

"I sure do miss them," she said, trying to sound forlorn. "Why, do you know that I was the first woman Dougie and Tommy had ever been with? That's something you don't forget. And Frank, well, he was wild. Even more passionate than Evan."

"You let them pass you around, huh?" Lucas asked, his voice full of derision.

"Of course not. I told you, I was in charge. I picked who I wanted to be with and when."

"Where did you stash the payrolls?"

She shrugged a shoulder and plucked at a loose thread in the bedspread. "You don't really think I'm going to tell, do you?"

He pushed to his feet and started unbuckling his gun belt. "You seemed eager enough to cut Evan in on your little plan." He dropped the leather and Colts to the floor. "I'll bet if I tickled you in just the right spot, you'd tell me where the money is."

For the first time since she'd come up with the absurd idea of confessing to a crime she hadn't committed, Megan felt a tug of apprehension. She watched as Lucas started slipping the buttons of his shirt through their holes.

"No. No." Her voice squeaked. "I wouldn't tell you a thing."

The shirt fell away from his bronze skin in a puff of white. His fingers moved to the top button of his trousers, and Megan truly began to panic.

"Don't you dare," she said. "You're a lawman. You can't become involved with a prisoner."

"I don't wear a badge. I'm just doing a favor for a friend, remember? He didn't say anything about keeping my hands off."

"Well, I'm saying it. Keep your hands off."

He laughed, long and deep. "You don't have a choice in the matter."

Megan pulled the quilt up to her neck and scooted back against the headboard. Lucas came to the side of the bed, his pants completely unbuttoned now.

"Come on, honey. It's not like you haven't done this before." He grabbed a corner of the spread and gave it a little tug.

She tried to get the quilt away from him, but his grip only tightened. The more she fought, the harder he yanked. Megan had to either let him pull her close or abandon the blanket altogether. And somehow she didn't think running around the room naked would raise her odds any.

With one strong tug, he brought her flush against his body. The bedspread suddenly seemed terribly thin, for she could feel the heat from his skin burning her own. She squeezed her eyes shut and prayed to disappear.

His warm breath on her cheek alerted her to the nearness of his mouth. Then she felt his lips brushing hers. At the soft touch, some of her fear fled on a breathy sigh. The tip of his tongue darted between her slightly open lips and began a slow exploration of her mouth. He took his time, kissing her fully, sliding a hand inside the blanket to cup one breast.

She moaned and instinctively pressed upward to allow his callused hand better access to the sensitive flesh. He kneaded the mound, flicked the pebbled nub with his thumb. When he released her mouth, she gulped for air, struggling to regain her equilibrium. But what sanity she had left disappeared the minute his tongue circled her nipple. She gasped, let go of the bedspread, and ran her hands over his back, twisting her fingers in his hair.

He moved to her other breast, giving it equal treatment. Then his hands slid over her dampened skin, enticing her every nerve ending to the surface until her body became an exquisite conductor of his lightest touch.

He broke away and lifted his head to meet her eyes. Megan dug her nails into his shoulders, silently begging him to continue his bewitching ministrations.

"Where's the money?" His chest heaved; his voice rasped.

She shook her head, unwilling to let anything tear away the web of pleasure he'd spun around her.

He kissed her again, hard and demanding, letting his weight push her into the mattress. She could feel his arousal pressing against her thigh.

"Tell me."

"I don't know," she said, only half aware of what he was asking.

"Tell me where you stashed the money, Megan."

"I don't know."

"You do. Tell me."

"I lied." She closed her eyes, letting her arms fall to her sides. "I don't know where the money is. I wasn't in on it. I lied."

Chapter Seven

Lucas stared down at Megan a moment longer, then shoved himself up from the bed. He rebuttoned his trousers and moved back to the chair, picking up the gun belt to rest it on his thigh.

Damn, but he'd almost lost control. A second longer and he would have forsaken everything to be buried inside her. He swore and reached for his shirt, just about ripping it in his haste to get it on.

His gaze returned to Megan. He watched her chest rise and fall as she tried to calm her breathing. It didn't matter how many other men she'd spread her legs for. She was right. He was playing the role of a lawman, and as such he had no right to have intimate contact with her. Even if her dark eyes and firm breasts seemed to call to him. Even if he couldn't be within ten feet of her without remembering that he hadn't been with a woman since Annie's death.

Five years. Five long, celibate years. Damn, those years were taking their toll now.

He ran a hand through his hair, vaguely registering its new shortness. He stood and took a step toward the bed, only to see Megan grab the spread, wrap it around her body, and shrink into the pillows.

A knock sounded at the door. He gave a weary sigh, buttoning his shirt before going to answer it. He opened the door only a crack, using his body to shield Megan's blanket-covered form.

"Got your packages here, Mr. Campbell."

Lucas held the door in place with his foot and took the paper-wrapped bundles. "Thank you."

"The dinners will be up as soon as possible, sir. Should I send someone to retrieve the bath?"

Lucas nodded. "That would be fine," he said before closing the door. Then he lifted the ivory-handled knife out of his boot and cut the thin strings binding the packages.

"Here." He pulled back the paper for Megan to see her new skirts and blouses, tossing them onto the bed. "Everything you need should be there."

Megan sat up and peered over the edge of paper. "These are all for me?" she asked softly.

"I'm wearing my new clothes," he said, holding up his arms and looking down at the now-wrinkled cotton shirt. "The lady over at the mercantile didn't seem to think you could get along with anything less." He shrugged. "I don't know much about women's clothing, so I let her decide what I should purchase."

She looked up at him. Her eyes held a trace of moisture, and Lucas felt decidedly uncomfortable.

"Thank you."

"Whatever," he said gruffly. "Better get dressed before they come for the tub."

She gave a little smile, grabbed the packages, and ran behind the satin and mahogany dressing screen, the long quilt trailing behind her.

Within minutes, several young men came to remove the porcelain bathtub. Lucas took a seat in a brocade chair near the window and let them do their job. A moment later, the maid bustled in, giving orders to an older black man who carried a small square table. He set the table where the maid told him, covered it with a pristine white lace cloth, and arranged the flatware and a vase of fresh-cut flowers.

The woman clicked her tongue and waved the man out of the way. She brought in two plates heaped with boiled potatoes, green beans, and thick, blackened steaks, then gave a wink and backed out of the room.

Lucas chuckled at the maid's motherly manner. He looked at the bouquet in the center of the table, then at its reflection in the mirror above the bureau. A movement caught his eye, and his breathing all but stopped.

In the mirror, he could clearly see Megan behind the screen. She seemed unaware of her nudity, comfortable and relaxed. She'd laid out all the different pieces of clothing, studying each. Lucas watched, mesmerized. He couldn't have looked away if a thousand-pound bull had charged him head-on.

She picked up the yellow skirt and held it to her waist, then set it down. She stepped into a pair of silk drawers that shimmered in the bright lamplight, tying them at the waist. Then she slipped the matching camisole over her head.

Lucas thought he would be disappointed to see her finely proportioned figure covered, but the white of the undergarments only accentuated the paleness of her flesh, drawing his attention to the length of her shapely legs.

She put on the ruffled blouse, leaving it open at the neck. Lucas expected her to don the yellow skirt she'd picked up earlier, but instead she chose the red. And he'd been right. The color set off the auburn highlights in her hair.

As she piled the rest of the unworn clothing together, he noticed that she had opted not to wear the corset. For some reason, that pleased him. She rolled the sheer silk stockings into a ball and set them aside, along with the garters.

Lucas sat up straighter when she came around the dressing screen and into view. He cleared his throat. "Does everything fit properly?" he asked.

"Fine, thank you." She tugged at the skirt, as if wearing feminine attire were alien to her. "You shouldn't have gone to so much trouble."

"You needed something to wear while your other clothes are being laundered."

"Still, two skirts, two blouses." Her cheeks turned an attractive shade of pink. "And the other things. It's too much."

He got up, dragging the second armchair to the table, setting it opposite his own. "Sit down," he said. "Your dinner's getting cold."

She came forward and sat, sweeping the skirt aside to fold one leg beneath her. Lucas saw a bare foot sticking out and smiled.

"I don't think two changes of clothes are too much if you can wear them," he said, returning to their earlier conversation.

"That's just it," she said. "I probably won't wear them once I get my old clothes back."

"You don't like dressing like a lady?"

She shifted in the chair, cutting through the crisp crust of her steak. "It's not very practical to wear expensive gowns while trying to run a business. Layers of petticoats tend to get in the way."

"So you choose to wear men's clothes."

Megan swallowed before answering. "I didn't used to. My mother would have swooned if I'd dared to wear trousers. But Mother is in New York, and I have to keep the Express afloat. You get more respect from people—especially men—if you face them on their terms. Do you really think my drivers would pay a whit of attention to me if I was wearing a frilly, lacy gown and fanning myself? No. They would humor me and then go behind my back to Caleb."

"Your brother?"

"Yes. But he doesn't own the Adams Express. I do. Papa left it to me in his will."

"Did your father always want you to take over for him?"

Megan laughed and speared a chunk of potato. "Hardly. At first he fought it tooth and nail. I started by working on the books at home, keeping all the figures straight. After a while, it seemed second nature for me to be in the depot. Caleb didn't really want the business, anyway. He tried to get involved to make Papa happy, but it wasn't in his blood. Cattle ranching suits him better, I think."

She looked up and met Lucas's gaze over the rim of his glass. "Did Annie always wear dresses?" *Good Lord, where had that come from?*

The same thought must have gone through his mind, for he choked a bit before managing to swallow his mouthful of wine.

"Did she?" Megan asked again.

"Do you always blurt out whatever comes into your head? Or do you just enjoy probing people's personal lives?"

"I didn't think it was such a difficult question. It could be answered with a simple yes or no."

"Until the next question, of course, which I'm sure you'd fire off within seconds."

She pursed her lips. "My mouth has always run a bit rampant. I don't seem to be able to help myself. I think most people have a sort of sieve in their brains that keeps them from saying things they shouldn't. My sieve is broken, I believe."

Lucas broke into laughter.

"It's not funny. Truly, it's caused me nothing but trouble. I should probably see a doctor. Maybe there would be something about it in his medical books."

"You think he could look up a cure for a broken strainer in your head?" he asked, still chuckling.

"Not a strainer," she corrected. "A sieve."

That caused Lucas to clutch his belly in amusement. He all but doubled over and fell to the floor.

"Well, don't think of it as a sieve, then. How about a door? Yes, that's better. Most people have a door in their mind that closes and keeps them from blurting out foolish things. My hinges must need greasing, because the door has ceased to swing shut."

In silent, helpless mirth, Lucas slapped a hand on the table, causing the silverware to jump and jingle.

Megan sat back, crossing her arms in front of her chest in vexation. What had come over him? She didn't find a brain disorder at all humorous.

When his booming guffaws subsided to hiccuping chuckles, Megan focused once again on her meal. The outside of the thick steak looked burned, but the inside was pink and tender. She popped a bite into her mouth and stoically ignored the arrogant man sitting across from her, chuckling now and again.

Long minutes passed, and they had all but cleared their plates before he said, "Always."

She raised her eyes and stared at him. "Excuse me?"

"Annie always wore dresses," he clarified.

"Oh." Megan had almost forgotten that she'd asked. "She must have been a real lady."

"She was. I don't remember her ever looking mussed or tired. Even after a full day of backbreaking work."

Megan's fingers tightened around her fork. She didn't know why it should matter, but she suddenly felt like a scruffy waif overshadowed by the beautiful, always proper Annie McCain. Then a stab of guilt hit her midgut. Good God, how could she possibly feel inadequate compared to a dead woman?

But then, Annie had evidently been so wonderful. Beautiful, gracious, soft-spoken, kind. She'd won Lucas's heart and borne him a son. Megan had thus far called him every vile name she could think of and slowed him down in his race for vengeance. Oh, yes, comparisons were called for. And clearly, compared to Megan, Annie McCain was like a sparkling new yellow-fringed surrey parked next to a pile of horse manure.

Megan waved a hand in front of her face, suffering the sudden, overwhelming sense that flies were buzzing around her head.

"It's too bad you're stuck with me," she said, a hint of bitterness entering her tone. "I'm sure you'd rather pass the time with a lady."

"And you aren't?"

"Do I look like a lady to you?"

"That depends. If I were to judge by your clothes, I'd have to say that the outfit you're wearing is plenty pretty. The skirt brings out the red in your hair and the sparkle in your eyes. But then, it is a mite less extravagant than what most 'ladies' would wear. And your trousers—no lady would be seen in them."

"There you have it," Megan said grimly, draining her goblet of wine.

"Of course," Lucas continued, "anyone with an ounce of sense would know you're a lady just by the way you carry yourself."

His words caught her attention. She glanced up. His eyes shone like sapphires, deep and fathomless.

"Your spine is always ramrod straight. Even now, with one leg tucked underneath you, you're not touching the back of the chair. You hold your head high and look people in the eye when you address them—whether it's with polite words or foul names."

She had the courtesy to blush at the mention of her rude language.

"And I happen to know you were brought up to be the most proper of ladies, living in New York City until you were sixteen."

"How do you know so much about me?"

"Brandt Donovan filled me in. I don't like surprises." He waited a moment, then continued. "Maybe it's the West that tarnished your image a bit. Made you thicken your skin to protect yourself. Wearing trousers ensures that you're taken seriously as owner and operator of the Adams Express. I'll bet it also protects you from the attentions of certain men."

"What men would those be?" she asked sardonically.

"The ones who would be pounding down your door if they ever saw you cinched up in a proper gown."

"Hmph."

"You don't believe me?"

"No one's come knocking at my door for some time now."

"How about Evan and the boys?"

"I told you that was all a lie. I made it up to convince you that the idea of me being involved in the robberies was ridiculous. Unfortunately, it failed."

"Miserably."

"Yes."

"So tell me about the men in your life. Other than 'the boys' that is."

"No."

"No?"

She shook her head. "There are none to tell you about."

"You mean to tell me that no one, not a single man, has called on you? Even before you stopped wearing dresses?" He sounded almost incredulous.

"Well, there was Bobby Spencer. But that hardly counts."

"Why not?"

"He was six years old." She turned her head to avoid seeing Lucas burst into another fit of mirth. To his credit, he kept his laughter under wraps. But his voice wavered a bit, and she knew he was fighting a chuckle.

"Six?"

"Yes, he was six. And I was seventeen. He used to follow me home from Sunday services to bring me flowers. His mother had to come collect him more than once."

"That's a cute story, but I still don't believe that nobody has at least *tried* to court you. I'd have bet the railroad payroll that you had to beat callers off with a stick."

"Nope. I suppose Caleb might have had something to do with it. He does have a way of towering over people and making their knees knock if he so much as looks at them sideways."

"I know the feeling."

"Really? Someone was tall enough to intimidate you?"

"Not since *I* was six years old," he said, grinning. "I was talking about you. You have a glare that can be so cold, people might want to start striking matches."

"And has it chilled you?"

"Once or twice," he said. "And you've got the staff of this hotel convinced you're a truly dangerous woman."

She gasped. "That's not true."

"Sure is. That poor chambermaid was quaking in her boots when I came up the stairs."

"Well, if you hadn't handcuffed me to the bathtub, I wouldn't have had to put up such a fuss."

"No, you'd be twenty miles from here by now."

"I told you I wouldn't have run away."

"Of course not. You like being in my company, especially knowing that I'll put you in jail at the first opportunity."

"Things could be worse," she said.

"How so?"

"I could have been kidnapped by Frank." The very thought made her skin crawl.

"He was a sight, wasn't he? How many different bugs do you think lived in that mangy hair?"

"Ugh. I don't want to know."

Lucas laughed. Then he pushed back his chair and rose. "Were you planning to go to bed soon?"

"I'm not very tired," Megan said, shifting to set both feet on the carpet.

"That poses a bit of a problem, then," he said with a frown.

"What problem?"

"I need to go out, and I can't leave you alone without cuffing you or tying you up."

"Where are you going?" She stuffed her hands under her legs to keep from fidgeting.

"To Big Springs."

"Why can't I go with you?"

"It's better that you don't," he answered vaguely.

"Why are you going?"

85

"You know why."

"Because you think that's where Silas Scott is?"

"If he's not there now, he will be soon. He won't leave the area without visiting Nelly."

A wave of fear washed over her at the thought of Lucas confronting Scott. "Can't you just tell the law where to find him? It would be so much safer."

His jaw locked. "No."

"Lucas," she said, rising. "It isn't worth it. You could be hurt. Killed. And then what would it matter if you were the one to finally track him down?"

"What's it going to be?" he asked, turning away. "Rope or cuffs? I'll have to tie both hands if I use rope, only one if you choose the handcuffs."

"You don't need to use either. I won't go anywhere."

"Pick one, Megan. I don't have all night. Where do you want to be for the next few hours?"

"Can you at least let me get ready for bed first? I don't want to sleep in these clothes."

"Make it fast."

She darted behind the screen and shed the skirt and blouse. Lucas hadn't thought to buy a nightgown, and sleeping naked under the present circumstances was absolutely out of the question. So she left the chemise and drawers in place.

"Close your eyes, please," she called.

"Not on your life," Lucas returned.

"At least turn around. It's not gentlemanly to make a lady parade by in her unmentionables."

"Blasted unmentionables again," he mumbled.

"What?"

"Nothing. I'll turn around, but keep talking so I know where you are." He moved to the dresser, facing the door.

"Are you looking?"

"No," he lied, watching for her reflection in the mirror.

"I'm coming out now," she warned.

Lucas watched as she stuck her head around the screen and checked to see that his back was turned.

"Start talking," he said to keep her attention away from the mirror. God only knew how devastating her wrath would be if she discovered his secret.

"All right. I'm coming out from behind the screen now. Don't look."

"I won't."

"I'll climb into bed, get under the covers, and then you can put on the handcuffs. I'd really rather you didn't, though."

He watched as she crept across the room, reached the bed, and jumped onto the mattress, quickly pulling the sheets up to her neck. He had already touched her bare flesh, even suckled her breasts, and she worried that he might see her in her drawers. She would be none too happy if she found out he'd watched her get into those drawers in the first place.

"You can turn around now."

He waited a second, then did just that. "Get comfortable," he said. "You'll have to stay like this for a while."

She wiggled around, rearranging the pillows. "All right," she said, raising one arm toward a bedpost. "Cuff me."

Chapter Eight

What in hell had possessed him to bring Megan along? Lucas asked himself for the hundredth time. He should have simply reported back to Brandt and told him to go after her. She hadn't suspected that anyone knew of her tie to the payroll bandits, so she wouldn't have been likely to run. Brandt could have talked to the Leavenworth marshal, gone down to the Adams Express, and taken her into custody. But no, Lucas thought. He'd had to be some big hero, bringing in the leader of the outlaw gang and killing Silas Scott all in one fell swoop. But Megan had turned out to be more trouble than she was worth.

Lucas swore and urged his horse into a faster lope.

Still, he wouldn't have traded the sight of Megan tucked up to her ears in bed for anything. She'd looked almost like a little girl waiting for her parents to come wish her good night. Until she'd reached toward the bedpost, and the blanket had fallen to reveal the full swell of her breasts.

He'd wanted to say to hell with Silas Scott, throw off his own clothes, and crawl under the covers with her. But he'd retained just enough of his senses to secure Megan and get the hell out of the room. In his whole life, no one had ever tempted him as much as Megan Adams did.

Remember Annie! his mind screamed. *Sweet Annie. Quiet Annie. Your wife, the mother of your child.*

Annie had been a good wife, always willing to open her arms and allow Lucas his husbandly rights. Still, he had never wanted Annie the way he wanted Megan. And he'd never felt she truly enjoyed making love. Tolerated it, perhaps even found fulfillment a time or two. But she had never thrown her head back and called his name—the way he envisioned Megan would. She had never let him make love to her in the kitchen while biscuits baked. Sex was to be had only in the bedroom after they retired.

He pictured Megan being game anytime, anywhere. He already knew she possessed a wellspring of hot, wild passion. Now he wanted the chance to taste that ecstasy. He wanted to watch her flushed face as she found her pleasure.

He mumbled under his breath and slowed his horse to a walk. Dismounting, he tethered Worthy to the lowest branch of a nearby tree. He checked both Colts to make sure they were loaded before starting toward the lone cabin in the distance. The rickety building stood surrounded by small trees and shrubs, washed in moonlight.

Lucas circled the shack to make certain there would be no surprises that might foil his plans. He spotted a horse tied at the front and frowned. Scott didn't ride a paint. Where was his old, scarred black gelding?

Maybe Scott's mount had floundered or gotten worn out. There was no law that said a man had to stick with the same horse his entire trip across the state. Lucas shook off a nagging thread of doubt. He pushed up on the balls of his feet and peered in the tiny square window above his head.

A small, grimy cook stove littered with pans and dishes hunkered in one corner of the room. Against the far wall, two figures groped and rolled around on a narrow cot. A dirty sheet hid all but their legs and the groans of frantic lovers on a creaking bedframe.

Lucas went to the door and waited until the noises ceased. Blood pounded in his ears. His heart raced. Finally. After chasing Silas Scott for so many long, tortured years, he would finally be able to stare down the barrel of his gun and shoot the bastard right between the eyes.

Annie and Chad would finally be at peace.

He would be at peace.

With a low growl, he raised a foot and kicked in the door, oblivious to the crash it made as it bounced against the wall. The occupants of the bed sat up, startled, grappling for the stained sheets. The woman shrieked. The man held up his hands in surrender.

Lucas lowered his gun a fraction of an inch, his muscles contracted in rage. The man in bed with Nelly was not Silas Scott. He was a kid, no more than eighteen by the looks of it.

"Get your clothes and get out," he said through clenched teeth.

The young man grabbed his pants from the floor and started struggling to get them on.

"Dress on your way," Lucas ordered. "Leave it there," he said when he saw the boy reaching for his gun belt.

The kid's face contorted in fear and embarrassment, but he did what he was told, clutching the pile of clothes in front of him as he ran out of the shack. Lucas kept his eyes trained on Nelly but held the door open until he heard the boy's horse gallop off.

Having had time to compose herself, Nelly sat across the bed, the sheet covering her from breast to hip. She ran one foot along the length of her other leg and smiled.

"You didn't have to do that, honey. I could have had him out of here in two shakes and still been ready for you."

"Where's Silas?"

Her smile wavered. "Who?"

"Don't play games with me, Nelly," he said in a barely

controlled voice. "Scott wouldn't come this way without dropping in to see you."

"What do you want with him?" She sat up a little straighter.

"I'm going to kill him. But that shouldn't surprise you. I imagine a lot of people would pay good money to see the bastard hang. Now tell me where he is."

"I don't know."

He took a step closer, aiming his gun at her heart. "Don't test me, Nelly. I'm not in the best of humor these days, and as far as I'm concerned, killing you would be good practice for when I finally do meet up with Scott."

"I don't know where he is."

One side of his mouth lifted in a grin. He cocked the hammer on his Peacemaker. "Too bad. There's a shortage of good whores in these parts."

"Wait!" she cried. "He came through here earlier. The son of a bitch wanted a quick tumble before he got back on the trail. Said he was headed for Wichita."

"You'd better not be lying to me, Nelly. If you are, I'll be back."

"I ain't lying. I don't owe Silas a thing. He told me ten years ago he was gonna take me away and make me his wife. But I'm still here."

Lucas released the hammer and slid the gun into its holster. He watched Nelly McFadden a moment longer, then turned for the door.

"Hey, mister. When you find Silas, tell him I said I hope he burns in Hell."

"I'll do that," Lucas said, touching the brim of his Stetson.

Lucas slipped into the hotel room well after midnight. He discarded his boots and gun belt in the dark, not bothering to light a lamp.

He climbed into bed, still fully clothed, leaning across Megan's sleeping form to remove the metal cuff from her dainty wrist. She mumbled incoherent words under her breath and rolled to her side. Tucking her head into his shoulder, she threw an arm over his midriff. He watched her, sure she would awaken at any moment and run screaming from his nearness.

Several minutes passed. He relaxed as best he could with her body rubbing against his and tucked her more fully into the crook of his arm. The thin material of her chemise did little to keep his mind from wandering, and his body quickly followed the forbidden path.

He closed his eyes, adjusting his internal clock to wake him in three hours. That's about all the time he could spare before getting back on the trail after Scott. God help Nelly if she'd lied to him.

Megan muttered several long sentences, mingled with sawlike snoring. The only words Lucas could decipher were *steak, money,* and *bastard.* He was thankful he didn't understand the rest.

She inhaled deeply and snuggled closer, drawing one leg up until her knee rested just below his groin.

Forget about Nelly McFadden, he thought, trying to keep his breathing even. God help him to resist the soft, fascinating woman in his arms.

"Get up."

Megan moaned and covered her head with a pillow.

"Get up, Megan. We've got a lot of miles to put behind us today."

She cracked open an eye and focused on Lucas, who sat with his back to her, tugging on his boots. It took less than a minute for her to register the fact that the room was still dark. Not even a tiny shaft of light filtered in through the drapes.

"What time is it?"

"Four."

"In the morning?" she squeaked.

"Come on, we've got to get moving."

She rolled to the other side of the bed. "Leave me here," she groaned.

The mattress shifted as he stood. A smile touched her lips. He was such a sweet man to let her sleep.

"Up!" she heard him bark, and then a draft of chill air hit her body.

She sat up, rubbing her arms. Lucas stood at the foot of the bed, holding the blankets that he'd just yanked off her.

"Give those back," she ordered.

Instead, he dropped the bedcovers to the floor and tossed her clothes into her lap. "Your shirt and trousers were waiting outside the door when I got back. They're clean. Get dressed."

"Where are we going?"

"After Scott."

Her heart skipped a beat. "I thought you went after him last night."

"He'd already left." Lucas tightened the strings of his holster around his thighs, then moved to the door. "Look, I don't have time to explain it right now. I'll be at the livery, saddling our horses. Be dressed and in the lobby with your things in ten minutes—or I'll come up here to collect you."

The door closed behind him. Megan wasted no time in following his orders. She didn't even bother removing the silk chemise and drawers but threw her clothes on over them. She bound her hair at the nape of her neck with a fraying pink ribbon she'd had since childhood. It took her several minutes of painstaking work to get all her belongings stuffed into the one set of saddlebags Lucas had left.

He had been thoughtful in buying her so much. Her eyes had stung with tears when she'd seen the small bottle of rosewater on top of the pile of undergarments. No one had ever given her anything that special before. Oh, she had always been provided with perfumes and anything else she wanted, but by her parents. It felt different when the gift came from a man. A very handsome, rugged man. Megan refused to let the moment be ruined by the knowledge that that same man had kidnapped her and was even now keeping her prisoner.

She threw the bags over her shoulder and started out of the room, looking back one last time to be sure she hadn't forgotten anything before heading downstairs.

The lobby was deserted. No clerk sat behind the high counter. It suddenly hit her that she had a perfect opportunity to escape. How hard could it be to sneak out the back of the hotel? There were probably a dozen good places she could hide until Lucas rode out of town. He certainly wouldn't waste time searching for her. Finding Silas Scott was more important to him than turning her in to the law.

She glanced at the doorway that most likely led to the kitchen, then out the back of the building. But her feet didn't move. No matter how loud it reverberated through her head that now was the time to run, she couldn't make a move.

"Megan."

The voice startled her. She swung around to meet Lucas's hard gaze. He stood inside the double front doors, feet apart, hands on his hips. A guilty blush crept up her neck as she worried that he might read her earlier thoughts.

"Ready?"

She nodded.

He moved forward, taking the saddlebags from her. "Let's go."

The horses stood at the hotel's hitching rail, looking every bit as awake as Megan felt. "Don't worry, girl," she said, patting the mare's neck. "Lucas and Worthy will lead us, and we can sleep."

Lucas helped her mount, then went to his own horse. "We'll start out at a pretty quick pace so we can cover a fair amount of ground before the sun comes up. Then we'll slow it down to a walk to keep the horses from tiring out."

"Where are we going?" Megan asked again, hoping that this time he would answer.

"Wichita."

"Wichita!" she almost screamed. "That's more than a hundred miles away."

"Yep, it is. And the sooner we get going, the sooner we'll arrive."

"Oh, God," she moaned as Lucas kicked Worthy into a lope. She desperately wanted to turn back the clock and take advantage of that lost opportunity to run away.

Chapter Nine

"I thought you said Scott wouldn't pass through Topeka without stopping to see Nelly McFadden." Megan popped the last bite of rabbit into her mouth and rubbed her greasy fingers on her pant leg.

They had crossed the Neosho River just as the sun was setting, then traveled a few miles farther to make camp on the bank of the Cottonwood. Tomorrow, Lucas said, they would find a shallow spot to cross the rapid waters and move on toward Wichita. Everything seemed to be going along in much the same vein as the last time they'd stayed the night beneath a blanket of bright Kansas stars.

"He visited her, all right. But someone else was in bed with her by the time I got there."

Megan's eyes widened. "And you believed her when she said Scott was headed for Wichita? Wouldn't she, of all people, have reason to lie?"

"Probably, but she had a new bruise under her right eye."

"Oh, well then," Megan said, as though his statement

made perfect sense. Then she frowned. "What does that have to do with anything?"

"I think Scott knocked her around. If that's true, then she might just be angry enough to point me in the right direction."

She watched as he finished off his own portion of meat and washed it down with a swallow of clean, cold water from the river. "Isn't that quite a stretch?" she asked. "I mean, are you really going to travel all the way down to Wichita on the word of your enemy's . . . you know?"

"What the hell do you expect me to do?" he asked in a sudden burst of anger, tossing the canteen away from him. "For the past five years, I've done nothing but track the son of bitch back and forth across Kansas and Missouri. Christ, every time I get close to him, he disappears. What else am I supposed to do?"

Megan waited a moment for his temper to cool. She saw the heaving of his chest slow to a regular breathing pattern, the muscles in his jaw slacken. "How can he be so hard to find?" she asked quietly.

"Beats the hell out of me. I swear to God, this guy is like a ghost. Just when I think I've got him cornered and there's no way he can get away, he vanishes." He ran splayed fingers through his light hair. "It's damn frustrating. So now I've got two choices. I can either take the word of Nelly McFadden and go to Wichita, or I can go to the nearest town and wait around until a report comes in to the marshal on where he was last spotted. Of course, by then he would probably be in the next state."

He turned his ice-blue gaze on Megan. "What do you suggest I do?"

She swallowed, feeling properly chastised for second-guessing his decision. "All right," she said. "You get to Wichita, then what?"

"I wait."

"For what?"

He shrugged and got to his feet. "For Scott to show up

97

in the local saloon. For someone to recognize him from his wanted poster."

"Don't you think that's dangerous? What if he sees you first and shoots you in the back?"

"I'll take my chances," he said, arranging the bedroll next to the fire.

The sinewy muscles of his back moved beneath the fabric of his shirt. Megan blinked but didn't turn away. "That's the stupidest thing I've ever heard. You're going to get yourself killed."

He didn't answer.

"Don't you care that this man is a ruthless, cold-blooded killer? He could shoot you down and never blink an eye."

He turned to pierce her with a steely glare. "Like I said, that's a chance I'm willing to take."

She threw up her hands in defeat. "God save me from senseless, out-for-justice, idiotic men. You in particular," she said, jabbing a pointed finger in his direction.

A short chuckle filled the night air, but then his face once again fell into an unemotional mask. "I thought you understood what I have to do."

"I do. Or at least I understand why you *think* this has to be done. What I don't understand is how you can go through life caring for nothing but revenge. Look around," she said, waving an arm to encompass their surroundings. "Do you even see it? Do you see all the stars twinkling above your head? The moon lighting up the night sky? Do you hear the swift current of the river as it rushes by? The birds chirping? The rustle of leaves?" Her voice rose with the mention of each of nature's individual delights. "Do you ever notice any of it, or are you too obsessed with murdering Silas Scott?"

She took a deep breath, trying to calm the blood rushing through her veins. Lucas stared into the distance, but he didn't seem to be focusing on anything in particular. Her heart plummeted with the knowledge that her words had fallen on deaf ears.

"I see it," he said finally. "I see the moon and the stars. I hear the river and the birds. And all I can think is that Annie and Chad won't enjoy those simple pleasures ever again."

"What about you?" Megan didn't know what caused her to press on. She only knew that if she could get Lucas to realize what he was missing, she might be able to convince him to put aside his quest for vengeance and start living again.

"Annie and Chad are gone," she continued. "No amount of grieving, no selfless act of revenge is ever going to bring them back. But you're here, you're alive, and there's so much good that you could do."

"Like what?" he scoffed. "My ranch is gone. Everything I worked so hard for—everyone I loved—has been destroyed."

"You could start another ranch," she suggested.

"I won't go back there," he said through gritted teeth.

"There are plenty of other places to build a home. And what about your talent with a gun? You were a bounty hunter, so I'm assuming you're a decent shot. You could get a position as sheriff or marshal in some small town. I'm sure they'd be grateful to find someone with your abilities. If all else fails, you could open a mercantile. Or ask your friend Brandt to get you a job with the railroad."

"I don't think Union Pacific would appreciate having someone like me on the payroll."

"They would be crazy not to hire you."

"Yeah, but they won't like knowing they've got a murderer in their midst. And I'll be one just as soon as I take care of Scott."

Megan jumped to her feet and faced him, hands on hips. "Haven't you heard a word I've said?" she yelled. "You don't have to kill him! You can give all the information to the marshal in Wichita and let him take care of Silas Scott. Scott's already wanted; I'm sure a lawman would be happy to bring him in and hold him for trial."

"Scott killed my family," Lucas said evenly. "It's my responsibility to see that he pays."

All of a sudden the air went out of her argument, and she dropped onto the scratchy blanket. "Fine. Go after him. Drag me along. But don't expect me to support your decision."

"I never asked you to," he said, lying down beside her. "In fact, I never asked you for a damn thing. I think it's about time you remember that you're my prisoner. What I say goes. I don't need your opinion or your approval."

She remained silent for several long minutes, searching for a comfortable position. Lucas had his back to her, and though his breathing sounded deep and even, she knew he was still awake.

"My mother told me once that roses are the hardiest of all flowers." She spoke softly, sure he could hear her in the dark silence, with only the campfire crackling at their feet. "In winter, snow and ice cover them, sometimes so brutally that you think nothing could possibly live for months under those conditions. Then spring comes, and the snow melts. And before you know it, tiny rosebuds appear. It seems like a miracle—until you realize that all they really needed was a little sunshine to melt the ice. It's like a never-ending promise from God. A promise of roses to bloom every spring.

"The ice will melt someday, Lucas. All you have to do is let a little sunshine into your heart."

Lucas rose before dawn the next morning, having gotten no more than a pinch of sleep here or there. Too many things plagued his mind, not the least of which was Megan's speech the previous night. Her words bothered him more than he wanted to admit. He found himself wondering if she was right, if he should try to put the past behind him and start over. And then he pictured Annie and Chad the way he'd found them that day. So much blood everywhere. He remembered the goading tone of

Scott's note, and he knew he could never put things behind him until Scott was dead.

The hatred began once again to swirl through his body, making him ever more determined to see Silas Scott suffer for his crimes.

He had half a notion to leave Megan behind. He could drop her off in the next town and go on without her. She was becoming too much of a burden to him, knowing about his past, trying to change his mind about what he knew had to be done. And yet he didn't want to continue the journey alone. Or maybe it wasn't that he didn't want to be alone but that he didn't want to be without her.

Christ, she was driving him insane.

Despite his urgency to find Scott, he almost looked forward to bedding down these days—whether on the hard ground or in a comfortable hotel room—because he knew that sometime during the night Megan would roll onto her stomach and drape herself across his long body. And, damn, he liked that. He liked the way she felt, the way she smelled, the way she mumbled in her sleep.

He still grinned like a schoolboy whenever he remembered her admitting to having a brain disorder. A broken sieve, for Christ's sake! What would she come up with next?

He stared at her for a moment, memorizing the way her hair fell in total disarray all around her. No matter how much tossing and turning she did throughout the night, it still looked as becoming as hell.

Lucas took a deep breath, then crouched to shake her awake. He knew from experience that it would take at least five minutes—another ten if he waited for her to start speaking coherently. But it had been his decision to bring her along.

Funny. He wasn't a bit sorry.

"Another day, another hotel room," Megan said, staring up at the sign for Gray's Hotel. "How long will we be staying?"

"As long as it takes." She muttered the much-used line at the same time Lucas did.

"Are we Mr. and Mrs. Luke Campbell again?"

"Sure are, darlin'," he said, taking her elbow. He guided her into the lobby past several curious onlookers peering at them from behind their newspapers.

"We'd like a room, please," he said to the man behind the desk. The clerk asked him to sign the ledger and handed him the key.

"Will there be anything else, sir?"

Lucas spared Megan a glance, then nodded. "A bath for my wife would be nice. Where can I get one of those papers?" He inclined his head toward the many men reading copies of the *Wichita Gazette*.

"I can have one sent up with the bath, if you'd like, sir."

"Good. What time will the dining room be open for dinner?"

"Five o'clock. Chicken and dumplings tonight." The clerk smiled and patted his stomach.

Lucas put a hand on Megan's back, leading her upstairs. Their room was at the center of a row of six others on the second floor. He opened the door and ushered her in.

"My goodness," she breathed. A step up from the Eat 'n' Sleep, the room exuded elegance. From the heavy velvet drapes to the pale pink satin and lace bedspread, everything was done with exquisite taste and an eye for detail. And all the pieces matched.

"Do you think all the rooms are like this?" she asked.

"Probably. Unless we looked like newlyweds to the clerk."

She turned to face him. "I'm sure he got that impression from the elegance of my dress."

Lucas took a step forward, leaving her just enough space to breathe without touching him. "It may not be a wedding gown, but I think you look mighty good in those trousers."

A trickle of excitement ran down her spine, but she

quickly squelched it, moving away to unpack the saddle-bags. She laid her things out on the bed before hanging them in the small wardrobe and folding them into the bureau drawers.

Lucas hadn't moved. He stood just inside the door, watching her. "Aren't you going to get settled?" she asked, trying to keep her voice even.

"Why don't you put my things away?" he said, tossing his set of bags to the bed. "I don't have much."

She put her hands on her hips. "If I remember correctly, I'm your prisoner, not your wife." She picked up the leather pouch and threw it back at him. "And I wouldn't do it even if I were your wife. Put them away yourself."

He advanced, staring down at her. "I could make you," he said in a tone meant to intimidate.

She cocked her head and held his gaze. "You could try."

A moment passed before he stepped back, grinning. "You're a real spitfire. Has anyone ever told you that?"

She didn't answer.

He opened the bag and pulled out his shirt, shaking it a few times before stuffing it into the dresser. Then he went to the bed, sat down, and kicked off his boots. He was about to lean back against the pillows when a knock sounded at the door.

"That's probably your bath," he said, rising.

He opened the door and let two young boys carry in a brass tub, followed by several buckets of steaming water.

"Mind if I watch?" Lucas asked when they were once again alone.

"I most certainly do," Megan answered haughtily.

He chuckled. "Well, I don't feel like locking you up, so I guess I'll have to stay. Pity there's no dressing screen."

A blush spread over her face, down past her collar. "You can't mean to watch me bathe. That . . . that . . ."

"Sounds like a damn good idea to me." She was flustered. He liked that.

She set her shoulders, making her breasts press even

more fully against the cotton of her shirt. "I think you should go."

"And miss the show? Uh-uh."

"Lucas . . ."

"I ain't leavin'. But I won't look, either." He went back to the bed and laid down, crossing his feet at the ankles.

"How can I be sure you won't peek?"

He lifted the hat off his head and placed it over his face. "Better?" he asked, his voice muffled by the hollow Stetson.

"All right. But if I catch you looking . . ."

"You won't," he said. He wouldn't get caught. Hell, he didn't even plan on watching her from under the brim of his hat. But a man couldn't help it if his imagination ran a little wild. If an ethereal image of Megan stark naked should happen to creep into his head, what could he do about it?

A soft, lilting sound reached his ears, and he tipped his head to hear better. At first it came in short, quiet spurts, then grew louder by degrees, filling the room. It took him a minute to figure out that Megan was humming. He didn't recognize the song but soon picked up on the melody enough to follow along in his head.

He pictured her relaxing in her bath, soaping one long, slim leg and then the other. Rinsing with a squeeze of the washcloth over her sudsy skin. He didn't know if the light tinkle of dripping water was real or imagined, but the sound had a disastrous effect on his body.

He took a deep breath to steady his dwindling control, only to be accosted by the heady scent of roses. He couldn't take any more. With a growled curse, he leapt up from the bed and stalked toward her, his forgotten Stetson falling to the floor.

Megan gasped when she saw him coming. She clutched the small square washcloth to her breasts in a useless attempt to cover herself.

"What—" she began.

"Fire! Fire!" The shouts came from outside their door. A rush of frightened footsteps filled the hallway.

"Damn!" Lucas grabbed Megan's arm and pulled her to her feet. He yanked the bedspread loose, wrapping it around her wet body. Lifting her into his arms, he ran out of the room.

Guests of the hotel clustered together in the street, all staring at the building, as if they expected it to collapse at any moment. But not a hint of smoke billowed out the windows; no red-orange flames licked at the walls.

"What the hell is going on?" Lucas muttered.

Megan felt like a rag doll, cradled in his strong arms. She held the blanket closed at her neck. The looks she got from the people milling about made her want to curl into a ball and disappear.

"You can put me down now," she said quietly.

He glanced at her as though he only now remembered he was holding her. His eyes just as quickly returned to watching the hotel. "You don't have anything on your feet."

She raised a leg, seeing her bare foot sticking out from the hem of the quilt. "Put me down."

"Hush." He tightened his arms about her.

"It's all right, folks." The call rose over the voices of the crowd. A pudgy, gray-haired man stood at the front of the building. "A small fire in the kitchen is all. No harm done. You can return to your rooms now."

People began trickling in, eyeing the hotel warily. "It's all right," the man said again, ushering patrons into the lobby. "Sorry for the inconvenience, ladies and gentleman."

The man's face turned a dark shade of red when Lucas stepped up on the boardwalk. He kept his gaze averted from Megan's blanket-clad form.

"Dinner still at five?" Lucas asked with an air of nonchalance.

"Yes, sir. On the dot. The kitchen sustained little damage. It will be cleaned up in no time. Chicken and dumplings tonight," he added.

"So I heard." Lucas shifted sideways to keep from cracking Megan's head on the doorframe. They made their way back upstairs, following a line of other guests doing the same. When they reached their room, the door stood open from their hurried departure. Sunlight streamed in through the far window, brightening the flowered wallpaper and cascading over the pristine white sheets of the bed.

Megan lifted her head to gaze at the man holding her. His face seemed more weathered than she'd first noticed. Tiny lines wrinkled his otherwise smooth forehead and marred the flesh about his gentle eyes. She froze, her heart skipping a beat when her perusal led to those cerulean orbs and she found them staring back at her.

She turned away, slightly unnerved. "Could you . . . put me down now, please?" The words sounded forced, even to her own ears. She couldn't help it. Her throat felt thick and scratchy, as if she'd just tried to eat a bale of cotton. And she wasn't so sure she wanted him to put her down. She liked the way his arms held her close, strong and steady beneath her. The heat of his body soaked through the bedspread, warming her.

Her legs slid downward as his grip loosened. It seemed forever before the fuzzy carpeting met the tips of her bare toes. One of his arms remained around her back, keeping her flush against his chest, her breasts pressed between them.

She swallowed. He was too close; she couldn't concentrate. Her mind seemed hazy, her thoughts jumbled. All she knew was that she didn't want to move yet. She wanted to stay this way for all time. Locked in his arms.

"Megan."

He whispered her name a moment before his lips brushed hers. His tongue trailed the line of her bottom lip, and she opened for him most willingly, wanting to get closer, to be one with him. The heat of his mouth, the grappling of tongues overcame her. She moaned low in her throat. Her fingers tightened around his biceps, the nails digging in. She closed her eyes and let the intimate sensations of his touch wash over her.

Lucas pulled away, breathing hard. She followed his movement, her body swaying forward. He put his hands on her waist, keeping her in place when he took a step backward.

She opened her eyes and stared at him, confused.

"I think you'd better get dressed," he said, reaching for his hat where it had fallen on the floor beside the bed. He walked to the door, stopping with his hand on the knob. "I'll be back for you before dinner."

Megan watched the mahogany panel close on his departing form, wondering what it was about her that offended his delicate sensibilities. It seemed that every time she offered herself to him, he walked away.

Not that she made a practice of seducing men. She had never made love before. No man had ever even kissed her the way Lucas did—hot and passionate and full of wicked delight. There was just something about Lucas that made her want to be with him.

She knew all about what took place between a man and woman—beyond what she and Lucas had already done. And if the rest felt half as good as his kisses, she definitely wanted to experience it.

But with only one man. Only with Lucas McCain.

Chapter Ten

Dressed in the yellow skirt and plain, unadorned blouse Lucas had bought her, Megan sat cross-legged on the bed, waiting for him to return. It amazed her that he'd left her alone for so long. Didn't he realize she could have climbed out the window? Why, by now she could have been partway back to Leavenworth.

She ran her fingers through her hair, brushing the tangles out as best she could before attempting to braid the long locks. Styling hair had never been her forte. She tended to leave sprigs sticking out all over the place, if she could even manage to keep the arrangement from being lopsided.

The thought of Leavenworth—or, more specifically, the Adams Express—depressed her. She could just imagine how far the business had plummeted with Hector holding the reins. Perhaps, if God chose to smile down on her, Caleb would take over. Her brother couldn't care for things as well as she did, of course, but he would be able to keep the Express running until she got back. Whenever that might be.

She gave the yellow ribbon at the end of her finished braid a brutal tug. She had to get back. She didn't care that Lucas intended to turn her in for robbing her own stages. She didn't care that he kept her under lock and key. With a little planning and a lot of luck, she could escape.

Of course, he would know exactly where she was headed, since she didn't really have anywhere else to go. But what did that matter? Lucas's obsession with finding Silas Scott would overrule his need to find her. By the time he got around to coming after her, she would probably be able to prove her innocence.

Unfortunately, that reasoning was weak, to say the least. Lucas didn't even know where Scott was at the moment. And what made her think her armed guard wouldn't spare a few hours to track her down and drag her back?

Megan groaned and collapsed full length on the mattress. It was hopeless. Even if she did manage to get away from Lucas, she had no way of knowing that the Adams Express hadn't already gone out of business.

"Ready?"

She sat up, startled by Lucas's sudden appearance. She hadn't heard the telltale grating of the key before he entered.

Her brows knit. "You didn't lock the door, did you?"

A grin lifted one side of his mouth. "Nope. Are you disappointed?"

"Of course not." She almost told him that she wouldn't still be sitting here if she'd known, but she thought better of it. No sense alerting him to the fact that she planned to escape. "I'm just surprised you trusted me."

He chuckled. "Don't get your hopes up, sweetheart. I was just outside the door. I would have heard you if you'd tried to leave."

"Oh."

He held out an arm. "Are you ready to eat?"

109

She put her hand in the crook of his elbow and let him lead her through the hotel. They met several other guests in the hall, all on their way to dinner. The dining room turned out to be average-size with dark wood paneling. Red-and-white checked cloths covered the round tables that crowded the room.

Lucas chose a table in the corner, holding a chair out for Megan. She noticed that he purposely seated her facing the wall. He sat opposite her, keeping the entire room in view.

"Do you expect trouble?" She had to call his name before he looked at her.

"What?"

"I asked if you expect trouble."

He shook his head. "Old habit, I guess. I like to be aware of my surroundings."

"Good idea. After all, you never know when the cook might come out and try to bludgeon you with a dead chicken."

"Exactly," he said, as if that were an everyday occurrence.

An older woman came to their table, a pristine white apron tied at her waist. "What will you have?"

Megan wondered why the woman bothered to ask, since evidently the only thing being served was chicken and dumplings. She looked up to see Lucas's mouth curved into a small smile. He winked.

"Let's see," he said. "I have a hankering for pot roast."

"Mmm." Megan went along with his game. "That sounds divine. With potatoes and carrots and thick, creamy gravy."

"Lots of gravy," he agreed.

"We got chicken and dumplings," the woman said, unmoved.

"Well," Lucas said, "if you pile on lots of gravy, I doubt I'll know the difference."

"You want coffee with that?"

He nodded. "What about you?" he asked Megan.

"Please."

The woman moved to the next table, getting that order more quickly than Lucas and Megan's.

"Have you heard anything about Scott yet?"

Lucas shook his head. "I think I'll take a walk over to the saloon later. Somebody may have seen him. If I can't find out anything there, I might have a word with the marshal."

"I thought you didn't want anyone to know you were in town."

"I'd rather they didn't, but it may be the only way I can pick up on Scott's trail. I can probably trust the marshal not to tell anyone about me."

They had eaten dinner and were just finishing a healthy slice of apple pie when the clerk from the front desk came to their table.

"Excuse me, Mr. Campbell." He nodded to Megan respectfully. "I forgot to send a paper up to your room. Here it is now, sir. Please accept my apology." He placed an issue of the *Wichita Gazette* on the table, then hurried out of the dining room.

Lucas stood, putting the paper under his arm. He held out his other for Megan.

"You can be very charming when you want to be," she said as they ascended the stairs.

He gave a disbelieving snort.

"I mean it," she insisted. "When you're not strapping me to a saddle or dropping me in the dirt, you're quite a gentleman. You've been nothing but polite all evening."

Lucas moved closer to whisper in her ear. "We're supposed to be married, remember? It wouldn't do for these fine people to think we're not getting along."

"I don't believe that has anything to do with it. I think you're basically a very nice man. Certain situations just bring out your barbaric side."

"Barbaric, huh?" They reached their room, and he opened the door, gallantly waving Megan in before him. "What barbaric act have I ever committed?"

"Stage robbery, taking part in a kidnapping, then kidnapping me again." She ticked off the crimes on one hand, quickly moving on to the other set of fingers. "Tied me to a horse, left me sitting outside a saloon alone and vulnerable." Another long-suffering snort interrupted her. She frowned but continued with the list. "Dropped me to the ground from your horse—which was quite a distance, as I recall. Handcuffed me to a bathtub, tied me to the bed—"

"Okay, okay." He held up his hands in surrender. "I thought you were going to point out barbaric things I've done to other people. You don't count."

Her eyes widened. "I don't count? And just why not?"

He leaned toward her, tapping the tip of her nose with his finger. "You're my prisoner, remember?" He moved past her to one of the brocade armchairs situated before the window.

She crossed her arms over her chest, pretending to be offended. When Lucas didn't seem to notice, she gave up and went to the mirror to unbraid her hair. Removing the yellow ribbon, she set it on the bureau. Only then, when she caught the reflection of the room in the mirror, did she notice that the tub was missing.

"The staff at this hotel is wonderful," she commented, turning to face Lucas, who sat reading the newspaper, his boots propped on the footstool. "They removed the tub without being asked, and the bed is made."

Lucas spared the four-poster a glance before returning his attention to the paper.

"Much nicer than the people at the Eat 'n' Sleep. It took them forever to retrieve the bathtub, and they never did make the bed. I swear, they looked at me as though I had a set of horns growing out of my head."

"They thought you were crazy," he said.

She put a hand on one hip in an annoyed gesture. "Well, that's absurd. That first night, when you cuffed me in the bath, and I protested . . . vehemently . . . well, I can understand them thinking I was a little touched in the head. But after that, everything was fine, and they still gave me strange looks."

"No," he said, refolding the paper and setting it aside. "You misunderstood me."

One side of his mouth quirked up in a grin. Megan had learned that that particular expression meant trouble. He knew something she didn't, and the half smile was a guarantee that she wasn't going to like it, whatever it was.

"I mean they really thought you were crazy. Demented."

"Why did they think that?" she asked warily.

"Because I told them so."

Her mouth fell open, and her tongue all but rolled onto the floor.

"I knew you would put up a fuss when I cuffed you, and I didn't want them breaking into the room to set you free, so I made up a story to keep them out."

"You did what?"

He chuckled, remembering. "I told the maid you'd once been kidnapped by a band of vicious outlaws. And with your fragile disposition"—he made a face—"you never recovered."

He started laughing. "You should have seen the poor woman when I told her you sometimes had to be restrained. I thought her eyes were going to pop right out." He slapped his knee, overcome with laughter.

Megan started counting. She concentrated on her breathing, imagined all the ways she would revel in torturing him. Nothing worked. The blood pounded in her ears a moment before she completely lost her temper.

She picked up the silver-backed brush from the dresser and hurled it at his head. "You are the meanest, most vile creature God ever put on this earth! You disgust me!"

She avoided the matching mirror but had no qualms about throwing the soap cup from his shaving kit. It hit the wall, pieces of thick clay flying in every direction.

"How could you *do* something like that?" she ranted. "You kidnap me, drag me halfway across the state, and then have the gall—the *gall*—to tell people I'm unstable." Darting across the room, she grabbed his saddlebags, heavy with the payroll money. Leaning back, she swung the leather at him with all her strength. The satchel hit him in the stomach, causing him to double over with a grunt of pain.

A smile of victory spread across her face. "I hope you burn in hell. I hope the Devil himself comes for you. I'll cheer when you go. No," she said, "I'll organize a parade. With elephants and tigers and a snake. Oh, but we can't have a snake, because you'll be *gone*. And you're the biggest snake of them all!"

Lucas straightened, fixing her with an ice-cold glare. He took a step forward.

She retreated, uncertain of what he might do. "You deserved to be punched in the gut," she said. "That was a mean trick you pulled back in Topeka."

He moved closer.

He was intent on catching her, she thought. Heaven knew what kind of punishment he'd cooked up in that pile of dung he called a brain.

When his arms snapped out, she shrieked and ran as fast as she could. She leapt onto the bed, skittering away on her hands and knees like a jittery colt. He stood at the end of the bed, ready to block any move she might make.

"Don't touch me," she said.

He advanced until the fronts of his legs came in contact with the footboard.

She wiggled back several inches, the soft mattress and her skirts impeding her progress. "I'll scream. I swear to God, I'll scream so loud, the roof will cave in."

"So scream," he said. "I'll just tell them the same story I told in Topeka. My dear, distraught wife still has nightmares about being kidnapped by that group of ruffians. Is it any wonder I sometimes have to tie her to the bed? It's for her own good, of course. The townspeople would understand that."

"You're a real bastard, Lucas McCain."

"It's about time you figured that out."

He lunged forward in a blur of motion. Megan opened her mouth to scream, but his hand quickly muffled the attempt. His body pinned her down, keeping her still.

"I'll let go if you promise not to scream."

She tried to tell him to go to Hell, but her words were indecipherable.

"Tut-tut," he said with a laugh. "I'm not sure what you said, but I know it wasn't nice. No wife of mine should talk like that."

Megan launched into a string of curses, all of them cut short by his hand over her mouth.

"I'm going to let you go, but you're going to behave yourself," Lucas said.

She managed to open her mouth enough to get a fair amount of his skin between her teeth. With a smile that he couldn't see, she bit down.

He yelped. When he sat up to stare at his injured palm, Megan rolled off the bed and stood, her breathing labored.

"That ought to teach you not to touch me."

He cradled his hand on one thigh. "Oh, I think I've learned my lesson."

She smiled, proud that she'd managed to get away. But her feeling of triumph didn't last long.

With lightning speed, Lucas reached out and grabbed a handful of her bright-yellow skirt. Then got to his feet and backed her up against the wall.

He stood over her, his hot breath on her neck sending shivers down her spine. She watched him, saw the raw emotion in his eyes. Still, at that moment, fear was the furthest thing from her mind. She no longer wanted to evade Lucas. She wanted very much to be here, up against the wall, his body pressing into her own. Her lashes fluttered as her eyes drifted closed.

"You know I want you, Megan."

The words blew through her like a cool summer breeze. Gooseflesh broke out along her arms.

"Do you understand what I'm saying?"

She understood. She wanted it, too.

"I want to take you to bed." His voice was low, strained. He put a finger under her chin and raised her eyes to meet his. "Will you let me make love to you?"

Megan tried to smile. He talked too much. She wanted him to shut up and kiss her. She wanted him to make love to her.

"Yes," she whispered. "Make love to me, Lucas."

Chapter Eleven

A moment later, his lips descended to capture hers in a passionate, undisciplined kiss. His tongue darted into her mouth, caressing every inch of its secret recesses. Megan kissed him back, her tongue tangling like an errant vine with his.

Her hands went to the buttons of his shirt, slipping them free until her fingers came in contact with the smooth, warm flesh of his bare chest. Her thumbs flicked over his tiny male nipples, teasing them to hard pebbles. His hands ran up her arms to her shoulders, kneading them a moment before he began unbuttoning her blouse.

Her top and skirt soon billowed around her feet on the floor. She didn't feel the least bit self-conscious standing before Lucas in her stockings and camisole. She'd given in to temptation this evening and donned the silk leggings, feeling devilishly feminine as she put them on, securing them with pristine white garters. It wasn't often that she dressed up anymore, so she took great pleasure in wearing them on this rare occasion. She hadn't known at the time that Lucas would ever see them. But now, knowing that he would, her stomach fluttered, and a jolt of excitement washed through her body.

Their kisses became fevered, hard and hot, until the world seemed to tilt on its axis, tossing her senses out of control. They broke apart, gasping for breath. Megan pulled the tails of Lucas's shirt out of his pants, shoving the material over his back until it joined her clothing on the floor. He yanked at her camisole until she feared he would tear the delicate material. She covered his hands with her own to help remove the impeding garments. She bent to her garters, but he stopped her.

His firm fingers brushed up the back of her leg. "Leave them on."

So the stockings remained, increasing the eroticism of their encounter.

"Come with me," he whispered, pressing tiny, biting kisses along her neck and collarbone.

His fingers dug into the back of her thighs, lifting her legs around his waist. The handles of his matching Colts pressed into her flesh, driving her higher above him. She looked down at him, liking this position, this feeling of power. Her hair fell all around them in a black curtain as she lowered her head for another soul-searing kiss.

He took her to the bed, letting her body slowly arch backward to meet the mattress. He let go of her to remove his gun belt, and she moaned in frustration, wanting his hands on her every moment. He pulled off his boots and shucked his pants, his movements jerky and rushed.

Megan rose up on an elbow to watch. He stood before her in all his naked glory, letting her look her fill. His clothes didn't do justice to the sinewy form beneath, she decided. Every inch of him was taut muscle and golden bronzed skin. She opened her arms, beckoning him.

He came closer, putting a hand on each of her knees. She reacted to the slight pressure, letting her legs part. He came to lie between them, resting his weight on one arm. She wiggled nervously when he didn't touch her.

Her whole being seemed to tremble with the need to feel him near.

Staring down at her, he touched one nipple with the tip of a finger. It swelled and tightened. "You're beautiful," he said.

The fire he started in her breast spread throughout her body, settling at her innermost core. "Lucas," she moaned. "Please."

He claimed her mouth once again as his hands fondled and caressed her. His warm fingers teased her nipples into peaks of desire. He stroked her belly, her hips, her inner thighs, venturing closer to that center of her being that cried out for his tender attention.

He brushed a hand over the crisp curls, making her strain toward his touch. She whimpered when one finger delved inside.

"Oh, God," he groaned. "You're so wet. I want you so much."

Megan ran her fingers through his hair. "Please," she whispered.

He raised his head. "Are you sure?"

She nodded.

He pressed a soft kiss to her lips. His mouth trailed across her cheek, down her neck. His hands moved to her sides, and he held her still as he positioned himself above her. In one swift motion, he buried himself inside.

She gasped at the painful, burning sensation that ripped through her. She was about to try to get away from Lucas when he stilled, tensing in her arms.

He put his lips to her brow. "It's okay. Don't move, and the pain will go away."

At that moment, she didn't believe him. But within seconds, the burning passed, replaced by the sensation of a deep, dark void she knew only he could fill. He pulled back slightly, and she dug her nails into his shoulders, wanting him to stay.

"It's all right," he whispered, brushing a kiss over her cheek. "I'm not going anywhere."

His lips touched her own. First soft and tender, then more urgent as his tongue delved into her mouth, sweeping and sucking. Rough, firm fingertips caressed her stomach, the undersides of her breasts. Then he started moving. Slow, short strokes.

Every nerve in her body sprang to attention. Megan moaned low in her throat. Of their own accord, her legs lifted to hug his undulating hips. She arched her back to meet his strong thrusts.

Lucas trailed a path of hot, openmouthed kisses along the side of her neck. His arms wrapped behind her back, supporting her as their movements became more frantic. She let her head fall back as a desperate moan echoed through the room.

Her need was like a fiery inferno, begging to be put out. But his damp skin on her own only added to the heat between them. His hard length throbbing and thrusting inside her only fueled the flames.

An overwhelming pleasure washed over her, making her cry out. She threaded her fingers through his hair, clutching the damp tendrils in an attempt to ground herself.

A moment later Lucas stiffened with a long groan before falling limply upon her.

They lay there, motionless, for some time. Megan's fingers ran through his hair in a comforting, unconscious gesture. She smiled when she felt tiny kisses on her shoulder and neck.

With another groan, Lucas rolled to his side, taking Megan with him. It took some doing to pull the sheets and bedspread from beneath them, but he finally got the covers loose enough to cover their naked forms.

Megan snuggled closer, drawing her leg up over his thigh. She glanced up, expecting to see a contented male smile adorning his face. Instead, the corners of his mouth turned down. His brows knit together as though he were deep in thought.

"What's wrong?" she asked, pushing up on one elbow.

He shook his head. His mouth evened into a straight line, but the wrinkle in his forehead remained.

She pulled away, moving to the other side of the bed. "Well, I thought all that grunting and groaning meant you were having a good time, but I guess I was wrong." With a solid punch, she puffed the pillows and arranged them behind her back.

He turned to look at her, wondering what had gotten into her all of a sudden. "And I suppose that was some other woman screaming in my ear."

"I did not scream," Megan denied, crossing her arms under her breasts.

The sheet puffed out, giving him a clear view of her ample charms. He tamped down the urge to reach over and brush a thumb over one of the raspberry nipples.

"You did scream. I'm sure the people in the next room would be happy to back me up." He rapped his knuckles on the wall above the headboard.

"Maybe I did, but only because *I* was enjoying myself. I wasn't simply making use of the nearest male to slake my animal lust."

"What the hell is that supposed to mean?"

"It means I've seen happier faces on men heading to the gallows. I didn't expect you to be grinning from ear to ear, but the least you could do is pretend you enjoyed the encounter."

Leaning over her, he pressed his lips to the curve of her shoulder. "What makes you think I didn't?"

"Your frown the size of the Arkansas River."

He raised his head to meet her eyes. They sparkled, flashing daggers of gold in the low light that filtered from the lamp beside the armchair where he'd been reading the *Wichita Gazette*.

"I wasn't frowning," he said.

"No? Then why was your brow more wrinkled than these sheets?" She snapped the covers back angrily, leaping out of bed.

Lucas took a moment to watch as she leaned down to

retrieve her abandoned clothes from the floor. She had no inhibitions, not even considering the fact that she was parading around naked. Annie had never done that. Hell, she had always put her nightdress back on after they'd made love, assuring him that no proper lady would ever sleep in the altogether.

With the memory of Annie came dawning understanding of Megan's upset. Immediately after he'd collapsed atop Megan, he'd begun thinking of Annie. Of how he was betraying her by being with another woman. Megan must have seen him frowning about that.

He sat up, touching his feet to the carpeted floor. Megan started away, but he grabbed her arm.

"Wait a minute."

She struggled, getting in several light punches to his biceps and chest.

"Damn it, I said stop." He pinned her arms, dragging her into the V of his legs.

She stiffened, standing straight as a pin. She clutched her skirt and blouse, along with his things, tightly to her chest.

He dropped his head between her breasts, taking in the seductive scent of her—roses and sweat and the smell of their lovemaking. He waited for the right words to form on his tongue. And waited.

When nothing came to mind, he lifted his face to look at her. Tears brimmed her eyes. He realized the rarity of such emotion in this beautiful woman and knew he had hurt her deeply.

"Megan."

She continued staring over his head at the opposite wall.

"Megan." He took her chin between his thumb and forefinger, tipping her head so she would be forced to meet his eyes. "I'm sorry. I wasn't frowning about what happened between us."

She swallowed, licking her lips before speaking. "Then why were you?"

He moaned, returning his forehead to her chest. He

was surprised to feel the clothing drop to the floor and her fingers twine through the hair at the back of his neck.

"Can't I just say it didn't have anything to do with making love to you and leave it at that?"

"All right."

His head snapped up. Could he have imagined what Megan had just said? The words had been soft, but he didn't think he'd misheard her. Still, he couldn't comprehend the idea of Megan—Megan Adams, his Megan, the same Megan he'd been with twenty-four hours a day for the past week—letting the subject drop so easily. No fight, no screaming, no objects being hurled across the room at him, just a simple "all right."

"All right?" he asked almost timidly.

She nodded. "As long as you promise to tell me if I ever disappoint you."

He stared at her, dumbfounded.

She moved closer, wrapping her arms around his neck, pressing her breasts to his chest. She kissed his ear, then began to gently draw on the lobe. "I didn't disappoint you, did I?"

He gave a strangled, raspy laugh. Already his body was burning again, desperate to make love to her once more. "Disappoint me? Christ, woman, if I were any more disappointed, I'd be dead."

She gazed at him a minute before a wide smile spread across her face. "Good."

Then she kissed him, full on the mouth, teasing and tempting with that slick tongue of hers. It took every ounce of willpower he possessed to push her away.

"No. Megan, no," he insisted, gripping her upper arms. He saw the confusion in her eyes. "I don't think it's a good idea for us to be together again."

When a wounded look replaced the confusion, he hurried to reassure her. "You're bound to be sore."

"Uh-uh," she said, trying to kiss him again.

He kept her at arm's length. "We can't, Meg."

She stepped back, breaking his hold. "Why not?"

He knew he was hurting her, but he didn't know what else to do. Making love to her had been a mistake. Oh, he wasn't sorry—or not as sorry as he should have been. She had been hot and willing, and he had enjoyed every damn minute. But that didn't excuse the fact that she'd been a virgin. His prisoner and a virgin. He'd stepped over two lines this night. And that didn't include the gnawing guilt that ate at his gut—guilt for his unfaithfulness to Annie, the woman he'd promised to love and cherish forever.

He couldn't make love to Megan again, no matter how much he wanted to. Blood rushed through his veins, causing his body to stiffen in protest, reminding him of just what he would be missing.

Grabbing his clothes from the floor, he stepped into the trousers. He left his shirt unbuttoned, pressing a light kiss to her cheek. "It's not a good idea right now."

He picked up his boots, gun belt, and hat and went to the door. "Get some rest. I'll be back in a while."

With that, he walked out of the room, leaving Megan standing naked—except for her disheveled stockings and garters—beside the bed. She felt her face flush in embarrassment.

Used. Discarded. Abandoned.

Well, if Lucas McCain didn't want to stay with her, that was his problem. She didn't need him, didn't even want him.

Except that she did.

She rubbed her upper arms, suddenly cold. And it had nothing to do with the temperature in the room.

Muttering a few choice words under her breath, she stripped off the stockings and tossed them on the bed. How dare he leave her after what they had shared?

What did you expect? a voice in her mind taunted. *A marriage proposal? A declaration of undying love?*

"Hardly," she answered aloud. "But he didn't have to race out of here like he'd just discovered I had the pox."

She went to the dresser and pulled out her old shirt. Its tails reached her knees, so she felt adequately covered.

Especially since she was all alone, thanks to one inconsiderate, ill-bred bounty hunter.

She was hurt and offended by his quick disappearance, but she was most definitely not sorry that they had made love. Perhaps she could have chosen a better partner—someone who wouldn't have run off with his tail between his legs—but she wasn't sorry. And in all honesty, she didn't think she could have let another man touch her the way she'd allowed Lucas to.

From the moment he'd lowered his bandanna at the outlaw hideout and she'd gotten a good look at his face, she had been attracted to him. Why, she didn't know. Maybe because he had the bluest eyes she'd ever seen. Or maybe because he had a way of looking at her that made her skin tingle.

She plopped down in the brocade armchair, unfolding the paper Lucas had been reading earlier. Her eyes skimmed over the headlines and local happenings. Anyone interested in bringing a dessert to the annual Harvest Festival should see Mrs. Walter Evergreen at the general store. A sorrel gelding had wandered into town; the owner could pick it up at Sam's Livery.

She turned the page, bored with the town's activities. Wichita man travels to Capitol. Miss Tulsa May Carter to wed local feed-store owner. Kansas stage robbed; driver taken hostage.

Just as she was about to move on, the bold words in the middle of the third page registered. Kansas stage robbed; driver taken hostage. It couldn't be. Why would the Wichita paper have an article about a Leavenworth stage being robbed? Surely it wasn't the biggest news of the week. Leavenworth was more than a hundred miles away. She held the paper up to the light, shocked to see her own face staring back at her. Turning up the lamp's wick, she read carefully.

Last Thursday, at precisely 10:29 A.M., a Concord stagecoach carrying three passengers was robbed by a band of five outlaws. One witness said that the bandits

125

must have been "dumber than a box of rocks" because as they conversed with one another, they revealed their Christian names—Douglas, Tommy, Evan, Frank, and Luke. A strongbox carrying the Kansas–Union Pacific Railroad payroll was taken. The passengers were not robbed—another mistake by the outlaws, claims the same source.

The stage, owned by one M. Adams of the Adams Express Stagecoach Line, had been accosted three times before on its run from Leavenworth to Atchison. It is suspected that all four robberies were committed by the same group of men. Descriptions from the passengers were given to the local marshal. The Union Pacific Railroad is offering a reward of $1,000 for any information leading to the capture of the gang.

Perhaps even more disturbing than the robbery, however, is the fact that the stage driver, along with the strongbox, was taken by the outlaws. The driver was a woman, though no one is quite certain why a female was allowed to drive the Concord. (This reporter has been assured that the matter will be fully investigated.)

Megan Adams, the abductee, pictured above, is approximately five feet, six inches tall with brown eyes and long black hair. She is most likely wearing men's clothing. If anyone has seen this woman, please contact the nearest law official, Marshal Thompson of Leavenworth, or Mr. Caleb Adams, also of Leavenworth.

Mr. Adams, the victim's brother, is offering a $10,000 reward for her safe return. He has also been quoted as saying, "If [the outlaws] touch one hair on my sister's head, I will personally [harm] each one of them."

Megan chuckled, easily deciphering *exactly* what Caleb had said. At least someone still cared about her well-being. It had taken the *Gazette* two long paragraphs before even *mentioning* her kidnapping. No doubt her brother had something to do with the story reaching such faraway newspapers. She wouldn't be surprised if the residents of Missouri were also out looking for her—terribly concerned, she was sure. It took a strong person to brush off $10,000. Which was about as much as Caleb had in the bank without wiring back to New York for Mother's help.

She continued reading. *The Adams Express has slowed business, making only six of its usual twenty runs per week. Caleb Adams has taken over the company, since M. Adams cannot be located at this time. The railroad is thus far refusing to risk another of its payrolls with the company, and many passengers are afraid to travel by way of the Express. It is not likely that the line will be able to stay in business beyond the end of the month.*

Megan threw down the paper, rushing to the dresser to dig out the rest of her clothes. She would not let a pack of stupid, mangy outlaws run her stage line into the ground. She had to get back—*now*. Just let Lucas *try* to stop her.

She put on her boots, pinned her hair up under her Stetson, and headed for the bed. It was time for some quick thinking. And a stealthy escape.

Chapter Twelve

With her teeth and nails, Megan gnawed and tugged at the edge of the white sheet until it began to rip easily. She repeated the process over and over, gathering strips of material and tying them together to make a ramshackle rope that would get her out the window and close enough to the ground that she could jump the rest of the way without serious injury.

Satisfied with the length, she tied one end around the foot of the massive bed, then quickly shoved pillows under the covers to look like someone sleeping. If it fooled Lucas for only a few minutes it would put her that much farther ahead of him on the trail. She turned down the gas lamp, casting the room into darkness before going to the window.

The heavy glass stuck at first, and she had to jiggle the frame to get it open. She leaned out, gauging the distance to the ground. It didn't look to be all that far, but she said a quick prayer just in case. Throwing down her makeshift knotted ladder, she climbed onto the window ledge.

She began begging God to see her safely down the side of the hotel, but when that became too wordy, she simply resorted to a litany of, "Please, please, please."

The whole ordeal lasted no more than a minute. Hanging on to the rope for dear life, she used the outer wall of the building to walk her way down. She landed on both feet, kicking up a small cloud of dust.

She felt a sharp stab of regret as she looked back up at the window of the room she'd just vacated. But she had no choice. Even if she wanted to stay with Lucas—which she didn't, of course—she couldn't let her business go under without a fight. If she lost the Express, she would lose everything. Her independence, her security, her way of life.

It took her a moment to decide to risk going to the livery. She went around the back to avoid being seen, then sneaked in a side door. She found her mount, saddled her, and walked the mare out into the night.

No one seemed to be about. The only noise came from a tinny piano inside the saloon down the street. At the edge of town, she climbed into the saddle and kicked her horse into a gallop. She wanted to get as far from Wichita and Lucas McCain as possible. Fast.

Needing time to cool off, Lucas made his way down the boardwalk at a leisurely pace. Or as leisurely as one could get with the fire of passion still burning in his gut. Damn, but he wanted to return to the room and make love with Megan again. She had a way of making a man forget everything, even his own name.

Lucas surely had. He'd forgotten that Megan was his prisoner, that he was responsible for her until he could turn her in to the proper authorities. He'd forgotten about Annie. About how much he cared for her and about how he'd promised to always be true. Hell, he'd even forgotten about Silas Scott. It had taken him a good five minutes to recall just why it was so damned important that he find and kill the man.

But now his head was on straight again, and he did

remember. He remembered everything. And he had to be sure that what had happened in the hotel room this evening never happened again. No matter how damn pretty Megan was. No matter how good she smelled or felt in his arms.

A strangled groan filled the otherwise silent night. If he didn't get his mind on something else, he would end up making love to Megan again.

He crossed the deserted street, heading for the jail. He didn't exactly like the idea of letting the marshal know he was in town, but if the man could give him information on Scott, it would be well worth the risk.

A man with a badge pinned to the front of his black leather vest sat with his feet propped on the desk, reading a newspaper.

"You the marshal?" Lucas asked.

"Yup." He held out a hand in introduction. "Oliver Ingalls. What can I do for you?"

"Name's Luke Campbell. I'm a bounty hunter."

The marshal arched a brow in curiosity. "There some trouble I ought to know about?"

"No, sir. Leastways, not yet." Lucas pulled an available chair in front of the desk and straddled it, crossing his arms over the back. "I'm not even sure the man I'm looking for is in town. That's why I stopped in. Thought maybe we could exchange a bit of information."

"I'll be honest with you, mister. I don't care much for bounty hunters. Most real lawmen don't, if you know what I mean. You may bring in a criminal now and again, but you do it for money, not because you care about upholding the law."

"I have to agree with you there, Marshal. And since you've put your cards on the table, I guess it's only fair that I do the same. I'm looking for someone all right—a murderer—but not 'cause I want to collect any reward. This one's personal."

The marshal leaned back in his chair, twining his fingers together over his stomach. "Care to share a name with me?"

"Silas Scott."

"Can't say I've ever heard of him."

"You probably have his poster up." Lucas stood, moving to the tackboard covered with pictures and notices. He found the one for Scott beneath several others. He took it down, handing it to Ingalls.

Ingalls cringed at the scruffy, bearlike image on the page. "Good-lookin' fella," he said sardonically.

"Yeah," Luke agreed.

"Well, I haven't seen him, but I'll be sure to keep an eye out from now on. My deputies will, too."

"I'd appreciate it." Lucas went to the door. "I'm staying over at the hotel in case you need to find me."

"Mind if I ask why you want this guy so bad?"

Lucas's hand tightened on the doorknob. "Like I said, Marshal, it's personal." He tipped his hat and walked out.

That's why he hated working with lawmen. Not that they weren't good men, it was just that they always wanted to know the whole story. Ingalls had probably already figured out that Lucas didn't plan to turn Scott in. For that reason, the marshal might choose not to tell him even if he did see Scott. But he might, and that was better than nothing.

He continued down the street, deciding a drink would hit the spot. The Whiskey Barrel looked to be a fairly clean establishment. Three men sat at a corner table playing a game of poker. A rather well-endowed blonde stood nearby, waiting to refill glasses or take the winner upstairs to celebrate. He didn't recognize any of them or the few other customers milling about.

The bartender gave Lucas a smile, wiping the counter with a dirty gray rag. "What'll it be?"

"Yuengling, if you've got it."

"Sure do." He filled a glass from the tap.

Lucas pushed a coin forward, taking a sip of the lukewarm beer. In the mirror behind the barkeep, he saw a slim, curvy brunette coming down the stairwell. With every step, her off-the-shoulder, hip-hugging, royal-blue gown fell open to reveal a long, shapely leg. She walked over to the card game, giving the poker players a small smile and a few words of encouragement. Then she made her way to the bar and stood beside Lucas.

"I've never seen you in here before," she commented. "Care to buy me a drink?"

Her voice sounded like melted butter, warm and smooth and inviting. But he took a close look and couldn't help comparing her with the woman waiting for him back at the hotel. Where Megan's eyes revealed her every emotion, this woman's showed nothing. Neither happiness nor sorrow. She was pretty enough, though, without the usual heavy makeup or thick, cloying perfume most prostitutes wore. He imagined she would clean up real nice if she ever got out of this kind of environment.

After a moment he shrugged, seeing no harm in granting her request.

She rested one satin-slippered foot on the small ledge that ran along the bottom of the bar. Her dress fell open, exposing that stocking-clad leg Lucas had admired when she first came down the stairs.

"Brandy, please, Pete," she said softly.

The bartender poured a glass, giving her a sharp look. "Don't be teasing the customers, Willow. They get real testy when you do that."

"I'm not teasing anyone, Pete." She turned violet eyes on Lucas. "Am I teasing you, sir?"

Pete straightened his well over six-foot frame. "She ain't no whore, mister, so don't be thinking you can take her upstairs."

"If she's not"—Lucas searched his mind for the right word; the last thing he wanted to do was insult the lady or incur Pete's wrath—"available," he said, "then what's she doing here?" He almost added "looking like that" but thought better of it.

"She works here—singing."

"Singing, huh?" Lucas turned to Willow. "You any good?"

A spark of life lit her eyes. "I've been known to draw a crowd."

He scoped the room. "Not tonight."

A smile tugged at the corners of her mouth. She took one last sip of brandy before sauntering over to the piano. Lucas didn't even try to stop himself from watching the sway of her hips. Some things a man just couldn't be expected to ignore.

She leaned over to whisper something in the piano man's ear, then climbed a set of narrow side steps to the stage. Her heels echoed on the rough planks.

The notes started, slow and precise. The piano sounded raw and tinny by itself, but the minute Willow opened her mouth and began to sing, everything else melted away. Her clear, satiny voice filled the saloon. The men at the corner table turned over their cards, giving her their undivided attention.

"Fair as the morning, bright as the day,
Vision of beauty, fade not away;
Over the mountain, over the sea,
Come in sweet dreams to me."

The swinging doors opened to admit a group of men. All eyes were on Willow, her voice drawing them. They shuffled in along the wall, careful to make no sound that might intrude upon her singing.

Above, leaning over the balcony rail, appeared half a dozen women in various states of dishabille. Two or three men joined them, shirttails hanging out over loose trousers.

Lucas couldn't believe it. Not only did the girls without customers emerge from their rooms to listen to Willow's performance, but men who had already paid for a good time also flocked toward the sound of her voice.

133

When the song ended and the tinny plucks of the piano strings faded away, a roar of applause filled the room. Lucas clapped until his hands were numb. He had never heard anything in his life as beautiful as Willow's singing.

Her efforts were wasted in this cowtown, he thought. She ought to travel out to California or east to New York City. There she might find an audience worthy of her talents.

Willow gave a curtsy and blew a kiss to the crowd. The piano man helped her down from the stage, and she made her way back toward Lucas.

"What do you think, cowboy?"

"I think that deserves another drink."

Her laughter tinkled like a thousand silver bells. Pete even let down his guard long enough to chuckle. He refilled both their glasses before serving the customers who had poured in during Willow's performance.

Lucas studied her out of the corner of his eye. She didn't belong here, that was obvious—even more so now that he'd heard her sing.

"Why are you here?" he asked.

"What do you mean?" She put the glass of brandy to her lips.

"You're not a prostitute; Pete made that perfectly clear. You're a damn good singer, but I think we both know you're wasting your time here."

"Wasting my time? Sir, I'm offended." She put a hand over her heart. "I like to think I've brought at least a smidgen of culture to this town."

"It would take more than one pretty songbird to do that." She chuckled.

"So tell me the truth. What are you doing here?"

"Why do you ask?"

"Let's just say I have a healthy dose of curiosity."

"You and every other lonesome wanderer with empty pockets and a headful of dreams. What is it *you* want, mister? A house filled with the pitter-patter of children's feet, or never-ending adventure?" Willow shot back the last of her brandy. "Sorry, but I'm not interested in either. I don't need some man to ride in on his white steed and sweep me off my feet."

"I didn't offer," Lucas said. He took another sip from his mug of frothy beer. "But that's quite a speech you've got there."

Her cheeks brightened to a handsome shade of pink. "It's a necessity around here."

"So why do you stay?"

"You don't give up, do you?"

"Nope."

She smiled. "I'm waiting for someone."

"Here?" He didn't bother hiding his surprise.

"My brother left home a few years back, when he turned eighteen. At first we got letters from him at least once a week, and then they just stopped. I promised my parents that I would find him. This is the last place he was seen."

"And you're hoping he'll show up again."

She shrugged one smooth, bare shoulder. "Either that, or I'll get some word of where he could be."

With every fiber of his being, Lucas wanted to warn her off such a path. It would only lead to hard times and heartache. But then, who was he to give advice on the matter? He was doing almost the exact same thing. At least her motives were pure.

Pete passed by, and Lucas caught his attention. "Got a piece of paper?"

Pete gave him a disgruntled look before going off to search for some. He returned a minute later with the label off a can of beans.

Lucas flipped it over to write on the back. "How about something to write with?"

Pete cursed. "Would be nice if you asked for everything at once so's a man didn't have to keep running to the storeroom."

"Sorry," Lucas said with a laugh.

Pete handed over a short, well-used pencil stub, and Lucas began writing.

"I'd like to stick around and help you find your brother," he told Willow. "But I'm looking for somebody myself." He ripped a section from the label, sliding it along the counter to her. "Brandt Donovan is a friend of mine. If you ever need anything—anything at all—I want you to write to him at this address. He'll help you out or get a message to me."

Willow stared at the paper in her hand. Then she lifted her eyes to meet his. "Why are you doing this?"

"It's just an address. I wish I could do more. At least this way you'll be able to contact me."

"No, I mean, why are you doing any of this? Most people would shrug off my search as just another sad story they heard in a saloon."

"Maybe I know what it's like to lose someone you love. Or maybe I just want to help." He dug into his shirt pocket, pulling out several folded bills. "Keep this. If you get news about your brother, you may need it for a train ticket or something."

"I can't accept this," she said, handing it back.

He folded her fingers over the money, giving her hand a squeeze. "Take it. Just don't go wasting it," he said with a wink. He slid several coins onto the bar for their drinks.

"Let me know when you find him." He refrained from saying *if,* knowing hope was sometimes the only thing that kept a person going. He pressed a small kiss to her cheek. "Good luck."

He left the saloon without looking back. There was nothing he could do for Willow right now. He had his own course to follow, his own problems. And one of them was back at the hotel waiting for him.

How would he meet Megan's eyes and tell her that what they had shared meant nothing? How could he look at her without wanting to make love to her again? Christ, this job was getting difficult.

Infiltrate the gang, Brandt had said. Get the goods on Megan Adams so she can stand trial, he'd said. If Brandt were standing in front of him this minute, Lucas knew he'd strangle the bastard. His friend owed him for this one—owed him big.

Lucas tipped his hat to the clerk behind the desk in the hotel lobby as he made his way up to the room. He wondered if Megan was over his abrupt departure yet. Most women would rant and rave and cry their eyes out. Megan, he thought, would be more likely to throw something. Like a chair or table.

He winced at the thought. Perhaps she'd fallen asleep. His head tilted heavenward in a plea for that one small favor. He didn't make a habit of asking the Almighty for much, but this was an exception. He didn't think he could handle an irate Megan just now.

Turning the key slowly, silently, he unlocked the door. He opened it a crack, peeking inside. The room was dark. He listened but heard no signs of movement. With a relieved sigh, he entered.

Megan was sleeping—or feigning sleep—he realized when he saw a slight mound beneath the covers. Maybe by morning all the emotions over the whole incident would have passed. They could start over, revert to being simply prisoner and guard.

He removed his gun belt, then went to the bed, sitting on the edge so as not to disturb her. He shucked his boots, then tossed his shirt and hat onto the bedside table. Unbuttoning his trousers, he leaned back against his pillow, arms folded beneath his head.

He soon became convinced that Megan was only pretending to be asleep. She had a habit of rolling all over the place, and she hadn't so much as shifted an inch the entire time he'd been on the bed. He'd expected more trouble from her. A few cuss words, a flying hairbrush. But silence was good. He could handle that better than some in-depth, emotional confrontation.

He was just drifting off when he realized an unfamiliar noise seemed to be filtering into the room. A wispy, breathy sound. With it came the unmistakable *ping-ting* of the saloon's piano.

His brows met. He opened his eyes, seeing pitch black. There was more. A nagging sense of things being out of place. The hairs on the back of his neck stood on end.

And then it hit him. Megan wasn't breathing. The woman who sniffed, snored, and cursed in her sleep hadn't made a peep since he walked into the room.

He sat up, fumbling with the lamp until the wick was burning full force. Turning back, he ripped the bedcovers down, only to find a pillow stuffed underneath them to resemble a sleeping person. Across from the bed, he saw a knotted length of material leading out the window.

"Son of a bitch!" He jumped off the mattress, grabbing for his clothes and boots, at the same time trying to buckle on his matching Colts. He didn't know where Megan thought she could run, but he vowed to find her. If it took until his dying breath, he would find her and bring her back.

He let his anger build, knowing that if he stopped to think things through too thoroughly, he would get scared. There was no telling what Megan might run into out there. A woman on her own drew trouble like ants to a picnic. And no matter how tough she pretended to be, even Megan couldn't handle some things.

Damn. He had to find her.

He rounded the bed, running a hand over the rope of torn sheets. She was one damned ingenious woman, he'd give her that.

The best way to track a person was to follow their exact trail whenever possible. For that, he'd have to climb out the window, too. He cursed her to hell and back for choosing such a narrow exit.

He lifted a leg through the opening, shifting and turning until he could back his way out. His hips rubbed against the sides, impeded by the Peacemakers strapped to his thighs. He wrapped his foot around the makeshift ladder to help his descent and clutched the windowsill for dear life. Oh, yes, she would pay for this one.

A billowing summer breeze swirled the curtains into his face. The newspaper on the floor fluttered.

For the second time that night, Lucas found himself frowning. He distinctly remembered folding the *Gazette* and setting it on the table beside the armchair. Turning the air blue with curses, he struggled to get back into the room. His graceful choreography landed him with his head on the floor, his feet sticking up in the air over the bed.

He righted himself and crawled to the newspaper, slapping a hand on the pages to keep them from rattling. The rough sketch of Megan immediately caught his eye. Damn it! He'd hoped she wouldn't see the article.

Well, at least now he knew where she was headed.

Chapter Thirteen

Megan stumbled to a stop, letting go of the reins and dropping to the hard earth to empty her boots of dirt and stones. She didn't know where she was, exactly, but it wasn't far enough from Wichita to ease her mind. Her horse had thrown a shoe only a few miles outside of town; she'd been walking the mare ever since. It didn't help, either, to know that Lucas had most likely discovered her missing by now.

She pulled her boots back on and got to her feet, brushing a straggling lock of hair out of her eyes. There had to be a town nearby. Somewhere she could get her horse reshod or find a fresh mount.

After another half mile or so, she heard the rush of running water. A stream, she thought with delight. She could get a drink and wash her face. Oh, what she wouldn't give for that small pleasure. Poor Girl—as she'd taken to calling the mare—would appreciate fresh water, too.

When she finally came upon the bubbling brook, she

almost fell to her knees to kiss the ground in thanks. Poor Girl kept going, dragging the reins out of Megan's hand.

Exhausted, Megan crawled to the edge of the stream. She scooped several handfuls of cold water to her mouth before her thirst was sated. Then she slid open the top few buttons of her shirt to splash water over her face and neck. She moaned in delight.

"Well, lookee what we got here, boys."

She swung around to face three men. She had been so thrilled to find the creekbed that she hadn't paid much attention to her surroundings or heard anyone nearby.

The first man had shoulders as broad as a barn. A long, ragged scar ran down one side of his face, through his right eye. He didn't bother wearing a patch to cover the puckered skin around the dead orb.

His two companions were less formidable, scrawny even. But their slight build didn't fool Megan for a minute. She sensed that they were mean and very, very dangerous.

"You lost, honey?" the big one asked.

She didn't answer but took a step backward, reaching blindly for Poor Girl's reins.

"You ain't goin' somewheres without answerin', are ya?"

"Of course not," she answered, hoping to stall for time. "In fact, I think I am lost."

"Oh?" The man to the left of the leader moved closer. "Where is it you're going?"

"Wichita," she said, wanting them to think she was on her way to a town close by, not someplace a hundred miles away like Leavenworth.

"That's right interestin'. There's tracks leading to this creek, but they're heading away from Wichita. Looks like a horse come up lame and the rider's been walkin' him. Wouldn't be you, now, would it?"

"No. My horse is just fine." She took the opportunity to turn and grab Poor Girl's trailing reins, never taking her eyes off the three slowly advancing men.

141

When they were no more than a yard away, Megan leapt into the saddle and spurred her horse forward. The mare raced across the stream, onto the opposite bank, but the missing shoe slowed her down, made her gait awkward.

Megan felt herself flying through the air before she realized one of the men had caught the back of her shirt. The force of her fall knocked the air from her lungs. The pain kept her immobile for several seconds.

She regained her breath and began fighting the man holding her down on the ground. With a solid kick, the heel of her boot met a shin bone. Her nails dug into his stubbly face, her teeth into his forearm. He swore violently, letting go to rub the raw and bleeding skin. While he was preoccupied with his small wounds, she pulled back and punched him in the jaw. He fell to the side, stunned.

The other two men pounced, trying to impede her movements. But while they fought to subdue her flailing arms, she landed a crippling blow to the groin of the bull-like man. He groaned, covering his injury with both hands.

That left one. He stared at his partners with wide eyes. Megan shoved him away, bounding to her feet. When he got to his knees and lunged at her, she cracked him under the jaw with one well-placed kick.

She watched them carefully while she caught her breath. Poor Girl stood beside a cottonwood tree, looking on, fear blazing in the whites of her eyes. Megan patted the mare's neck and began leading her away. The men were coming around. She needed to get away as fast as possible. But with the limp Poor Girl now had from their fouled attempt at escape, there was no way Megan could ask her to carry added weight.

"Come on, Girl," she said, clicking her tongue. She would think of something.

"Not so fast."

Megan turned, only to find herself looking down the

barrel of a revolver. The broad-shouldered man stood not three feet away, the gun shaking a bit in his white-knuckled hand.

"I don't take kindly to no uppity bitch makin' me look bad."

"You don't need an uppity bitch to do that," she retorted.

He moved forward with his arm up; she was sure he meant to strike her. She took a step backward, prepared to run but ready to fight if necessary.

A shot rang through the night, stopping her attacker in his tracks. He whirled around, raising his pistol to ward off this newest threat.

"If you want to live to see tomorrow, I suggest you drop the gun."

Megan had never been so happy to see anyone in her life. Lucas stood on the other side of the stream, aiming both ivory-handled Peacemakers at the group of men.

"Drop it," he warned again.

The Remington faltered in the big man's grip, but he didn't loosen his hold. Another bullet rent the air. All eyes turned to see one of the thinner men clutch his leg before doubling over. His .44 tumbled to the ground.

"Who wants to be next?"

Both men threw their guns toward the bank of the creek.

"Good. Now pick up your friend and ride out of here."

They lifted the wounded man by the armpits, half dragging, half carrying him across the stream.

The staccato beat of galloping horses faded into the distance, leaving them alone in the night. Except for a scant amount of moonlight filtering through the treetops, all was dark.

Lucas stood stock-still for long minutes. His body hummed with unreleased fury and deep-rooted fear. When he'd come upon Megan being approached by that burly, unkempt man, he saw red. He wanted to rip the bastard's throat out. Now he couldn't seem to move.

Megan was all right. A little shaken, from the looks of her, but not hurt. It seemed to take forever for his heart to pick up a normal rhythm.

As he watched, Megan closed her eyes and slumped to the ground. Suddenly, Lucas wasn't so sure she was okay.

He reholstered his Colts, splashing through the calf-deep water to the other side of the creek. He reached her in three long strides. His hands shook as he gripped her upper arms.

Then she lifted her head and smiled. A wide, radiant smile.

"Christ!" he swore, releasing her. "I thought you were hurt."

She struggled to her feet, wiping dust from her pant legs. "I'm fine."

That's when he noticed her ripped shirt. All the buttons down the front were missing, and the collar hung open haphazardly, torn at the seam.

He stared hard at the rent fabric. "Did they hurt you?"

She shook her head. "No. I'm fine."

Lucas clenched his teeth, biting back the need to go after those bastards, to kill them for even daring to touch her. The haze of anger slowly began to fade. But the remnants of fear remained.

He grabbed Megan's shoulders, his fingers digging into her soft flesh as he shook her. "Are you crazy? What the hell were you thinking, running away like that? You could have been killed!"

She looked up at him, tangled hair falling in her face, her brown eyes big and bright. Then she lifted a hand to his face, her lips turning up at the corners. "But I wasn't."

It took a minute for her words to sink in. Longer for him to realize she was right—she hadn't been killed. Hadn't been raped or beaten or any of the other thousand things he'd imagined as he rode around looking for her.

"Christ," he said and drew her against him. His mouth devoured her, drinking, plunging, reaffirming. He couldn't seem to get close enough to stop the tremors that raced through his body. His hands ran over her face, her arms, reassuring himself that she was unharmed. He'd never been so afraid in his life as when he'd seen her standing at the business end of that bastard's pistol.

Lucas lifted her into his arms, took hold of the mare's reins, and crossed the stream. He lowered Megan, letting her slide down, causing a sweet friction to build between their bodies. His tongue traced the gentle curve of her lips. Keeping her hand clutched tightly in his own, he tied her mount to his gelding.

Lucas kissed the tip of Megan's nose, then picked her up by the waist to deposit her at the front of his saddle. He climbed up behind. With a soft click, he set Worthy into motion toward town, the reins knotted and secured about the pommel.

He put one arm around Megan's waist. The other slipped into the opening of her shirt to cup one of the heavy globes concealed there. His fingers teased the nipple while he rained small, openmouthed kisses along her neck.

Megan whimpered when he nipped her earlobe. His breath against her hair, the silky warmth of his tongue made her insides burn. Her flesh was alive with wanting.

He released her breast, sliding his hand over her stomach and out of the shirt. She was about to voice her disappointment when his other hand circled the opposite mound. His right hand rested on the waistband of her trousers. Expertly, he undid the buttons there, slipped his hand inside her satin drawers, and cupped her.

She gasped when his fingers touched the bud of desire hidden within, slick and ready for his ministrations. She let her head fall back against his shoulder. Her hands curled beneath his thighs, as though at any moment she might otherwise be wrenched up and tossed through the air.

"Oh, God," she moaned as his finger slipped inside her.

"It's okay, baby," he whispered above her ear.

He circled her ultrasensitive nub with his thumb, all the while moving his finger in a steady rhythm. Ecstasy

145

built to an almost painful plane. She groaned and writhed on his lap, begging him to cease his sweet torture.

"Lucas. Lucas."

"Easy, baby. Let it come."

He kicked the horse into a faster gait, driving them together more forcefully. His motions increased. A brilliant array of stars broke out before her. She screamed his name, riding his finger as uncontrollable spasms washed over her.

She let out a strangled sigh, limp and replete in his arms.

"Did you like that?"

She tried to laugh at his wicked question. *Like* was not the word she would use to describe what she had just experienced.

Only after she began to recover did she become aware of Lucas's own arousal pressing into the small of her back. He didn't seem inclined to do anything about it, but he had given her such pleasure, she wanted to do the same for him. Even in the awkward position of riding on horseback, there had to be some way. . . .

"Lucas?"

"Hmm?"

"Are we alone?"

"You don't see anybody else on this horse, do you?"

She rolled her eyes at his smart-aleck answer. "I mean, is there anyone else around? Can anyone . . . see us?"

"Nope. It's just you, me, and the horses."

"Good." She swung her leg over Worthy's neck, bumping Lucas's arm from her waist.

"What do you think you're doing?" he asked, his voice sounding confused and more than a little miffed, as if she were abandoning him there in the saddle.

"You'll see." Balancing herself in the crook of his legs, she started to wiggle out of her pants.

She almost fell, and Lucas yelled at her. "What the hell are you doing?"

"You'll see," she said again. It took some doing, but she finally managed to get her trousers off without removing her boots. She slung the pants across Worthy's rump, then got up on her knees. The horse's easy gait and Lucas's hands were the only things keeping her from toppling over.

"Megan, if you don't—"

She cut him off. "Do you want me to do this or not?"

"I can't imagine what the hell it is you're trying to do!" he snapped. "If you don't sit down, you're going to fall off and break your damned neck."

Megan ran her fingers through the hair at his temples, leaning close to the solid wall of his chest. "Shut up and make love to me."

"How do you expect me to do that?" The words were meant to be rough, but his tone revealed just how much he wanted to.

"Easy." She bent her head, pressing her mouth to his full, pouting lips. He tasted of the lingering remnants of ale. Her hands slid down the front of his shirt to his gun belt. She unbuckled it, letting it drape over the saddle behind him. He didn't seem to notice he was no longer properly armed as his hands moved beneath the silk of her drawers to cup her rounded bottom. She loosened the buttons of his trousers, allowing his hardened length freedom from the binding confines.

Lucas pulled his mouth away but held her derriere even more tightly. "Megan, we can't."

She ignored him, closing her fingers around his pulsing shaft.

He groaned. "This isn't going to work, Megan."

She took the end of his ear into her mouth, suckling gently. "Take off my drawers."

"Huh?" He pushed the collar of her shirt aside, kissing the sensitive flesh of her shoulder.

"Take my drawers off, Lucas."

He seemed to get the message that time, for he removed his hands from her bottom. He fought to find the waistband of her drawers beneath her shirt, which hung to midthigh. Finally he found the tie. For long minutes he struggled with the knot, cursing more foully than Megan had ever before heard.

She chuckled, still massaging his rock-hard arousal. "Hurry, Lucas," she whispered, curious to see just what he would do.

She didn't have long to wonder. With a savage tug, the string snapped. He leaned back, lifting her so the silken undergarment could fall away, leaving her naked from the waist down.

When he set her down, she spread her legs to straddle him, her legs resting on his thighs.

"I can't wait, Megan. I can't."

She wrapped her arms around his neck just as he lowered her onto his throbbing member. They both gasped at the contact. Sweet, electrifying bolts of lightning shot through their bodies.

"Tell me if I go too fast." He grasped her hips, lifting and lowering her.

Megan thought she would die. Her stomach clenched; her breath caught. A wave of untamed heat spiraled through her, causing her to cry out.

Hearing Megan's shout, Lucas thrust faster, bringing them together with added force. It happened before he could think to stop it or even slow things down. White-hot pleasure washed over him. He clutched her close as he came, filling her with the hot liquid of his climax.

When he could once again manage to breathe air into his paralyzed lungs, he swore. "Christ. I think I died and went to heaven." He felt Megan's chest move against his own as she laughed.

She raised her head from his shoulder, meeting his eyes. Lucas pushed long, errant curls out of her face, then kissed her. Soft, slow, not so much with uncontrolled passion as with gentle caring.

A few flickering lights in the distance alerted him to their nearness to town. He pulled the tail of her shirt down as far as it would go, covering her, loathe to let her go. He reached behind him for her trousers. "You'd better get dressed."

She took her pants, turning sideways on the saddle. "Where are my drawers?" She looked around, patting him down in case they were tangled in his clothes.

"My guess is, somewhere back there." He arched a thumb over his shoulder.

"Back there?" Her eyes widened. "You mean . . . back there . . . on the ground?"

"Yep." One side of his mouth lifted. "Unless some horny little raccoon grabbed them up."

"Lucas!" She slapped his chest. "That's terrible. How could you lose them like that?"

He ran a hand up under her shirt to tease one pearl-tipped nipple. "I had more important things on my mind. Care to repeat the experience?"

"No, thank you." She snapped her trousers in the air, struggling to get them on over her boots. She did not, however, ask him to remove his hand. It remained on her breast until they arrived at the outskirts of town. Then Lucas rebuckled his gun belt, and Megan straightened in the saddle.

Her face flushed guiltily, he noticed, even though no one was around. Had the main street been brimming with people, he didn't think anyone would possibly guess what had occurred on the trail. Only he and Megan knew. And he wasn't damned likely to forget. He suspected he would carry the memory with him long after he'd cocked up his toes and moved on to the here-after.

The livery was dark when they arrived. Lucas stabled their mounts and scrawled a short note to the owner, asking him to have Poor Girl reshod.

They walked to the hotel, through the empty lobby, and up to their room. Lucas struck a match, lighting the bedside lamp.

Megan felt suddenly self-conscious. About her failed attempt at escaping Lucas and returning to Leavenworth. About her boldness in making love to him, especially *that way,* out in the open for God and all the world to see.

149

Her cheeks turned hot just thinking about it. If he mentioned it—said one word—she would burn up from embarrassment.

She reached up to pull the brim of her Stetson down, hoping to hide her reddening features, but her hand met with only soft, tangled curls.

"What the . . . Where is my hat?" She whirled around, as if it might be hovering behind her, making faces, and she had to catch it.

"What?" Lucas asked from beside the bed.

"My hat. It's gone."

He glanced at his. It rested on the dresser where he'd put it when he came in earlier that evening, forgotten in his rush to find Megan. But hers was nowhere in sight.

"I must have lost it," she said. "Damn. I loved that hat, too."

"I'll buy you a new one in the morning."

"But—"

"In the morning, Megan. For now, can we please get some sleep? I don't know about you, but I'm exhausted."

She shrank back a step, clutching her hands behind her. "You're not going to cuff me again, are you?"

He answered her question with a question of his own. "Are you going to run away again?"

"I might."

"Then I'll cuff you."

"But I might not," she offered.

"Then I won't."

"But how will you know—"

"Get into bed, Megan."

She shrugged out of her trousers, making sure the shirt covered as much exposed skin as possible. She didn't know why she bothered, since Lucas had already seen her, touched her, made her cry out, and . . . Good, Lord, she had to get her racing pulse under control.

Lucas whipped back the covers, pointing to her side of the bed. She climbed in, drawing the bedspread over her bare knees as she puffed the pillow behind her back.

He turned down the wick of the lamp, casting the room into a dim yellow-orange glow. Then he moved to the other side of the room, in front of the bureau mirror.

"Aren't you coming to bed?" she asked quietly.

"In a minute."

She watched him a second longer before snuggling under the covers and nodding off to sleep. Her last conscious thought was that it seemed colder, even under the quilted blanket, without Lucas's arms around her.

Chapter Fourteen

Lucas yawned, raising a hand to rub his eyes. The misty gray of early morning peeked through the hotel window. He turned his head to glance at Megan. Her dark hair fell over her face like a veil, fluttering slightly each time she exhaled.

He rolled out of bed without disturbing her. By the time he dressed, shaved, and strapped on his matching Colts, the sun was up and people were milling about town. Tucking his well-worn hat on his head, he slipped out of the room.

He stopped at the mercantile, purchasing a new beige Stetson for Megan. He figured it was at least partly his fault that she'd lost the old one. He smiled at the memory. The last thing he'd been thinking about on the ride back to Wichita was her hat.

He was on his way back to the hotel when he noticed a man vigorously sweeping outside the saloon. Something in his brain sparked. The back of his neck tingled. He'd been a bounty hunter long enough to know not to ignore instinct. He crossed the street, stepping up on the opposite plank sidewalk.

When he got closer, he recognized the bartender from his earlier late-night visit to the Whiskey Barrel.

"You're out awfully early, Pete," he said casually.

"Damn rowdies," Pete swore, swinging the broom even more violently than before.

"Sounds like I missed all the excitement."

He huffed. "No excitement. Just a down-and-dirty brawl."

"What happened?" His voice was calm, but he felt as if he were trying to squeeze blood from a turnip.

"Some mean-ass drifter came in about midnight, one o'clock. Trouble started when he decided to take another cowboy's girl upstairs."

"Anybody hurt?"

"Not 'less you count me." Pete pulled back the collar of his shirt. A thick red welt ran across his chest and shoulder. "Bastard tried to take me out with the leg of a chair."

"What did you do?" Lucas asked. He could just imagine.

"Let's just say he'll be walkin' funny for a while."

Lucas chuckled for a moment, then probed for more information. "What did this guy look like?"

"The meaner side of ugly," Pete said. "Had a face a mother would have trouble loving. I don't even want to think about what the rest of it looked like under that beard."

Lucas stiffened. "Black hair going gray? About six feet tall?"

Pete shrugged. "Guess so."

"Did you see the horse he came in on?"

"Yep. Made sure he rode out on it, too."

"What did it look like?"

Pete stopped sweeping, leaning on the broomstick. He gave Lucas a curious look. "It was a black, scraggly old thing. Probably shoulda been put down long ago. Why do you ask?"

"I've been looking for someone," he said quickly, not offering more. "Did his horse have an old scar across its left flank?"

"Sure did."

Blood rushed to Lucas's brain. His palms began to itch with anticipation of the kill. "Which way did he go?"

"He was headed east, but I overheard him telling one of the girls he was on his way to Missouri. Lexington. No, that ain't it. Started with an *i* . . . Independence," he said, slapping his leg. "That's it. Said he was on his way to Independence. Hey, where you goin'?" he called.

Lucas didn't hear Pete or any of the other sounds of a town waking to a new day. His mind was on blood. Damn it, if he hadn't had to go running after Megan last night, he'd have been around to catch Scott.

But then, there was no guarantee that he'd have even known the bastard was in town, he reasoned.

He knew now, though. And all he had to do was catch up with Scott on the trail to Independence.

The thought that Independence, Missouri, was two hundred miles away didn't dim his determination. He finally had a decent lead, and he was not going let Silas Scott get away.

He strode into the hotel room, letting the door slam behind him.

Megan sat up with a startled yet sleepy expression on her face. "What's going on?" she asked groggily.

"We're leaving. Get dressed."

She fell back against the pillows with a moan. "Not again," she complained. "Can't we ever stay in a town more than one night?"

"This time is special," he told her, stuffing their things into his saddlebags.

She gave an unladylike snort.

"I'm taking you home."

Suddenly she was wide awake. She stared at him with mammoth, disbelieving eyes. "Really? You're taking me back to Leavenworth?"

"Yep. But only if you're dressed and ready to ride in two minutes."

She leapt out of bed and dragged on her trousers, not bothering to tuck in the shirttail. "Why the sudden change of heart?" she asked, struggling to jam on her boots.

"No change of heart. I got a new lead on Scott that takes me through Leavenworth." That wasn't the complete truth, but he figured Leavenworth was close enough to Independence that he could drop Megan off at the marshal's office without losing too much time. And without her slowing him down, he could cover a lot more ground.

He went to the door, holding it open. "Ready?"

"Ready." She pushed to her feet and left the room ahead of him.

Before she slipped out of arm's reach, he brought the new Stetson up behind her and dropped it on her head. With a pat to the hat and one to her bottom, he ushered her out of the hotel.

The closer they got to Leavenworth, the more anxious Megan became. Lucas hadn't said half a dozen words to her the entire trip, and she could almost feel the cold iron bars of a jail cell closing around her. She was sure he still intended to turn her in. Why should a few hours spent in carnal splendor change his mind?

But the thought of sitting in jail didn't bother her nearly as much as the distance that seemed to have grown between the two of them overnight.

She had almost begun to believe that there was more to Lucas than the hard exterior he presented to the world. More than vengeance and bloodlust in his heart. Now she feared she'd been wrong. All that truly mattered to him was finding Silas Scott and killing him for what he'd done to Annie and Chad. And while Megan understood his anger, hatred, and need for justice, she couldn't quite fathom a fury that consumed one's whole life, one's whole soul.

She glanced to the side, taking in Lucas's stiff form, his hardened jawline.

"You're still going to turn me in, aren't you?"

"Yep," he answered without looking at her.

"And there's nothing I can do to change your mind?"

"Nope."

So much for bargaining, she thought.

She took a deep breath. "All right, then. I know you're only doing your job, so I'll go along quietly."

That brought his head around. He stared at her, eyebrows raised. "No arguments?"

"No arguments."

"No kicking, screaming, and threatening to see me hanged?"

"None of those things," she promised.

Lucas didn't take his eyes from her. Something was brewing in that devious mind of hers; he was sure of it. He didn't let himself believe for even a minute that she would let herself be locked up without a fight.

"What's the catch?" he asked.

"No catch. Just a small favor."

He grunted, facing forward again. "No deal." He'd rather drag her to jail kicking and screaming than make a deal with the Devil herself.

"Please, Lucas. It's not a big favor, just a little one. It would mean so much to me."

He didn't look at her, didn't respond.

"I promise to let you turn me in to Marshal Thompson without so much as a tear if you'll just let me see my family first. I don't want them to find out about all of this by word of mouth. I want to be able to tell them myself so it's not such a shock. Please, Lucas."

He gritted his teeth for a moment, thinking her proposition through. He supposed it wouldn't hurt to let her visit her brother one last time before he took her to jail. The most he would lose was a few hours. He let his eyes stray to Megan's face. Damp black curls stuck to her skin where they'd escaped the confines of her hat. A bolt of desire ripped through him, hot and intense.

He swore under his breath. He was going to miss her more than he cared to admit. How could he possibly say no when all she asked was one last visit with her family before an indefinite prison stay?

"All right. But when it comes time for me to turn you over to the law, I don't want even a peep of argument. Got it?"

"Oh, yes, I promise," she said, bringing her horse closer to his. Without warning, she threw her arms around his neck, hugging him close.

He held her tight as she slipped from her horse to his. Setting her sideways on the saddle in front of him, he let the heat of her supple body seep into his. Yes, he was going to miss her, he thought a second before their lips met.

Lucas let his eyes drift across the expanse of Caleb Adams's ranch. The large white house was nestled in a valley between two crests of pasture land. A few head of cattle grazed on the hilltop. The lawn was strewn with toys. A hobbyhorse, a red wagon missing a wheel, the remnants of a corn-husk doll, and proof of a bloody battle between wooden cowboys and Indians.

As they rode up to the hitching post, Lucas noticed two sets of fingers wrapped around the porch railing. His hand moved automatically to the Colt at his hip.

"No," Megan said, covering his hand with her own. "It's just little Zachary." She dismounted and moved toward the house.

When the small boy recognized Megan, he popped up and ran yelling happily down the porch steps, launching himself into her arms.

"Aunt Megan! Aunt Megan!"

"Hey, there, Zach." She picked him up and spun him around, kissing him atop his light-brown hair.

"Where've you been, Aunt Megan? Mama and Daddy have been awful worried 'bout you."

"I know, but—"

"Zachary Adams, what on earth are you yelling about? You're going to wake your sister if you don't—"

A woman with hair the exact color of the boy's stopped in midstride. The screen door fell closed, hitting her behind. "Oh, my God. Megan." She flew down the steps.

After several minutes of happy embraces and excited chatter, the women broke apart. Megan set Zachary back on his feet, turning to Lucas.

"Lucas," she said, taking his hand and drawing him closer. "This is my brother's wife, Rebecca, and their son, Zachary. This is Lucas," she said by way of introduction.

"Zachary," Rebecca said, "go to the barn and find your father." The little boy ran off without further urging, leaving a trail of dust in his wake.

"Come inside." Rebecca took Megan's hand and guided her through the front door. "Sit down, both of you." She waved to the settee in the middle of the parlor.

Megan took a seat on the sofa while Lucas sat in an armchair off to the side.

"Are you all right? We've been worried sick about you," Rebecca said.

"I'm fine," Megan answered, smiling. "When Caleb gets here, I'll tell you everything. How's Rose?" she asked.

"She's napping. Unless Zachary woke her with all that screeching. Maybe I ought to check on her."

"I'll go with you." Megan followed her sister-in-law to the stairs leading to the second floor. "I'll be right back," she mouthed to Lucas.

He sat back in the chair, exhaling a deep breath. The women were gone no longer than five minutes when heavy footsteps echoed on the porch. A tower of a man with dark hair and brown eyes stepped into the room.

"Megan!" he barked. "Megan?"

The little boy scooted around the man's legs and hopped onto the sofa.

"Caleb!" Megan came clattering down the steps, throwing herself into her brother's arms.

Rebecca appeared a second later, carrying the baby.

"You're all going to give poor Rose nightmares if you don't hush." She bounced the child gently in her arms, cooing quietly.

"Where have you been, Megan?" Caleb asked. His tone was rough, but he kept his voice low. Then his eyes darted to Lucas. "And who the hell is he?"

"This is Lucas McCain," Megan said. "He works for Union Pacific. They sent him to find out who was stealing the payrolls."

"So what is he doing with you?"

"Union Pacific thinks I had something to do with the robberies," she told him.

Caleb gave her an odd look.

Without batting an eyelash, she blurted out, "Lucas is taking me to jail."

Chapter Fifteen

"What?" Caleb stormed forward, his eyes burning with fury.

"Shit." Lucas leapt to his feet. He drew his gun without thinking of the women and children standing witness.

"Caleb, Caleb, Caleb." Megan put herself between the two towering men.

"Move!" Lucas barked, pushing her out of harm's way.

"Don't use that tone with my sister," Caleb threatened.

"Don't use her as a shield," Lucas countered.

"I don't need a woman to protect me, you bastard."

"Stop it! Stop it!" Megan used her body to pry them apart. "Caleb, sit down. Lucas, put that gun away before somebody gets hurt."

The men faced off a moment longer.

"Sit!" she yelled, putting a hand to each of their chests, moving them physically.

"Don't get all worked up, Caleb. There's a perfectly good explanation for why Lucas is taking me in. And, you," she said, turning on Lucas. "How dare you draw

Thrill to the most sensual, adventure-filled Historical Romances on the market today…

FROM  LEISURE BOOKS

As a home subscriber to the Leisure Historical Romance Book Club, you'll enjoy the best in today's BRAND-NEW Historical Romance fiction. For over twenty-five years, Leisure Books has brought you the award-winning, high-quality authors you know and love to read. Each Leisure Historical Romance will sweep you away to a world of high adventure…and intimate romance. Discover for yourself all the passion and excitement millions of readers thrill to each and every month.

SAVE AT LEAST $5.00 EACH TIME YOU BUY!

Each month, the Leisure Historical Romance Book Club brings you four brand-new titles from Leisure Books, America's foremost publisher of Historical Romances. EACH PACKAGE WILL SAVE YOU AT LEAST $5.00 FROM THE BOOKSTORE PRICE! And you'll never miss a new title with our convenient home delivery service.

Here's how we do it. Each package will carry a 10-DAY EXAMINATION privilege. At the end of that time, if you decide to keep your books, simply pay the low invoice price of $16.96 ($17.75 US in Canada), no shipping or handling charges added*. HOME DELIVERY IS ALWAYS FREE*. With today's top Historical Romance novels selling for $5.99 and higher, our price SAVES YOU AT LEAST $5.00 with each shipment.

AND YOUR FIRST FOUR-BOOK SHIPMENT IS TOTALLY FREE!

IT'S A BARGAIN YOU CAN'T BEAT! A Super $21.96 Value!

LEISURE BOOKS A Division of Dorchester Publishing Co., Inc.

GET YOUR 4 FREE* BOOKS NOW— A $21.96 VALUE!

Mail the Free* Book Certificate Today!

---

4 FREE* BOOKS & A $21.96 VALUE

Free Books Certificate

YES! I want to subscribe to the Leisure Historical Romance Book Club. Please send me my 4 FREE* BOOKS. Then each month I'll receive the four newest Leisure Historical Romance selections to Preview for 10 days. If I decide to keep them, I will pay the Special Member's Only discounted price of just $4.24 each, a total of $16.96 ($17.75 US in Canada). This is a SAVINGS OF AT LEAST $5.00 off the bookstore price. There are no shipping, handling, or other charges*. There is no minimum number of books I must buy and I may cancel the program at any time. In any case, the 4 FREE* BOOKS are mine to keep—A BIG $21.96 Value!

*In Canada, add $5.00 shipping and handling per order for first shipment. For all subsequent shipments to Canada, the cost of membership is $17.75 US, which includes $7.75 shipping and handling per month.[All payments must be made in US dollars]

Name _____

Address _____

City _____

State _____ *Country* _____ *Zip* _____

Telephone _____

Signature _____

If under 18, Parent or Guardian must sign. Terms, prices and conditions subject to change. Subscription subject to acceptance. Leisure Books reserves the right to reject any order or cancel any subscription.

Get Four Books Totally
F R E E* —
A $21.96 Value!

PLEASE RUSH
MY FOUR FREE*
BOOKS TO ME
RIGHT AWAY!

Leisure Historical Romance Book Club
P.O. Box 6613
Edison, NJ 08818-6613

AFFIX
STAMP
HERE

your weapon in this house? There are two children present who could get hurt. Do you want Zach to think gunfire is the best way to resolve conflict?"

"Did you see that?" Her nephew tugged on his father's sleeve. "That was fast, wasn't it, Daddy?"

Caleb's face hardened, but he nodded and said, "Yes, it was fast."

"Wow! Can you teach me to do that, mister?" Little Zach pointed his finger, aiming at different spots in the room. "Bang! Bang!"

"Zachary, don't you want to show Aunt Megan the pretty new rocks you found in the pasture?" Rebecca suggested.

"Mama," he groaned. "They're stones, not rocks."

"I'm sorry," she apologized. "Why don't you go up to your room and find them, and stay there until I call you down. Your father and Mr. McCain have some things to discuss."

Zach thrust his bottom lip out in an attempt to pout.

His mother stood firm. "Go. Bessie?" She turned to the girl standing in the doorway of the kitchen, intently watching the standoff between Caleb and Lucas. "Put on a pot of coffee for dinner, will you, please?"

When only the four of them—and the baby—were left, Rebecca turned to Megan. "Maybe it would be best to tell us everything. From the beginning."

"I think you're right." Megan took a deep breath, then began. "Well, I was driving the stage the day I disappeared because Hector was afraid of the outlaws who had been robbing us of the railroad payrolls. Before we got five miles out of town, the gang stopped us, took the money, and kidnapped me. At first I thought Lucas was one of the bandits. But then, after he kidnapped me from them, I found out he was working for Union Pacific. You might remember that the railroad's head of security, Brandt Donovan, paid me a visit not long ago to discuss the robberies. Mr. Donovan just happens to be Lucas's best friend. I guess he believes I've had something to do with all the stage holdups. I haven't, of course, but I can't convince Lucas here of that. Brandt Donovan sent him to find me, and Lucas darn well intends to turn me in to the law. I promised to go quietly if he let me come to see you first. He kept his end of the bargain, and I'll keep mine.

"Anyway, before Lucas could turn me in to Marshal Thompson, he had some personal business to take care of. So we traveled to Topeka, and then down to Wichita. Now the person he's looking for is headed into Missouri. Independence, isn't it, Lucas?"

He didn't answer.

That didn't stop Megan from continuing. "Lucas decided to leave me here before moving on."

Caleb's eyes narrowed. "The railroad thinks you had something to do with the string of payroll robberies?"

She chuckled. "Not exactly. It's more like they think I planned the whole thing."

"What?" Caleb and Rebecca asked at the same time. The baby started to fuss. Rebecca rubbed the child's back, whispering some soft, meaningless chatter in her ear.

Megan shrugged a shoulder. "I know. It's ridiculous. I would never have anything to do with something like that. But Lucas doesn't know that. And in all fairness, I have to tell you that it's not Lucas's fault he has to put me in jail. He's only doing what his friend asked him to do. He doesn't know all the details, and Brandt Donovan seems determined to see me pay for my crimes."

Lucas almost swallowed his teeth when he heard that. Megan had spent the last two weeks fighting him at every turn, trying to convince him of her innocence. Now suddenly she seemed resigned to sitting in a prison cell. She was defending him to her family, for Christ's sake.

"Everything is going to be fine, though," she told them. "You don't have to worry. Obviously, I didn't organize the robberies. I didn't so much as let it slip that a strongbox was being transported. The railroad people won't be able to prove anything, and they'll realize they made a mistake."

"I'll wire New York," Caleb said. "Mother will hire the best lawyer available. You won't be in jail more than a day."

Megan smiled. "Thank you. But it really doesn't matter. A jail cell actually sounds comforting after sleeping on the ground for the past two weeks."

"You had to sleep on the ground?" Rebecca gasped. "You poor thing."

"It wasn't so bad, to tell the truth. And we stayed in a couple of hotels."

"Together?" Caleb asked sharply. "Alone?"

"Don't get all provoked, Caleb. We had to stay in the same room because, technically, I'm his prisoner. But Lucas was a perfect gentleman. He acted very professionally, making his pallet on the floor after handcuffing me to the bed."

"He handcuffed you?" Rebecca looked about to faint.

"It all sounds much worse than it actually was, I swear. I'm in perfect health. See?" She stood and did a pirouette. "And now that I've told you everything, let me hold my niece."

Megan cradled the child in her arms, swaying back and forth, humming a soft little song. "This is Rose," she said, turning to Lucas. "Say hi." She lifted Rose's tiny hand, waving it in his direction.

Lucas found himself waving back. Then a scowl broke out across his brow, and he lowered his arm. If it didn't seem so pointless, he'd have cursed. But no amount of swearing would erase the effect Megan had on people—especially him.

"Megan," Rebecca said, "why don't you come into the kitchen and help me with dinner? We'll leave the men alone to talk."

Megan seemed to hesitate. She glanced first at Lucas, then at her brother.

"Do you think that's a good idea?" she asked her sister-in-law.

"It's a wonderful idea." Rebecca took her arm and steered her toward the kitchen.

Megan glanced behind her as the two women went through the swinging door. Lucas saw the warning in her eyes, the desperate plea for him not to get into a fight with Caleb. He almost winked to let her know everything would be fine. But then, why not let her think the worst for a while? Maybe then she would choose her words more wisely rather than spitting out the first thing—and everything else—that came to mind. He could only imagine all the misunderstandings her bluntness had caused over the years.

Why, just now, she'd sure as hell nearly gotten him killed. Telling her brother that he intended to throw her in jail. That he'd made her sleep on the ground. That he'd cuffed her to a bed. Jesus! Her brother was big. Tall, broad-shouldered, dark, and . . . angry. Lucas usually brushed off such threats, knowing that a bullet could cut down the largest of men and that he happened to be fast enough on the draw not to worry much about quarreling with most anyone.

But Caleb Adams was different. Somehow he didn't think Megan would be very forgiving if he shot her brother in the middle of the parlor.

He felt Caleb's brown eyes on him. In a slow, calculated movement, he turned his head to meet those cold, judgmental orbs.

"Did you touch my sister?"

Lucas fought to keep his shock from showing. He'd expected questions, but he thought the man would at least work his way up to something as personal—and life-threatening—as *Did you touch my sister?*

What was he supposed to say? *Yeah, she was the best I've ever had—for a virgin.* He could just picture the shade of red her brother's face would turn before Caleb strangled him with his bare hands. He could hardly blame him. If some travel-worn ex–bounty hunter had kidnapped and seduced his little sister, he would be mighty angry, too.

"Don't you think that's a topic you'd best discuss with her?"

Caleb's jaw locked visibly. "I'm asking you."

Lucas didn't want to have to kill anybody today. It was

bright and sunny and fairly peaceful. He didn't want to ruin it by spilling blood. But Caleb had asked. And Lucas rarely lied.

He got to his feet, hands at his sides but well away from the Peacemakers. "Yes. And if you want to do something about that, I suggest we go outside. No sense messing up this nice, clean house."

"Sit down."

Lucas remained standing. "Listen. If you want a piece of me, you can have it. It's only fair, seeing as how I deflowered your sister. But I don't intend to let you hit on me without getting in a few punches of my own. I'd rather not have Megan or your wife or your little boy watch while I crack your skull open. So let's take it outside."

"I said, sit down." Caleb's fingers were white on the arms of his chair, but he made no move toward Lucas.

Lucas watched closely, not quite sure Adams wasn't planning a sneak attack. He backed up a step, returning to his seat. He didn't know what to make of the man sitting across from him. He seemed unreasonably calm, considering.

"My sister is a big girl, Mr. McCain. I've known for a while now that she's got a mind of her own. She can take care of herself—for the most part."

"So I've learned."

"But she's also naive. She has a tendency to believe what people tell her. If she loves you and thought you were in love with her, if you filled her head with dreams of marriage and happily ever after, she'd likely let you do anything."

Lucas put a hand up. "I know where you're going with this, but I didn't promise her any such thing. In fact, I made it perfectly clear that there is no future for us. I have a job to do, and that just happens to be turning her into the law. After that, there's some personal business to take care of. I don't have time to settle down and start a family. She knows that.

"But I didn't force her, either." The muscle in his jaw tensed. "I'm not that kind of man."

A hint of a smile played at the corners of Caleb's mouth. "I didn't think you were. Besides, I know my sister better than that. *If* you forced her, she'd make sure you paid. You'd be black-and-blue from head to foot. And if she hadn't succeeded in killing you by now, she'd have told me to do it. So, you see, I have no doubt that you had Megan's permission to do . . ." His lips thinned. "Whatever it is you did. However, I am concerned about her emotional state."

"I don't think you need to worry. Megan doesn't seem to be the type of girl who would lock herself in her room for months on end, crying over a lost love."

"Then you don't know her very well," Caleb answered solemnly.

Lucas wondered at that. Would Megan miss him? Would she spend her days weeping over his absence?

Caleb continued. "As I said, Megan's a big girl. As long as she seems happy, I'll stay out of it."

"That's noble of you."

"But if you hurt her, I'll break every bone in your body."

"Come away from that door," Rebecca chastised.

"I'm trying to hear what they're saying."

"That's eavesdropping," Rebecca said, drawing Megan back to the counter. "Besides, as long as we don't hear breaking glass or grunts of pain, we shouldn't fret."

Megan blinked worriedly. "What if we do?"

"Then we douse them with a bucket of cold water."

"Hmph." She scraped the skin off a carrot with sharp, angry strokes.

"Do you want to tell me about him?"

Megan's head snapped up. "Who?" she asked evasively.

"Who?" Rebecca clicked her tongue. "Mr. Tall, blond, and gorgeous."

"He is gorgeous, isn't he?" She couldn't keep from grinning like an idiot.

"Aha. I take it from your smile that there's more going on than meets the eye. Would it have anything to do with those nights alone on the trail?"

"No," Megan answered honestly.

"What about the hotel rooms? I must admit the handcuffs piqued my interest."

"You're terrible! What would Caleb say if he heard you?"

"He'd probably wish you all a good night and carry me upstairs to bed."

While Megan laughed, Rebecca asked Bessie to go out to the vegetable garden for a basket of green peppers.

"Now," she said. "We're alone." She glanced at little Rose, playing with her toes in a bassinet in the corner of the kitchen. "Or as alone as we're likely to be. Tell me what's going on between you and this Mr. McCain."

"He's wonderful." Megan clasped her hands over her heart, smiling. "He's handsome and brave, and when he touches me . . . Oh, I shouldn't be telling you these things. If Caleb found out, he'd kill me. Or, worse, he'd kill Lucas."

"You don't think *I'm* going to tell him, do you?" Rebecca put down her paring knife and sat at the table.

Megan hopped atop one of the chairs, sitting with her legs folded beneath her. "I think I fell in love with Lucas the first time I saw him. Really saw him, I mean. He wore a bandanna over his nose and mouth when he rode with the others to rob the stage. But then, when he pulled that brown neckerchief down . . . Lord, he stole my breath away. Does that sound too silly? Too girlish?"

"Not at all. The first time I met Caleb, I was so unnerved, I made a complete fool out of myself by cursing and kicking his desk. I think I broke a toe on the blasted thing."

"He has the bluest eyes. Did you notice?"

"Caleb? I'm pretty sure he has brown eyes."

"No," Megan groaned. "Lucas. Lucas has the deepest, bluest, most beautiful eyes I've ever seen." She waved a hand. "Who cares about Caleb?"

"Well, I do," Rebecca said. "But go on."

"And he has the nicest, um . . ." She pointed behind her and down. "Bottom."

"You looked?"

"I rode behind him for miles and miles. It was sort of hard to miss."

"Yes, well, nice backsides do count for something."

"He didn't want to make love to me at first." She stopped, eyeing her sister-in-law. "I can talk about this, right? You won't say anything to Caleb?"

"Not a word." She crossed her heart. "I promise."

"All right." Megan leaned forward, lowering her voice to a whisper. "I wanted him to touch me, even though I knew it was wrong. But I've never felt this way about a man before. As if we were destined to meet. He keeps telling me we don't have a future together, that he has to track down Silas Scott. That's the man who murdered Lucas's wife and son," she explained.

Rebecca gasped. "What?"

"Oh, it's a very long story. Suffice it to say that Lucas won't stop until he's found and killed this man. And, truly, who can blame him? But I get the oddest feeling, Rebecca. It's as if I don't really believe Lucas will ever be gone. But I know he will. I know he's leaving. And somehow even that's okay. I think, even if I never see him again after today, it will all have been worth it. I wouldn't trade the time we've spent together for anything. I'll be lonely, but I'll have my memories. I'll always be able to look back and remember how sweetly, how tenderly he made love to me."

"I hope you don't think you'll spend the rest of your life alone. Any man would be lucky to have you. If Lucas isn't smart enough to realize that, some other man will be."

Megan shook her head at Rebecca's statement. "I won't ever be with another man. I could never feel this way about anyone else."

"But maybe—"

"No. There will never be anyone who even comes close to Lucas. Would there be another man who could fill Caleb's shoes?"

"You're right. I'm sorry for mentioning it. Of course no one could ever take Caleb's place. And if you love Lucas half as much as I love your brother, I can understand your wanting to be a spinster rather than settling for less."

"I never said I was going to be a spinster. Lord, that word puts me in mind of a little old lady dressed in gray with tiny spectacles perched on the tip of her nose. No. I may never marry, but I'll never be like that, either."

Bessie returned then, her straw basket filled to the top with shiny green peppers.

Rebecca smiled. "Zach can help you wash those, Bessie. Where is he?" She looked around a moment before her hand flew to her mouth. "Oh, my goodness. I forgot I sent him to his room. He's probably wondering why it's taking so long for me to call him down."

"I'll get him," Megan said. She headed for the door. "He can show me his new rocks." She cupped a hand to the side of her mouth. "And this will give me a chance to check on Caleb and Lucas."

"Would you like another slice of meat?" Rebecca asked over Zachary's constant chatter.

Lucas stabbed a thick slab of beef from the platter she offered. "This is delicious, Mrs. Adams." He piled an extra serving of potatoes, carrots, and gravy onto his plate, too.

"Thank you. And you really must call me Rebecca."

He nodded, but he wouldn't do any such thing. First names were too personal. He didn't want to like these people. Not when he knew he had to take Megan away from them. He'd already come to grudgingly respect Caleb, and as far as he was concerned, that was more emotion than he could afford.

"Will you be taking Megan with you directly after dinner, or will she be allowed to spend the night?" Rebecca asked.

Lucas chewed a bite of beef, waiting to swallow before answering.

"We'll be leaving after we eat," Megan said. "Isn't that right, Lucas?"

He nodded.

"We shouldn't have stayed this long," she said. "But I did so want to see you."

"You seem to be in an awful hurry to go to jail," Caleb said sharply.

She smiled at her brother. "Not at all. But the sooner Lucas turns me in and wires Brandt Donovan, the sooner this whole mess will be cleared up."

"Well, I'll be wiring Mother first thing in the morning. She'll probably faint dead away when she finds out you're under arrest."

"I don't know why she'd be surprised." Megan popped a bit of carrot in her mouth. "She always said I would be the death of her. She probably has an attorney lined up just waiting for word that I'm in trouble."

"Probably."

Megan's fork stilled. She pinned her brother with a sharp gaze. "Caleb, how is the Express?"

He shifted in his seat, refusing to meet her eyes. "Fine."

"The truth, Caleb."

"All right." He threw his napkin down beside his plate. "The truth is, not so good. Hector is taking only half his runs, swearing up and down that the stage line is cursed. As soon as the passengers find out the Adams Express is the express they've been hearing such terrible things about, they opt to find another mode of transportation, even if it means staying in Leavenworth an extra week. If things go on in this vein much longer, we'll go under. There, are you satisfied?"

Megan frowned. "Not at all."

Caleb's tone softened, and he covered her hand with

his own. "Megan, I've done my best. Things weren't all that great before you were kidnapped. You can't expect a miracle."

"I don't expect a miracle." She sniffed and looked away. "I just expect people to realize that I am not an ogre. I am not at fault for the stage being robbed." Her fist came down on the tabletop, rattling silverware. "No one—not a single passenger—has ever been harmed on one of my stages. You'd think that would count for something."

"I guess no one wants to take the risk of being the first person shot by the outlaws."

With the conversation heading in such a sensitive direction, Lucas began shoveling his dinner into his mouth twice as fast. He wiped his lips with the linen napkin before rising from the table. "You about ready?"

"The least you could do is let her have a decent meal before you haul her off to the gallows," Caleb said.

"I'm finished," Megan said, standing.

"Are you sure you don't want anything more?" Rebecca asked. "There's apple pie for dessert."

Megan's eyes widened. She nibbled her bottom lip. "I shouldn't. We really have to go. But, oh, your pies are so good." She turned a pleading gaze on Lucas. "Just one slice, I promise."

"Bring it with you," he said, eager to be gone.

"I'll wrap up the whole thing. You might get hungry later tonight, anyway."

"That wasn't very nice," Megan told Lucas later when they were mounted and ready to ride into town.

"What wasn't?"

She raised an arm, smiling and waving to her family, who stood on the front porch. "Leaving before dessert. Her apple pies are really delicious. You don't know what you're missing."

"Maybe I'll confiscate the pie before I turn you in to the marshal."

"Over my dead body," she said, clutching the dish closer to her chest.

He had to admit the pie smelled good. God, didn't her family have any faults? Her sister-in-law seemed to be a saint—the perfect mother, a fabulous cook, sweet and charitable. Halfway through dinner, he could have sworn he saw a halo glowing above Rebecca Adams's head.

Even Megan's brother seemed faultless. Sure, he'd been hard-pressed not to knock Lucas into the next county, but his anger was justified. He only wanted to defend his sister's honor. Christ, Lucas was starting to feel like a jackass just for doing his job.

He glanced at Megan, riding beside him at an even pace.

"You've got a nice family." He hoped the statement would assuage his guilt. It didn't.

She beamed at him. "They are wonderful, aren't they?" She reached out to cover his hand where it rested on the reins. "Thank you so much for taking me to see them. You can't imagine how much I missed them the past few weeks."

Yes, he could. If his family had been like the Adamses, he'd have missed them, too. But the only time his father had paid him any attention was when he disciplined—with the back of his hand. And his poor mother had been so afraid of the bastard, she never tried to stop him from beating her only son. It was no wonder he'd run away at the age of eleven.

They arrived in town just as the sun was setting on the far horizon. Megan, he noticed, had tightened her grip on both the reins and the apple pie. She sat ramrod straight in the saddle, but she didn't balk. She didn't make a run for it or try to change his mind.

Damn her. Why couldn't she argue with him, cry like a baby, beg him to let her go? If she spurred her horse into a gallop at the last minute, he would at least be able to build up enough anger to drag her back and into the marshal's office.

But she kept her promise, making no attempt to get out of going to jail.

"Damn!"

She jumped, startled. "What?"

"I just remembered something I have to do."

"Now?"

"Right now." He threw his leg over Worthy's rump. "Stay here." He saw her swallow. "Don't move."

"Shouldn't I go in? Explain things to Marshal Thompson?"

"No. I'll take care of it when I get back. You stay where you are. Don't move a muscle." Confident she would obey, he turned and strode down the boardwalk. His long strides ate up the distance between their horses and the telegraph office. He looked behind him before entering the building, checking to see that Megan was still where he'd left her. She'd pulled her hat down to shade her face from curious onlookers, but other than that, she hadn't budged.

In curt syllables, he told the clerk he wished to send a telegram. He filled out the necessary form, then slid it across the countertop, along with the proper coin payment. He waited for the man to tap the message over the wire. Satisfied, he left the office and headed back for Megan.

Only she wasn't there.

Chapter Sixteen

He blinked, sure his eyes were playing tricks on him. She wouldn't defy him. She wouldn't dare run. Oh, but she would, a voice in his head reminded him. He quickened his steps.

"Lucas."

The husky whisper reached him before he could mount Worthy. He looked toward the alley between the jail and the bank, trying to pinpoint the source of the sound. He stepped back onto the boardwalk. His eyes narrowed, and his hand moved to the butt of his revolver.

"Lucas," he heard again. "Over here."

This time he recognized the voice as Megan's. The only question was, what the hell was she doing crouched in the alley? He asked her just that.

"Shh!" she said, motioning him into the shadows. "Get down."

He balanced on the balls of his feet, not sure why he bothered. "What the hell is going on? I told you not to move."

"See those men over there?"

He followed the tip of her finger with his eyes. Three old men in overalls sat on a bench in front of the general store. They all scratched at their beards around corncob pipes. "Yeah. So?" he asked, agitated.

"They sit there for hours, keeping each other—and anybody else who'll listen—informed about town goings-on."

He waited for her to continue. When she didn't, he snapped, "Who cares?"

"I do," she whispered harshly. "Everyone in town knows I was kidnapped by the stage robbers. If those men see me, they'll come over to make sure I'm all right. If they find out I'm being arrested, it will be all over Leavenworth by sundown."

Lucas looked at the horizon. "That's in about ten minutes."

"My point exactly."

"What are we going to do, sit here until they leave?"

"Yes. I don't know why they're here so late. They usually gather there in the afternoon, then go home for supper."

"Megan," he said, his teeth grating together. "I'm not going to crouch here all night. My feet are already falling asleep."

"We can't let them see me." She clutched his arm. "Please. I don't mind going to jail—honest I don't. But please don't make me a spectacle in front of the whole town."

He ran a hand through his hair. "Christ. What did I do to deserve this? Why couldn't I be saddled with some prim and proper miss who wouldn't lower herself to hiding out in an alley?"

"Because a prim and proper miss wouldn't be suspected of feeding payroll information to outlaws in the first place," she said, answering his rhetorical question. "She wouldn't run her own stagecoach company or drive her own stage or let you handcuff her to a bed. And she would rather die than let you touch her the way you—"

"Never mind." He looked toward the other end of the alley. "What's that way?"

She looked behind them in the direction he indicated. "Nothing. Just the backs of these buildings."

"Is there anything to keep a person from riding around?"

"No." Her brow wrinkled. "What are you thinking?"

He moved forward on his haunches, keeping clear of the old men's line of vision. "Stay here," he said. "And I mean it this time."

At the corner of the bank he straightened, walking to Worthy as though there weren't a woman huddled in the alley, waiting for him to get her away from prying eyes. He mounted, grabbed the mare's reins, and started toward the end of town at a lazy gait. As soon as he was out of the geezers' sight, he made a half circle, coming around behind the jail to the alley. Megan still crouched against the wall of the jail, watching the old men on the bench. The pie teetered precariously on her knees.

"Mount up."

She swung around, a hand pressed to her heart. "You scared me, Lucas."

"Mount up," he repeated.

She did as he told her, and they started away from town. "Where are we going? If we just wait, I'm sure the men will leave. Then you can turn me in to Marshal Thompson like you planned."

"Plans change."

"What?"

"Where's your house?"

"What?"

He sighed at the thickness of her skull. "Your house. You did say you owned one. That you live there. Alone."

She nodded.

"So where is it?"

"About three miles outside of town."

He made a flourishing gesture with his arm. "Lead the way."

A Promise of Roses

* * *

The house was just what he expected from her lengthy description. Two stories, painted white. Black shutters closing off the windows. A white picket fence surrounding a nice-size yard. A small barn stood off to the side, empty now. According to Megan, her brother had moved her livestock and the one hired hand over to his place when she disappeared. They'd also locked the place to keep out unwanted guests.

"I'll take care of the horses. You go inside." He walked the animals into the dark barn, fed them, and bedded them down for the night. Then he started up the front porch steps, taking them two at a time.

The inside of the house was darker than the barn. He heard rather than saw a match flare to life and followed the sound to find Megan lighting an oil lamp on a table beside a red brocade settee.

"Nice," he said.

The crystals hanging from the lamp glittered in the yellow-orange haze. She moved across the room to start the wick of another, much plainer lamp.

"This is the parlor. My mother likes this room best. Personally, it's a little too . . . stuffy for my taste. But I left everything the way it was before Papa died. I'm not here much, so it doesn't really matter how the furniture is arranged.

"I should probably go around and open all the shutters," she added.

"Leave them closed. The fewer people who realize we're here, the better."

She shrugged a shoulder, uncaring.

"Show me around the rest of the house." He didn't want to see the other rooms as much as he wanted to get a feel for the place. He wasn't comfortable in a new location until he knew every possible exit, every corner a person could hide in, any area that might harbor a possible danger.

She left the parlor, carrying a lamp with her rather than

177

lighting new ones every time she entered a room. Crossing the foyer, they entered the dining room. Through another doorway stood a large kitchen.

He immediately noticed the door at the far end of the room. "Where does that lead?"

"Outside."

He turned the key, opening it to look around for a moment. Then he pulled it closed and made sure it was locked tight.

She retraced their steps, leading him up the stairwell to the second floor. "That's Papa's bedroom." She pointed to the door at the end of the hall. At the next one, she said, "Caleb and Rebecca stayed here before they built their own house. That's the guest room." She waited for him to open and inspect all three.

"This is the best of all, though," she said with a grin. "The water closet. Papa got it into his head that we needed one." She opened the door, holding the lamp for him to see. Inside sat a large porcelain, claw-footed tub, a pedestal sink with an oval mirror hanging on the wall above, and a commode. "There's no water for the sink or tub yet. Papa died before it was completed, and I haven't had the time yet to add all the finishing touches."

"Wallpaper and dried flowers are finishing touches," Lucas commented. "Running water is more a necessity."

"Not for me," she said. "I'll have pipes put in when I get around to it. Until then, I'll make do."

She left the door open as she moved down the hall to the first door on the right. "This is my room."

A four-poster oak bed with a pink floral canopy and matching bedspread filled the center of the room. Along one wall was a dresser, complete with sparkling gold fixtures. In the corner behind the door stood a cheval glass and a changing screen made of the same fabric as the curtains and bedclothes.

"Nice." Except he could hardly picture this as Megan's domain. Something less frilly and more practical would better suit her tastes, he thought.

"Thank you." She lit the wick of the lamp beside her bed, and light blazed through the room. "It's been this way since I was sixteen. I guess I never got around to redecorating."

"No, it's nice."

She pulled off her hat, tossing it atop the dresser. "Yes—for a sixteen-year-old, terribly romantic dreamer. These days, when I get home from the Express, I just want a place to sleep. Give me a blanket and a hardwood floor, and you'll hear me snore."

He chuckled, knowing that to be true enough. But the humor caught in his throat when Megan unbuttoned her shirt, letting it fall to the floor.

"I know you have a thing about being the only one to know what's going on," she said. "But do you think you could enlighten me?"

His eyes slid to her creamy shoulders, the lift of her breasts beneath the soft material of her camisole.

"Lucas?"

He snapped his head up, returning his attention to her face. "Huh?"

"Enlighten me." Her boots now lay haphazardly on the floor. She husked her trousers down her legs. "Tell me why you all of a sudden decided to bring me here instead of turning me over to the marshal."

"What are you doing?"

"Taking off my filthy clothes. How about you?"

"I'm still dressed."

Like the tinkle of a bell, her laughter filled the room. "I can see that. But why—"

"I changed my mind."

Her hand stilled as she was reaching into the wardrobe. Slowly, she turned to look at him. "What do you mean?"

"You're doing this on purpose, aren't you? Getting undressed in front of me," he said in a slightly choked voice.

"Actually"—she walked toward him in a fluid movement—"I was hoping to convince you to do me a little favor."

"I knew it." His voice rasped.

She tucked her index finger into a gap between two buttons of his shirt. Her lashes fluttered. She gave him what she hoped was a sensual smile. "Do you think you could please pump a few buckets of water so I can take a bath?"

"Another bath? Christ, I never met a woman who takes as many baths as you do." Actually, he had. Annie. And he didn't care how many baths Megan took when they stayed at hotels, but it was something different altogether when he was expected to fetch and heat the water.

She pulled away from him, going back to dig in the wardrobe. "Well, I wouldn't need so many if you didn't drag me all over tarnation. The trail is dusty. I'm dirty and need a bath."

"Fine," he said, the sexual tension in the room broken. "Where's the pump?"

"In the kitchen."

"And the tub? I suppose you want me to lug bucket after bucket of hot water all the way upstairs so you can relax in the expensive new tub that you haven't bothered hooking up to running water."

"No. You can bring in the tub from the shed behind the house."

He threw up his hands. "Now I have to go outside?"

"Oh, it won't kill you. And you can wash up as soon as I'm finished." Her voice softened. "I'll have a pot of coffee and a slice of warm apple pie waiting for you when you're done."

"Hmph."

"You should be glad I didn't ask you to fill the tub up here." She smiled while she piled her nightclothes over her arm. The grin remained as she followed a grumbling Lucas to the kitchen.

With the first pot of water on the stove to heat, Megan watched Lucas pump and pour several bucketfuls into the small metal tub. The towels sat on the edge of the table, within reach.

"Anything else, Your Royal Highness?" he asked.

"How about building a fire in the parlor?"

He dropped the empty bucket to the floor with a clatter. "Want me to shoe the horses, maybe build an addition onto the house while I'm at it?"

She shot him a sugar-sweet smile. "Only if you have the time."

He glared daggers as he stalked out of the room.

She allowed herself only a moment to revel in the warmth of the bathwater before dipping her head under to scrub her hair. She refrained from using her favorite rose soap and bath oils, knowing Lucas would want to use the water afterward. Making quick work of the task, she washed, dried, and changed into her nightdress.

"Your turn," she yelled.

He pushed through the door just as she belted her robe.

"I'll be in the parlor." She started past him.

He caught her arm. "Oh, no, you don't. I expect that coffee and warm pie you promised."

"I'll fix it as soon as—"

"Uh-uh. You said you'd have it ready when I finished washing up. I want them on the table, both hot enough to take my breath away, the minute I step out of this tub."

He was doing a pretty good job of taking *her* breath away, she thought, struggling to draw air into her lungs. He turned her toward the stove and gave her a little shove.

She put the pie in the warmer, then threw grounds and water into the coffeepot and set it on to boil. All in all, she did a pretty good job of ignoring the fact that Lucas was discarding his clothes directly behind her.

A boot dropped to the floor. The distinct rustle of denim met her ears. Her nails dug into the counter. She'd seen him naked before, she told herself. No sense looking at him again.

Oh, bloody Hell! She swung around just as he lowered himself into the tub, and she got no more than a glimpse of his tan, sinewy back. Then he sank farther into the tub, and even that small pleasure was taken from her.

Blast it! She turned away.

Control yourself, Megan. You're beginning to act like a harlot.

Who are you to criticize? she countered. *You're the one who wanted him to make love to you in the first place.*

Yes, but I'm in love with him. I have been from the very beginning.

Ha! You didn't even know him. For all you knew, he was a murdering, raping, pillaging outlaw.

That's not true. From the moment I looked into his glimmering, crystal-blue eyes, I was in love with him.

You didn't look into his shimmering blue eyes. I did.

Then you must be in love with him, too.

I'm not.

You are.

I tell you, I'm not. He's a bounty hunter, out to kill a man. He'll never settle down. And if you think I'm going to keep following him across the country the way I have the past couple of weeks, you're crazier than I am for talking to myself.

Admit it, Megan. You love him. He's everything you've ever wanted in a man. Strong, handsome, virile. Rugged, tender, noble. Just like the heroes in all those penny dreadfuls you used to read. You'd follow him to the ends of the earth if he asked you. You're in love with him.

"Stop saying that!"

Water lapped behind her. "I didn't say anything."

She swung around to face Lucas, who'd turned his head to look at her. She frowned. "What?"

"You told me to stop saying that, but I didn't say anything."

Her brow remained furrowed. "I wasn't talking to

you." She found a dishrag to wrap around the handle of the coffeepot and took it off the stove.

"Then who were you talking to?"

She set the pot on the table, along with two mugs. "Nobody. Somebody else. Oh . . . Not you, all right?"

"Is that sieve acting up again?"

She looked at him crossly. "What sieve?"

"The one in your head. The one that's always making you say things you don't mean for people to hear."

Her cheeks flushed. "No, my sieve is not acting up, thank you very much. Will you just take your bath and shut up?"

"Yes, ma'am," he said with a chuckle.

She took the pie out of the warmer, slamming it down on the counter. Her knife ripped into it, nearly destroying the beautiful artwork Rebecca always created with her crusts. She took a deep breath to calm herself and serve the slices with at least a shred of dignity.

Busying herself at the other end of the kitchen, she waited for Lucas to finish his bath and change into clean clothes from his saddlebags.

"You can look now."

"Of course I can look," she said sharply, crossing the room to take a seat at the table. "It's my house. I can do anything I like."

Lucas cut into his piece of pie with his fork. Oblivious to the steam wafting up from it, he popped it into his mouth and chewed. "Mmm. This is good." He took another bite, then washed it down with a swallow of scalding black coffee.

She stared at him, making no move to eat her own dessert.

"What just bit your behind?"

Strong, handsome, virile. Rugged, tender, noble. Too bad her criteria didn't include vulgar. He'd fit right in.

She left the table, her pie untouched. The kitchen door swung on its hinges as she moved into the parlor.

Why had that stupid little voice in her head decided to

speak up now? She'd been completely prepared to be dropped off at the jail, never to see Lucas again. But then he'd brought her here. To her home. Where they were alone together, giving her too much time to think, to imagine.

She sat in the corner of the sofa, her legs tucked beneath her.

She didn't want to think. Every time she did, she started coming up with wild, crazy ideas. Like this love business. What kind of idiot would fall in love with a man like Lucas McCain?

The voice in her head opened its big mouth. You would, it said.

"Shut up. Just shut up. When I want your advice, I'll ask for it."

"Okay. I won't say another word."

She turned to see Lucas standing in the doorway. He'd stacked his dessert dish on top of his coffee cup, holding the fork in his other hand.

"Mind if I join you?" he asked.

"Do I have a choice?"

"No." He plopped down beside her on the settee.

"I thought you weren't going to say another word."

"I lied."

"Why does that not surprise me?"

He shrugged, returning his attention to his slice of apple pie.

She watched the flames in the fireplace leaping, snapping, and blazing bright orange. "You never did tell me why you decided not to take me to jail tonight. It couldn't have been because of those three old men. You're not the type to let an audience disrupt your activities."

A lascivious grin curved his lips. Lips now dusted with cinnamon and brown sugar.

"You know what I mean," she complained.

He waited until his mouth was empty to answer. "I told you before, plans change."

"But not without a reason."

"I have one."

"And that would be . . ." she prompted.

"I changed my mind."

"About what?"

"I'm not turning you in."

Chapter Seventeen

She couldn't possibly have heard him right. For some bizarre reason, she thought she'd heard him say he wasn't taking her to jail. But of course he was. That's why he'd dragged her with him all the way to Wichita and back. There was no way he would change his mind now. Was there?

Just to be safe, she asked him to repeat himself.

"I'm not turning you in," he said again.

If she hadn't already been sitting, she would have crumpled to the floor. "Why? Why change your mind all of a sudden?"

When he shrugged and started on another bite of pie, she wanted to slap him. This was her life they were talking about, not what crop to plant next spring!

She took a deep breath, hoping to alleviate the murderous urges flowing through her bloodstream. Then she grabbed his chin and turned him to face her.

"I'm going to be polite and warn you that my nerves are not in the greatest condition right now. For instance, at any moment, I might snap and bludgeon you to death with that fire poker." She pointed to the cast-iron stand beside the fireplace. "So ask yourself whether you would rather risk that fate or just give me a straight answer." She held up a hand. "No, think about it for a minute."

He continued chewing, unruffled and silent.

"All right. Now, keeping in mind what I've told you, I am going to ask you a question. You can answer me, or you can start spreading a blanket to keep the floor from being stained with your blood."

"Ask," he said without looking at her.

"Why did you change your mind about turning me in?" Her heart almost stopped beating as she waited.

He shrugged his other shoulder, and she lurched off the sofa, going for the poker.

"Hold it! Hold it!" he yelled, putting his arms up in self-defense. "I'm getting to it. Lord, you're a real powder keg tonight, aren't you?"

"I gave you fair warning." She stood over him, poker raised above her head.

"Yeah, I guess you did. Do you want to sit down so I can explain, or are you going to hover over me with that damn thing?"

She positioned the poker on her shoulder like the rifle of a sentry officer on guard duty.

"Okay," he said. "But I may get too scared to remember everything."

She snorted.

He patted the cushion beside him. "Come sit down?" It was a question, not an order.

Reluctantly, she gave in. But the fire poker remained in her hand, ready in case he angered her again.

"I changed my mind because Brandt asked me to track down the outlaws, infiltrate their gang, and discover their identities and how they were operating in cahoots with you. I did that. Trapping you was just an added bonus."

"I know that," she said. "I've known that from the

beginning. But it didn't seem to matter before, so why does it now?"

"Because I hadn't met your family before."

She frowned, lost.

"It doesn't make much sense, I know. Before we got into town, I didn't give a grouse's tailfeathers about your family or your business or your future. I had it in my head that you were the brains behind the stage robbery outfit. End of story. And our . . . being intimate didn't change that. Until I met your brother and his wife and kids. I don't see how anyone with a family like that could turn to a life of crime. Now, if you had a father like mine, one who beat you just for looking at him cross-eyed, I could understand. But you . . . Even if you lost the Express, you'd still be okay. You could go live with your brother, or with your mother in New York. From what I've heard and seen, you're far from being poor."

"But—"

"You wanted to hear the whole story, so be quiet and let me tell it." He stared into the orange flames of the fire a second before continuing.

"I can't let you go free. I made a promise to a friend, and I have to honor that no matter what. Besides, I already told him I had you in custody. But I'm not going to be the one to turn you over to the law. I wired Brandt when we were in town earlier. If he wants to see you stand trial for your crimes, he can come down and turn you in himself. I can direct him to the outlaw hideout, too, but he'll have to capture the boys. I'm done with this. As soon as I hear from him, I'll head for Independence."

"What are you—we—going to do until you hear from him?"

"You can do anything you like as long as I'm with you. But you don't leave the house unless I give the okay."

"I see. I'm free as a bird—in a wrought-iron cage."

"It's either that or a jail cell." He got up from the sofa with his dirty dishes. "Your choice," he said before going to the kitchen.

When he was out of sight, Megan gave in to the childish whim to stick out her tongue.

Freedom, she thought. She could go anywhere, do anything—as long as she asked permission first or took Lucas along. Well, it was better than a jail cell, she supposed. But she'd be damned if she'd ever admit that to him.

"When do you expect to hear from Brandt?" Megan asked a short time later.

"Tomorrow at the earliest. The end of the week if he's on a special assignment for the railroad."

She sipped at her cup of lukewarm coffee. Settled at opposite ends of the settee, she and Lucas stared at the dwindling embers in the fireplace rather than at one another. Since his heart-stopping announcement that he wasn't going to turn her over to the marshal, Megan found it difficult to carry on a conversation, let alone look him in the eye.

Why did he have to shake up her life so much? She had been perfectly happy with the idea of sitting in prison until the whole payroll robbery mess could be cleared up. Well, maybe not happy, but at least she'd prepared herself for it.

Then Lucas had swaggered into the parlor and turned her world topsy-turvy again. Just like he'd swaggered into that outlaw hideout. All maple-syrup smiles and sexy, sky-blue eyes twinkling with mischief.

"What is it that Brandt does, exactly?"

"He's head of security for Union Pacific."

She rolled her eyes. "I know that. And if I hadn't, I'd definitely have gotten that impression from the way he jumped down my throat about the robberies. You'd have thought I called his mother a wallowing warthog, he acted so offended—as if the money being stolen was a personal affront to his manhood or something."

"Well, in a way, it is. As head of security, he's responsible for the safety of persons and property transported by rail. And it was Brandt who talked his employers into

189

using the Adams Express to get the payrolls from Kansas City to Atchison. Union Pacific bigwigs are bound to come down hard on him for that."

Megan flushed guiltily for having judged Brandt Donovan to be an obnoxious, pea-brained railroader after meeting him only once. And that hadn't been under the best of circumstances.

"I didn't realize," she said. "I may have to apologize the next time I see him." She'd thrown a few choice words—as well as a pot of coffee—at the man during his visit. And as much as it galled her, she knew it was only right to say she was sorry—and to thank him for his recommendation of the Adams Express.

It seemed that everyone had something to lose in this venture. She, her business; Brandt, his job; Lucas, Silas Scott's trail.

"Apologizing won't keep him from taking you to jail," Lucas said. "He's like a bloodhound. Once he picks up a scent, he'll follow it to the ends of the earth. No amount of weeping or batting your eyelashes will change his mind, either."

"I wasn't going to weep *or* bat my eyelashes," she protested, putting down her coffee cup. "Simply make amends for the things I said the day he came to my office. I'm afraid we didn't exactly hit it off."

"No, I can't imagine you did. I see you and Brandt getting along about as well as a lamb and a wolf." After a second of silence, he winked. "You being the wolf, of course. Poor Brandt wouldn't stand a chance against your razor-sharp tongue."

She glared at him.

"Matter of fact," Lucas continued, "I'd better warn him of what he'll be up against, trying to take you prisoner. I'll show him my bumps and bruises. He'll figure things out right quick."

"What bumps and bruises?" She jumped up, provoked, her fists on her hips in the billowy lawn of her nightdress and robe.

Lucas scoffed. "How about the ones I got trying to fit out that hotel window when you ran away?"

"Ever hear of a little thing called the stairs? I didn't tell you to climb out that window, you dumb ox. I only went that way because you had me locked in the room."

"I wouldn't have had to chase after you at all," he bellowed, "if you hadn't been stupid enough to run in the first place." He rose from the sofa, and they stood nose-to-nose in the middle of the parlor.

"You didn't have to follow me. I would have been fine."

"I'm sure those three mangy cowboys planned otherwise."

"I can take care of myself. I handled those men just fine, with no help from you."

"It didn't look that way when I showed up. I seem to remember the three of them surrounding you. And I don't think they planned to play ring-around-the-rosy."

"What would you care?" Megan yelled. "What difference would it make to you whether you brought me in dead or alive? It might even be easier to manage a dead prisoner than a live one."

Lucas moved so fast, she cried out in surprise when he grabbed her arms. His blue eyes turned as dark as stormclouds, glittering with barely controlled fury. "Don't say that." His voice sounded ragged, the words forced through tightly clenched teeth. He caught her chin in one hand, his grip almost crushing. "Don't ever say that."

Megan swallowed, her heart constricting when she thought she saw a hint of moisture surrounding his deep pupils. "I'm sorry," she whispered.

"Don't ever talk about you dying." His voice was softer now, pained. "Not even as a joke."

"I won't."

"Not ever again."

"I won't," she promised.

His hold on her chin lightened, and his thumb began a slow, downward stroke.

She stared into eyes that had returned to their gentle

blue hue, thinking of how easy it was to read his emotions—if one knew him well enough. After spending twenty-four hours a day with him for the past two weeks, she felt she knew him fairly well. But she wanted a chance to know him better. Much better.

The voice in her head was right. She was in love with him.

"Lucas, I—" She opened her mouth to tell him, but he cut her off with soft, warm lips. She groaned deep in her throat at the power of his kiss, the strength of his arms wrapped around her waist.

He lifted his head, his breath still warm on her face. "I lied before," he said.

"About what?"

"I didn't just change my mind about turning you in." He ran the tip of one finger over her cheek, retracing the movement with his mouth. "I wanted a few more days with you. The two of us, alone." He emphasized each statement with a kiss. His mouth trailed over the slant of her jaw, up to the lobe of her ear, across her lashes. "I don't want to think about your guilt or innocence. I don't want to think about what will happen once Brandt shows up. I just want to make love to you until neither one of us can find the energy to stand."

"Mmm. Sounds promising."

Lucas chuckled. "You're the most unusual woman I've ever met."

She smiled. "Really? Why?"

"Because you're not afraid of sex."

Her smile fell, drooping into a frown. "That's it? My sole claim to uniqueness is that I'm not afraid of sex?"

"Yep."

"You sure know how to stir a girl's heart."

"I'm serious. I've never met anyone as open about sex as you are. The first time we made love, you were a virgin. Every other virgin I've ever known has whined and whimpered and acted as if she were selling her soul to the Devil."

"Maybe they were." She cocked her head. "And just how many virgins have you been with?"

"Enough to know you were different."

"Oh, yeah?"

"Yeah. You're the only virgin who's ever attacked me, that's for sure."

"I never attacked you! You attacked me."

He raised an eyebrow. "Not the way I remember it."

"That's not surprising, since you seem to forget your real name every time you ride into a new town."

"If it wasn't an attack, then what would you call it?"

"I would call it being taken advantage of. You caught me off guard."

"Ha!" Lucas backed away to better see her face. "You wanted it as much as I did."

"I never said I didn't."

He blew out a tempered breath, running splayed fingers through his hair. "Then what the hell are we arguing about?"

"You said what made me unusual was not being afraid of sex. I disagree. I have a lot of unique qualities."

"One of which is the ability to drive me completely mad," he griped.

"Precisely," she said. "But there are others. Yet the only one you seem to care about is that I'm not shy about letting you take me to bed."

"I seem to recall a time we didn't bother with a bed."

Her cheeks filled with color. "That is not the point I am trying to make here."

"There's one very specific point I'm trying to make, but it just seems to keep floating right over your head." His tone had a sharp edge to it, his patience nearing an end.

"And what would that be?"

"Exactly what I said. You're the most special woman I've ever met. You swore you were innocent of my accusations, and still you understood that I had to do my job. Except for that one time I secured you to the bathtub while you were asleep, you went along with me even

193

when I had to handcuff you in a hotel room. And I don't know of another woman who would risk her life by openly defying a gang of armed bandits. Granted, most of them turned out to be harmless, but you didn't know that when you dared them to shoot you."

"I thought you believed I was in on it with them."

He blinked, as if he didn't understand what she meant. Then he stiffened. "I do."

"But you just said I couldn't have known the disposition of those outlaws. That means you don't think I knew them ahead of time."

"I didn't say that."

"Yes, you did."

"Look, I thought I told you already: It doesn't matter what I think. I'm doing a favor for Brandt Donovan. Once I turn you over to him, if he wants to let you go, that's fine. But if he wants to see you charged with robbery, that's his choice. Got it?"

Megan fought a grin. "Got it." She didn't think Lucas believed her guilty anymore. Oh, he was loyal to a fault, so she would probably still go to jail if that's what his friend Brandt wanted, but it meant a lot to her to know Lucas was no longer convinced she'd orchestrated the entire string of holdups.

She stepped forward, looping her arms around his neck. "I seem to remember you saying something about making love until neither one of us can stand. Just so you know, my legs are feeling a bit weak already."

Chapter Eighteen

Lucas scooped Megan up in his arms and headed for the stairs. She ran her fingers through his hair, kissing his temple, cheekbones, eyelids, distracting him until he stumbled and could only pray they didn't fall down the steps in a tangle of legs and the soft lawn of her night-clothes. On the landing of the second floor, he groped for the knob to her room, kicking the door closed behind them. He hoped his memory of the house proved accurate and he hadn't just walked into the water closet instead of her bedroom.

When his knee hit the footboard of her bed, he gave a sigh of relief and let Megan slide down the length of his body. She sat on the mattress, moving so that her legs were on either side of him, never breaking the passionate loveplay of their lips. Her hands roamed over his back and buttocks, teasing with light strokes, kneading with strong motions.

Lucas groaned into her mouth, running his fingers through her untamed hair. He loosened the belt of her robe, pushing it over her shoulders and arms to lay in a heap on the bed. Then his hands went to the hem of her gown, tugging it up her slim legs to her hips. She shifted slightly, allowing him to hike the material to her waist. Her arms lifted, and he removed the nightdress completely, tossing it aside.

Megan sat on the edge of the mattress in naked splendor, her head tilted back to stare up at him, adoration shining in her eyes. The tip of her tongue darted out to moisten her dry lips. He watched her, wanting to wrap his arms about her and somehow absorb her into his very being. He wanted to carry her in his heart forever.

Eager for his touch, she reached up and brushed an errant lock of sandy-blond hair away from his face. "Lucas . . ." she whispered.

It was all the encouragement he needed. He ripped open his shirt, uncaring of the buttons that popped and flew in every direction. Before he could manage to remove his belt, Megan's soft touch stopped him. Her fingers deftly unbuckled the strip of leather, moving to the buttons of his trousers. She undid them with aggravating slowness, torturing him by letting her knuckles rub erotically over the hardened flesh trapped within the confines of his britches.

"Megan," he growled, gripping her shoulders, sure he could stand no more.

She simply smiled, a smile that told him she knew exactly what she was doing—and didn't intend to stop.

Lucas closed his eyes, struggling for control of his raging senses. Not an easy task when his body screamed for release.

Megan seemed to surround him. The erratic beat pulsing through his fingertips was her heartbeat. The breathy, catlike purr that met his ears was her sigh. The sweet scent of roses that tickled his nostrils, the scent of warm, impassioned flesh and sunshine combined formed a fragrance completely feminine, uniquely Megan.

Her fingers slid beneath the material of his trousers, covering him. His body jerked with the spark that ran through his veins. His hands clenched at his sides. "God, Megan," he groaned. But he didn't touch her.

She wrapped her legs around his thighs, locking her feet together to bring him closer to the bed. Her fingers stroked the hard evidence of his desire, exploring, caressing. Then she kissed his chest, her tongue darting over a male nipple at the same time her hand squeezed his pulsing shaft.

He inhaled sharply, his eyes flying open. "Christ," he swore.

"Do you like that?" she asked. Merriment danced in the ginger depths of her eyes.

"What do you think?" he countered raggedly.

She beamed up at him. "I think I like tormenting you."

A low growl emanated from his throat. With one lightning-quick movement, he pushed Megan on to her back on the mattress, her legs still looped around his hips.

"I think it's about time for the shoe to be on the other foot," he said.

She glanced down the length of his body to where his legs dangled off the end of the bed. "Then shouldn't you take off your boots?" she questioned innocently.

"Don't worry about my boots, honey," he drawled. "I have something much more interesting in mind."

She quirked an eyebrow. "Really? What?"

He dipped his head, taking the tip of one breast into his mouth while his hand trailed down her belly.

"Oh," she said, arching toward the warm pleasure of his lips.

His fingers drew circles on her belly, hips, and legs. Then his hand roamed to her inner thigh, coming dangerously close to the triangle of curls that covered her feminine mound.

She expected him to touch her there next, lifted her hips in anticipation. But he only continued the tiny, fluttering strokes on her leg. His face lifted, and he grinned. Then he began to lap at her other breast, surrounding her nipple with the moist heat of his mouth.

"Lucas," she moaned, her fingers clutching at fistfuls of his hair.

He paused, raising his eyes to hers. "Do you like that?"

"What do you think?" she asked, tossing his earlier words back at him.

One side of his mouth lifted in a grin. "I think you need to experience a little more torment." With that, he ran his fingers over the dark curls at the apex of her thighs—lightly, almost imperceptibly. She gasped, wriggling on the bed.

He brought his hands to her waist, holding her in place while he kissed the smooth expanse of her stomach. Then his lips traveled lower.

Megan froze when she felt his hot breath between her legs. Surely he couldn't mean to . . .

But he did. His fingers parted the feminine petals of flesh, and his tongue darted over the bud of desire hidden within.

Her eyes closed, and her legs tightened of their own accord about his upper body. His tender onslaught continued, driving her mad with wanting. He licked and nipped, circled and tugged until she thought she would explode. Her fingers dug into his scalp. A tortured moan caught low in her throat.

He gave her a moment's repose, sliding back up to lie at her side. "Had enough?" he taunted.

All she could manage was a strangled sigh.

He smiled, grabbing her up for another hard, mindless kiss. Then he positioned himself between her thighs and thrust deep. They both groaned at the exquisite pleasure of his entry.

Lucas held her close, keeping his lips locked with hers as he moved within her body. She writhed beneath him, reaching for that earth-shattering release she knew he could bring her.

His hands moved to her hips, anchoring her. He began to thrust faster, harder. All thoughts disappeared as he buried his face against her shoulder, anticipating the impending climax. Her nails dug into his back. She screamed above his ear, tensing in his arms. He withdrew, then thrust home, again and again until his body stiffened with an exultant cry.

He remained on top of her for what seemed like hours until he regained enough strength to roll aside. They lay there, staring up at the ceiling for several minutes, the room filled only with the ragged sounds of their shallow breathing.

"You okay?" Lucas finally managed.

"Mmm. Better than usual, I'd say," she mumbled.

He hefted himself up on one elbow to look down at her. A satisfied smiled edged her mouth. "Oh, really?"

"Mmm." She tilted her head in his direction. "But I thought you said you were going to make love to me until I didn't have the energy to stand."

"Did I say that?"

"Uh-huh."

"Think your legs will hold you?"

A devilish light twinkled in her eyes. "I think I could manage a few teetering steps."

He caught her lips, delving into the sweet honey of her mouth. Then he lifted his head and fixed her with a serious gaze. "Then I'd say I still have a job to do, huh?"

"I'd say," she quipped.

He smacked her lightly on the side of her bare bottom. "Watch your mouth, woman, or I'll withhold my ample talents."

She shrugged a petite shoulder. "I guess I'll just have to find someone else to warm my bed, then."

"Ah!" he gasped, clutching at his heart as though wounded by her words. "You injure me, my lady. What must I do to regain the honor of your favor?"

She wound her fingers in his hair, trying to stifle a grin. "Shut up and kiss me, you lout."

"Gladly." His head bent to hers, and he swept her up into yet another vortex of unbridled passion.

* * *

Many hours later, Megan stretched languidly. Her finger-tips brushed the smooth breadth of Lucas's chest as they lay haphazardly across the feather-soft mattress.

"Are you awake?" she asked, wiggling her feet over the side of the bed.

Lucas groaned. "I don't think I'm alive."

She leaned over to pinch his inner thigh.

"Ouch!" he yelped, yanking his leg out of reach. "What was that for?"

"You thought you were dead," she said. "I figured if you could feel that, you'd know you weren't."

He snorted. "Thanks."

She grinned and propped her arms on his chest, resting her chin on folded hands.

"Now what?" he asked warily, watching her through half-closed eyes.

"I'm hungry."

"Not again." He let out a long-suffering groan. "Go easy on me this time, will you? I don't think men were built to endure this much punishment in one night."

She punched him in the shoulder, levering herself up to a sitting position. "I'm hungry for food, you dolt. I've had enough of you for one night." With that, she hopped off the bed and began searching for her discarded night-clothes.

"Where did that stupid robe go?" she muttered to herself.

"Did you look under the bed?" he offered.

She got down on all fours, but her hair fell around her face, obstructing her view.

Lucas reached out, gathered the long strands in one hand, and held them out of her way.

"Thank you," she said brusquely. Then, "Aha!" She crawled forward a few steps, stretching an arm under the bed and coming back with a handful of very wrinkled white lawn. Getting to her feet, she tossed aside the nightdress and wrapped the robe around her bare body.

"Where do you think you're going?" Lucas asked as she marched for the door.

"Downstairs. There's still half of Rebecca's pie left, remember? And I'm hungry enough to eat the whole thing." She threw a look of challenge over her shoulder before leaving the room.

"Shit." He leapt out of bed and ran after her, naked as the day he was born.

By the time he arrived at the kitchen doorway, Megan already had the pie in her hand. She moaned in delight over a mouthful of soft apples and cinnamon while readying another bite with her fork.

"Aren't you going to share?" Lucas asked.

She shook her head.

"Aw, come on, Megan. I'm hungry, too."

"Too bad," she said, popping another forkful between her lips.

He stalked forward. She stepped away. He started opening and closing drawers, rooting around for a fork. Finally he found one.

He turned to her, holding the utensil as if wielding a mighty sword. "I want that pie, Megan."

She arched a delicate eyebrow. "Is that a request or an order?"

"An order."

She raised the other brow in disbelief. "Then come and get it."

He moved to her right. She twisted, keeping the pie out of reach. He moved left. She dodged his attack. He caught her around the waist with one arm, bringing his fork around with the other. She squealed, holding the prize as far away from him as she could manage.

He made a stab with the fork. It missed, sliding across her forearm. She gave a yelp of outrage, then wielded her own fork, grazing him in the upper thigh.

He yelled but kept his hold on her waist.

She struggled to break free without upending the pie. Switching hands, she brought the fork around, aiming for his other leg.

This time he let go, clutching his injury.

201

He looked down to see four beads of blood welling up in a straight line. "You stabbed me," he said in an accusatory tone.

"You scratched me first," she defended, holding up her slightly scraped arm as proof.

"But you stabbed me." He leaned against the counter and slid to the floor. He sat there, staring at the wound, his face a mask of astonishment. "I can't believe you actually stabbed me. With a fork."

"Oh, it isn't that bad," she said, setting the pie on the counter above his head and kneeling next to him.

"It is," he whined. "I could die."

He sounded like a spoiled child who hadn't gotten his own way. "Oh, don't be such a crybaby," she scoffed.

"What if it gets infected?"

She rolled her eyes. All this from a man with more scars on his body than she had hairs on her head. And one, white and puckered high on his right shoulder, she was pretty sure came from a bullet.

"Oh, let me look at it, for heaven's sake." She moved closer, absently tossing her hair behind her.

Slowly, he moved his hand, revealing the small dabs of red on his upper thigh. Barely as big as pinpricks, she thought, though her conscience was accosted with a rare jolt of guilt.

She decided to play along with his "poor me" scenario. "Oh!" she gasped. "It *is* bad." Jumping up, she went directly to the flatware drawer, returning with a sharp, serrated steak knife. "I may have to operate."

His eyes widened, but he didn't respond.

She ran a thumb over the injury. "Yes, I think that's best. Let's see." She leaned back to contemplate her next move.

"I think it would be best if I cut right . . . about . . . *here*." Her fingers wrapped around his flaccid manhood. It jumped and stirred beneath her touch. She lifted her eyes to Lucas, waiting for him to react.

His features remained calm. He didn't move so much

as a muscle. "I don't think that's such a good idea," he finally said.

"Oh, no?"

He shook his head.

"Why not?"

He shrugged, a wicked grin touching his lips. "You may want to use it later."

Chapter Nineteen

She did indeed.

They made love again, right there on the kitchen floor, both the pie and their battle for it forgotten. Afterward, Megan made a half-hearted attempt to gather her robe around her bare torso, but with Lucas resting between her thighs, her effort was useless. And she really had no desire to shield herself from him anyway.

"How will Brandt know where to find you?" she asked, breaking the silence in the room.

He gave a grunt, shifting to his side to lean back against the row of cupboards. She rolled with him, her head on his shoulder, one leg sandwiched between his.

"That's what you've been thinking about all this time?"

"I haven't been thinking about it all this time," she said with undisguised innuendo. "Just the last few minutes."

"Did anyone ever tell you that you're hard on a man's pride?"

"No. Why?"

He inhaled deeply. " 'Cause a man likes to think he's pleasured a woman so well, she won't be thinking of anything else for a good, long while."

"Oh. Well, then, pretend I didn't ask about Brandt Donovan, and I'll just lie here all glassy-eyed and swooning." She let her muscles go slack, her head lolling to the side.

Lucas chuckled. "No good," he said. "I already know you've amply recovered from my ministrations. So go ahead and ask your questions."

She scrambled up on one elbow, her fingers teasing over his chest. "How will your friend know where to find us?"

"He won't. I'll find him."

"And just how will you manage that?" she asked doubtfully.

"In the wire I sent this afternoon, I told him to get a room at the hotel when he gets to town, which should be in a couple of days. I'll ride in to get him and bring him out here to your place."

"Why not just have him ask for directions? Everyone in town knows how to get here."

"Do you want people getting suspicious? All I need is for somebody to figure out that you're here in Leavenworth rather than a hundred miles away, tied to the back of some bloodthirsty outlaw's horse. I can see it now: a mob of angry townspeople marching toward this house with lit torches, demanding to know why you're holed up in here with me. No doubt they'd lynch me for defiling you."

"Well, now, how would they know you'd done that?"

He chuckled. "They wouldn't have to know it. They'd assume it. A lone woman in the same house with a lone man means trouble—in this case, for the man. Folks take one look at me and think rape. Hell," he scoffed, "they'd probably think I was one of the bandits who nabbed you to begin with."

"Poor baby. Your future is beginning to look rather bleak."

Her soft words caused his brows to come together. "You don't sound too worried about it."

"I'm not. After all, if they hang you, I won't have to go to jail. What's so bad about that?"

He moved to hover over her, barring escape with his arms on both sides of her waist. "But if I'm dead," he said, his mouth close to her ear, "there won't be anyone around to make you scream." For emphasis, his tongue licked lightly up her neck to the hollow beneath her ear.

She ran her hands over the thick muscles of his upper arms, enjoying the warm, tingling sensations his touch created. His was not to be the last word, however. Her head fell aside to allow him better access as she purred deep in her throat.

"That's true," she said. "But I'll bet Brandt Donovan would be more than happy to take your place."

Lucas froze. Then slowly, ever so slowly, he raised his head. "If he even thought about it, I'd kill him."

"But he's your best friend."

"Friends share a lot of things, but not women. Never women."

"But if they hang you, won't it be his duty to take your place?"

"No," he answered curtly.

"You can't expect me to be alone forever," she said.

But as she said it, she no longer found the conversation amusing. Suddenly she wasn't joking anymore. She meant what she said. She couldn't lock herself away just because Lucas wasn't there. When he left, it would all be over. As hard as it might be, she would have to go on with her life.

"You can't expect me to be alone forever," she said again, her throat raw, her eyes burning.

He moved off her, getting to his feet. When he spoke, his voice, too, sounded pained. "I know." Then, with no concern for his nakedness, he walked through the swinging kitchen door and out of sight.

Megan rolled onto her side, clutching the soft material of her wrap close. *I will not cry,* she told herself. *I will not cry.* But no matter how hard she tried to follow her own dictate, tears seeped through her lashes and down her temple, soaking the sleeve of her robe.

An hour later, Megan composed herself and went in search of Lucas. She had to apologize. Not for what she'd said—she'd meant that—but for seeming to complain about his impending departure. She wasn't a little girl anymore, believing in fairy tales and happily ever after. He would leave, and she would go on with her life. In her head, she knew that. She just couldn't seem to convince her heart.

She found Lucas sitting on the settee, staring into the last embers of the fire. He must have gone upstairs first, because he was now dressed, though his shirt and trousers were left unbuttoned. He didn't move when she touched his shoulder. She wrapped her arms around his neck from behind, touching her lips to his ear to whisper, "I'm sorry."

He didn't say anything, but his hands came up to cover hers.

"I know you have to leave," she continued. "I shouldn't have brought it up."

He leaned his head against her shoulder. "You have a right to be angry," he said. "You deserve more than a few quick tumbles and a wave farewell as I ride off in search of Silas Scott. You deserve forever. But that's one thing I can't give you."

"Shh," she whispered, pressing a kiss to his jaw. "I'm old enough to make my own decisions, Lucas McCain. I don't need you to protect my delicate sensibilities. When we made love that first time in Wichita, I knew you weren't planning on sticking around. I knew it wasn't forever, and I still chose to fall in love with you. That was my decision, Lucas. And I think it was a pretty darn good one.

"And I'm going to make another right now. I want to be with you. For as long as I've got. If you ride out of town tomorrow morning, then I want tonight. If you stick around for a week, I want seven days. After that, I won't try to make you stay. I can't say I won't be sad when you leave, but I can promise that I won't regret one moment of the time I spend with you."

She straightened, running a hand through his crop of sandy hair. "If that isn't enough to convince you to come up to bed with me, then I give up." Turning, she walked from the room.

Halfway up the steps, she stopped to listen. The low creak of the sofa told her he'd stood. She smiled as she rushed up the remaining stairs. She wanted to be naked and waiting when he arrived at her door. She had promised not to try to make him stay, but she was damn well going to let him know what he'd be missing when he left.

A noise awoke Lucas. He shot straight up in bed, dumping Megan's head off his shoulder as he reached out an arm in search of his pistol. The holster rested where he'd put it in the middle of the night, on the table beside the bed. His fingers closed around the butt of the gun.

He listened, and again he heard something. Peacemaker gripped in his right hand, he struggled into his trousers.

On the bed, Megan came more fully awake. "What is it?" she asked, brushing tangled hair away from her face.

"Shh!" he hissed harshly. Grasping her fingers, he thrust a gun into her hand. "Use this if you have to." Then he picked up the matching pistol and sneaked out of the room.

Slowly he made his way down the stairs to the front door, where the noise seemed to be coming from. Suddenly the door opened, catching on the chain Lucas had

had the sense to latch last night before following Megan upstairs.

"Son of a bitch," he heard. Followed by a higher, lighter, "Thun of a bitch."

"Don't let your mother hear you talking like that," the deeper voice chastened.

Lucas's brow wrinkled. What the hell was going on?

Megan's cry from behind him brought his gun up, cocked and ready. Then the door burst in, crashing against the wall, and Lucas found himself once again face-to-face with—and aiming a gun at—a furious Caleb Adams. Right beside him stood little Zach and Rebecca, holding baby Rose.

"Jesus!" he swore, immediately lowering the revolver.

"First you threaten to shoot me!" Caleb roared. "Now you point a gun at my wife?" He moved forward, looking as if he was about to do murder.

Lucas held up a hand, about to explain.

"Lucas!" Megan came flying down the stairs, a robe hastily wrapped around her nude figure, the Peacemaker dangling from her hand at her side. "I heard Zachary," she said breathlessly as she threw herself into his arms. Then she looked around at the others.

The minute she saw the unbridled fury in her brother's eyes, her arms fell away from Lucas's bare chest. "Caleb." She turned her head. "Rebecca. What are you *doing* here?"

"I was about to ask you—and your friend, here," Caleb growled, looking pointedly at Lucas, "the same question."

"I was under the impression that this was Megan's house," Lucas said. "I hardly think she has to apprise you of her comings and goings."

Caleb took a menacing step forward.

"Caleb!" Megan and Rebecca both cried at the same time. He stopped, but the angry flush in his face didn't fade.

"What are you doing here?" Megan asked again.

When Caleb chose to stare down Lucas rather than answer his sister, Rebecca sighed and shifted Rose to her other arm. "We went to the jail first thing this morning to check on you. You weren't there," she said, as though it were some huge revelation. "Marshal Thompson didn't seem to know what we were talking about when we told him Mr. McCain had planned to turn you in for stealing those railroad payrolls."

By Rebecca's second sentence, Megan was shaking her head. "Lucas decided not to turn me in. He wired his friend Brandt Donovan, who's head of security for the railroad, instead. If Brandt still thinks I was involved in the robberies, he'll take me to the marshal."

"Why the sudden change of heart?" Caleb asked, his tone of voice making it clear he didn't trust Lucas any more than he would a bull with its ass in a dander.

"No change of heart," Lucas said. He made a point of keeping his words and attitude light. He wasn't going to back down from a direct confrontation with Caleb, but he also didn't want to stir up too much trouble. The man was, after all, Megan's brother. Funny how many times he seemed to be reminding himself of that fact.

"I just decided the railroad wasn't paying me enough to track down the outlaws and turn in their leader. If Brandt feels that's necessary, he'll have to do it himself."

"They're paying you enough to sleep with the prisoner, though, aren't they?"

Lucas's jaw tightened, and it took every ounce of his patience not to smash his fist into Caleb's smug face.

"Caleb! Watch how you talk in front of your son," Rebecca reminded him.

All eyes turned to Zach. His smiling face peeked out from behind his father's pant leg. It was plain to see that he loved listening in on adult conversations.

"If you want to discuss that sort of thing, I suggest you and Mr. McCain go outside," Rebecca offered.

"That won't be necessary," Caleb said. His glance moved to Megan. "You okay, sis?"

"I'm fine. Just surprised to see you here, is all. What time is it, anyway?"

"About nine," Rebecca supplied.

"Already? My goodness, it's so hard to tell with all the shutters closed. Lucas didn't want anyone to know we were here, so we didn't open them."

Rebecca rolled her eyes. "There would've been a swarm of people here for sure if they had suspected someone was staying in the house. The citizens of Leavenworth are busybodies," she told Lucas. "They pride themselves on knowing everything about everyone else."

"He figured as much," Megan said. "Especially since I was supposed to be off to God knows where being kidnapped. Would you like some coffee?" she asked, changing the subject.

"Yes."

"No."

Caleb and Rebecca answered at the same time.

"No," Rebecca stated more firmly. "We didn't mean to disturb you. We only wanted to make sure you were all right. We'll pack up a box of food and such and bring it over later. Would tonight be all right?"

Megan blushed, knowing Rebecca was as much as asking if they'd be out of bed by then. "Tonight is fine."

"How about seven o'clock?" her sister-in-law asked, doing her best to turn her husband and son around and usher them out the front door.

"That's fine. You can stay for dinner."

"Oh, no," Rebecca said over her shoulder as she crossed the threshold. "We've got an awful lot of work to do around the house. It's best we just drop off some things for you. If you need anything, though, you know where to find us."

Megan started out the door after her family, but Lucas put an arm around her waist to pull her back. She gave him a look of annoyance.

"You're not dressed," he whispered in her ear.

She looked down, aghast to find that the robe she'd so hastily thrown on hid next to nothing of her nakedness. Her face flamed as she turned and fled upstairs, leaving a loudly laughing Lucas behind.

"Are you crazy? What are you doing leaving her alone with that man?"

"Exactly that," Rebecca said.

"There's no telling what he's doing to her in that house."

She chuckled. "Oh, I think it's pretty obvious what they've been doing."

"That's it!" Caleb did an about-face, ready to charge to his sister's rescue.

Rebecca grabbed his arm, doing her best to control her husband and keep from jostling the baby at the same time. "Caleb, don't you dare. I seem to recall your sister turning twenty-one not long ago. She's old enough to take care of herself and make her own decisions."

"She's just a kid. And that bastard is taking advantage of her."

"Zachary, get into the buggy," she said, hoping to get him farther away from his father's less-than-exemplary language. "You told me you *grew up* when you were only sixteen. Megan has waited much longer than you did."

"It's not the same thing," Caleb argued, his jaw clenched tight. "She's a girl. And he's got to be nearly twice her age."

She laughed at his overexaggeration. "I hardly think he's that old, Caleb."

"Well, he's at least five years older than she is. And he's taking advantage of her. How long do you think he'll stick around, Rebecca? Huh? Not long, I tell you. He'll run off and leave her with a broken heart. Or worse." The muscle in his jaw jumped. "I don't want to see her hurt."

"Neither do I. But she's a smart girl, sweetheart. She knows he'll leave. But she still wants to be with him. I think you need to let her make her own decisions. After all, if he makes her happy—even if it's only for a little while—shouldn't we let her be happy?"

Caleb wrapped an arm around her waist and pulled her close. He buried his face in her hair. "Did I ever tell you that I hate it when you're right?"

She smiled. "You only hate my being right because it means you're wrong."

He lifted his head and helped her into the buggy. "Let's get going," he said. "The sooner we get home, the sooner we can be back here with that box you promised Megan."

Chapter Twenty

"Don't you think we should get out of bed now?"

Lucas pulled her closer, wrapping his arm more tightly around her waist. "Why?"

She propped herself up on his chest to stare down at the peaceful contours of his face. His eyes remained closed even as he carried on a conversation. "Because we've hardly moved from this bed in four days," she reminded him.

"We got out this morning."

"We fell out. That doesn't count."

"I remember," he said, his lips curving. "It counts."

"My brother wants to kill you."

"He can try."

"He probably thinks I'm no better than a harlot."

He gave her waist a squeeze. "But you're *my* harlot."

"That's not funny, Lucas," she said, slapping his chest playfully. "My reputation is at stake here."

"Nobody but your brother knows you're here. I doubt he'll be the one to spread rumors."

She let the subject drop, knowing it to be a lost cause. "What about your friend Brandt?" she asked instead.

He groaned but, other than that, didn't move. "What about him?"

"Shouldn't he be here soon?"

"When did I send the wire?"

"Thursday."

"What day is this?"

"Tuesday."

He groaned again. "Shit. We've been in bed that long?"

"Except for the time you chased me into the backyard."

"I didn't chase you. You ran away. And I don't recall your complaining when I made love to you in the flower garden."

"It was the vegetable garden, and I was much too pre-occupied to complain."

Several minutes passed silently. Then Lucas asked, "What were we talking about?"

"Brandt Donovan."

"Think he made it into town yet?"

"Where was he coming from?"

"The Union Pacific office in Missouri."

"It's only a day's ride by train. He's probably been in town for the past few days."

"Damn."

"Don't you think you ought to go look for him?"

"Probably." But he made no move to do so.

"Should I be wearing a dress when I meet him? I hate the blasted things, but it might make a better impression than my trousers. Of course, I probably made a pretty good impression the day he came to the Express." She paused, nibbling her lower lip.

Lucas cracked open one eye to look at her. "What did you do?"

"I threw a pot of coffee at him."

His chest rumbled with laughter.

"It wasn't hot," she defended herself. "I would never throw hot coffee at anyone."

"Why not? You stabbed me with a fork."

"You deserved that, and you know it. Now, are you going to go after your friend or not?" She sat up. The sheet dropped to her waist. "I'd better wash and dress. Lord, I hope I can find a gown that fits; I haven't worn one in ages."

She crawled over Lucas and across the bed on her hands and knees. "Maybe I'll just wear one of the skirts you bought me."

An arm wrapped around her waist from behind, hauling her back down on the mattress. She let out a cry of surprise, then settled comfortably against Lucas's warm chest.

"Maybe that can wait until later."

"But Brandt is waiting for you in town."

He nibbled the lobe of her ear, stroked his palm over her stomach. "Let him wait."

Brandt Donovan stood at the bar of the Dog Tick, minding his own business, sipping a drink. Next he'd try a shot of whiskey. Maybe that would taste better than the glass of flat, warm beer in his hand.

Then maybe he'd go track down that no-good friend of his. *I'll wait for you in Leavenworth,* Lucas had said in his wire. *Meet me at the hotel.* Brandt had been waiting for three days, and still no sign of McCain.

He made a face, pushing aside the tasteless beer. With a flip of his wrist, he signaled the barkeep. "Whiskey," he said to the older, thick-middled man. He tipped back the shot glass, disappointed to find he had been wrong. The whiskey wasn't any better than the beer.

So maybe he'd give up on drinking altogether. A woman, that's what he needed. His eyes roamed the length of the mirror behind the bar, stopping on the painting of a very beautiful, very naked dark-haired woman on the opposite wall. Too bad she wasn't around, he thought. He could easily spend a long, luxurious hour in her arms.

His gaze returned to the reflections of a gaggle of giggling, large-bosomed women leaning over the arms of

216

several half-drunk, rowdy cowboys. He decided on the petite blond one. She didn't look too used, and he guessed she was even a bit afraid of men, judging by the way she drew back at any sudden movement. He'd give her an hour or so of pleasure without fear. After all, the only thing about him that had ever frightened women was the size of his manhood. He drew himself up to his full height, puffing out his chest. And he'd always been able to caress away their doubts, make them glad he was so big.

He turned around, prepared to offer the blonde a tidy sum for the night, when he saw what had to be a mirage. A vision. His imagination. Unless his mind was playing tricks on him, the woman in the painting had just come to life. And she was headed in his direction.

Brandt swallowed, silently thanking his friend for not showing up yet.

"Looking at anything particular?" she asked, wetting her lips in a slow, sensual motion. She seemed to enjoy the fact that he openly ogled her breasts where they nearly overflowed from the bodice of her skintight, bright-red gown.

He regained his equilibrium just before his mouth fell open and his tongue rolled to the floor. Raising his eyes to her face, he assumed a relaxed position against the bar. "I was thinking of taking that little blond piece upstairs," he said, nodding his head in the girl's direction.

"Madge," the dark-haired woman said. "Sweet, but not nearly as experienced as some of the others."

"Oh? Then whom would you suggest?"

She inspected his form from head to toe, taking her time, thinking it over. "For a man like yourself—tall, strong, intelligent—I'd offer someone with a little more . . . finesse."

He raised an eyebrow at her choice of words. He almost laughed out loud. She was the first person he'd met in this cowtown who could put a sentence together without using *ain't*. He couldn't wait to tell Lucas that

217

Leavenworth's prostitutes were better educated than its shop owners!

"Do you have anyone who fits that description?" he asked.

Her right shoulder lifted in a casual shrug, causing the thin strap of her dress to fall down her arm. "There is one, I believe."

"Ah. Tell me about her."

"Tall," she said, stepping closer to show that her height all but equaled his own. "Dark hair. Smooth olive skin. A lithe, shapely figure." She pressed herself to his chest, letting him get a feel for her ample offerings. "More than enough to fill a man's . . . fantasies. I think it would be fair to say she can take care of any man's needs—all night long."

"And just how much would this enchanting creature cost me?"

"There's no need to talk about that now," she said, running her arm around his elbow. "We can take care of all that after I take care of you."

At this point, he was too damn hard to argue about it. And he figured he could afford it, whatever the price. So he followed her through the crowd, up the flight of hollow, rickety steps, and into a room at the farthest end of the hall.

For a whore's bedroom, it was quite large. But then, this one did have her likeness—every last detail—hanging downstairs for all the world to see. Maybe that had something to do with the accommodations.

"You sure like red, don't you?" he asked.

She only laughed.

Red carpet, red curtains, red sheets. Her red dress, red shoes, and red stockings should have clued him in. But he could deal with all that. After all, he didn't plan on spending too much time studying his surroundings.

"What's your name?" he asked, having always had a strange need to know the name of a woman before he slept with her.

"Ruby," she said.

Not surprised in the least, he rolled his eyes.

That's when the mirror caught his attention.

How it stayed secured to the ceiling he didn't know, and, truth be known, he didn't particularly care.

"I'm starting to like it here," he said. "Any town that has a room with a mirror above the bed can't be all bad."

Ruby threw him a coy glance as she tossed her mane of hair over one shoulder, giving him her back. "Slip this dress off, mister, and I'll show you exactly why that mirror is there."

He smiled and took a step forward. She didn't have to tell him twice.

In the doorway, Ruby leaned close to plant a hard, wet kiss to Brandt's cheek. He pressed a couple of extra bills into her palm with the promise that he would return. And he would. There was no way he'd leave town without enjoying a repeat performance. He was seriously considering having a mirror installed above his own bed back in Boston.

He left the Dog Tick whistling, not the least perturbed that the buttons of his shirt didn't seem to be in the proper holes. He stepped off the plank sidewalk, about to cross the street to the hotel, when a heavy, solid object nudged him square in the back.

"Keep walkin'," a low voice behind him commanded.

Brandt kept to an easy pace, walking straight ahead until the gun barrel pressed into his spine directed him otherwise. They stopped in the alley between the hotel and the dry goods store, away from prying eyes.

"Hate to disappoint you, mister," Brandt said, "but I just spent my last dollar on a whore over at the saloon. The best I can give you is this ring." He held up his left hand to show the gold band on his little finger. A circle of tiny diamonds surrounded the letters UP.

The pressure of the gun at his back lessened. "What do I want with your stupid ring? For all I know, Union Pacific was too damn cheap to use real diamonds."

"Oh, they're real all right." Slowly, Brandt turned around. "I thought you said you'd meet me at the hotel."

"I did. You weren't there."

"I've been waiting three days. A man can't be expected to go that long without a little feminine companionship."

"That kind of pastime will get you killed one day. Your guard is always down after you leave a woman's room."

"Which is pretty damn often," Brandt admitted, grinning broadly.

Lucas shook his head. "You're lucky to have made it this long."

"Have you been over to the Dog Tick?" Brandt asked.

"Not yet."

Brandt gave a long whistle, tucking his hands into his pants pockets as he rolled back on the heels of his boots. "There's this girl named Ruby," he said. "She's got a mirror hanging above her bed." His brow furrowed. "I wonder if any of the other rooms have mirrors. Maybe I ought to go see."

"Check it out later," Lucas said. He grabbed his friend's arm and pointed him in the direction of the hotel. "Right now you need to get your things so I can take you out to the house."

"What house?" Brandt asked, balking. "Where have you been all this time?"

Lucas didn't answer but kept walking.

"Hey. I'm not taking another step until you tell me what the hell is going on. You wired me less than a week ago, telling me to haul my ass down to Leavenworth as fast as I could, but when I get here, *I* end up waiting for *you*. Care to explain that to me?"

Lucas shook his head, fighting the urge to hit something—or someone. "First Megan, now you," he mumbled instead.

"Megan?" his friend asked, bewildered. And then it dawned on him. "Oh, yes, Megan. The infamous Miss Adams. You've had her in custody all this time." His eyes widened meaningfully. "No wonder you're late."

"I got held up, all right? I'm here now, so let's go." He took a step forward, only to be stopped in his tracks by Brandt's next question.

"Did you sleep with her?"

"Why is everyone so damned concerned all of a sudden about who I take to my bed?"

"So you did."

"I didn't say that," Lucas snapped.

"You didn't have to. She's a criminal, Lucas. For all you know, she orchestrated the entire string of robberies, had power enough over five men to get them to carry out her plans."

"Or maybe she was just in the wrong place at the wrong time. Did you ever think of that, Brandt? Or are you too damn thick-skulled to admit that you were wrong to suspect her in the first place?"

"Do you have any evidence to prove she's not guilty?"

"Do you have any to prove she is?"

Brandt sighed. "What's going on with you, Lucas? I've never known you to start second-guessing. You told me yourself, it's not your job to decide guilt or innocence; you get paid to bring a man in. Do you think that just because she's a woman she could never commit a crime?"

"You've met her," he said. "Does Megan Adams seem to you to be the fragile, feminine type?"

Brandt cringed. "She threw a pot of coffee at my head."

"She stabbed me in the leg with a fork."

"Definitely not a lady given to swooning. Which only makes me believe all the more strongly that she's capable of setting up a band of thieves to steal the railroad payrolls."

"I don't think she has it in her."

"Why? Because she turned out to be a good lay?"

"Be careful, Brandt," Lucas warned, his lips drawn tight in displeasure. "Be very careful."

"So it's more than that," his friend observed. "Are you in love with her?"

Lucas averted his gaze. "You know better than that."

"Maybe I don't. Annie and Chad have been gone a long time, Lucas. You're allowed to stop grieving. You're also allowed to give up on finding Silas Scott."

"I won't give up until that bastard is dead." His jaw throbbed from being clenched so tightly for so long.

Brandt softened his tone. "Then why are you still here? Why didn't you drop the Adams woman off at the marshal's and continue on this path of vengeance you've set for yourself?"

Lucas met his friend's eyes. "Because she would have been convicted and hanged—or, worse yet, thrown in some hellhole of a prison for the rest of her life—without anyone ever giving her a fair shake. I'm not asking you to set her free, Brandt. I'm just asking you to hear her out, give her the benefit of the doubt. After you talk to her, if you still think she was in on the robberies, drag her back to the Union Pacific headquarters. Or to the marshal. You can pay me for my time, and I'll set out after Scott again."

Brandt thought it over a minute, shifting from one foot to the other. "No hard feelings?" he asked finally.

"None."

"Then, let's get my things so I can go talk to Miss Adams."

Chapter Twenty-one

Megan paced the length of the foyer, back and forth, back and forth, until she was sure she'd worn the wood down at least half an inch. She went to the window for the fourth time in as many minutes and looked out. No sign of Lucas. Where was he?

She tugged at the bodice of her powder-blue dress, the only one left in her closet that still fit. Rebecca had sewn it for her not six months ago for the annual Harvest Festival barn dance. The bodice seams were straight, the skirt ironed to perfection, the hem even and just a fraction of an inch from the ground. She looked fine. She looked like a lady.

She felt like a little girl playing dress-up in her mother's clothes.

It was bad enough that her family knew she'd been holed up in the house alone with a man—for five days, no less—but now she had to come face-to-face with Brandt Donovan. Lucas's best friend. The man who thought her responsible for the railroad's payrolls being stolen. She only hoped this meeting with the head of Union Pacific security went better than the last, when she'd thrown a pot of coffee at him.

Her heart plummeted at the memory. Things didn't seem too promising. Still, with Lucas there, maybe Brandt wouldn't be so quick to judge her. Or maybe she should pack up her mother's china and send it back to New York—because she was going away for a long, long time.

The sound of horses coming up the drive startled her out of her gloomy thoughts. She ran for the front door but stopped short of opening it. Again she straightened the bodice of the dress over her breasts, flattened the front of her skirt, then smoothed a hand over the swept-up curls she'd arranged only an hour ago.

The door opened just as her hand reached out for the knob. She smiled until her skin refused to stretch any farther. The look on Lucas's face almost sent the corners of her mouth falling into a frown, but she caught herself, stiffened her spine, and prepared herself for whatever followed.

Brandt Donovan entered right behind his friend. He was half an inch or so taller than Lucas. Wavy chestnut hair fell to his shoulders, framing a handsomely chiseled face. His emerald-green eyes sought her out immediately. He took a step into the house, closing the door behind him.

The walls of the hall began closing in on her.

"Let's go to the kitchen for a cup of coffee," Lucas said. He started in that direction.

Brandt waved her ahead of him. She flashed him her pasted-on smile and all but dove through the swinging door.

The men took their seats at opposite sides of the oak table while she went for the coffee already boiling on the stove. Wrapping a towel around the hot handle, she carried the pot over.

"I'd like mine in a cup this time, if you don't mind," Brandt said.

Her eyes widened, but then she saw his grin. A furious blush climbed up her neck and face. "I do apologize for that, Mr. Donovan. I was out of line. I hope you'll for-give me."

"Apology accepted." Still, he held his cup out a good distance away from himself for her to fill. "In retrospect, I realize you aren't completely to blame for what tran-spired in your office that day. You had every right to become defensive when I came at you full steam ahead." He chuckled. "I'm not exactly the most diplomatic man you'll ever meet."

"That's for damn sure," Lucas agreed.

Brandt tossed him a quelling look. "Shut up." He turned back to Megan. "Perhaps if we had sat down and discussed things properly, our argument never would have reached such a volatile level."

It pleased Megan more than she let on to hear him admit he had been at fault, too. "I assure you, it will never happen again." If she got mad at him, she'd be sure to throw something harder than coffee at him.

"Good," he said, shifting in his chair and sipping his coffee *very* carefully.

Lucas gave a soft chuckle, but Brandt turned a serious gaze on Megan. "I won't waste any more of your time or mine by going over the past, Miss Adams. I think you know why I'm here."

Megan tried to swallow the lump of fear building in her throat.

"The crux of the problem is, you're suspected of con-spiring to commit theft of Union Pacific payrolls. It's my job to see you pay for your crime. However," he stressed, keeping eye contact, "Lucas here has some doubts about your involvement in the whole thing. And because he's a trusted friend, I've decided to let you tell me your side of the story. Now, I'm not saying I'll let you go scott-free. If I still believe you were involved, then it's my duty to see you tried with the rest of the gang. But I'm willing to hear you out."

Megan nearly bit a hole through her tongue waiting for him to finish his speech. She could tell by his tone and the set of his mouth that he was going to think her guilty no matter what she said. It took all her willpower to keep from smacking him square in the face with a rolling pin. If she could find the rolling pin to begin with.

In his own mind, the arrogant bastard had already found her guilty. She might as well go to Marshal Thompson and turn herself in rather than waste her breath explaining things to Mr. Donovan.

She glanced at Lucas. The lines in his face suddenly seemed more pronounced, as though he, too, already knew that the outcome of the situation was going to be bad for her. But he had tried so hard to help—even going so far as to postpone his search for Silas Scott so that he could stay with her and await Brandt's arrival—the least she could do was tell his friend the truth. Everything, from start to finish. What happened then was up to Brandt Donovan. And the law.

"Tell me again why you were driving the stage that particular day."

Megan groaned, running her hands over her face. Lucas paced behind them. "Because Hector refused to take the run."

"Why?"

"Because the stage had been hit by the bandits before—the last three times we'd carried the railroad payroll."

"And he knew the payroll was on the stage that day?"

"Yes."

"How?"

"I always tell the drivers. It's only right that they know they may be in danger. And I send Zeke along to ride shotgun."

"Where does Zeke live?"

"What?" she asked, wondering what that had to do with anything.

"Where does Zeke live? In town?"

"No."

"Then where?"

"About eight miles from here. Five from town."

"And how long before a run do you tell him he'll be needed to ride shotgun?"

She shrugged her shoulders.

"Think, Megan. This is important. A week before? A day? That very day? When?"

"A day or two before," she said, her voice rising. "I usually ride out to talk to him a couple of days before I put the payroll on the stage to Atchison. If he's busy, I hold it back a while."

"So Zeke sometimes knows days ahead of time when you'll be transporting the money."

"Yes. At least one day before."

She raised her head to see Brandt looking pointedly at Lucas. Lucas came to a halt in the middle of the kitchen.

"What does that have to do with anything?" she asked. Then understanding dawned. "Oh, no. I know what you're thinking, and you're wrong. Zeke is a good man. He'd never steal a penny from anyone. Besides, I pay him well to ride along."

"Goodness and prosperity often have little to do with a person's reasons for theft. The richest man in the world could still be caught stealing. It's all about greed."

"I don't care what you think. Zeke doesn't have anything to do with this."

"You seem to be in an awful hurry to turn suspicion away from him. Especially when all fingers are pointed in your direction." He shoved a finger in her face for emphasis.

"If you don't move your hand out of my face," she warned in a low, calm voice, "I'll rip it off and feed it to my dog."

"Listen here, you little—"

"All right," Lucas broke in, "that's enough. Brandt, get your hand away from her. Megan, all Brandt is trying to say is that Zeke had knowledge of the payrolls before they were actually transported."

She opened her mouth to protest.

He held up a hand to stop her. "That doesn't necessarily mean Zeke is guilty of anything. It could just be that he mentioned the job he was doing to someone in passing, and they planned the holdups. We have to look at every possibility."

"Fine," she said, crossing her arms over her chest and slumping down in her chair. "But I'm telling you, you're wrong. It's not Zeke."

Brandt sighed but started back in with his questions. "When do you tell the drivers they'll be hauling a strongbox?"

"Not till they show up for work."

His forehead wrinkled in a frown. "Why?"

"Zeke is an old man. He does his job without complaint and knows enough to keep his mouth shut about certain things. That's why I don't think he had anything to do with this," she added with a glance at Lucas. "But the drivers are younger. If they know they're transporting a large sum of cash the next day, they have a tendency to go over to the Dog Tick and brag about it to anyone who'll listen. They like the men to think they're important and the whores to think they're rich. Next thing you know, I've got folks hanging around the office waiting to see the payroll loaded. The fewer chances I have to take, the better.

"That's why I had to drive the stage that day. When I told Hector the payroll was on board and he refused to take the run, I didn't have time to hire another driver. I either took the run myself or gave the passengers back their money. And if you knew just how bad business is these days, you'd understand why refunding wasn't an option."

"So you decided to drive the stage from Leavenworth to Atchison. And back?"

"Of course back."

"You wouldn't have hired a driver there to get the stage back to town?"

"Why would I pay someone to do that when I'm perfectly capable?"

"Then when did you plan to meet the others?"

"What others?" she asked.

"The men you recruited to rob the stage at gunpoint."

She leaned forward, her arms on the table. "I'm going to say this one more time. Slowly, so you can understand. I did not gather or hire a group of cohorts to rob Union Pacific payrolls. I did not, in any way, have anything to do with the robberies. I swear it on my father's grave."

"Who's to say your father's really dead?"

"His grave is in the cemetery behind the church in town. I'd be happy to go with you if you want to dig it up."

He said nothing for several minutes. "If you didn't have anything to do with the robberies, and Zeke didn't either, then how did anyone know exactly when your stage would be carrying the payrolls?"

"I don't know! But I suppose anyone paying close attention would know when I'm carrying large amounts of money."

"How?"

She rolled her eyes at him. "Because a strongbox is loaded onto the stage in Kansas City. It's taken off here. If someone knew a payroll was being sent, he could very well follow it. Our schedule is public knowledge." She waited a moment for that information to sink in, then aimed the final blow. "Maybe the robberies were set up by someone at Union Pacific."

Brandt snorted, standing up so fast that his straight-back chair toppled to the floor. "That's ridiculous. Everything at our office is kept strictly confidential."

"So is the information at the Express," she said.

"It's unconscionable to think that someone working for the railroad would be committing the robberies."

"And it's so much more 'conscionable' to blame me?" She stood up to give him a full view of herself, for the first time that day thankful she'd worn a dress that made her look more ladylike and less capable of committing a crime.

"You've been wrong about me before, Mr. Donovan. The first time you walked into my office, you insisted I wasn't the owner of the Adams Express. 'No man,' you said, 'would be crazy enough to put a woman in charge of his business.' You couldn't even fathom the possibility that a woman might run her own business."

"Well, it was your father's business before he left it to you in his will," he pointed out.

"That's true," she said. "But I was running the Adams Express long before his death, and doing a damn good job of it, I might add."

"Until you decided to start stealing railroad payrolls."

She threw her hands up in frustration. "I didn't steal anything!" she yelled. Turning to Lucas, she said, "Would you tell him, please?"

He didn't answer.

"Oh, that's right. You think I'm guilty, too. Well, bully for you both. If you need me, I'll be upstairs." She headed for the kitchen door.

"Megan," Lucas said, stopping her.

She turned to look at him, waiting.

"Don't go anywhere."

Her eyes narrowed, and she growled low in her throat as she stomped out of the room, leaving the door swinging wildly on its hinges. "Bastards," she swore under her breath.

"What do you think?"

"I want to think she's innocent," Lucas answered honestly.

"But you don't."

"I don't see how anyone else could get the precise information she's privy to."

"Maybe the rest of the bandits will be able to tell us something."

"Yeah, something to further incriminate her," he said blackly.

Brandt lowered his eyes. "We'll never know until we

question them. They have to be brought in anyway. It's time. We have Miss Adams in custody."

Lucas ran a hand through his uncombed hair.

"Do you want to leave her here and lead me to their hideout?" Brandt asked.

"I don't think that's such a good idea. She's been known to run off," Lucas admitted.

"What are we going to do with her, then?"

They looked at each other, and Lucas nodded knowingly.

"I don't think she'll like that idea," Brandt said.

"I *know* she won't like it," Lucas answered, already starting for the stairs.

Chapter Twenty-two

"What?!?"

"It's just until we can bring the others in," Lucas said.

Megan stood inside the kitchen door like a warrior ready for battle. "Are you out of your mind?!"

"You knew this was coming. A week ago you seemed resigned to going to jail and standing trial."

"A week ago I thought I'd be able to come up with a way to escape!"

Lucas almost chuckled at that but thought better of it. Megan looked mad enough to skin him alive. He should have known there was something going on in that over-active mind of hers when she'd started being so complacent on the trail. Now he knew she'd just been buying time while she formulated a plan.

"I'm sorry," he said, meaning it. "But if I leave you alone in this house, I think there's a pretty slim chance you'll be here when I get back."

"You're damn right," she said. "The first chance I get, I'm hell and gone from here."

"Which is exactly why you'll be safer at the jail."

"Oh, now there's logic for you. I'll be much safer sitting in a jail cell waiting for some hangman to drop a noose around my neck than I would be in my own home."

"Megan—"

"No." She held up a hand to stop him. "God, I can't believe I ever trusted you. And to think I fell into bed with you like some two-bit whore."

"Stop it."

"Don't tell me what to do. Not ever again. You're the one who told me to tell Brandt Donovan I was innocent. A whole hell of a lot of good that did me. I might as well have strung myself up from the nearest tree."

"I'm sorry," he said again. "But this really is for the best."

"Ha! This is just the easiest way to get me out of your hair and off your conscience. If you turn me over to the marshal, at least you can tell yourself you were just doing your job. Well, I don't buy it. I'm innocent, Lucas. And even if no one else on God's green earth ever believes me, I want you to know it's the truth.

"So throw me in jail. Let them accuse me of crimes I didn't commit. But while you're out there tracking down Silas Scott and chasing after the ghost of a wife you're never going to hold again, I hope the knowledge of my innocence eats away at you."

With that said, she slammed out of the kitchen.

Lucas let her go, knowing there was nothing he could say to make any of this easier. Still, he tried to think of something, anything, to help her understand why he and Brandt had made the decision they did. Why she was going to jail.

A second later, Brandt stuck his head through the doorway. "Is it safe?"

"She's gone," Lucas answered.

"I know. I heard her storm upstairs. But I expected you to be tearing the place apart."

"Why? I'm not the one going to jail," he said with derision.

233

"No, but I know you, Lucas. I don't think it sets well that you have to turn the woman you love in to the law."

"I told you before," he said, fixing Brandt with a glare. "I'm not in love with her."

"When I asked if you were in love with her, you said I knew you better than that," he pointed out. "And you're right on that count; sometimes I think I know you better than you know yourself. At least I'm smart enough to admit something when it's plainer than the nose on my face. You love her. No matter how far you run with the excuse that you're after Silas Scott, that's not going to change. And don't tell me you can't love Megan Adams because you feel it's your duty to remain faithful to Annie's memory."

Brandt softened his tone. "That's it, isn't it? Your twisted sense of loyalty is the only thing keeping you from telling Megan you love her. Lucas," he said, touching his friend's arm, "you weren't this loyal to Annie when she was alive. You told me yourself that she'd tricked you into the marriage in the first place. When she told you she was pregnant, you did the right thing by marrying her. I think you're to be commended for not tossing her out in the street when you found out she'd lied. And then, when she did get pregnant, you stayed married to her. You didn't love her, yet you stayed in the marriage because it was your duty."

"It was my baby," he said.

"I know, but a lot of men wouldn't have stuck around long enough to find that out."

When Lucas didn't respond, Brandt continued. "When are you going to stop blaming yourself for their deaths? You didn't even know Scott had escaped from prison, so how could you have known he'd come after you? And how could you know he'd kill them instead?"

Something inside Lucas snapped. He paid no mind to the stinging behind his eyes as he slammed a fist down on the countertop. "I should have been there, God damn it! She begged me not to go. She begged me not to leave her alone again. But I just couldn't let the chance at a thousand dollars pass me by. It was that much more to invest in the ranch."

He turned away from his friend, trying to get his raging emotions in check. Finally, he forced himself to face Brandt again.

"Do you know what the worst part of it is?" he asked. "Do you?"

"I know how much it hurt to lose Chad."

"Besides that." He shook his head, running a hand over his face in agitation. "It's that it didn't hurt enough to lose Annie," he said bitterly. "Seeing the pain she'd suffered on my behalf—that hurt. Seeing little Chad—" He broke off. "But being without Annie didn't hurt nearly as much as it should have."

Brandt remained silent.

"I thought I'd convinced myself that I hated her for tricking me into marriage. But I didn't. The truth is, I understood why she did it. It was the only way she could get away from that bastard of a father of hers. He beat her, and he'd started touching her, and she was scared to death he would come into her room one night and rape her. How in God's name can you blame a young girl for doing the only thing she could think of to escape that?

"I'd known her for years. We grew up together. When she came to me and said she was in trouble, I did what I thought was best. I knew it wasn't my baby. Hell, I'd never even touched her."

Lucas paused, trying to collect his scattered thoughts, giving Brandt a chance to digest everything he'd just said. Brandt was his best friend, but even he hadn't known the whole story.

"She died thinking I hated her, Brandt. We had a huge fight when she told me she'd lied to get me to marry her, and I told her I hated her. I never told her differently after that."

"Don't you think she knew you'd forgiven her? I saw you with her, and with Chad when he was a baby. I didn't see a man who hated his wife. I saw a man who cared for her. Maybe you didn't love her as a woman, but you loved her as the mother of your child. You were good to her." He put a hand on Lucas's back, adding softly, "I think she knew."

Lucas cleared his throat and straightened.

"Why don't you let Silas Scott go?" Brandt ventured. "His deeds will catch up with him eventually. Why don't you concentrate on Megan and the rest of your life?"

The muscle in Lucas's jaw twitched. "I may not have been able to tell Annie I loved her, but I can damn well get the bastard who killed her."

"Isn't there another way to make amends?"

"I think you're forgetting he killed my son, too. I'm going to make him pay."

Brandt gave a defeated sigh. "I guess I'm not going to change your mind any more than the woman upstairs did. I just hope you know what you're giving up."

"I'm not giving up anything," he said, bristling. "I'll tell you how to get to the outlaws' hideout, but I'm not going with you," he announced suddenly. "I'm getting the hell out of here before someone else tries to convince me I'm in love with a woman who's been nothing but trouble since the minute I took a shot at her."

A soft knock at her bedroom door startled Megan. She sat up on the bed, wiping her eyes with the sleeve of her dress. "Come in," she said, steeling herself to face Lucas once again.

Brandt Donovan stepped into the room.

"What are you doing here?" she asked bluntly, too surprised and upset to be polite.

"I came to see if you were all right." His gaze moved around the dark room, taking in every feminine detail from the flowered curtains to the lacy bedspread.

"I'm fine," she said, sniffing once to make sure her tears weren't overly obvious.

"In that case," he said, shifting uncomfortably, "we really ought to be going."

"Where?" she asked, as though she didn't already know.

Brandt met her gaze for the first time since entering the room. "You know where."

"You mean Lucas isn't even going to come up for me?" she asked, her voice dripping with sarcasm. "I expected at least that from the man determined to see me behind bars."

Brandt shifted, looking away. "He isn't here."

Her heart stopped, and it took a moment to get it started again. "What do you mean?"

"He isn't here. He left about an hour ago."

She was hearing things, she thought. Lucas wouldn't leave without saying good-bye. Would he?

Crossing to the dresser, she tried to remain calm. "We can wait for him to get back." She twisted the silver-backed hairbrush in her hands. "You're not in that much of a hurry to turn me in, are you?"

"I'm sorry, Megan," Brandt said quietly. "He isn't coming back."

Her fingers turned white as they tightened around the brush handle. She closed her eyes and told herself not to panic. "Where did he go?"

"After Scott, I suppose."

She turned to Brandt. "You don't think he's *ever* coming back, do you?"

He shrugged. "It's hard to say with a man like Lucas. He could be gone for ten years and then all of a sudden show up on your doorstep."

"But you don't think he's ever coming back, do you?" she asked again, determined to get an answer.

Silence filled the room. Then Brandt sighed and shook his head. "No, I don't think he's coming back."

She felt like crying, and she cursed Lucas for making her feel so lonely and bereft. In the past day she had cried more than she had in her entire life. She straightened her spine. If she ever did see Lucas McCain again, she'd make damn sure he paid for that.

"I guess that's it, then," she said. "If you'll just give me a minute to change clothes, I'll be happy to accompany you into town."

Nodding, he turned the knob and stepped into the hall. "Miss Adams," he said before closing the door behind him, "I'm sorry."

She turned away, unable to answer, unable to handle the pitying look on his face. When she heard the door click closed, she set down the hairbrush and began unbuttoning her dress.

Not wanting to wear a dress or her old dungarees and man's shirt when she walked into the jail, she changed into one of the skirts Lucas had bought for her. She refused to allow herself to think she might be wearing it as a remembrance of her time with him.

Brandt awaited her at the foot of the stairs. He gave her a smile, but she couldn't find the will to reciprocate.

"Ready?" he asked.

"As ready as I'll ever be," she answered, knowing it to be the truth.

Offering his arm, Brandt led her out the door onto the porch. In the yard stood her father's black-and-gold carriage, her mare hitched to the front, Brandt's sorrel tied at the back.

"I hope you don't mind that I hooked up the buggy. I didn't think you'd want to ride into town on horseback. And to tell you the truth," he said as they descended the porch steps, "I'm not too eager to climb into the saddle again myself."

Ignoring his attempt at conversation, she allowed him to help her into the carriage. She slid as far as possible across the seat, staring out at the horizon, seeing nothing.

For a long time, they both remained silent. Then Brandt cleared his throat. "I want you to know I'm not enjoying this," he said. "The idea of sending a woman to prison doesn't sit well with me."

She didn't answer.

"If I could find another way to handle the situation, I would."

Megan almost reminded him that it was his idea to turn her in in the first place. Hadn't Lucas told her more than once that it was Brandt who thought her guilty, Brandt who wanted her brought in, Brandt who expected her to pay for her crimes? But when it came right down to it, and he was the one having to turn her in, he changed his tune. Now it seemed that Brandt's conscience was getting the better of him.

Good. She hoped he choked on it.

"If you need anything," he added, "anything at all, don't be afraid to contact me."

She couldn't contain a snort of disgust at the offer. "I'd rather eat cow droppings."

He cleared his throat again. "I just mean that you don't have to feel cut off from the world. If you need anything, if you just want someone to talk to, you can get in touch with me."

"I have a family, Mr. Donovan. People who love me and believe me when I tell them the truth. Whyever would I need to contact you?" She used a sharp, scathing tone, hoping to dissuade him from any other attempts at easing his guilty conscience.

It worked. They arrived in town just before sundown without another syllable spoken between them. Brandt held her hand as she alighted from the carriage, but she quickly shook off his touch, choosing to walk into Marshal Thompson's office of her own volition.

"Miss Adams!" the marshal said, leaping up from his chair.

She supposed it was rather shocking to see her in anything other than men's clothing.

"It's good to see you back and safe. What can I do for you, Miss Adams?"

"Not for me, Marshal," she answered. She stood in front of his desk, waiting for Brandt to explain. She might be cooperating, but she sure as all-fired hell wasn't going to turn herself in for something she hadn't done.

"Marshal," Brandt said, holding out his hand to the

older gentleman. "My name is Brandt Donovan. Head of security for the Union Pacific Railroad."

"Glad to meet you," Thompson said. "Have a seat. What can I do for you?"

Megan sat in silence, her lips pursed as Brandt recounted all the events leading up to this moment. She didn't interrupt with the truth or even try to defend herself. But it pleased her no end that Marshal Thompson obviously didn't believe a word Brandt Donovan said. The longer Brandt talked, the more the marshal's mouth fell open.

"Megan?" he asked, dumbfounded. "You think Megan Adams is responsible for your troubles?"

"I'm afraid so, sir," Brandt answered. "We've investigated several avenues, and each leads back to her."

"Megan Adams?" the marshal asked again, his eyes wide with disbelief. Then he turned to her. "Is any of what he says true?"

"Parts of it," she said. "Like the fact that the payrolls have been stolen, and that I was driving the stage the day I disappeared. But if you're asking me if I had anything to do with the robberies, my answer is a resounding no. No, I did not plan the robberies. No, I did not give any information to the thieves."

"Then why are you here?" he asked. "I'd never take you to be the kind of person to sit still and let your reputation be slandered."

She smiled at his perception. "It's a very long story, Marshal. Suffice it to say that I decided I would be found innocent sooner rather than later if I allowed myself to be brought in. If I put up a fight or tried to run, things would only be harder. I'm innocent. It's up to Mr. Donovan and Union Pacific to prove otherwise."

"But you know that if I put you in a cell, everyone will think you're guilty."

"There's no helping that, I guess. But I am innocent, and I believe that will be proven in time."

The marshal drummed his fingers on the desk. "Your brother will have my hide if I lock you up."

"Her brother has nothing to do with this," Brandt said, a hard edge entering his voice. "She's a criminal. It's your job to put her behind bars."

"I don't guess you've met Caleb Adams," the marshal muttered.

"No, but—"

"It's all right," Megan said. "I've already talked to Caleb. He knows everything and is, at this very moment, finding an attorney to represent me."

"I see." The wrinkles in Marshal Thompson's forehead deepened in thought.

"Are you going to arrest her or not, Marshal?" Brandt asked.

Thompson looked at Megan, then at Brandt, then back at Megan.

"It's all right, Marshal Thompson," she said. "I don't mind."

Brandt threw up his hands, kicking back his chair. "I don't believe this! She's a criminal, for God's sake, and you wait for her permission to arrest her? What kind of lawman are you?"

The marshal came to his feet slowly. "The kind that doesn't take kindly to you coming in here accusing a lady of stealing."

"I don't give a good God damn if she's the queen of England. She broke the law, and it's your job to see that she pays for it."

"Now, you listen here, sonny-boy," the marshal said, pointing a finger at Brandt's chest. "Right now I'm more likely to lock *you* up for insulting an officer of the law and being an all-around pain in the ass." His gaze darted to Megan. "Sorry, Miss Adams."

"That's all right, Isaiah."

He returned to upbraiding Brandt. "Nothing boils my blood faster than you city folk coming into my town and telling me the way things ought to run. So I'm giving you fair warning: Show some respect, or I'll send your mangy carcass back to your big city in a pine box. Got it?"

Brandt didn't answer, but his face burned with indignation.

"Miss Adams is a fine, upstanding citizen," the marshal continued. "Her father started one of the first businesses in this town. Got the place up and running, he did. Megan ain't got no reason to take anyone else's money. You remember that.

"Now," he said, smoothing the front of his vest, "I'm going to put her under arrest, but only because she thinks it's for the best. If I had my way, I'd set her free and let *you* cool your heels for a couple of hours in that cell."

He came around to the front of the desk, holding a hand out to her. "Miss Adams," he said, "if you'll come with me." He led her to an iron-barred cell in the corner. "Folks might not see you so easy back here," he told her.

"Thank you. And, Marshal," she said as she entered the cell that would be her new home for a while. "If my brother and Rebecca should come—"

"I'll send them right back to see you."

She thanked him again, then, touching his sleeve, whispered, "Don't be too hard on Mr. Donovan. He's only doing his job."

He grunted. "He needs to learn his place, if you ask me," he said before returning to his desk and a very unhappy Brandt Donovan.

She smiled when she realized he'd left the cell door open.

Chapter Twenty-three

Lucas drew a deep breath, held it, then exhaled a long stream of tobacco smoke. He'd been standing outside the saloon for nearly an hour. The stamped-out remnants of a dozen cigarettes attested to that. He only smoked when he was anxious. And he figured waiting for Silas Scott counted.

It had taken him nearly a week since leaving Leavenworth to find the bastard. He'd crossed over into Missouri and traveled through Kansas City and Independence before finally tracking him to the outskirts of Chilhowee.

And he had missed Megan every inch of the way.

Damn it, why couldn't he get her out of his head? One minute he was sure he wanted nothing more than to strangle Silas Scott with his bare hands. The next he found himself imagining those same hands splayed over Megan's firm bottom and full breasts. More than once he'd been tempted to turn Worthy around and go back for her.

As if she would be happy to see him! He had all but

locked the cell door on her himself. How could he possibly expect her to forgive him for that? Even if she could—by some miracle—get past the fact that he'd put her in jail, she would never be able to forget that he hadn't trusted her enough to believe her when she said she was innocent of the crime.

A loud ruckus behind the bat-wing doors of the Tommy Two Fingers Saloon snapped him out of his thoughts of Megan. He pulled his hat down another fraction of an inch, not wanting to be recognized. Not that that was likely, but he'd been a bounty hunter long enough to know that outlaws sometimes showed up in the least likely places. At any moment one of them might point a finger, and every criminal in town would be on him like quills on a porcupine.

He concentrated on rolling another smoke, trying to hear through the commotion of drunk cowboys and giddy prostitutes for any hint of Scott's departure. Striking a match on the side of the building, he held the flame to the tip of his cigarette. With a few short puffs, the tobacco caught. He shook out the match and tossed it into the street.

He whirled around at the scrape of a shoe on the plank sidewalk behind him. A tall, leggy blonde had emerged from the shadowy alley next to the saloon.

"You've been out here a long time, mister."

He took another drag on the cigarette.

"Care to join me inside?" She twisted a fat sausage curl around her index finger.

"Nope."

Hips swaying, she moved forward, touching a hand to his chest. She fiddled with one of the buttons on his shirt. "You sure? I can make it worth your while."

"Truth is, sweetheart," he said, catching her hand before it could venture below his gun belt, "I'm broke."

The sides of her mouth turned down in a pout.

"But if you help me out, I might just be able to find me a little cash."

She smiled a bit. "How?"

"Have you seen a man in there, about yea high"—he

held up a hand to show Scott's approximate height—
"with a black-and-silver beard?"

"Ugly as a boar hog's behind?" she asked.

"Real ugly."

"Yeah, I think I saw him with Penny."

"He still in there?"

"If he's with Penny, he is. What do you want with him?"

"He owes me some money," Lucas lied easily. He put
an arm around her waist, pulling her close. "You see, if I
can get my money back from him, then I just might be
able to spend an hour or so upstairs with you."

"Oh, goody." She grinned. The curls piled atop her
head shook precariously as she bounced up and down.

He didn't let himself think for one minute that she was
excited about getting him into bed. She wanted his cash,
and that was all there was to it.

"There a back entrance to this place?" he asked, knowing
there had to be if she'd been able to sneak up behind him. "I
don't like to call a man a debtor in front of other men."

She grabbed his arm and tugged him through the alley
to a small, worn door hanging from loose hinges. She led
him up a set of squeaky back stairs. A long hallway
stretched before them, rows of doors on either side.

"This is Penny's room," she whispered when they got
to the fifth door on the right.

He fit his ear to the wooden portal. From the moans
and groans echoing inside, he decided the room was most
definitely still occupied.

"Come on," the girl urged, pulling on his arm.

He shook her off, wanting to stay and wait for Scott to
finish his business and come out so he could finish his.

"Come on," she said again. "There's another way in."

Lucas gave up and followed. She led him farther down
the hall, around one corner, then another, until they
seemed to be almost back where they'd started.

"Not everybody knows about this room," she said, her
hand turning on the knob. "But sometimes we bring customers in here when they, you know . . . want to watch."

It took a minute for Lucas's eyes to adjust to the darkness of the tiny space. A long chaise lounge took up the center of the room. Thick, heavy draperies covered one whole wall. "What is this?" he asked.

Her fingers curled around the cord to the curtains. She pulled, and the deep cherry-red pieces of material slowly began to part. "It's the viewing room," she told him, smiling.

A huge window appeared before his eyes, and the stunning sight before him drove him back a step. His legs hit the edge of the chaise. He dropped to its soft cushion with a plop.

"How did this get here?" he asked, as though it might have dropped from the sky.

"Sally had it put in. She saw one like it when she worked in Reno and said it would be a big success here. We don't tell everybody about it, though, or they'd all want to use it. And this is the only one we've got. Penny gets the room next to it 'cause she gets the most customers. And she'll do things the rest of us won't."

Lucas could see that. From each bedpost hung sets of thick iron shackles. Several quirts and whips of various sizes lay scattered about the room. And he didn't even want to know what she did with the horse harness sitting in the corner.

Her activities with Silas Scott, however, seemed fairly tame, though from the grunts and groans they emitted, one would think they were building a barn or doing some other strenuous work. With her back to him, legs straddling his hips, she rode him with an ease born from years of experience.

The blonde sauntered forward, stroking Lucas's shoulder and chest. "Do you like to watch?" she asked in a low, husky voice. She didn't wait for him to answer. Her fingers drifted down his torso, across his hard thigh. "You can pay me later," she offered. "I don't mind."

The sounds inside Penny's room crescendoed, reaching an ear-splitting peak. Then all was silent. Lucas pushed the blonde away and reached for his Peacemaker, moving to the door he'd noticed as soon as he set foot in this secret room.

His companion opened her mouth to speak, but Lucas shushed her with a finger to his own lips. He turned the knob, opening the door inch by agonizingly slow inch, praying the hinges would remain silent long enough for him to get the drop on Scott.

"Thanks, darlin'," Scott said, reaching for his pants.

"My pleasure," Penny returned, sliding toward the headboard. She tossed her mane of fiery red hair over one shoulder. As she did so, she caught a glimpse of Lucas and gasped.

"Glad you two are feeling so amicable," he said, stepping from the shadow of the secret doorway. "Maybe you won't mind standing up for me, Scott. Nice and easy," he said, motioning with the barrel of his gun. "Keep your hands where I can see them."

"I hope you said your prayers, McCain," Scott sneered. "Because I'm going to send you to your Maker."

"Not if I send you to Him first."

"Look, fellas," Penny said, standing at the end of the bed completely naked. "I don't know what all you've got against each other, but keep me out of it." Lowering one arm, she grabbed the corner of a sheet, dragging it up to cover her nudity. "I've already been paid, so I'll just leave you two alone to work out your differences."

Lucas let her sidle her way to the door. She opened it and started out, only to stick her head back in. "Hey, mister," she said to him, "try not to get too much blood on them sheets. Laundry day ain't till Monday." With that, she closed the door behind her.

Lucas stared at Silas, taking in every wrinkle and roll of his old, abused body. For the first time since his quest for vengeance had begun, he wondered what could have happened to turn Scott into such a blackhearted, cold-blooded killer. Surely he had started out like any other child, innocent and pure.

"Go ahead and pull the trigger, McCain."

"Don't rush me," Lucas said. "I've been waiting for this a hell of a long time. I intend to make it last."

The sounds of running feet began below them, climbing until they reached the second floor.

"I wouldn't wait too long, if I was you," Scott warned.

Lucas's finger tightened on the trigger, but he didn't shoot.

In the second of his hesitation, chaos erupted. The door burst open. A crowd of people flooded the room, Penny jostling about in the mass. Scott struck out, slapping Lucas's gun arm with the trousers in his hand. He dove for the window, grabbing the holster on the bedside table on his way out.

Lucas raced for the window, reaching it in time to see Scott struggling into his pants as he ran down the alley. "God damn it!" he swore, pounding the sill with his fist.

"What the hell's going on in here?" the hulk of a man at the front of the crowd demanded.

Lucas took one look at him and knew he'd rather take his chances flying out the window than fighting this Goliath. "Just a friendly chat," he answered.

The giant took a step forward.

Lucas holstered his weapon, at the same time preparing to jump. With a smile and a pleasant good-night, he flung himself out the window.

Lucas followed Scott's trail for seven hours. By the time the sun appeared on the horizon, he was so tired and so disillusioned, he could hardly see straight. Dismounting, he ran his hands through his hair in frustration, then dropped to the ground in a heap of exhaustion. He was never going to find Scott. He was never going to avenge Annie and Chad's murders. He was never going to be at peace. The only time he'd ever even glimpsed tranquillity was when he'd been with Megan.

That knowledge couldn't have winded him more than a horse's hind kick to the gut.

Megan had been right. She'd told him that someday he'd realize revenge wasn't the answer. One day, she said, he'd discover that he no longer hated as much, no longer wanted to dedicate his life to finding and killing a man.

He could hear her speaking of roses in winter as though she were there with him, whispering the words in his ear. *In winter, snow and ice cover them, sometimes so brutally that you think nothing could possibly live for months under those conditions. Then spring comes, and the snow melts. And before you know it, tiny rosebuds appear. It seems like a miracle—until you realize that all they really needed was a little sunshine to melt the ice. It's like a never-ending promise from God. A promise of roses to bloom every spring. The ice will melt someday, Lucas. All you have to do is let a little sunshine into your heart.*

The ice will melt someday. All you have to do is let a little sunshine into your heart.

Lucas wondered if Megan realized just how strong her love really was. As brilliant as the sun, shining day and night. Warm enough to melt the icy shield of hatred guarding his heart.

He got to his feet, dusted off the back of his pants, and reached for the reins. "Well, Worthy, old boy, what do you say?"

The gelding shook his head, pawing the ground.

"Me, too," Lucas agreed. "Let's go home."

"Full house."

"Son of a bitch!" Thompson threw his cards down on the table. "How'd you get so good at poker?" he asked.

"Practice," she answered.

"Does your brother know you gamble?"

She shot him a bright smile. "Who do you think taught me?"

"Deal me out," he said. "I've played cards with your brother, and if he taught you, there's no way I'm going to risk my whole paycheck. Travis, if you know what's good for you, you'll quit, too."

"She's just a gal," the deputy said, scratching his scalp beneath the rim of his sweaty Stetson.

Marshal Thompson gave a hoot of laughter as he got up to stretch his legs. "Don't say I didn't warn ya. You want some coffee, Meg?"

"Sure. You staying in, Deputy?"

"Yep. I ain't lettin' no girl beat me at cards."

Another guffaw reached their ears from across the room, where Thompson was pouring coffee.

Megan dealt out five cards to Travis, five to herself, then waited for him to trade. She traded two of her own, and the betting began.

The kitty had reached almost fifty dollars before Travis called. "Three of a kind," he said, proudly displaying his hand.

She started to spread her cards on the desk. "That's better than—"

Travis let out a loud whoop and began gathering his winnings before Megan could finish her sentence.

"You win, boy?" the marshal asked.

"Sure did."

"Wait a minute," Megan said. "What I started to say was that three of a kind is better than you've gotten so far." She tapped her cards. "But it still doesn't beat a flush."

"Son of a bitch," Travis swore, shoving the money toward her.

"Watch your mouth in front of the lady," Marshal Thompson warned, forgetting he'd used the same curse only moments earlier.

"What's all the racket in here?" a deep male voice boomed.

"Caleb!" Megan leapt up from her seat, running into her brother's arms.

"Are you corrupting my sister, Marshal?"

"It was her idea to play poker for cash."

"Who won?"

"I did," she answered happily.

"Thatta girl," Caleb said. "Mind if I talk to my sister alone, Marshal?"

Thompson waved to the cell. "Be my guest."

With Caleb's arm around her waist, they entered the small space and sat down on the cot.

"This isn't very comfortable, is it?" he asked, hitting the straw mat.

"It's better than sleeping on the ground," she said, knowing from experience.

His deep blue eyes met hers. "Are you okay?"

"I'm fine."

"Honestly? If you need anything, if anyone's bothering you, I'll . . ."

"Caleb, I'm fine. Marshal Thompson has been very accommodating. He only locks me in the cell when he and Travis are both gone. Rebecca brought plenty for me to read the last time she stopped by. She even gave me some embroidery." She rolled her eyes heavenward. "As if I could ever be bored enough to sew. And you visit at least once a day. What more could I need?"

"Freedom would be nice."

"I'll have that just as soon as the lawyer you hired gets here from New York City."

"It's going to take more than just his presence to get you out of this mess."

"I know, but it's a start. Marshal Thompson already told you that if Union Pacific wasn't putting up such a fuss about keeping me locked up, he'd have let you bail me out days ago."

"Instead you're sitting here like some kind of criminal."

"They think I am a criminal," she reminded him. "Please, let's not go through this again. I don't like it any more than you do, but there's nothing else we can do right now. What really bothers me is that I'm stuck here while the Express is about to go under."

"I took care of that."

"Caleb, what did you do?" she asked anxiously.

"I transferred five thousand dollars to your account."

"What?"

"I figure that ought to keep you in business for a while. Even if you don't have much coming in, you'll have money in the bank to keep the Express open. At least until we clear your name and you can run things yourself."

She threw her arms around his neck. "Oh, Caleb, you're the most wonderful brother in the world."

"You won't think so if I can't get you out of jail."

"I'll always think so," she promised. "If it weren't for you, the Adams Express would have gone out of business already."

" 'Scuse me. I don't mean to rush you, Caleb, but Travis and I need to go on rounds pretty soon. You know how Friday nights are around here," the marshal said. "If it weren't so rowdy, I wouldn't even worry about it."

"That's all right, Marshal. I was about to leave anyway." He hugged Megan close. "I'll see you first thing in the morning."

"Tell Rebecca and the children I said hello."

"You're sure you're all right?"

"I'm sure."

He gave her one last squeeze before leaving the jailhouse.

"I'm gonna have to lock the door," Thompson said, fitting the big skeleton key in the cell door. "You have everything you need for the night?"

"I think so."

"If it gets too noisy, pull that blanket over the window. And you have the other blanket for privacy," he said, pointing to the heavy quilt he and Travis had hung earlier in the week. All she had to do was stretch it over the rope and her cell was closed off from the rest of the building.

"I'll stop back later to see how you're doing."

"Thank you," she said as he moved away from the door. "Good night."

She settled down on the corner of the cot and picked up one of the books Rebecca had given her. After only three pages, she realized she didn't have a clue as to what she'd just read. Her mind was on other things. One other thing, to be precise. She couldn't help but wonder where Lucas was, what he was doing, if he was all right.

So much for washing your hands of him, she thought. With a sigh, she picked up the sewing supplies Rebecca had sent. What better way to keep her mind off Lucas than embroidery? After all, she could hardly concentrate on him if she was jabbing herself with a needle every other stitch.

Chapter Twenty-four

"Psst."

Megan rolled to her side, away from the noise that threatened to rouse her from her deep, comfortable sleep.

"Psst."

She waved a hand in front of her face, thinking an annoying little insect had gotten through the blanket covering the cell window.

"Wake up," she heard.

That was definitely not an insect. Annoying, yes. Insect, no. At least she had never met a mosquito that could talk. She threw off the covers, standing on the cot to tear the blanket from the window. Through the bars she saw only the shadow of a face. But she would have known that voice anywhere.

"Lucas! Oh, God, Lucas." She thrust her hands through the bars, ready to throw her arms around his neck and kiss him into oblivion.

Then she remembered that he was the reason she was behind bars to begin with. She curled her fingers around the cold metal instead. She might have missed him like the blue blazes, but he had only been gone a week. A week wasn't nearly enough time to forgive him for not believing in her.

"What are you doing here?" she asked, forcing herself to remain calm and keep her voice steady.

"I came back."

"Obviously," she said, not giving him the satisfaction of seeing how much it pleased her.

"I'm going to get you out of there," he said. "Is anyone standing guard?"

"Yes, the marshal, but—"

"Stay put. And keep away from the window."

"But—"

"Shh. Don't make a sound. I don't want them to get suspicious. Now stand back."

She retreated a step, watching as his form moved away from the window. Then she turned and pulled aside the quilt divider, walking out of the open cell. She tiptoed past the marshal dozing at his desk and out into the dark of night. Rounding the corner of the building, she saw Lucas tying one end of a rope to his saddlehorn. The other end was already secured to the bars of her cell window.

"Need some help?" she asked.

"No. You just keep quiet and stay away from the window."

She shrugged and backed up a few feet. If he wanted to tear the jail apart, so be it.

He lifted a foot to the stirrup. And then, so fast he almost fell, he spun around to face her.

"What are you doing out here?" he asked in a harsh whisper, his eyes as wide as saucers.

"I came out to see if you needed any help."

"But you're . . . But they . . . But you . . ." He swallowed and tried again. "You're supposed to be locked up. In jail. Behind bars." He looked toward her cell. "How did you get out?"

"The door was open," she answered casually, as

though every prisoner had the opportunity to walk about freely.

"But the marshal . . . he . . . you . . ."

"Don't start that again," she warned.

He put his hands on his hips. "You're supposed to be locked in that cell. I was coming to break you out. How the hell can you just prance out here like an average, everyday citizen?"

"Simple," she said. "The marshal didn't believe a word of Brandt's accusation."

He stared at her as though he'd suddenly gone simple-minded.

She went on. "He's keeping me in custody because the railroad pressed charges, and it's the law. But he pretty much gives me the run of the place."

"So this is just like a holiday to you. Sure, it's not as fancy as you're used to, but you get good service and can come and go as you please."

She refused to remark upon such sarcasm. She didn't owe him any explanation. What she owed him was a good, swift kick in the pants.

"If you care to continue this discussion, we'll have to go in." She rubbed her arms to fend off the evening chill. "Marshal Thompson trusts me to stay inside. It wouldn't do to let him find me out here talking to a man who was about to help me escape."

"Little did I know you didn't need my assistance."

"How could you?" she asked sardonically. "You didn't stay around long enough to find out what happened. For all you cared, I could be hanging from a tree at the other end of town." With that, she returned to her cell.

Lucas followed a minute later, after untying the rope from the window bars. He moved silently past the marshal to the other end of the jail. Noticing the rope and blanket hanging across the front of the cell, he yanked the partition closed, casting them into semiprivacy.

For a moment he just looked at her, taking in every inch

of her beautiful body. Ebony hair lighted by the moon, eyes glowing bright even in the darkness of the cell.

A pang of loneliness hit him, even though she was standing three feet in front of him. Lord, he'd missed her. And he loved her. There was no reason to deny it anymore. No need to protect her from the hurt he would cause when he left—because he was never leaving her again.

"Megan," he said, holding out his arms as he took a step toward her.

"Don't even think about it."

Her words stopped him cold.

"I'm not going to let you just waltz back into my life after the way you treated me. You left. Just left. No note, no explanation, not even a good-bye. You disappeared from my life as rudely and abruptly as you entered it."

"Megan, let me—"

"Go to hell," she snapped. "Do you have any idea how much it hurt when Brandt told me you were gone? Brandt Donovan, of all people. Kind of like pouring salt on the wound, wouldn't you say, Lucas?"

"Megan, if you would—"

"All because you're obsessed with finding Silas Scott so you can avenge Annie's death. Well, fine," she ranted. "If you'd rather spend your life alone, in the saddle, searching for something you're never going to find—and I don't mean Scott—then you go right ahead. But I hope you know what you're missing. I hope you know that you're giving up the best thing that's ever happened to you. When you're ninety years old, you'll finally realize you weren't searching for Silas Scott all those years, you were looking for satisfaction. Contentment. Peace. Maybe a little piece of happiness. But that comes from love, companionship, and understanding. You won't find it out there," she said, pointing into the distance.

"I know," Lucas answered simply.

"And don't even try to tell me it's your duty to track down Scott. That excuse is wearing thin. You're just running away, and someday you're going to have to admit it."

"I know," he said, a little louder this time, though neither of them had spoken above a whisper since entering the jail.

"That's such a—" She stopped and looked at him—really looked at him for the first time since his return. "Did you say you know?"

He nodded.

"You know what?" she asked warily.

"I know you're right. Every word you said is the truth. Why do you think I came back?"

"Oh, no!" she gasped. "You killed him, didn't you? You finally found Silas Scott, and you killed him."

"I wanted to," he said between clenched teeth. "But I didn't."

The air left her lungs in a rush of relief. "Then why did you come back?" she asked, crossing her arms beneath her breasts. "Because you felt guilty leaving me here to face a hangman's noose alone?"

"No," he said matter-of-factly. "I came back because I love you."

Her eyes widened in disbelief, and her whole body went rigid with shock. He thought that if he sneezed, she would probably fall over.

"Do you remember what you said to me that night we made camp by the Cottonwood River? About roses?"

She narrowed her eyes. "No," she said, though he could tell by her expression that she did.

"You said that every winter snow and ice cover the roses. And every spring the sun melts the ice, and the roses bloom again, as big and as beautiful as before." He stepped close, putting his hands on her arms. "And then you told me that my heart was like those roses. It was covered with so much pain and hatred that I thought it was dead. But then I met you, and just like the sun melts the snow, you melted the ice around my heart.

"I love you, Megan. It finally penetrated my thick skull. I finally figured out that I'm not searching for vengeance so much as I'm trying to find peace. I won't get that by killing Silas Scott."

Tears brimmed in Megan's eyes, but she made no move to embrace him. "I'm glad you finally came to your senses."

Lucas's eyes widened. "That's it? You're not going to throw your arms around me and tell me how much you missed me?"

She made a noise that seemed to be part sniff, part scorn. "Not bloody likely," she retorted.

All the images in his head of a soft, feminine, loving, ecstatic Megan disappeared like mist off a lake on a warm summer day. His eyebrows drew together, and his mouth turned down in a frown. "You mean I rode without stopping, night and day, just to be with you again, and all you can say is 'not bloody likely'?"

"That's right."

He shook his head as if to clear it. "Didn't you hear me?" he asked. "I said I love you."

"I heard," she said solemnly. "It just doesn't matter anymore."

Lucas started mumbling under his breath. Somehow he'd gone from being the man of her dreams to the dirt she scraped off her boots after walking through a cow pasture. "What in God's name is going on?" he asked aloud.

He saw her spine straighten and knew he was in trouble.

"I'm in jail, and you're leaving."

He stood his ground. "I'm not going anywhere until you tell me what the hell is going on."

"Nothing is going on, Lucas. Now, if you'll excuse me, I'd like to go back to sleep."

"A week ago you were telling me that you loved me, begging me not to leave."

"I never begged," she clarified.

Ignoring her statement, he continued. "Now you're acting as though I'm the last person on earth you ever wanted to see again."

"You are."

"Why? I love you—I told you that. What more do you want from me?"

She laughed, a short, wild laugh. "Do you really want to know?" she asked.

"*Yes!*" He wanted to know what the hell was going on.

"All right, I'll tell you. I want to be the most important thing in your life."

"You are," he said, as though everyone in the world knew it. As though it had been prophesied thousands of years ago, written upon ancient stone tablets as proof for all time.

"No," she said. "No, I'm not. Otherwise you wouldn't have left again to go after Silas Scott."

"You know why I went, Megan."

"Yes, I know. And I understand. But what I don't understand," she said, her tone sharpening, "is how you can love me and still think I'm responsible for the payroll robberies."

His eyes widened. "That's what this is about? Those stupid payrolls?"

She huffed, frustration seething from every pore. "No, Lucas, this is not about the payrolls." She paced the length of the cell. "It's about trust. It's about believing what another person says, even if your logical mind says it can't be true. You claim to love me, but you obviously don't trust me, or you would have believed me when I told you I had nothing to do with the robberies. You never would have turned me over to Brandt, knowing he was going to put me in jail."

"He hired me to track down the bandits, and he said you were their ringleader. When I found you with them, it was my duty to bring you in."

Megan's whole body shook from the effort it took not to hit him. She took a deep breath and tried yet again to get through to him. "Yes. Yes, Lucas, it was your duty to Brandt and the Union Pacific Railroad to turn me in. But what I'm saying is that if you loved me, you would have believed me when I told you I was innocent. You would have tried to convince Brandt of my innocence. You would have tried to help me prove my innocence. Instead, you threw me to the wolves and went off on your misbegotten search for Silas Scott."

"But now I'm back," Lucas said. "And I do love you."

"Do you believe that I didn't have anything to do with the railroad payrolls being stolen?"

His slight pause told her all she needed to know. Even if he wanted to believe her, he still wasn't completely sure.

"I think you'd better leave now," she said quietly.

"Megan—"

She put a hand to her temple. "I'm tired, Lucas. Just go."

After several long minutes, she heard the rustle of the blanket as he slipped out of the cell, his footsteps as he left the jailhouse. She laid down on the cot and pulled the scratchy wool cover up around her neck, feeling even more desolate than when she'd realized she would actually be going to jail.

Chapter Twenty-five

Lucas still didn't know what had crawled under Megan's skin to make her so ornery. He thought the only thing women wanted was to hear "I love you." He'd said it, and she'd kicked him out like she would a dog with muddy paws.

He crossed the dusty street, stepped up onto the next sidewalk, and headed into the lobby of the Wilkes Hotel. The young man at the front desk straightened his slouched posture, coming forward from his seat in the corner.

"Can I help you, sir?"

"You got a Brandt Donovan staying here?" he asked, sliding the sign-in register closer to take a look for himself.

"That man the railroad sent? Sure do. I don't think he'll be wanting visitors this time of night, though."

Lucas searched out the room number next to Brandt's name. "He'll see me," he said, tapping the page before starting up to the second floor.

When he got to Brandt's room, he lifted his fist and pounded on the door. Black curses colored the air. Lucas grinned and pounded some more.

"This place had better be on fire," he heard just before the door flew open.

Clutching a tangled sheet to his waist, Brandt squinted at Lucas. "Christ," he swore, slamming the door in his friend's face.

Lucas turned the knob and walked in behind Brandt, who was crawling back into bed.

"What the hell are you doing here?" Donovan muttered into a pillow.

"I need a little favor."

"Me, too." Brandt punched the pillow before burying his face deeper into the center of it. "I need you to leave me alone so I can get some sleep."

Lucas reached over to steal his friend's sheet. Brandt remained still, not caring that he was now completely naked.

"That's what you get for spending all night at the saloon."

"Like you haven't done the same thing," Brandt said, rolling over. "And give me back the damn covers."

Lucas handed back the sheet. "I just hope you didn't spend all your cash on some sweet-talking blonde," he said, knowing his friend's penchant for fair-haired women. Light hair meant light skirts, or so Brandt had always claimed.

Finally realizing Lucas wasn't going to leave, Brandt struggled into a sitting position. He tucked the sheet around his hips and rested his head against the headboard. "Why do you care how much I spent?" he asked, dragging a hand across his face.

"I need a little loan."

Brandt groaned. "I'm not giving you any more money to waste on your wild goose chase for Silas Scott. If you're broke, get a job. Hell, I'll even get you a position with Union Pacific security, if that's what you want."

"I don't want a job. And I don't want the money so I can keep after Scott."

His friend sighed. "Then what do you need it for?"

"A ring."

Brandt's eyes slowly opened. "A ring. What kind of ring?"

"An engagement ring. With a big diamond—as big as I can find around here, anyway."

"An engagement ring. A diamond engagement ring." Brandt repeated it as though he'd never heard of such a thing. Then he jumped up from the bed, the sheet covering him forgotten. "Holy Christ, you did it, didn't you? You really did it."

"Did what?"

"You came back for Megan. You asked her to marry you."

"I came back for Megan," Lucas said. "But I didn't ask her to marry me."

"Why not?"

"I didn't get the chance. She kicked me out."

"What?"

"You heard me. I told her I loved her, and she told me to go to hell."

"I've been telling you that for years," Brandt said under his breath.

"Don't you think you ought to get some pants on?" Lucas asked, irritated.

Brandt looked down. "Oh, yeah." He reached for a pair of tan trousers wrinkled into a ball on the floor. "Why did she boot you out?"

"She said that if I really loved her, I would have believed in her innocence."

"And?"

"And I wouldn't have left again to go after Scott."

"Oh, God, I almost forgot." Brandt's usually dark complexion paled. "If you're back, that means you did it. You killed Scott."

Lucas moved to the window. He took in the whole

length of the town. At one end stood the church that doubled as a schoolhouse. In the middle was the mercantile, the hotel, and the Adams Express. Then came the saloon, the livery, and the jail. Not a bad little town. He supposed he ought to get used to it if he was going to put down roots here.

Brandt's voice interrupted his thoughts, repeating the question he'd been trying to avoid.

He'd given up on personally tracking down and killing Scott. That he could deal with. But it didn't mean the bastard didn't deserve to die. That fact still ate at his gut, no matter how hard he tried to tamp it down.

"Oh, God. You *did* kill him, didn't you? You tortured him and killed him, and now you're running from the law."

"Will you lose your job if UP finds out you're harboring a fugitive?"

"You're damn right." He started pulling on an equally wrinkled white cotton shirt. "Look, Lucas, you're my best friend. You know I would do almost anything for you. If you needed food or money, I'd give it to you. Hell, I'll even help you find a place to hide out. But I'd rather the town marshal didn't find you here. Christ, I'd be out of a job before you could say *jackrabbit*."

"Take it easy," Lucas said. "I'm not wanted by the law, and I didn't kill Silas Scott."

Brandt looked up from tugging on his boots. "You didn't?"

"No, I didn't. Jesus, why does everybody think I murdered the bastard?"

"Forgive me," Brandt said in a sarcastic tone, his body relaxing visibly. "You've only been saying you were going to kill the guy for the past five years. I don't know where I would have gotten the idea that you actually intended to do it."

Lucas flinched, feeling properly reprimanded. "You're right. I apologize."

"So if you didn't kill him, what are you doing back here?"

"I guess you could say I came to my senses."

Brandt snorted. "That'd be a first."

Lucas shot him a quelling glance. "I had him, Brandt. I had my gun pointed right at his chest."

The room fell silent. Brandt's fingers dropped away from the boot he'd been tugging on. "So what happened?" he asked.

"I don't know. God help me, I wanted to kill him. My finger was on the trigger, ready to blow the bastard to kingdom come. Then I thought of Megan and how vengeance wouldn't keep me warm on a cold night. By the time I shook off that damn niggling sense of doubt, Scott was gone. Oh, I followed him, but I didn't get very far. My heart just wasn't in it anymore. When I stopped and took a good look around me—at the deserted trail, the trees, the dark sky—I realized that wasn't where I wanted to be. I wanted to be back here, with Megan in my arms."

He shook off his bout of nostalgia. He'd made the decision to come back for Megan, and he wasn't the least bit sorry. He just wished he could know that somewhere down the road, Silas Scott would get what was coming to him.

"So what do you say? Are you going to lend me the money to buy a ring or not?"

"Do I have a choice?" Brandt asked.

"Not really."

Brandt opened a drawer and reached inside for his billfold. With it came a silky black stocking and a red satin garter. Lucas began to roar with laughter. Brandt cleared his throat and stuffed the feminine items back in the drawer.

"Didn't know I'd taken those with me," he explained. And then a devilish light entered his eyes. "Guess I'll have to track the lady down and return them."

He handed Lucas several folded bills. "So what are you going to do after you buy the ring, if she's still mad at you?"

Lucas shrugged. "I'll just have to show her how much I love her."

"How are you going to manage that?" he asked.

"By proving her innocence."

"Haven't you got anything nicer than these?" Lucas asked the mercantile proprietor. The rings in the black velvet case were fine, just not what he had in mind for Megan.

"Got another box," the older gentleman said. "They're mighty expensive, though. Don't sell many of those 'round here."

"Let me see them."

He opened the case to see a dozen gems sparkling back at him. A large, square-cut emerald caught his eye immediately. He lifted it from its velvet cushion and held it to the light. Leaf-shaped etchings curled around the gold band like a trellis of climbing ivy. The green of the emerald would set off Megan's hair and skin coloring perfectly, he thought.

"I'll take this one," he said.

"That one's gonna cost ya," the slope-shouldered man warned.

Lucas ignored him. "This is the one I want," he said. Only the best would be good enough for his wife.

Ha! They weren't even married yet, and already he thought of her as his wife. More importantly, though, he thought of her as his. And she was. Forever. Even if she hadn't quite figured that out yet.

He paid the proprietor, refusing his offer to wrap the ring. Instead, he slipped it into the breast pocket of his leather vest. With a little pat over his heart, he headed back to the jailhouse.

Outside the telegraph office, a freckled boy of about ten stepped in front of him. "Paper, mister? Hot off the presses."

Lucas hesitated.

"C'mon, mister. It's only a nickel."

"All right," he said, smiling. He reached into his trouser pocket for a coin. "Here you go."

The boy handed him a newspaper and continued on his way.

Lucas unfolded the pages, deciding to glance through them on his way back to the marshal's office.

But the first bold headline stopped him in his tracks.

Chapter Twenty-six

LEAVENWORTH WOMAN JAILED FOR SUSPICION OF RECENT PAYROLL ROBBERIES.

"Son of a bitch!" he swore, reading on.

Megan Adams, owner of the Adams Express Stage-coach Line, sits in a Leavenworth jail cell at the time of this printing. With the encouragement of a Union Pacific Railroad representative, local marshal Isaiah Thompson has taken Miss Adams into custody for conspiring to steal railroad payrolls being transported by her stage company from Kansas City to Atchison, Kansas.

Lucas didn't bother reading the rest. It took all his willpower not to march over to the newspaper office, find the louse who wrote the article, and punch him into a spiral of unconsciousness. He stomped to the jailhouse, slamming the door closed behind him.

"Have you seen this?" he asked, throwing the paper down on the marshal's desk.

Marshal Thompson read in silence for several seconds.

Caleb and Megan appeared from the row of cells. "What's going on out here?" her brother asked.

"Christ!" Thompson swore, passing the paper to Caleb.

Lucas grabbed Megan's hand, hauling her back to her cell. "Gather up your things. I'm getting you out of here."

"What?" she balked. "Lucas, what's going on?"

"They know you're here."

"Who?"

"Everybody," Caleb answered, handing her the newspaper. "How the hell did they find out? I thought we were trying to keep it a secret."

"We were." The marshal joined them. "I swore Travis to secrecy; we didn't tell anyone. I've even been letting the regular drunks and such go this week so they wouldn't see her in here."

Lucas started throwing Megan's belongings into the middle of the gray blanket covering the cot, tying them up into a knapsack of sorts. "I'm not going to let her become some sideshow freak for this town. I'm getting her out of here." He straightened and faced Thompson. "Is that going to be a problem?"

"If it was, you'd both be locked in that cell right now." He moved away from the door, giving them room to pass. "Go out the back so no one will see you. You got a horse?"

"Worthy's out back," he said, more to Megan than the others. He took her hand, pulling her past Caleb and the marshal. "Come on."

"Wait a minute," she said, refusing to budge. "If you think I'm guilty, why are you going to such pains to protect my reputation?"

One corner of his mouth curved. "No wife of mine is going to be an ex-convict," he said. Then he kissed the tip of her nose. "Now move."

"Hey," Caleb called out. "Where are you taking her?"

"I haven't quite figured that out yet."

"How about the Express office?" Megan offered, ignoring his comment about marriage.

Three sets of disbelieving male eyes drilled into her. "Isn't that a bit obvious?" Lucas asked.

"Not really," she answered. "If I had stolen those payrolls, it would be stupid of me to return to the Express, right? Well, that's exactly what everyone else will think, too." The men still looked skeptical, so she continued. "There's a room above the office. I use it to store old schedules and files and spare parts for the coaches. I doubt anyone even realizes the room is there, let alone would think of it as a place for me to hide."

"She's got a point," Caleb said. "If anyone starts to close in, we can persuade them to look in another direction. Or at least get word to you so you'll have a chance to get out of there."

Lucas shifted his weight to his other foot. "You really think it'll work?"

A silent moment passed. And then Caleb said, "I think it will."

Myriad voices and heavy footsteps on the wood sidewalk outside distracted them. The rest of the town had obviously just gotten wind of the newspaper article.

"Shit!" Lucas swore, pushing Megan out the back door. He hefted her onto Worthy's back and climbed up behind her. "We'll ride out around town," he told Caleb. Marshal Thompson had stayed inside to fend off the approaching crowd. "When it looks safe, we'll come at the Express from behind."

"You need to unlock the door from the inside," Megan told her brother.

Caleb nodded. "Be careful," he said as Lucas kicked his mount into a gallop and sped off toward the edge of town.

"What's wrong?" Lucas tossed the stub of his cigarette away from the boulder where he stood. They'd been watching for more than three hours, watching and waiting no more than a mile outside of town.

"What makes you think anything's wrong?" Megan

asked, discarding the stem of a bright-pink wildflower she'd plucked all the petals from.

He lowered himself to the ground beside her. "You haven't said a word since we left town."

"What-makes-you-think-anything-is-wrong," she said again, counting off each word on her fingers. "Seven words. See? I said something."

"Megan." He gave her a look meant to intimidate.

She jumped to her feet, dusting off the back of her calico skirt. "All right. You want to know what's wrong? I'll tell you. I'm tired of being treated like a criminal. It's one thing to sit in jail waiting for some high-class lawyer to come and convince everyone you're innocent, but it's another when people suddenly don't care whether you are or not. Whoever wrote that newspaper article didn't care about the truth. He never came to the jail to see if I was actually there. He never sat down with the marshal to get the whole story. He only cared about writing a story that would sell papers.

"As a result, the people who read that article won't care about the truth, either. They'll only want to see me behind bars so they'll have something to titter about behind their hands. Why, I'm probably the best topic of gossip they've had for months.

"And don't even think about trying to placate me," she said when he opened his mouth to speak. "You're worse than all of them put together."

"Me?"

"Yes, you. You walked into that jail cell last night all puffed up about telling me you loved me, but you still think I'm guilty. You've always thought I was the one responsible for the robberies."

"That's not—"

"It is true! And even if it weren't, you'd still have turned me in. Because Brandt Donovan asked you to." She settled tight fists on her hips and began to pace. "God help him if I find out he was the one who gave that story to the reporter. I'll split him open like ripe fruit and rip out his heart."

"Megan."

"Then I'll cook it up and feed it to him for dinner." She did an about-face and paced back.

"Megan."

"Or maybe I'll have him drawn and quartered. Yes, that sounds promising."

"Megan."

She stopped in midstride. *"What?"*

"If you didn't plan those robberies, why haven't you tried to refute the charge and prove your innocence?"

Her eyes widened. "Maybe it has something to do with the fact that you kidnapped me and wouldn't let me out of your sight for two weeks. And then you threw me in jail—oh, I'm sorry, I mean you had *Brandt* throw me in jail. When, exactly, was I supposed to find time to gather evidence in my defense?"

Lucas ignored her sarcasm. "You really think you can find proof that you're innocent?" he asked, pretending he hadn't already made the decision to try to find evidence that pointed to someone else setting up the robberies.

"I don't know. But it wouldn't hurt to look."

"Where?"

"What?"

"Where would you look? Where do you think you could find evidence to clear your name?"

"I don't know that, either. The only place I can think of is the Express office. That's where all the paperwork is— schedules, payroll transport records, every piece of correspondence I've ever gotten from the railroad. If there's anything that would prove my innocence, I guess that's where I'd find it."

"Well, then," he said with a smile. "Things are working out better than I expected."

Megan frowned. "What does that mean?"

"It means it's a good thing we'll be hiding out at the Express for a while. That'll make it easier to search the place without being discovered."

She simply snorted and gave him a look to let him know she thought he'd lost his mind.

The sun was just beginning to set as Lucas and Megan crept up to the Adams Express building and plastered themselves to the rear wall. Through the thin wood they heard voices, one decidedly Caleb's. They strained to make out the words.

"—else, sir?"

"No, that will be all, Hector, thank you."

Feet shuffled. "You sure I can't do that for you, Mr. Adams?"

Caleb paused. "No. I'm going to stay just a little longer to work on the books."

"You shouldn't bother with that," Hector continued. "I don't mind taking care of it for you."

The legs of a chair scraped across the floor, followed by heavy, receding footsteps. "I don't mind," Caleb said firmly. The bell on the front door jingled. "Have a nice evening, Hector. See you in the morning."

The building fell into silence. Then they heard the slight rustle of blinds being drawn. Caleb's steps grew louder until the back door swung open.

"Get in here," he whispered harshly.

Lucas pushed Megan ahead of him, taking one last look around before ducking into the darkened room himself.

"Is that damn Hector always so hard to get rid of?" Caleb asked bluntly.

"He was just trying to help," Megan answered.

They stumbled through the clutter of the back room, which was used mostly for storage, and up a flight of stairs. Caleb carried a lantern at his side, keeping the wick low for fear someone would notice the light from outside.

The room above the office left a lot to be desired. It looked as if it hadn't been used—or cleaned—since the Adams Express had opened twenty years before. Their passage left footprints on the dirt-covered floor, and the dust in the air made them cough.

"Quite a little housekeeper you are, Meg," Caleb commented.

She punched her brother's arm. "I never saw you up here with a broom when you worked with Papa."

"It's your business now, remember? I seem to recall your making several threats against my wife and family if I ever interfered."

"That's right. And I suggest you remember those threats before you say anything else about the condition of this place."

"It is a mess, Megan," Lucas put in.

Caleb tried to quiet a chuckle.

"Oh, shut up," she told them both. "It isn't so bad." She crossed to an old iron cot in one corner, plopping down on the mattress. A cloud of dust floated up around her. Both men stared at her as if to say "I told you so" while she coughed and sputtered and turned blue in the face.

"You should be safe up here," Caleb said. "You can probably even get away with walking around at night as long as you keep the lantern low. It'll be harder during the day. You'll have to be careful not to make a sound. These walls are as thin as paper. If you so much as sneeze, anyone who happens to be downstairs will know you're here."

"I'll have to make sure Megan doesn't fall asleep, then. No offense, but your sister snores like a runaway train."

"So does Rebecca. Don't worry, you'll get used to it in twenty or thirty years."

"I doubt it."

"Excuse me," Megan said, clearing her scratchy throat. "I am in the room, you know."

"How could we forget?" Lucas asked rhetorically. "You've been hacking like a mule with pneumonia for the past ten minutes."

She raised one eyebrow. "Oh, you'll pay for that one."

Even in the dark of the room, they stared one another down.

Caleb chuckled. "I can see you two will get along fine up here. Alone. Completely isolated." He handed the lantern to Lucas. "Good night."

Silence followed him down the steps and out the front door.

"So what are we going to do all night in this dark room?"

Lucas smiled wickedly. "I can think of a few things."

"Ha!" Megan scoffed. "You're fooling yourself if you think I'm going to let you touch me after that remark about my snoring."

"You'd melt in a second if I so much as kissed you."

"Is that what you think?"

"It's what I know," he challenged.

She stretched out on the cot, feigning a yawn. "If I weren't so tired, I just might make the effort to prove you wrong."

"I guess that means you aren't interested in going downstairs to search for something that might clear your name."

She sat up, fairly leaping off the bed. "Of course I am. Let's go."

"All right," he said. "But first, there's one thing . . ."

"What?"

He wrapped an arm around her waist, leaning in for a kiss. His lips suckled as his tongue darted inside, twisting and dancing with hers. She moaned. Her knees bent, and she went slack in his arms.

Lucas straightened. When he was sure she could stand on her own, he slipped his arm from around her back. "You're right," he said, wiping his lips with the back of one hand.

"About what?" she asked, still slightly dazed.

"I could never make you melt." He turned around and began descending the stairs.

"Of course not," she said, her voice weaker than she'd have liked. "My constitution is much too strong for any such nonsense."

But her lips still tingled, and she had trouble negotiating the steps as she followed him down to the front office.

Chapter Twenty-seven

Lucas sat at the desk, concentrating on the figures in the most recent Adams Express ledger. The low lamplight did nothing to hurry the aggravatingly slow process.

Megan's head appeared from the other side of the desk, where she knelt on the floor sorting through Express records. She slapped another pile of papers in front of him. "What are we looking for, anyway?"

"Anything. I'll know it when I see it."

"Great," she said, bending over the stack of letters and telegrams from Union Pacific once again. "He doesn't know what he's looking for, but he'll know it when he sees it. Now there's a plan if ever I've heard one."

"What are you babbling about over there?"

"I am not babbling."

"Sounds like babbling to me."

"Well, I wouldn't be too concerned then. After all, you don't even know what it is you're looking for."

"I'll know it when I—"

"—see it. Yeah, yeah. Just don't expect me to be overly confident. Lucas, we could be days at this."

"Yep."

The short answer, along with the change in his voice, made her stop. She peeked over the edge of the desk to see him studying one page of the ledger more closely than the others. "Did you find something?"

"Maybe."

She jumped up and rounded the desk, coming to stand behind him. "What? Lucas, what is it?"

"I thought you were the only one who worked on the books."

"I am. Except for the past few weeks when Caleb has been taking care of things."

"And you've always kept this ledger under lock and key, right?"

"Yes."

"Then why does the handwriting change every few entries starting six months ago?"

"What?" She leaned closer.

"It's not very noticeable, but look." He used his fingers to compare two separate columns. "Your writing flows, while the other is blockier. The numbers are different, too. You make figure eight's, while this person uses two circles, one on top of the other. Your two's are smooth with a loop at the bottom. Whoever wrote this made a sharp angle at the bottom of his."

"I don't pay much attention to the ledger except to make sure that each day's incoming and outgoing funds come out right. Maybe Caleb did make some entries before now, and I just forgot."

"No." He flipped ahead several pages. "Caleb's writing is more fluid, like yours. See? Who else could have gotten to your records?"

"No one. Well, Hector, I suppose, but—"

"Hector. The one Caleb had trouble getting rid of tonight?"

"Yes. He's my regular driver."

"How would he have access to the ledger?"

She tucked her chin against her chest guiltily. "Well, he sometimes mans the office for me. Like the day I drove the stage because he refused to."

Lucas's brow wrinkled. "Do you think you could find anything with a sample of Hector's handwriting on it? Maybe we could compare something you know he wrote to the writing in the ledger."

Megan rifled through some papers on the desk, next moving to a set of cabinets along the far wall. The more she came up with nothing, the faster her movements became. As a last resort, she checked the shelves beneath the ticket counter. "Aha!" she cried out, her voice still low for fear of someone discovering their presence.

She handed Lucas a slip of paper. A note from Hector letting Megan know he wouldn't be able to take a week's worth of stage runs because his brother was visiting from Texas. Lucas folded the page, isolating one line of writing, then held it next to a line in the ledger.

"Oh, my God." Megan felt a wave of dizziness sweep over her and clutched the back of Lucas's chair. Not Hector. He'd been working for her too long. She'd entrusted him with too many duties. She'd *trusted* him.

"There has to be some mistake," she said. "Maybe Hector was only keeping the records up to date to help me out. He knows how hard it's been for me to keep the Express going. People just don't want to do business with you when they find out a woman is running things."

"I don't think 'helping' includes breaking into a locked drawer, do you? And I'll bet if we go back through the numbers, redo the math, and compare them with your bank account, we'll find inconsistencies. My guess is, he's been skimming the profits for some time now."

"I don't believe it," she said matter-of-factly. "There has to be some kind of mistake. I'm sure if we ask him, he'll have a perfectly good explanation."

"Oh, I'm sure he will. He's had six months to make up a believable story."

"Do you have any idea what you're saying, Lucas? You're telling me that my right-hand man, a person who's worked for me since he was sixteen years old, has betrayed me. You're saying he set me up to take the fall for something he's done."

"That's exactly what I think is going on."

"Can you prove it?" she asked, turning his own logic back at him.

"Not yet. But his handwriting in this book does prove one thing."

"What?"

"If Hector got to this ledger and made these entries, he probably knows a lot more about what goes on around here than you think he does."

She stared at Lucas for a long minute. Then quietly she asked, "You think he's involved in the payroll robberies, don't you?"

He met her gaze steadily. "I think so."

"Oh, God," she said again, covering her face with her hands. Pain thrummed behind her eyes. "How can this be happening? I can't believe—"

"Shh!" Lucas clamped a hand on her thigh, turning his head to listen more closely.

This time Megan heard the noise, too. A low, grating sound just beyond the front door. Lucas shoved the ledger back into the drawer and with a quick twist locked it away. Taking the key with him, he blew out the lamp, grabbed her hand, and made a silent run for the back of the office. But before they reached the stairs, the front door opened. With a quick shove, Lucas pushed her behind the row of oak cabinets, hunching down beside her. He held a finger up to his lips, warning her to remain silent.

From their hiding place, they could hear footsteps, the shuffling of papers, the opening and closing of drawers.

"Hurry up!" someone whispered.

"I'm hurrying," someone else replied.

Megan slumped when she recognized one of the

voices. Even though the words were low and muffled, she knew beyond a doubt that the man breaking into the office was Hector.

As if reading her thoughts, Lucas nudged her elbow, mouthing a one-word question. "Hector?"

With dread weighing heavily on her, slowly, regretfully, she nodded.

Another drawer slid open, and a sigh of relief reached their ears.

"Now tear out those pages," the other man ordered. "I can't believe you were stupid enough to write in the company records."

"I had to cover my tracks," Hector said. "Otherwise she would've figured out that I was taking money out of the cash drawer."

"What the hell did you do that for, anyway?"

They heard paper ripping as Hector tore pages out of the Express ledger. " 'Cause you take too long gettin' me my cut of the payroll money. You and the guys stop at every saloon between here and the hideout to buy whiskey and women. I'm lucky to get anything by the time you show up."

"You get your share."

"Yeah, but I deserve more. Without me, you wouldn't know when to stop the stage. I'm the one who finds out when the railroad is shipping the payrolls via the Adams Express."

"And you're paid well for your trouble."

"Not well enough. Don't you care that Ma and I can hardly keep food on the table?"

"Doesn't the Adams woman pay you for driving the stage?"

"Sure, but that doesn't go far. Especially with Ma being sick and all." Hector's tone became more serious. "She's your ma, too, Ev."

A wave of nausea rushed over Megan. She couldn't believe what she was hearing. The conversation swirled through her head like a bad dream. Discovering that Evan was the other intruder shocked her enough. But the rest . . . Not only was Hector responsible for the payroll robberies, but he and Evan—the leader of the outlaws who had kidnapped her—were brothers.

She felt like such a fool. She hadn't even known Hector's mother was ill. If only he had told her, confided in her, she would have managed to give him a raise. Or even lend him the money he needed until they got back on their feet. Maybe then he wouldn't have been so easily convinced to betray her trust.

"Shut up and let's go," Evan said. The ledger pages crinkled as he shoved them into his pocket. Footsteps sounded across the wooden floorboards. The front door whispered closed behind them, and Megan heard the key turn in the lock, leaving them alone in the building once again.

She released a breath she hadn't realized she'd been holding. Lucas patted her back and helped her to rise. He lit the lamp on the desk, then opened the drawer, which the two men had forgotten to relock. The key they had used, a duplicate to Megan's, still rested in its hole.

"Now do you believe me?" he asked.

She nodded, feeling sick to her stomach.

He flipped open the ledger. The rough edges of torn paper remained where pages of records used to be. "There goes our evidence," he said grimly.

"What do we do now?" She didn't have much hope that they'd be able to prove her innocence with the only evidence of someone else's involvement missing.

He answered her with a conviction she found comforting, even through her gloom. "We get Brandt and the marshal and tell them what we found."

"What will it matter?" she asked. "The proof we found is gone. Hector and Evan took it."

Lucas eyed her for a moment. The corner of his mouth lifted in a half smile. "Then we'll just have to get it back."

The light blazed brightly inside Brandt Donovan's hotel room, though it was nearing three o'clock in the morning.

Megan sat in a maroon medallion-backed armchair beside the window while Lucas tried to convince his friend to go along with his plan.

"Absolutely not." Brandt paced the length of the room, occasionally spouting a string of choice phrases at Lucas's proposition. "Are you crazy?"

"It's the only way," Lucas explained again.

"It can't be the only way. You'll get yourself killed trying to walk back in there."

"That's why I need you at my back."

He stopped in midstride. "I'm telling you, it's crazy."

"We have to get back the evidence that will clear Megan."

"Ever think of leading the marshal to their hideout and letting him take care of it?"

"No."

Brandt threw up his hands and resumed pacing. "Why not?"

"Because neither the marshal nor his deputy would get within two feet of the place before they shot 'em dead."

"What makes you think they won't do the same to you?"

He took a deep breath and tried once again to explain his plan. "The marshal and his deputy will be there. So will Caleb Adams and any other able-bodied men who want to join the posse."

Getting up from the bed, he stood in front of his friend, placing a strong hand on his shoulder. "I want you with me, Brandt. This is dangerous, I know, but I wouldn't trust another soul to guard my back."

Brandt held Lucas's gaze for several long seconds. Then he ran splayed fingers through his chestnut hair and shook his head. "Damn it, McCain, you make it hard for a man to say no."

Lucas chuckled. "That's the idea."

"All right, then. I'll go with you. But no funny business."

He nodded. "Agreed."

"And no heroics. We go in, take the outlaws into custody, and get the hell out."

"That's the plan."

Brandt went on listing conditions as though he didn't trust Lucas not to get himself killed. "We keep Marshal Thompson and the others at our backs. I'm not going in there if I don't know for damn certain there are half a dozen guns backing me up." He paused, his brow wrinkled in thought.

"Anything else?" Lucas asked, amusement radiating from his smiling eyes.

Brandt hesitated, then shook his head. "That's all."

From the other side of the room, Megan piped up. "I have a question."

Both men swung their heads in her direction, as though they'd completely forgotten her presence. Not surprising, since neither of them had ever known her to be silent for so long.

"What's that?" Lucas asked.

"What do you want me to do?"

Chapter Twenty-eight

Lucas and Brandt exchanged doubtful glances.

"I don't want you to do anything," Lucas said. "You're staying right here."

The minute the words left his mouth, he knew he'd made a terrible mistake. Megan's cheeks turned pink, and she rose from the chair. Her eyes narrowed, and her lips pursed.

She took a step forward, hands on hips. "Lucas McCain, I hope you're not saying what I think you're saying. I am not about to sit in this hotel room and twiddle my thumbs while you and Brandt and my brother ride off to apprehend those bandits. I'm going with you."

"Now, Megan," Brandt said, attempting to pacify her increasing fury. "I'm sure Lucas is only concerned about your safety."

"He ought to be worried about *his* safety," she threw back. "And you'd better think twice before siding with him against me, Brandt Donovan. Rile me, and I'd be mighty concerned about ever visiting Ruby over at the

Dog Tick again, if I were you." She let her gaze slide downward, making sure he understood exactly what she was implying.

He flinched.

"Don't let her intimidate you," Lucas told his friend. "She's more bark than bite."

"Is that so?" she said, stalking forward.

Brandt stepped aside, leaving Lucas to defend himself against her wrath.

"That's so," Lucas retorted.

They stood nose-to-nose in a vibrant clash of wills.

"Well, I've got news for you, mister."

"What's that?"

"You are going to take me with you."

"Oh, yeah? What makes you think so?"

"I'm a woman. I know these things," she said.

He snorted. "Try again."

"All right, then. How about this? If you don't take me along, Brandt won't be the only one limping for the rest of his life."

Lucas's face remained impassive. "Feisty, that's what you are."

"My mother calls me spoiled. Caleb says I'm wild." She moved closer, her breasts pressing against his warm chest. "I think I like being feisty best of all."

He didn't say anything.

"This is my life we're talking about, Lucas. I think I have a right to be involved in the outcome of your little plan."

Without warning, he bent down to place a firm, moist kiss on her lips. "What do you say, Brandt? Think we could use one more rider in our posse?"

His friend cleared his throat before answering. "I don't suppose it would hurt. Can she handle a revolver?"

Lucas and Megan shared a knowing look. "You'll just have to wait and see," he told Brandt with a laugh. "Just wait and see."

A Promise of Roses

* * *

An hour before daybreak, the eight-man–one-woman posse hid their mounts in a copse of trees just beyond the run-down outlaw hideout. At an order from Thompson, the deputy marshal sneaked closer to the shack. More quietly than a wisp of wind, he loosened the bandits' horses from a half-fallen hitching post and led them back to the others.

Lucas was relieved to see the four familiar mounts. Evan and the boys were still here. That meant none of them had gotten antsy; they still felt safe. The posse's attack would be a complete surprise.

Hector, though, seemed to be absent.

"All right, men," the marshal whispered. Then, with a tip of his hat, he added, "And Miss Megan. We're going by McCain's plan here, so what he says goes. Lucas?" he said.

Lucas surveyed the circle of faces, each eager and ready to take down the gang of robbers who had plagued their town for months. Caleb looked ready to throttle all four bandits with his bare hands.

"Brandt and I will go in first," he said, making his authority clear to Caleb. Not that Megan's brother didn't know what he was doing; he was just too personally involved. Even more so than Megan, because his temper and need to avenge his little sister ran so hot.

"I'm hoping they won't have time to draw their weapons if we can catch them off guard. Two of them are just kids, fellas, so let's try to keep the violence to a minimum. If anyone's going to give us trouble, it'll be Frank. Watch for a man with long, dirty black hair and a scar on his neck that runs from ear to ear."

"You sure there's no other way outta there?" one of the men asked. "Maybe a couple of us oughta go around back."

Lucas shook his head. "These guys are low on brains and high on confidence. They probably never even considered that someone might find their hideout. Chances are they're sitting inside right now, playing a hand of cards.

"Now," he continued, "Brandt and I will go first. The rest of you come in behind. Keep at least three feet back, no less. Got it?"

Six heads nodded in understanding. The men straightened, taking a step back to await Lucas's signal.

Before Megan could get away from him, Lucas grabbed her arm. "I want you well out of the line of fire," he told her. "It probably wouldn't be a bad idea for you to stay back here and watch the horses."

Her eyes narrowed. "Maybe I can check them for weapons, too," she taunted. "I'll bet a couple of those mounts are heavily armed. Wouldn't want them to get the drop on us, now would we?"

Lucas gritted his teeth, swallowing the urge to shake her senseless. But then, if nothing else did, her being here proved that she'd long ago taken leave of any senses God had seen fit to give her. "Megan," he said through a tightly clenched jaw.

"Lucas," she said with equal determination. "You have two choices. I either go in with you and Brandt, or I come in with the others. Either way, I am going to be a part of this."

"You're going to get yourself killed," he growled.

She smiled sweetly. "Then you'll get to say you were right all along." With that, she flounced off in Brandt's direction. "I'm going in with you and Lucas," she told him in a no-nonsense tone of voice.

His eyes widened, and she could have sworn he nearly choked on his own Adam's apple. "Did you clear this with Lucas?" he asked.

"I don't have to clear anything with him," she retorted. "But, yes, he said it's okay."

"I did not say it was okay," Lucas said in a harsh whisper, coming up behind them. "But, then, I don't guess I have much to say about it one way or the other." He turned to Brandt. "She's going in with us. At least that way I can keep an eye on her. It's either that or leave her back with the rest of the men. And there's no telling what might happen then. Caleb is the only one I'd trust to keep her safe."

Brandt looked doubtful but simply shrugged. "It's your call."

Lucas looked at Megan, who had joined the rest of the posse for the moment. "Don't let anything happen to her," he told his friend.

"I'll protect her with my life," Brandt said solemnly. Then, with a hint of laughter in his voice, he added, "But I won't be responsible if she shoots herself in the foot."

The men surrounded the one-room shack. Lucas stood outside the door, his hand on the rusty latch. Brandt and Megan maintained a position less than a foot to the right of the portal, ready to step in immediately after him.

The other six men formed a semicircle behind them. Guns drawn, muscles taut, they prepared to rush in at the first sign of trouble.

Lucas held up a hand, beginning to count down the seconds on his fingers. *Five . . . four . . .*

Megan took a deep breath. Her fingers tightened around the butt of her revolver. She could feel Brandt's strong hand at her back.

Three . . . two . . .

She uttered a quick, two-word prayer. *Please, God.*

Lucas's remaining finger went down. *One.*

The door burst open. Lucas stepped inside, flanked by Megan and Brandt. Four startled men jumped up from their chairs, overturning the rickety oak table.

"Evening, gentlemen," Lucas greeted them. "Ah, ah, ah. None of that," he said, waving his gun when Frank reached for the revolver strapped to his thigh.

"Luke," Evan said, shocked. "And Meggie. What's going on?"

"You're under arrest," Lucas informed them.

"For what?" Frank spat.

Brandt stepped forward, keeping his pistol leveled at them while he relieved them of their sidearms. "For holding up the Leavenworth–Atchison stage no fewer than four times and stealing Union Pacific payrolls."

Evan gasped, playing his act of innocence to the hilt. "That's ridiculous," he said. "We would never do any such thing. Would we, boys?" The two youngest shook their heads, more than eager to agree with anything that would get them out of this fix. "Why, just ask Luke, there. He's ridden with us. He knows we're not criminals."

Frank sneered at them. "You can't prove a thing."

Brandt returned to stand with Lucas and Megan. "Don't be stupid, Frank."

"Too late," Megan singsonged behind him.

Brandt tossed her a quelling glance before clearing his throat. "Like I said, don't be stupid, gentlemen. Lucas McCain wouldn't be here if he were one of you; he'd be locked in a jail cell back in Leavenworth. Which is exactly where you're all headed."

"McCain?" Dougie said. "You told us your name was Campbell."

"Shut up," Frank spat at Dougie, staring at Lucas with hate-filled eyes. "He's one of them, you asshole. He only joined us so he could find out where we were hiding. Ain't that right, McCain?"

"I always said you were the only one in this outfit with any brains," Lucas said by way of an answer.

"If you don't mind," Brandt interrupted, "I'd like to get this over with and get back to town so I can get some sleep. Marshal!" he called out.

Thompson and the others filed into the tiny shack until it was filled to overflowing. Lucas saw to it that the outlaws were properly restrained, then took Megan's arm and guided her outside. Brandt followed.

"Not bad," Lucas said.

"All in a day's work." Brandt preened with pleasure.

"So what do you think?" Lucas asked, his tone serious. "Will this prove her innocence?"

The "her" in question stood happily in the curve of Lucas's arm. She hadn't gotten the chance to show off her firearm skills in front of Brandt Donovan, but everything had gone off without a hitch, so she couldn't complain.

Lucas's question, however, brought her head out of the clouds and back to reality. She hadn't even considered that she might *still* be thought of as the leader of the thieves.

The look on Brandt's face didn't do much to ease her fears.

"If we can get these guys to talk, she'll be off the hook. But I wouldn't hold my breath. That Frank is going to be a tough one."

"Tell me about it," Lucas grumbled.

"And I think Evan is smarter than you give him credit for. I doubt we'll find a single thing in that shack to use as evidence against them. Your best bet, I'd say, would be to find Hector and those missing ledger pages. That, and your testimony as to what you heard in the Express office last night, will probably clear Megan of any involvement. But getting the gang convicted is another story altogether. I don't think we can do that without one of them breaking down and confessing everything."

"Work on the boys," Lucas said. "They're young. They're scared. It shouldn't take much to get them to talk."

Brandt nodded.

"What about Hector?" Megan asked nervously.

Lucas smiled wryly at Brandt. "Doesn't look like you're going back to bed any time soon, old friend."

Brandt groaned but didn't argue with what he knew had to be done.

Chapter Twenty-nine

"You know what to do, right?" Lucas asked for the tenth time in as many minutes. He sat on the edge of Megan's desk at the Express office, studying her closely for any sign of fear.

She was wearing the frilly white blouse and bright-red skirt with blue and yellow flowers that he'd bought her on the trail. Standing in the stream of sunlight that spilled through the storefront window, her hair pulled up in a twist, she looked absolutely radiant.

A warm sensation washed over him—a feeling Lucas was only now beginning to recognize as love.

"Everything will be fine," she told him. "Stop worrying."

He couldn't help but worry about her. He loved her. He'd give anything for this to be over. To be able to take her home and make hours worth of long, luxurious love to her. After he convinced her to forgive him, of course.

He shifted nervously. "Are you sure he'll come? What if he suspects something?"

"He won't suspect anything. He comes in every morning around this time. Chances are, he'd be afraid of making people suspicious by *not* showing up. And now that the whole town's seen that newspaper article, he'll come to catch up on the latest gossip."

"That's what I'm afraid of."

"Lucas, *stop worrying.* There are going to be four of you in the back room, all with guns trained right on poor Hector."

"*Poor Hector?* Let's not forget that *poor Hector* is responsible for almost single-handedly ruining your life."

"I know. I just can't help but feel sorry for him, is all." He snorted.

She smiled. "Are you done being worried?" she asked.

"No!" he answered emphatically.

"Too bad. Now, go hide with Caleb and Brandt and the marshal before you blow my cover."

Lucas pulled her close, wrapping his arms around her back. His tongue traced the outline of her lips, teasing and caressing, capturing her tongue with his own. The kiss turned from warm to scalding hot almost instantaneously. She purred deep in the back of her throat, flexing the fingers she'd woven through his hair.

For the first time since Megan had come up with the harebrained idea of confronting Hector in the Express office, he felt his tension ease. He wouldn't let anything happen to her—that was all there was to it. And Brandt and her brother, along with Marshal Thompson, waited in the storage room to back him up.

Someone cleared his throat behind them, and they inched apart—slowly, leisurely, not the least bit embarrassed.

Brandt didn't even try to hide his grin. "You'd better get in here, Lucas, unless you mean to get caught. Hector should be here any minute."

Lucas was loathe to release Megan. "You're sure you're going to be all right?"

"I'm sure."

He kissed her one last time, then followed Brandt to their hiding place in the back room.

Megan moved around to the other side of the desk, tapping her foot in irritation. Who did Lucas think he was to keep kissing her like that anytime it struck his fancy? And why did she keep *letting* him? Why was it that every time he came within breathing distance, she melted like grease on a griddle?

And that remark he'd made back at the jailhouse about her being his wife! *No wife of mine,* he'd said. Well, if he thought she was going to marry him after he'd doubted her honesty and run off and left her, he was nuttier than a chicken in a fox's den.

Never mind that he'd come back for her and tried to find evidence to clear her name. The fact remained that he'd left, and only now did he seem to believe she'd had nothing to do with the robberies in the first place.

A noise at the front door caught her attention. She rose from behind the desk and started forward.

Hector ducked his head in the door, eyes darting around nervously.

"Hector!" she called out, careful to keep her voice happy and relaxed. She pulled the door all the way open, urging him into the office by tugging on his shirtsleeve. Once he passed her, she closed the door behind them.

"Come in and sit down." She motioned him to the chair behind the desk. She leaned back against the ticket counter, keeping herself between Hector and his only avenue of escape. For all intents and purposes, he was now surrounded.

"How have you been?" she asked casually.

"Fine," he answered quickly, eyes shifting from place to place, never stopping on her figure straight ahead of him.

"And your mother?"

His head came up, as she'd known it would. They'd never really discussed his family before, so she knew the mention of his mother would catch him off guard.

"Sh-she's fine."

Megan gave a smile before dispensing with the polite

chatter. "Hector, I have a little problem, and I was hoping you could help me out."

"S-sure thing, M-miss Megan."

She took note of his sudden stutter. He'd never had a problem with his speech before.

"I've had a rough couple of weeks," she told him. "As you can probably imagine. Kidnapped from my own stage, accused of stealing the railroad payrolls, put in jail for a crime I didn't commit."

His eyes grew big as pancakes, finally stopping their random movements long enough to focus on her.

"That's right," she said. "I was none too happy about it, either. Especially since I didn't have anything to do with setting up the robberies." She crossed her arms over her chest, fixing him with a steady gaze. "The group of bandits has been taken into custody, and the authorities have decided to release me for lack of evidence," she lied. "But they still seem to believe that information about the payrolls must have been given to the outlaws by somebody at the Adams Express. Someone who knows the routine, has access to confidential records—that sort of thing.

"Now, if they've already cleared me of any wrongdoing, who do you think they'll investigate next? Caleb?" She shook her head. "They already questioned him. And everyone knows he doesn't spend much time in town, with a ranch to run.

"They've checked out Zeke, and Wally, and all the rest of the drivers," she said, counting them on the tips of her fingers. "So who does that leave?"

He swallowed, his Adam's apple bobbing up and down the length of his throat.

Straightening from the counter, she dropped the concerned-employer facade and went for honesty. "Why did you do it, Hector?"

He leapt to his feet. "I—I d-don't know what you're t-talking about, Miss Megan."

"I was hiding in the office last night when you and

your brother broke in. You tore some pages out of the Express ledger, remember, Hector?"

He started shaking his head, retreating slowly.

"But I'd already seen the ledger pages," she continued. "I know you were stealing money out of the cash drawer and fixing the records so I wouldn't know. And if you managed that, I have no doubt that you could have gotten into the confidential shipping records."

She saw Lucas step silently from the shadows of the back room. Brandt, Caleb, and Marshal Thompson followed suit.

"You did it, Hector. I just want to know why."

"You don't understand, Miss Megan," he pleaded. "I had to. My brother Evan made me. When he came up from Texas last year, he wanted money. Ma and I didn't have any, so he talked my little brother Dougie into going with him, and they got a gang together and started stealing. At first it was only small stuff. They'd swipe people's bags off of crowded trains, or break into hotel rooms. Then, when he found out you transported Union Pacific payrolls between railroad stations, he decided to try taking those. He said it'd be better pay for less work.

"I couldn't say no. He's my brother. And he gave me and Ma a good chunk of the money."

"So you did it out of greed?" she asked, astounded that anyone could push their knowledge of right and wrong aside to commit such a crime. "That money doesn't belong to you, Hector. Or to your brother and his friends."

"Ev said those railroad folks were rich enough already." He jutted out his chin in defiance. "It was our turn."

"And what about the people who were waiting for that money? Did you ever think of them? Most of the men who own stock in Union Pacific live back East, Hector, in New York City and Boston. The payrolls were on the way to people who work for the railroad. Good, hard-working people from these parts. Men with families to feed, children to clothe. People like your mother, who work hard for every penny they can get. How do you think they felt when their money didn't show up? What are they supposed to do about feeding their children when they don't get paid?"

Hector's eyes clouded with concern. He opened his mouth to reply, then spotted Megan's backup force out of the corner of his eye. "What's this?" he cried, whirling around. "You tricked me!" His accusation was aimed at Megan, who still stood behind him at the counter.

"I'm sorry, Hector," she said solemnly. "I didn't want to believe you were the one passing along confidential information. And I wouldn't have believed it if I hadn't been here when you stole those ledger pages." Her voice grew quiet. "I didn't think you were capable of such a thing. I trusted you, Hector."

He swung around, eyes wild.

The others watched Hector closely but made no move to apprehend him.

Megan saw him edging forward. She stepped into his only path of escape. "It's too late, Hector," she said.

"No!" he screamed, and bolted for the door.

Her arms stretched out to stop him, but the force of his body knocked her off balance. They both fell to the floor in a heap of skirts and flailing arms and legs. She tried to hold him down, succeeding only in keeping a tight grip on his pant leg. He dragged her with him, fighting to get to the front door and out of the Express office.

The minute Lucas saw Hector charging Megan, his heart stopped. He didn't know to what lengths Hector might go to get away. Horrid images filled his mind.

He rushed past Megan's prone figure on the floor, tackling Hector. The boy struggled for several seconds, yelling and lashing out. Then his body went slack as he realized the futility of his efforts.

The others surrounded them, hauling Hector to his feet. With only one thing on his mind, Lucas relaxed his hold and went to Megan. She sat with her back against a row of cabinets.

"Are you all right?" he asked, slightly out of breath.

"I'm fine," she told him.

He ran his hands over her limbs to assure himself of the truthfulness of her words. "Can you stand?"

"Of course I can stand," she snapped, taking the arm he offered for support.

Her sharp retort brought a smile to his face. Yep, she was just fine. But confronting Hector couldn't have been easy for her, he thought. She was surely suffering emotional if not physical pain at this point.

He wrapped his arms around her shoulders, keeping her close as they made their way to the jailhouse. A gale of angry curses filled the room when Thompson threw Hector into the cell next to his brother's gang. The boys were caught, and they knew it.

"We still don't have enough proof to convict them," Caleb said quietly as the captors stood around the marshal's desk.

"We have the duplicate key they left in the office last night," Lucas said.

"Not enough," Brandt said. "All that proves is that there were two keys to the same desk drawer."

"You heard Hector," Megan reminded them. "He admitted giving the boys the information they needed to set up the robberies."

"But will he recant in front of a judge?" Brandt asked, not much above a whisper. "Even with us witnessing that confession, he could take it back, say we're lying, that we'd all been there with the sole intention of framing him and taking him into custody. "Even if we testified under oath as to what we heard, it might not be enough to convict." He grimaced.

"But they're guilty!" Megan said, dumbfounded.

"I know it. You know it. We all know it," he said. "But unless we can prove it or get them to confess, they'll probably walk."

And she would still be a suspect.

No one said as much, but everyone knew. It hung over the room like an evil specter.

The door opened. They turned to see the deputy strut in.

"Travis," the marshal said with a nod. "Anything?"

He didn't answer but moved to Thompson's side, handing him several pieces of wrinkled paper.

"Yahoo!" Thompson slapped the pages down on the desk for all to see. "We've got 'em," he said. "Megan Adams, you're free to go."

Her head snapped up, the question naked in her eyes.

He nodded. "I sent Travis out to Hector's place on a hunch to see if he could find anything. These ledger pages, along with our testimonies, are enough to build a case against these boys. You're no longer a suspect." He threw Brandt a pointed glance. "Unless the railroad objects."

Chapter Thirty

In stunned silence, Megan turned to face Brandt. If even a flicker of doubt existed in his mind, Union Pacific could still try to press charges against her.

"Mr. Donovan?" she asked.

He held her gaze for a long moment.

She stopped breathing.

"The Union Pacific Railroad has no objections to letting Miss Adams go."

Caleb let out a loud whoop. Lucas squeezed her hand, which still rested in his.

Brandt bent at the waist, bowing regally. "Our most sincere apologies for any inconvenience this may have caused, Miss Adams," he said formally. Then he took her hand, pressed a soft kiss to it, and said softly, "I'm sorry for doubting you, Megan. Forgive me?"

Her insides warmed at his heartfelt apology. She smiled. "Just see that it doesn't happen again," she said. "Or I may have to throw another pot of coffee at your head."

His eyes widened, but he quickly broke into a grin. "It won't happen again, I assure you."

"Good. Then if you'll excuse me, gentlemen." She rose, breaking her contact with Lucas. "I'd like to get home. Caleb, will you drive me, please?"

"Absolutely," he said. Her brother went to hold the door open for her. "Rebecca will be ecstatic. We'll have a big celebration dinner."

Megan nodded, but she really had no desire to spend the evening with her family. She loved them dearly, but right now all she wanted was to crawl into her own bed and cry herself to sleep.

She was a free woman. Lucas didn't have to stick around any longer out of guilt for putting her in jail. Despite his protestations, he'd likely be back on Silas Scott's trail by morning, and once again she would be alone.

The thought brought a stinging mist to her eyes. She ducked her head and left the building before anyone noticed the gathering tears.

"Hey." A strong hand caught her arm before she could step off the boardwalk.

She turned to face Lucas. He stared down at her, his face unreadable.

"Where do you think you're going?" he asked.

She raised her chin a notch, determined not to let him see how much she hurt inside. "Home," she said. She loosened her arm from his grasp and started across the street. Caleb's buggy was hitched behind the Express office.

"Wait a minute," he called.

She quickened her pace.

He stalked after her.

Caleb and Brandt hurried to wish the marshal and deputy a good day before setting off after them.

"Megan," Lucas said sternly. "For Christ's sake, will you wait a minute!"

She stopped in the middle of the street, whirling around to face him. "Will you keep your voice down?"

she hissed. The last thing she wanted was to attract the attention of every busybody in town.

"No, I will not keep my voice down!" he said in what could have passed for a defiant shout.

She lowered her eyes, hoping the townspeople would, for once, mind their own business. But her prayer fell on deaf ears. People stopped on the sidewalks. Men, women, and children filtered out of buildings to watch the spectacle.

Her face began to color. She felt the warm blush streaking up from below the neckline of her blouse. Mortified right down to her toes, she tried once more to escape.

And once more Lucas caught her arm.

"Let go of me," she told him in a hushed voice.

"Not until you tell me where you're going."

"I told you, *home*."

He crossed his arms over his chest, leaning back to look at her. His gaze raked her from head to foot. "I hope you weren't planning on going without me."

Her eyes drifted closed. The fight washed out of her, leaving her weak. "I thank you for coming back," she said. "For helping to prove my innocence. But it's over now. You can go back to tracking down Silas Scott without feeling guilty."

"I don't want to go back to tracking Silas Scott."

She stared at him, confused. "It's all you've ever wanted."

He shrugged, resting his hands on her hips, bringing her flush with his body. "I used to think so. Before I hit a run of bad luck. See, I came across this shrew of a woman who caused me nothing but trouble." His lips quirked up in half a grin. "She ranted and raved and told me I didn't want revenge as much as I wanted peace. Of course, I thought she was crazy at the time."

He bent, warming her lips with his own. "But now I know she was right all along. Killing isn't going to bring anybody back. It will only turn me into what I despise most—Silas Scott.

"So I've decided to stick around," he said. "Marry up with that shrewish woman."

She slapped his chest. "I am not a shrew."

A full-fledged grin spread across his face. "Yes, dear."

Several knowing snickers from the men in the crowd reached their ears.

"Do you mean it? Are you really giving up chasing after Scott?"

"I'll hang up my guns altogether if you want me to."

She shook her head, knowing the Peacemakers were as much a part of Lucas as his hands or his feet.

"I've got something for you," he said quietly. He reached into the breast pocket of his vest. The huge, square-cut emerald glittered in the bright sunlight.

Megan gasped. "It's beautiful!"

"It's yours," he told her, slipping the circlet onto the ring finger of her left hand. "On one condition."

"What's that?" she asked, sure she could comply with his request.

"Promise never to take your sunshine away." His voice grew suspiciously rough. "I couldn't live without it."

She looked up to see moisture gathering in the corners of his eyes. And then her vision hazed, and she could see nothing at all. She threw her arms around his neck, hugging him tightly. "I promise. I'll never leave you."

"I love you, Megan."

"Oh, Lucas, I love you, too."

His mouth swooped down to capture hers. They stood in the middle of town, among hoots and hollers and cheers of happiness. But all they knew was each other.

His hands crept over her back, cupping her bottom to lift her off the ground. Their mouths devoured. Her tongue parried while his thrust in passionate combat.

Mothers covered their children's eyes, hurrying them away from the disgraceful scene. Men watched until even their cheeks turned red.

Brandt leaned closer to Caleb. "We should probably break them up," he said.

Caleb gave a bark of laughter. "Are you kidding? We should sell tickets." After another few minutes, though, he changed his mind. He cleared his throat.

Then again, louder. He and Brandt shared a glance before stepping forward.

Megan and Lucas reluctantly broke their kiss. She buried her face against his shoulder when she realized she'd made such a fervent display in front of the whole town.

"They'd better get used to it," Lucas said, guessing her thoughts. " 'Cause I intend to kiss my wife whenever the notion strikes me."

She smiled, licking her lips guiltily. Because she knew she wasn't going to mind a bit.

"Can we go now?" Caleb asked.

Lucas nodded, holding Megan close to his side. "We'll go to your place first," he said. "Then, after dinner, Megan and I will go home."

"Home?" she asked.

"I figure your house is as good a place as any to set down roots. You don't mind, do you?"

She shook her head, happier than she'd ever imagined one person could be.

"I thought I'd try my hand at ranching again."

Caleb groaned. "Just what I need, competition from my own brother-in-law."

"Don't worry," Lucas said. "It'll take me a while to get a good-size herd together." He pressed his lips to Megan's temple. "Besides, I have some home improvements to tend to first—so my wife can enjoy her endless baths. And then I plan to spend a lot of time working at starting a family."

"Just so you don't start it in the middle of the street," Caleb said, heading for the Express office. "Brandt, you're welcome to join us for dinner."

"I'd like that."

"I say we lose them at the next alley," Lucas whispered in Megan's ear as they trailed behind.

"That wouldn't be very nice."

"No, but I'm gonna have a hell of a time keeping my mind on food if you make me sit through a long meal."

She raised up on tiptoe to nip at his earlobe. "I'll make it up to you."

He groaned and pulled her closer.

"McCain!"

The shout rang through town, capturing the attention of anyone within whistling distance.

Lucas whirled, recognizing the voice immediately. He pushed Megan behind him, shielding her with his body.

Silas Scott stood not ten yards away, his sloppy girth straining the buttons of his silver vest. He swept his black jacket open to reveal two ivory-handled revolvers hanging low on his hips.

"I'm sick of you following me, boy. You shoulda done me in back in Chilhowee when you had the chance."

"Get out of here," Lucas told Megan harshly.

"No." She refused to budge. "I'm not leaving without you."

"Get her out of here," he yelled to Brandt and Caleb, who stood motionless several feet away.

They both came forward, each taking one of her arms. She put up a fuss, kicking and screaming, shouting the vilest of threats, but they dragged her out of harm's way.

"Hush! Megan!" Caleb snapped. He didn't mince words. "If you don't stop screeching, you'll break his concentration and get him killed."

That shut her up quicker than a bucketful of platitudes could have.

"Silas Scott is something he has to deal with," Brandt reassured her. But he clutched a revolver in his white-knuckled hand. He dug into his boot for a hidden weapon, then handed Caleb the smaller pistol. "If Lucas misses . . ." he began.

Caleb finished his thought. "Scott's still a dead man."

"Time to have it out, McCain," Scott challenged. "Here and now."

Heidi Betts

Lucas's fingers twitched over the butt of his Peace-maker.

"And when you're dead, maybe I'll make a prize of that little lady behind you."

Lucas kept his eyes on Scott, refusing to let the bastard bait him. Megan would be safe. Even if Scott managed to kill him, Caleb and Brandt would never let him lay so much as a finger on her.

"Your move," Scott called out.

Sweat rolled down Lucas's forehead, but his gaze never faltered. His hands remained steady above the revolvers strapped to his hips.

"I said make your move, McCain." Scott shifted uneasily.

Silence hung around them like a tomb, thick and heavy.

"I said *draw!*"

Epilogue

"You really scared me this afternoon," Megan said, stretching out atop Lucas.

They lay replete after a bout of wild lovemaking, though she still couldn't seem to get close enough to him. Almost losing him to a bullet only a few hours earlier had shaken her to the very depths of her soul. She loved him desperately and was completely sure she could not live without him.

Lucas had fired before Scott's gun even cleared leather. But she would never forget the agonizing moments after that shot. Waiting for one man to crumple, one to remain standing.

She thanked God Lucas hadn't been the one to fall.

His fingers ran through her long hair. "I'm sorry you had to see that."

"I wasn't worried about seeing a gunfight," she told him pointedly. "I was worried about losing you."

"You'd've missed me, huh?"

"Of course. I mean, who else would keep my sheets warm? And I need *somebody* around to draw my baths."

"Hmph. You probably would have sold the ring before my body was even cold."

"Oh, no." She held it up to the pale lamplight. "This beauty is never leaving my finger."

"Good."

"No matter who I marry."

"What?" His eyebrows drew together.

"Well, you haven't exactly proposed yet."

"What do you think the ring is for?"

"I'm not sure. I thought maybe you just wanted me to have it as compensation for all the trouble you've caused me."

"That thing cost a small fortune! If you're going to keep it, I sure as hell expect you to marry me."

"Well, then, you really should ask."

"Ask what?"

"Ask me to be your wife, you ninny."

He groaned, throwing an arm over his eyes. "You're going to make me do it, aren't you?"

"Yep. I expect a proper proposal of marriage."

"Fine. Megan, will you marry me?"

"You really should be down on one knee when you ask," she said.

He glared at her but got out of bed and down on one knee. "Megan, my love, will you be my wife?"

She chuckled. "You should be wearing pants, too."

"Look," he growled. "You're naked. I'm naked. This is going to be a naked marriage proposal, okay?"

She shrugged a bare shoulder. "Okay, but I don't think that's at all proper."

"Never mind," he said curtly. "Will you marry me or not?"

"You have to take my hand," she said, holding it out to him.

He ran splayed fingers through his hair, muttering a few choice phrases. Then he took her hand in his own.

"The very next word I want to hear out of your mouth is *yes*. Got that? *Yes*. Nothing more, nothing less. Just *yes*. Okay?"

She opened her mouth. He gave her a warning glare. With a sugary sweet smile, she licked her lips and said, "Yes."

"Very good," he praised. "Now, let's try this again." Kneeling next to the bed, he brought her hand to his lips for a light kiss. "Megan, my love, my life, will you do me the honor of being my wife?"

As soon as she started laughing, he knew he was in trouble.

"That rhymed," she said, giggling until she fell against him. They both toppled to the floor.

"That's it," he said, setting her aside and getting to his feet. "I give up. Find someone else to marry you."

"No, no," Megan cried. She grabbed his leg. "I won't laugh again."

Still skeptical, he slowly crossed his legs to sit on the floor in front of her. "Promise?" he asked.

Megan climbed into his lap, wrapping her legs around his waist. "Yes," she said. Her tongue trailed along the curve of his ear.

"And you promise not to interrupt me again?"

"Yes," she said, kissing the pulse at the base of his throat.

"What are you doing?" he asked.

She licked the outline of his lips. "Yes."

"That isn't an appropriate answer to the question."

"Yes."

"Did I miss something?"

She lifted her head. Her mouth tilted up in a grin. "Yes."

"Yes, what?" he tried instead.

"Yes, I'll marry you."

"Well, finally." He exhaled in relief. "I thought I'd have to propose to someone else just to get a straight answer." He rolled her to her back.

She smiled. "I hope you know that I'm not going to

309

curb my tongue just because you put a ring on my finger."
She held up her hand to emphasize her point.

"Pretty nice for only realizing I loved you four days
ago, huh?"

"Did you really only fall in love with me four days
ago? I think I've loved you forever."

"Well, I'm a man. You can't expect us to catch on as
quickly as you women do."

"That's true enough," she agreed easily.

He tweaked her nose. "Hush. No, I didn't just fall in
love with you. I think I've loved you since the moment I
shot your hat off. I saw that luxurious mane of black hair,
and I was lost. It was only four days ago, though, that I
realized I didn't want to go on without you."

"Even when I make your life harder than Hell?"

"Even then. Because—as any man who's been to Hell
and back can tell you—Heaven is oh, so much sweeter
when you finally get there."

"Lucas?"

"Hmm?" he asked, looking down into the brown
depths of her eyes.

"I love you."

He kissed her long and thoroughly, until neither of
them had the strength or the will to move. "I love you,
too," he whispered against her lips. "I love you, too."

Cinnamon and Roses
Heidi Betts

A hardworking seamstress, Rebecca has no business being attracted to a man like wealthy, arrogant Caleb Adams. Born fatherless in a brothel, Rebecca knows what males are made of. And Caleb is clearly as faithless as they come, scandalizing their Kansas cowtown with the fancy city women he casually uses and casts aside. Though he tempts innocent Rebecca beyond reason, she can't afford to love a man like Caleb, for the price might be another fatherless babe. What the devil is wrong with him, Caleb muses, that he's drawn to a calico-clad dressmaker when sirens in silk are his for the asking? Still, Rebecca unaccountably stirs him. Caleb vows no woman can be trusted with his heart. But he must sample sweet Rebecca.

Lair of the Wolf

Also includes the second installment of *Lair of the Wolf*, a serialized romance set in medieval Wales. Be sure to look for future chapters of this exciting story featured in Leisure books and written by the industry's top authors.

___4668-7 $4.99 US/$5.99 CAN

The Cowboys DREW

LEIGH GREENWOOD

The freedom of the range, the bawling of the longhorns, the lonesome night watch beneath a vast, starry sky—they get into a woman's blood until she knows there is nothing better than the life of a cowgirl . . . except the love of a good man.

As the main attraction for the Wild West show, sharpshooter Drew Townsend has faced her share of audiences. Yet when Cole Benton steps into the ring and challenges her to a shooting contest, she feels as weak-kneed as a newborn calf. It can't be stage fright—she'll hit every target with deadly accuracy—can it be love? Despite her wild attraction to the mysteriously handsome Texan, Drew refuses to believe in romance and all its trappings. But when the cowboy wraps his strong arms around her, she knows that she has truly hit her target—and won herself true love.

___4714-4 $5.99 US/$6.99 CAN

Dorchester Publishing Co., Inc.
P.O. Box 6640
Wayne, PA 19087-8640

TYKOTA'S WOMAN

CONSTANCE O'BANYON

Tykota Silverhorn has lived among the white man long enough. It is time to return to his people. Time to fulfill his destiny as the legendary tribal chieftain he was born to become. So what need has he for the pretty white woman riding beside him in the stagecoach, trembling beneath his dark gaze? Yet when Apaches attack the travelers, when one of his own betrays him, Tykota has to rescue soft, innocent Makinna Hillyard, teach her to survive the savage wilderness . . . and his own savage heart. For, shorn of the veneer of civilization, raw emotions rock Tykota. And suddenly, against his will, blue-eyed Makinna is his woman to protect, to command . . . to possess.

___4715-2 $5.99 US/$6.99 CAN

Dorchester Publishing Co., Inc.
P.O. Box 6640
Wayne, PA 19087-8640

Please add $1.75 for shipping and handling for the first book and $.50 for each book thereafter. NY, NYC, and PA residents, please add appropriate sales tax. No cash, stamps, or C.O.D.s. All orders shipped within 6 weeks via postal service book rate. Canadian orders require $2.00 extra postage and must be paid in U.S. dollars through a U.S. banking facility.

Name_____
Address_____
City_____ State_____ Zip_____
I have enclosed $_____ in payment for the checked book(s).
Payment <u>must</u> accompany all orders. ❑ Please send a free catalog.

The OUTLAWS: Rafe

Connie Mason

He is going to hang. Rafe Gentry has committed plenty of sins, but not the robbery and murder that has landed him in jail. Now, with a lynch mob out for his blood, he is staring death in the face . . . until a blond beauty with the voice of an angel steps in to redeem him.

She is going to wed. There is only one way to rescue the dark and dangerous outlaw from the hanging tree—by claiming him as the fictitious fiancé she is to meet in Pueblo. But Sister Angela Abbot never anticipates that she will have to make good on her claim and actually marry the rogue. Railroaded into a hasty wedding, reeling from the raw, seductive power of Rafe's kiss, she wonders whether she has made the biggest mistake of her life, or the most exciting leap of faith.

___4702-0 $5.99 US/$6.99 CAN

Dorchester Publishing Co., Inc.
P.O. Box 6640
Wayne, PA 19087-8640

Please add $1.75 for shipping and handling for the first book and $.50 for each book thereafter. NY, NYC, and PA residents, please add appropriate sales tax. No cash, stamps, or C.O.D.s. All orders shipped within 6 weeks via postal service book rate. Canadian orders require $2.00 extra postage and must be paid in U.S. dollars through a U.S. banking facility.

Name_____
Address_____
City_____State_____Zip_____
I have enclosed $_____ in payment for the checked book(s).
Payment <u>must</u> accompany all orders. ☐ Please send a free catalog.

White Nights — Susan Edwards

Eirica Macauley sees the road to better days: the remainder of the Oregon Trail. The trail is hard, even for experienced cattle hands like James Jones, but the man's will and determination lend Eirica strength. Yet, Eirica knows she can never accept the cowboy's love; the shadows that darken her past will hardly disappear in the light of day. But as each night passes and their wagon train draws nearer its destination, James's intentions grow clearer—and Eirica aches for his warm embrace. And when darkness falls and James stays beside her, the beautiful widow knows that when dawn comes, she'll no longer be alone.

Lair of the Wolf

Also includes the fifth installment of *Lair of the Wolf*, a serialized romance set in medieval Wales. Be sure to look for future chapters of this exciting story featured in Leisure books and written by the industry's top authors.

___4703-9 $5.50 US/$6.50 CAN

Dorchester Publishing Co., Inc.
P.O. Box 6640
Wayne, PA 19087-8640

Please add $1.75 for shipping and handling for the first book and $.50 for each book thereafter. NY, NYC, and PA residents, please add appropriate sales tax. No cash, stamps, or C.O.D.s. All orders shipped within 6 weeks via postal service book rate. Canadian orders require $2.00 extra postage and must be paid in U.S. dollars through a U.S. banking facility.

Name_____
Address_____
City_____State_____Zip____ _____
I have enclosed $ _____ in payment for the checked book(s).
Payment <u>must</u> accompany all orders. ❑ Please send a free catalog.

SNOW FIRE

NORAH HESS

She is lost. Blinded by the swirling storm, Flame knows that she cannot give up if she is to survive. Her memory gone, the lovely firebrand awakes to find that the strong arms encircling her belong to a devilishly handsome stranger. And one look at his blazing eyes tells her that the haven she has found promises a passion that will burn for a lifetime. She is the most lovely thing he has ever seen. From the moment he takes Flame in his arms and gazes into her sparkling eyes, Stone knows that the red-headed virgin has captured his heart. The very sight of her smile stokes fiery desires in him that only her touch can extinguish. To protect her he'll claim her as his wife, and pray that he can win her heart before she discovers the truth.

___4691-1 $5.99 US/$6.99 CAN

Dorchester Publishing Co., Inc.
P.O. Box 6640
Wayne, PA 19087-8640

Please add $1.75 for shipping and handling for the first book and $.50 for each book thereafter. NY, NYC, and PA residents, please add appropriate sales tax. No cash, stamps, or C.O.D.s. All orders shipped within 6 weeks via postal service book rate. Canadian orders require $2.00 extra postage and must be paid in U.S. dollars through a U.S. banking facility.

Name_____
Address_____
City_____State_____Zip_____
I have enclosed $_____ in payment for the checked book(s).
Payment <u>must</u> accompany all orders. ❏ Please send a free catalog.

PEGGY WAIDE
POTENT CHARMS

She is the most frustrating woman Stephen Lambert has ever met—and the most beguiling. But a Gypsy curse has doomed the esteemed duke of Badrick to a life without a happy marriage, and not even a strong-willed colonial heiress with a tendency to find trouble can change that. Stephen decides that since he cannot have her for a wife, he will convince her to be the next best thing: his mistress. But Phoebe Rafferty needs a husband, and fast. She has four weeks to get married and claim her inheritance. Phoebe only has eyes for the most wildly attractive and equally aggravating duke. But he refuses to marry her, mumbling nonsense about a curse. With time running out, Phoebe vows to persuade the stubborn aristocrat that curses are poppycock and the only spell he has fallen under is love.

___4694-6 $4.99 US/$5.99 CAN

Dorchester Publishing Co., Inc.
P.O. Box 6640
Wayne, PA 19087-8640

Please add $1.75 for shipping and handling for the first book and $.50 for each book thereafter. NY, NYC, and PA residents, please add appropriate sales tax. No cash, stamps, or C.O.D.s. All orders shipped within 6 weeks via postal service book rate. Canadian orders require $2.00 extra postage and must be paid in U.S. dollars through a U.S. banking facility.

Name_____
Address_____
City_____State_____Zip_____
I have enclosed $_____ in payment for the checked book(s).
Payment <u>must</u> accompany all orders. ☐ Please send a free catalog.

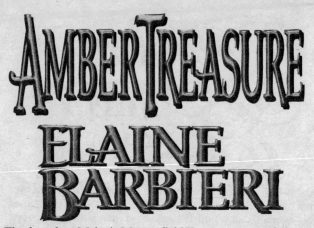

AMBER TREASURE

ELAINE BARBIERI

The last place Melanie Morganfield Young expects to fall prey to love is on the same sea that took her wealthy husband. Recently widowed, Melanie finds herself seeking solace with the captain of the very ship that was to have sailed her and her husband on a journey of discovery to the Orient. Melanie thinks she can never love again. But Captain Worth Randolph's passionate glances and surprising gentleness start to sweep away her defenses. Beneath his hard exterior, Melanie finds a compassionate soul. And gazing into his eyes, she finds the courage to finally let go of the past and surrender to the man who exposes the deepest treasures of her heart.

___52370-1 $5.99 US/$6.99 CAN

Dorchester Publishing Co., Inc.
P.O. Box 6640
Wayne, PA 19087-8640

Please add $1.75 for shipping and handling for the first book and $.50 for each book thereafter. NY, NYC, and PA residents, please add appropriate sales tax. No cash, stamps, or C.O.D.s. All orders shipped within 6 weeks via postal service book rate. Canadian orders require $2.00 extra postage and must be paid in U.S. dollars through a U.S. banking facility.

Name_____
Address_____
City_____State_____Zip_____
I have enclosed $_____in payment for the checked book(s).
Payment <u>must</u> accompany all orders. ❏ Please send a free catalog.

Taming Angelica

Alice Chambers

What is the point in having beauty and wealth if one can't do what one wants because of one's gender? Angelica doesn't know, but she plans on overcoming it. Suffragette and debutante, Angelica has nothing if not will. Lord William Claridge has a wont to gamble and enjoys training Thoroughbreds, but his older brother has tightened the family's purse strings. Strapped for cash, the handsome rake decides to resort to the unthinkable: Marry. For money. But when his mark turns out to be a more spirited filly than he has ever before saddled, he feels his heart bucking wildly. Suddenly, much more is on the line than his pocketbook. And the answer still comes down to . . . taming Angelica.

___4682-2 $4.99 US/$5.99 CAN

Dorchester Publishing Co., Inc.
P.O. Box 6640
Wayne, PA 19087-8640

Please add $1.75 for shipping and handling for the first book and $.50 for each book thereafter. NY, NYC, and PA residents, please add appropriate sales tax. No cash, stamps, or C.O.D.s. All orders shipped within 6 weeks via postal service book rate. Canadian orders require $2.00 extra postage and must be paid in U.S. dollars through a U.S. banking facility.

Name_____
Address_____
City_____ State_____ Zip _____
I have enclosed $ _____ in payment for the checked book(s).
Payment <u>must</u> accompany all orders. ❏ Please send a free catalog.